on
bone
bridge

ALSO BY MARIA HOEY

The Last Lost Girl

on bone bridge

maria hoey

POOLBEG
CRIMSON

Published 2018 by Crimson
an imprint of Poolbeg Press Ltd
123 Grange Hill, Baldoyle
Dublin 13, Ireland
www.poolbeg.com

A catalogue record for this book is available from the British Library.

ISBN 978-1-78199-8267

 www.facebook.com/poolbegpress
 @PoolbegBooks

Printed and bound by CPI Group (UK) Ltd, Croydon, CR0 4YY

www.poolbeg.com

About the author

Maria Hoey has been writing since she was eight years old. Her poetry has appeared in Ireland's foremost poetry publication, *Poetry Ireland,* and her poems and short stories have also appeared in various magazines. In 1999, Maria won first prize in the Swords Festival Short Story Competition. In 2010, she was runner-up in the Mslexia International Short Story Competition and was also shortlisted for the Michael McLaverty Short Story Award. Her debut novel, *The Last Lost Girl,* was published in 2017 and was shortlisted for the Annie McHale Debut Novel Award 2017 and the Kate O'Brien Award 2018.

Maria was raised in Swords, County Dublin, and has one daughter, Rebecca. She lives in Portmarnock with her husband Dr Garrett O'Boyle.

Acknowledgements

Once again, my thanks to all the lovely people at Poolbeg, in particular Paula Campbell and my superb editor, Gaye Shortland. My gratitude and love to all my family, especially my mother Mary and my father Noel who long ago taught me a love of books. My thanks also to my extended family, old neighbours, and friends, all of whom have cheered me on to finish this, my second book.

And again, my thanks and indebtedness to my early readers: my daughter Rebecca D'Arcy, my husband Dr Garrett O'Boyle and my sister Caroline Hoey-Edwards.

For Garrett who encouraged, endured and believed

Prologue

*Something bad happened on Bone Bridge when we were ten
years old, me and Violet-May Duff. It wasn't our fault. All we
did was to go for a walk. Rosemary-June came too, and of
course the little boy. What happened was an accident and
nobody was to blame – that was what they told us then, that
is what I have always told myself. Just a terrible accident and
it is best not to think about it, certainly not to dwell on it. Best
to forget ... but easier said than done, when what happened
that day changed our lives forever, me and Violet-May Duff
and Rosemary-June, and of course the little boy.*

Book 1

Chapter 1

Every story has to start somewhere, and it is not always at the beginning. Besides, who can say for sure where any particular story really begins? For me, this story began on Friday the 16th September 1983, although ask the others who were a part of it and I imagine they would say it began at quite another time. And so it did, for them. I only remember the date so precisely because it was exactly one week and one day to Violet-May Duff's tenth birthday, which also happened to be mine. At the time it seemed like more than a coincidence that we should not just share a birthday but be exactly the same age too; it seemed to me like a sign. Because in the ordinary course of things Violet-May Duff and I might never have met; she was one of the beautiful people. Despite being the same age, she started school a year behind me, on account of some kidney problem, which forever afterwards her mother would refer to as Violet-May's "weakness". As a result, she was forbidden to sit on the grass, walls, rocks, damp sand, park benches or even garden furniture without a cushion. She was also, from the first of September until the last day of May, forced to wear wool tights instead of the white knee-socks she loved. The year she turned nine, Violet-May was allowed to join her own age-group in my class. But even then, that whole year, she did not speak to me once. It was not that she was rude to me or ignored me, rather that I was simply of no interest to her one way or another. But all that changed that September afternoon.

As part of our homework earlier that week, we had been asked to write a composition on "The Most Exciting Day of My Life". I wrote about the day I ran away from home even though I had never run away from home nor had any desire to do so. But a great many of the children in the books I read had done so and I thoroughly enjoyed unleashing my imagination on the subject. I was asked to read my story to the class and our teacher praised it and told me I was a fine writer with a vivid imagination. As I sat back down, the bell for home-time began to ring, but while all about me girls were on their feet stuffing books into bags and rushing for the door I stayed where I was, basking quietly in the glow of my teacher's praise.

It was then that Violet-May came and stood before my desk. She smiled at me and said, "I liked your composition."

I am not sure if I answered her. I think it much more likely I only stared at her in silent surprise. Violet-May Duff was the prettiest girl I had ever seen. She had beautiful starry brown eyes – in fact, everything about her, from the top of her silky brown curls to the toes of her black patent shoes seemed shiny and perfect to me. If I could I would have swapped everything about myself to look as she did, especially my straight brown hair and my grey eyes. And now, this object of my admiration was talking to me and smiling at me and standing close enough for me to see each gleaming bead of her little blue necklace.

If Violet-May thought my silence odd or stupid or rude she showed no sign.

"Do you want to come to my birthday concert?" she said. "There's going to be a play and a party afterwards with an ice-cream cake and a soda-stream."

Again, I am not sure exactly what I said. "Yes, please," perhaps or I may have only nodded. I had a bad habit of nodding then, which my mother was constantly trying to correct.

"Good," said Violet-May. "And you could help me with the play too, if you like."

She made it, I remember, sound like an honour was being conferred on me. Even so I felt the need to admit somewhat worriedly that I had never written a play before, only stories and compositions.

Violet-May said that didn't matter. "It's the same thing," she said, "except that in a play the people say the words on a stage. My brother is going to make a stage for me."

I was happy again then and accepted the honour of being asked to help. "When is your birthday?" I asked.

When she told me the date I could not hide my delight, "That's my birthday too," I said.

Violet-May frowned. "Is it?" But almost at once she was smiling again. "That's nice," she said.

But I knew instinctively that she was not pleased and I suspected then what I now know to be true: Violet-May did not like to share.

My mother did not try to hide her surprise when I told her about the invitation.

"What's the Duff girl doing inviting you to her birthday party? I didn't know you were friends with her?"

"I'm not – I mean I wasn't. But she invited me and it's not a birthday party, it's a birthday concert."

"But it's your birthday that day too," said my mother. "Why would you want to go to someone else's party, or concert or whatever it is? Would you not rather have your own day, your own party?"

"No. I want to go to Violet-May's. Please can I go?"

"If you want," said my mother, "but it wouldn't be my idea

of fun. That little one looks every bit as stuck-up as her mother."

It was quite true that Mrs Duff was stuck-up. She quite literally held her head high and her chin up and all the children laughed at her behind her back, not only because of the things she said but the way she said them. Mrs Duff didn't have clothes, she had "costumes". She talked about her home as "our little country hideaway" and once, at the school's sale-of-work I had heard her say, "My children are my raison d'etre". I heard it as "raisin detra" and thought it was some kind of cake, that Mrs Duff meant she wanted to eat her children. I asked my father but my mother interrupted, saying, "It's French for up yourself."

And then there were the double-barrelled names she had given her girls, Violet-May and Rosemary-June. The boys made fun of them all the time. I had been known to join in too, but more, I must confess, out of envy than spite. Kay has never seemed to me a satisfactory name – it has no sooner begun than it is over. Long before I became friends with Violet-May, I had made numerous attempts to change it. I would come across a name I liked the sound of, mostly from the books I read or from the television, try it on in secret first to see if it was a good fit and then announce to my parents, "From now on I want to be known as ..." Courtesy of Enid Blyton, I had trifled with Darrell, Alicia, Gwendoline, Isabel and Georgina (answering only to George). I had also tried on Diana, Ruby, Heidi and Clara and, from the television, Christina, Cassandra, Marina, Miranda, Gloria, Dolores, Tiffany and Cleopatra. My father who indulged me in almost all things played along, but my mother would have none of it and refused to call me anything but Kay.

"But Cleopatra is so pretty," I remember wheedling, "and Kay Kelly is so boring, and so plain."

To which my mother replied, "It's quite pretty enough for you."

My mother had, I know without a doubt, a profound but unsentimental love for me. She took pride in my doings and sayings – she just rarely said so in my hearing. Her constant worry about me expressed itself almost as annoyance so that it often seemed to me that she blamed me if I got hurt or was sick. Even when I fell and hurt my knees, she would chide me, "How did you fall? Were you running again? What did I tell you about running?"

And then she would fuss and clean my scrapes and cuts, and her hands were deft and gentle while her face was creased with crossness.

But meanwhile the Duff girls had two first names as well as a middle name, which when they made their Confirmations meant they would have four names each. It just didn't seem fair.

But there was more to it than fancy names and fancy talk. Mrs Duff's ability to put people's backs up had its roots in the past and even as a child I was aware there was a story about Flora Duff, or Florence Flynn as some people insisted on calling her. I had sometimes overheard snippets of conversations between my mother and Mrs Nugent when she came in from next door for a cup of tea and a chat. Gossip was the breath of life to Mrs Nugent. As soon as my mother realised I was about, she would change the subject but even so I had strung together enough to work out that Florence Flynn had met Robert Duff while on loan from the home for unmarried mothers to scrub the Duffs' floors. Robert Duff had fallen for Florence much to the horror of old Mrs Duff, who I assumed was Robert Duff's mother and, according to Mrs Nugent, a controlling and domineering woman. Old Mrs Duff considered that an unmarried mother and skivvy was nowhere near good enough for her only son and threatened to leave the house forever if Robert went ahead and married one. I had no idea what a skivvy was – however, I gathered that skivvy or not Robert Duff had married Florence Flynn and

Mrs Duff was as good as her word and went to live with her sister. How people knew all these things intrigued me, but there was apparently a somebody who claimed to know another somebody who did know and who was only too willing to help fill in the blanks. I also knew that there was more to the story of Florence Flynn but this I had yet to find out.

"Violet-May wants me to go over to her house tomorrow to help with stuff," I told my mother. "Is it alright if I go?"

"What sort of stuff? I hope you won't let her have you doing the dirty work. You're not her slave, you know."

"No, it's just writing stuff," I said. "Part of the concert is to be a play and I'm helping Violet-May with that. She has ideas and everything – she just wants me to help her."

"Well, alright," said my mother, "go if you want to, but I smell a rat."

Chapter 2

As it turned out, there was nothing wrong with my mother's nose.

The following morning, in spite of it being a Saturday, I was up before I was called and by the time my mother put her head around my bedroom door I was already dressed and had my pencil case and a rolled-up fresh copybook stuffed inside my white shoulder bag. My mother insisted I eat some breakfast even though I was almost too excited to swallow and afterwards she came to the door and watched me over the top of the hedge until I reached the corner of our road and she could see me no longer. I believe now that she was anxious although there seemed no logical reason why she should have been. Violet-May's home was a five-minute walk down the road. But perhaps it was that, like me, she understood that I was venturing into a different world that day.

The Council had built our estate on a stretch of wasteland on the crest of a hill that overlooked the river valley and justifiably, which I find is not often the case in such matters, named it River View. The estate fronted onto a road known locally as Old Road which, narrow and hemmed in by trees and bushes, led in a circuitous route to the town. As it was not the main route, however, traffic was fairly light and so the road was generally considered safe enough, in those days anyway, for many of the children from River View to treat it as an extension of the estate. We walked up and down it on a daily basis, unaccompanied by adults, and it was along this road I walked that September Saturday morning, on my way to Violet-May's home.

The Duff house was invisible from the road, surrounded by a high stone wall – even the wrought-iron gates were set back from the road itself. I had walked past the gates many times and had even, when dared to do so by my playmates, ventured beyond them once or twice. I had never dared to go any further than the bend in the treelined avenue but today I passed through the gateway proudly, an invited guest carrying my head high, my bag swinging from my shoulder. The leaves of the beech trees had already turned to gold and the sunlight made them blaze, so that it seemed to me that I trod a magic pathway.

The canopy of trees ended, giving way on one side to a high bank of large flowerless shrubs with leathery-looking dark-green leaves. I remember thinking that I did not much like the look of them. Then I rounded a curve and the driveway opened up and split in two, curving around a circle of lawn. The bank of dark plants continued on my right all the way up to one side of the house and beyond.

I remember standing for a moment to gaze at Violet-May's home. To me that day, it looked like a mansion; in reality it was a very elegant granite Georgian house.

After a while I became aware of a dog barking somewhere and then my gaze shifted to the figure of a woman who was on her knees at the edge of the lawn, bent over a flowerbed in which she was digging. A boy was standing over her, his back to me and his arms waving about as though he were arguing.

As I came closer I heard him say, "Why is it the final word? It doesn't have to be the final word if we talk about it, does it?"

"There's nothing left to talk about, Robbie," said the woman and I knew from her voice that it was Mrs Duff – there was no mistaking that pitch and tone. "Dad and I made it very clear to you what would happen. Here you are, only a couple of weeks into the new term and –"

She must have heard me then because she abruptly stopped talking and looked around, shading her eyes against the sun.

"Can I help you?" she called.

"I'm Kay," I told her. "I've come to help Violet-May with the play."

"Then go and find her," said Mrs Duff. "She'll be with Rosemary-June in the second garage."

I remember she made the word *garage* sound foreign and posh. But, as I had no idea where the second garage was, I still hesitated. While I waited I thought about how the Duffs had two garages and we didn't even have a car.

The boy turned to me then and smiled, "Go round the back of the house and keep left," he said. He pulled a long face. "You'll hear them before you see them."

I had seen Violet-May's brother before but it was not until that moment that the bullet struck. Robbie Duff was fourteen at that time. He had Violet-May's dark-brown eyes but his thick wavy hair was a dark golden colour and sprang up over his left eye in a natural riotous quiff. He was tall and thin and walked with a slight stoop and that year was rarely seen out without a brown corduroy jacket, grey fingerless gloves and a black-and-white oversized PLO scarf around his neck. For whatever reason, in that moment, just a week short of my tenth birthday, I fell hopelessly in love with him.

When I didn't move, Robbie raised a hand and pointed. "That way," he said.

Then he turned back to his mother and I found my feet and let them carry me slowly away, looking back all the time. Robbie had returned to arguing again, I knew, because his arms were waving about once more and I watched as Mrs

Duff got slowly to her feet, her hand to the small of her back. I had once heard my father refer to her as "a handsome woman", but looking at her that morning, I remember thinking that she was getting quite fat.

I did hear them before I saw them. The garages, originally part of the stable block, were some distance away from the back of the house and as I rounded it the sound of the dog's barking grew louder. I became aware of another sound, a thin screeching which I followed across the lawn, past beds of flowers still summer-bright, to a cobbled yard.

The second garage, the smaller of the two, was farthest away. The door was open and as I came closer I could see Violet-May. She was sitting on a chair pulled up to a small table on one side of a makeshift stage which had been set up against the back wall. There was a second empty chair next to her. In the middle of the stage, Rosemary-June Duff was playing, or attempting to play, the violin.

Whenever I saw Rosemary-June next to her sister, I wondered how they could be from the same family. She was two years younger than us and, where Violet-May was dark, Rosemary-June was very fair, with ice-blue eyes, very big and very wide. In contrast to Violet-May's sulky mouth, Rosemary-June was all smiles. When she had finished playing, she began again.

"Stop," Violet-May snapped. "You need to practise, Rosemary-June. But go and do it somewhere else, you're giving me a headache. And, anyway, Kay is here now and we need to work on the play."

It was the only greeting I received from her.

Rosemary-June, in seemingly perfectly good humour, packed her violin into its case. Then she climbed down carefully from the stage and as she passed me fixed me with her great eyes and said, "Do you have a kitten?"

"No," I said, surprised.

"I don't either," said Rosemary-June. "I want one, but

14

Mummy says no. It's because we have a dog. But it's not my dog, it's Robbie's. I don't even want a dog, I want a kitten."

"It's not because of the dog," said Violet-May, "it's because of the baby. Mummy told Dad that she doesn't trust cats around babies. Forget about the silly old kitten, Rosemary, and go and practise. I told you that Kay and I need to work on the play."

"But nobody wants a baby," said Rosemary-June, "not even Mummy. I heard her say so. And I don't think I'll practise anymore. I don't feel like it."

"Well, go and talk with fairies then or something," said Violet-May. "Kay, come up here and sit beside me."

"Does Rosemary-June talk to fairies?" I asked, after she had gone and I had settled myself in the chair next to Violet-May.

"She says she does."

"Do they talk back?"

"I don't know, but Rosemary-June says they appear to her in a silver mist."

"Oh," I said.

It sounded so nice that I wanted to believe it. The thing was, looking at Rosemary-June, I used to feel that if fairies did exist she was exactly the sort of person they would choose to appear to. I don't think that Violet-May ever believed in fairies – she was firmly of this world.

The dog was still barking. "Is that Robbie's dog," I asked. "Why doesn't someone let him out?"

"Because he runs off into the fields every chance he gets," said Violet-May. "He rolls in mud and then he runs into the house. And he eats things, not food, just things. He's a mongrel. Robbie found him and brought him home. Now can we do the play, please, and stop talking about the stupid dog?"

So I opened my bag and took out my pencil case and copybook. "What's the play about anyway? Is it funny or sad?"

"Sad, I think," said Violet-May. "Yes, let's make it sad."

I looked at her in surprise. "Haven't you started it yet?"

"Well, I've been thinking about it and I have ideas – I just haven't written anything down yet. But I've made this." She picked up a square of blue paper that had been folded in two. "It's the programme for the concert."

I took it from her. The front cover had a drawing of daisies and daffodils and someone had written, in exquisitely curling letters, the words:

You are invited to Violet-May Duff's
Birthday Concert
on Saturday 24th September 1983 at 2.30pm

Inside, the same hand had set out the order of events:

Programme

Song One – Sung by Violet-May Duff
Poetry Recitation – by Violet-May Duff
Song Two – Sung by Violet-May Duff
Violin Recital – by Rosemary-June Duff
Play – The Unhappy Princess – written by and Starring Violet-May Duff

I looked up then and, as though she had read my mind, Violet-May said, "It was done before I knew you were helping me with the play. It's too late to put your name down on the programme now. Daddy took it to a printing shop and had photocopies made. But I'll tell everyone you helped me. Isn't the programme pretty? All the guests will get one. I drew the pictures and made it all up. Robbie helped me with the spelling and he did the fancy writing – it's called calligraphy."

I studied the programme with new respect. "It's beautiful," I said fervently. "Is Robbie coming to the concert?"

"If he feels like it, but he probably won't feel like it. He's in bad humour because he's being sent to boarding school."

"Why is he being sent to boarding school?" I am sure my dismay showed in my voice and my face.

"Because Mummy says he's not applying himself and she's afraid he's getting in with a bad crowd."

"Oh." I said nothing for a while as I processed this catastrophe. "When does he have to go?"

Violet-May shrugged impatiently. "Not until after Christmas. Now are we doing the play or not? We don't have much time to write it, only today and tomorrow." She looked at me anxiously. "You can come over again tomorrow, can't you? Tomorrow afternoon?"

"Yes," I nodded happily. "I can if you want me to. We can do it after school next week too, if you like?"

Violet-May shook her head. "I have things to do after school so we have to finish it by tomorrow."

We set to work then and it soon became clear to me that, other than knowing she wanted to speak most of the lines there were to be spoken, Violet-May had no ideas whatsoever. She did, however, seem to expect me to have a great many. I made some suggestions but at each Violet-May wrinkled her nose and looked disappointed.

I dug around a little desperately in my mind. "We could choose your favourite book and do something from that," I said.

"I don't have a favourite book."

I misunderstood and smiled sympathetically, "I know, there are so many it's hard to know which your real favourite is."

"I don't like reading very much," said Violet-May.

It is always difficult to learn that your idol has feet of clay and I was silent for a little while. "But you like plays," I said.

"Plays are different," said Violet-May. "Mummy took us to a play once. There was a beautiful lady on the stage and everybody was just sitting looking at her. When I grow up I'm going to be a famous actress. I'll be on the stage and on the television and in films and everyone will look at me too."

I forgot that Violet-May didn't much like reading. "I bet you'll be beautiful," I told her. "I promise I'll go and see you."

"Alright then," said Violet-May, graciously accepting my adoration as her right. "But what are we going to do about the play for the concert?"

"I still think we should do something out of a book," I said. "What about *Tom Sawyer* or *Huckleberry Finn* – we could probably make a play out of those."

"But those are boys," said Violet-May. "I don't want to be a boy. I want to be a princess, a beautiful princess in a beautiful dress. Mummy bought me a princess dress but I can't wear it if I'm a stupid boy, can I?"

A princess dress but no princess play – I remember thinking that Violet-May was, as my mother was fond of saying "putting the cart before the horse".

"Well, there are a lot of stories about princesses too," I said. "I suppose we could make a play out of one of them but it won't be so exciting."

"You can make it exciting," said Violet-May. "You're the best writer in the whole class and I just know you'll write the best play ever."

My happiness was complete.

"It's three o'clock and your daddy was about to go and get you if you'd been another fifteen minutes," was my mother's greeting when I got home.

My father, who was washing his hands at the sink, turned and smiled at me, as though to say that going to get me had not been his idea. I smiled back.

"I'm starving," I announced.

"Did they not give you anything to eat all that time?"

"No."

"Nothing at all?"

"No – but I didn't know I was hungry until I was on my way home. I never notice I'm hungry when I'm writing."

"But what about Violet-May? Didn't she have lunch?"

"I don't know. She may have. She wasn't with me all the time."

My mother rolled her eyes. "Well, wash your hands and sit down and I'll make you a banana sandwich."

Sitting at the table, watching my mother open a sliced pan and begin spreading butter on two slices of bread, I realised just how hungry I was. I could barely wait while she chopped the banana. Thinking about eating made me think too about Mrs Duff getting fat.

"Violet-May's mammy is having a new baby," I announced, "and Robbie Duff has to go to boarding school. I don't think that's fair when he doesn't even want to go."

"Oh well, only the best for Florence Duff," said my mother who was lining up discs of banana in careful rows on a slice of bread. "I heard she was pregnant again – how old is her youngest girl now?"

"Rosemary-June is eight. Mrs Duff doesn't want a new baby, nobody does."

"Don't say that," said my mother, "don't ever say that."

Her voice was so sharp that I looked up in surprise.

My father stopped drying his hands and came and patted her on the shoulder.

"I'm only saying what Rosemary-June said," I told them. I was feeling that sense of frustrated bemusement children experience when some mild wrongdoing elicits a response from adults disproportionate to the misdemeanour. I would be sixteen before I discovered that my mother had suffered three miscarriages and a stillbirth before I was born.

"She didn't mean anything by it, Liz," said my father and he smiled his gentle smile from one of us to the other.

"Yes, well, just don't repeat it," said my mother. "Now eat your banana sandwich. I can't believe they didn't give you so much as a biscuit." She slammed the plate down before me and then came and sat down opposite me and watched me

19

eating. "I suppose the house is beautiful?"

"It's beautiful from the outside," I said. "I didn't see inside."

"What, she didn't let you in?"

"No, we were working in the second garage, me and Violet-May. We nearly finished the play." I looked up anxiously. "I have to go back tomorrow afternoon, I promised Violet-May I would. Please can I?"

"Please *may* I?" said my mother. "You may if you want to." She looked at my father. "The second garage, did you ever in all your life?"

Chapter 3

I went back to Violet-May's house the following afternoon, annoying my mother by rushing my dinner in my hurry to get away. This time there was nobody in the garden and I got as far as the shiny yellow front door. My knock was answered by Violet-May's father and we stood and surveyed one another, him smiling down and me gazing up.

At that time Mr Duff would have been in his early sixties but to me he seemed an old man. He was stout and almost bald with a rusty-coloured head and face and slightly protuberant eyes. He also had a black-and-grey monobrow which held me close to spellbound every time I saw it. I could never see exactly where the two brows knit – to me it seemed all of a piece and so, anytime I was close enough to do so, I examined it minutely. But in spite of his facial affliction, I liked Mr Duff intensely on first sight.

That day, when he opened the portal to the interior life of the Duff house, I remember him looking at me as though, pleased enough to find me on his doorstep, he was uncertain what to do with me, now that I had come.

I decided to help him, "I'm Kay," I said. "I'm here to help with Violet-May's play."

"Kay," repeated Mr Duff. When he frowned his monobrow

descended toward his nose. He put a finger in his right ear and waggled it briefly. "Come to help with Violet-May's play."

"For the birthday concert," I said, and Mr Duff's brow climbed upward once more.

He took his finger out of his ear. "The birthday concert," he said. "Certainly there is to be a birthday concert. Perhaps you will step inside, Miss Kay, and we shall endeavour to find Miss Violet-May this instant."

Nobody had ever called me Miss Kay before. I liked the way it sounded very much so I happily followed him inside and gazed about me. The Duffs' hall was not like our hall at home – it was more like a room all of itself, a room that was bigger than our kitchen and sitting-room put together. The paintwork was light blue on top and palest yellow at the bottom and the walls were covered with pictures in big golden frames, of what I thought of as people from the olden days: whiskery men and women with silly expressions on their faces. I wondered if they were Violet-May's relations and thought that I wouldn't have liked any of them to be mine.

Ahead of me, beyond a pillared archway, the wide and elegant staircase rose up between its darkly gleaming wooden handrails. I thought everything was wonderful except perhaps the grey stone floor which to me looked cold and a bit dirty – we had carpet everywhere at home, except in the kitchen.

"Perhaps," said Mr Duff, "Miss Violet-May is to be found in the drawing room."

The drawing room – I had a glorious vision of Violet-May in a room filled entirely with colouring books, pencils, crayons and markers – but the room to which Mr Duff led me, although remarkable for its size, the great flood of light through the big windows and the enormous gleaming white mantelpiece, was a great disappointment to me. It held nothing more remarkable than pretty pink-and-gold sofas and a lot of chairs and tables and things.

"Not here," said Mr Duff and he waggled his ear again.

"Maybe she's in the second garage?" I suggested.

"The second garage," said Mr Duff. "The second garage?"

While he was considering this, Violet-May herself appeared behind us.

"Oh, you're here," she said. "Daddy, what are you doing with Kay? I need her. Come on, Kay, we'll go out through the kitchen."

As I walked away after Violet-May, I looked back at her father. He raised his arm and I thought he was about to wave to me so I waved to him first, but after all he was only going to waggle his ear again.

In the second garage we settled down to work once more on the play. This time there were refreshments provided: a plate of pink and white iced biscuits and a big glass jug of lemonade that had bits of the lemon still floating about. It didn't taste like the real lemonade you bought in bottles but it was nice enough and I drank a lot of it. We had been working for a while when a shadow fell across the open doorway. Looking up, I saw Robbie Duff standing staring in at us. He was dressed just as he had been the day before, the same black-and-white scarf and the grey fingerless gloves. But today he was wearing what looked like earmuffs, attached by wires to a small blue-and-silver box which he was carrying in one hand.

"*Have you two seen Prince?*" he shouted.

"*No!*" Violet-May shouted back. "*Robbie, when are you going to put up the curtain?*"

"*Later!*" shouted Robbie and he went away again.

"What's that thing on his head?" I asked.

"It's a Walkman."

"What's a Walkman?"

"It's for playing his music. That's all Robbie cares about – music and his stupid dog Prince. He promised he'd put up the curtain today."

"Maybe he'll come back later," I said hopefully.

23

But Robbie did not come back and we worked on until eventually Violet-May got up.

"I need to go inside for a minute," she said.

I wondered if she meant that she needed to go to the toilet. I did. I had needed to go for ages but had not liked to ask. It was, I thought, probably because of all that funny lemonade I'd drunk.

"Do you want to come and see my princess dress, the one I'm wearing for the play?" said Violet-May.

I nodded my agreement – if I was inside the house I would at least be closer to a bathroom.

"Come on then and I'll show you," said Violet-May.

Inside, the hall was cool and dim and quiet. As I followed Violet-May up that beautiful staircase, I remember reaching out my hand and letting it slide along the shining handrail.

"Your house is like a palace," I said.

"Is it?" said Violet-May, as though the thought had never occurred to her.

However, her bedroom when we reached it was not what I'd expected at all. The carpet was a nice shade of blue, if very faded, and the curtains were made of a silky blue material, but nothing was as pretty as I had imagined it would be. And yet, looking around me, I remember thinking that I wished this was my room. I had gone through a pink phase two years earlier and my Rainbow Brite themed bedroom had been given a makeover with pale-pink paint and darker pink curtains and duvet set. My matching dressing table and chest of drawers were white and had only recently been given a fresh coat of gloss.

The wardrobe from which Violet-May took her princess dress was enormous and almost black in colour and all the furniture in the room was dark and old-looking. But she had a rocking chair which I envied greatly and an enormous brass bed so high off the floor you had to climb up into it.

"Now, you can look but don't touch," said Violet-May as she laid the dress out over a chair for my inspection.

I put my hands behind my back as I approached but, in any case, the dress was safely under wrap and I gazed in some wonder at the diaphanous creation in its protective polythene bag. The bodice was made of blue satin trimmed with matching lace. It had off-the-shoulder sleeves and a skirt of pale-blue tulle spangled with shimmering silver butterflies, over a voluminous pale-blue net petticoat.

"There are matching blue satin slippers too," said Violet-May.

"You're going to be so beautiful," I said.

Violet-May nodded her head in happy agreement. "And wait until I show you my dress for the party," she said, "and my new shoes."

"OK," I said. Then, because I could hold it in no longer, I finally asked if I could go to the toilet.

Violet-May, who was putting her dress away in the cavernous wardrobe, said over her shoulder that I could.

I hesitated. "Where is it?"

"Down the hall, the second door on the right."

I remember walking down the hall to the biggest bathroom I had ever seen. The floor was bare wood and the bath was not attached to the wall – instead it stood by itself on four clawed feet in the middle of the room. The toilet had a dark wooden seat and a long chain that you had to reach up and pull. The door had no lock and this caused me great distress as it was impossible to sit down comfortably and relax for fear that someone might suddenly burst in. And what if that somebody should be Robbie Duff? The thought filled me with horror and, if my need to go had not been so pressing, I would have held it rather than take the risk. In the event, I perched nervously on the edge of the toilet seat, my pants around my knees, my gaze intently on the door and my ears pricked for the least sound of approaching footsteps. In that moment I thought very kindly of our little bathroom at home, all shiny white and sparkling silver and I decided that my mother, just like me, would not like this one at all.

I was washing my hands at the big sink when I heard a lot of screaming and shouting coming from beyond the door. When I came out I was just in time to see Robbie on his way down the stairs, ducking his head to avoid being struck by whatever it was that Violet-May had just hurled at him.

"*I'm going to kick that dog!*" she was screaming, "*I'm going to kick him and kick him and kick him!*"

Going back to join Violet-May at the door to her room, I could see that there were tears in her eyes.

"What's wrong?" I asked, and she held out her hand and I looked down at the chewed wreck of a shoe.

"Look what that dirty old mongrel dog did to one of my party shoes!" she said. "What am I supposed to wear to my party now? It's all Robbie's fault – Mummy told him not to let the dog into the house and now look what he's done. I'm going to kick that dog, I'm going to kick him so hard. I wish he was dead, I do, I wish that stupid dog was dead!"

She shoved the shoe into my hand then and turned away from me and into her room, banging the door loudly behind her. For a moment I just stood and stared at the door handle and wondered what to do.

"She won't come out for ages and ages," said Rosemary-June.

I turned to find her standing a little farther along the landing, watching me. I'd had no idea she was there. She was smiling which, considering her sister's plight, I found a bit surprising but perhaps, I thought vaguely, it had something to do with being able to see fairies – perhaps nothing really seemed to matter to her.

At that moment Mrs Duff appeared on the stairs, making her way slowly upward.

"What on earth is all this noise about?" she said. "Did Mummy or did she not ask you all to be quiet while she rested her eyes?" She stopped when she saw me. "Goodness me, Kay, are you here again?"

"I came to help Violet-May with the play," I said and realised how tired I was of those words, "but the dog ate her shoe and –"

"She locked herself into her room again," Rosemary finished my sentence for me.

I held out my hand so that Mrs Duff could see the evidence and she came closer and stared down at the remains of the shoe. I had never been that close to Mrs Duff before, and I could see the tiny cracks in her lips where the skin had peeled. Her eyes were brown like Violet-May's and her face looked sort of swollen. I remember thinking that I didn't like her, but I didn't really know why. I wondered if it was because her voice always sounded sort of bright, as though she was happy, but her eyes didn't look happy even though she smiled a lot and showed off her big bright teeth.

She was smiling now as she turned and spoke to Violet-May's door. "Violet-May, open the door now, please, and let Mummy come in."

"*Go away!*" screamed Violet-May.

Mrs Duff glanced back at me, still smiling. She put her hand to her head and kept it there as she tried once more. "But what about Kay? She's come specially to help you with the play. Now be sensible, Violet-May, and open the door and come out, please."

"*Tell her to go home!*" screamed Violet-May. "*Tell her I hate the stupid play!*"

I felt as if she had thumped me in the stomach. I remember staring blankly at the door and then I heard sounds coming from behind it, thumps and squeals followed by more thumps followed by a sort of snarling sound I had only ever heard a dog make. I looked in bewilderment at Rosemary-June who had come to stand next to me and was smiling fixedly at the door to her sister's room.

"She's having a tantrum," she said calmly. "She thumps her pillow and bites it and she –"

"That's enough, Rosemary-June," said Mrs Duff. She turned to me with her brightest smile. "Violet-May just needs some time to calm down. I'm afraid you had better go home, Kay."

Then she walked away down the landing, her hand to her head once more.

"Now no more noise, please, while Mummy has a little rest!" she called over her shoulder.

Then it was just me and Rosemary-June, standing on the landing looking at one another.

"I suppose I'd better go home," I said.

I said it loud enough so that Violet-May might hear but, if she did, it did not stop her carrying on.

Rosemary-June said nothing and, watching her, a thought crossed my mind.

"You don't think she'll really kick Robbie's dog, do you?" I said. "It wasn't really the dog's fault, not if the door was open."

"She probably will," said Rosemary-June. "She wishes he was dead, you heard her say so."

"But she didn't mean it," I said hopefully.

"He ate her shoe and made her angry," said Rosemary-June. "It's best not to make Violet-May angry."

Then she too walked away, and I was left alone on the landing. I stood there for a moment, unsure what to do next, but there was nothing to do but go home.

As I made my way slowly downstairs I saw the match of Violet-May's shoe lying on the step where it had fallen. It was pale blue with a gold buckle and it was perfectly beautiful. I picked it up and placed it next to its chewed-up match which I was still carrying. I looked at them sadly before carrying them both downstairs where I placed them together on a small table.

I was walking disconsolately to the hall door when Mr Duff appeared in the hallway behind me.

"We meet again, Miss Kay," he said. "Not going home so soon, I hope?"

"Violet-May doesn't want to play with me," I told him. "She locked herself in her bedroom."

"Ah," said Mr Duff and he waggled his ear. "Is that so? Well, well, what a pity, what a pity. But perhaps you might allow me to drive you home, Miss Kay?"

But I did not want to be driven home. The truth was that I still had hopes of Violet-May changing her mind and coming rushing after me.

"No, thank you, Mr Duff," I said. "I'd rather walk."

He said nothing more but he opened the door for me and stood aside as I went out into the sunshine, and then he walked with me as far the gate.

As we passed under the trees in the avenue I looked back several times, but there was no sign of a penitent Violet-May calling me back, back to the second garage and the play and the proximity of her brother Robbie.

Perhaps Mr Duff read my mind because when we reached the gate he gave me a little bow and said with a sad smile, "Never mind, Miss Kay, you must come again when the storm is over."

But looking at the sky I could see no sign of any storm, and as I walked away I remember wondering sadly whether Violet-May would ever want me to come again.

Chapter 4

We were watching *Knight Rider* when the car pulled up outside the house. Mrs Duff got out first then the passenger door opened and I saw Violet-May. I jumped up and my mother's eyes followed my gaze to the window.

"Sit down, Kay," she told me. "Sit down and wait until they knock."

I opened my mouth to protest but one look at her face told me not to waste my breath. I had not mentioned what had happened earlier but I had been quiet since getting home, and I think she suspected something because she made a point of giving me an extra slice of cake with my tea. Now she got up, walked slowly across to the television set and turned it off, then she came and sat down again and we both waited. Even when the knock finally came, she motioned to me with one raised finger and I had to stay where I was while she went into the hall alone to open the door. As soon as she was out of the room, I jumped up to listen at the door but I made sure to be back in my seat by the time all three of them came into the sitting room.

"Your home, Mrs Kelly, is perfectly lovely, perfectly lovely," said Mrs Duff. "And as for your garden, the flowers are perfectly lovely too – you will have to tell me what your secret is."

My mother's face lightened visibly at Mrs Duff's praise and I saw that her chin which had been up had come down again. My mother was fiercely house-proud. Our front steps shone, and not a petal of her Busy Lizzies or geraniums was allowed to lie a moment on the porch floor. The windows glittered, the net curtains were brilliantly white, elaborately looped and tied on either side with lace bows. The lino gleamed and she hoovered and polished every day. When she was not cleaning in the house, she was weeding; the small square of front garden and only slightly larger back one were pristine; our garden shed had net curtains in the window.

I had jumped up from the sofa by now and while Violet-May and I stood and stared at one another without saying a word, our two mothers talked about plants and flowers.

Mrs Duff turned to me with a big smile on her face, "Kay, Violet-May asked especially that she be driven here to apologise personally for her rude behaviour today."

I could see by the sudden rise of my mother's chin that this was unwelcome news.

Then Mrs Duff turned her smile on her, saying, "A little upset, Mrs Kelly, between Violet-May and her brother, nothing at all to do with Kay of course. Now, Violet-May, what do you have to say to Kay, who was kind enough to offer to help out with your play?"

I remember thinking that it was *our* play and that I had not offered, Violet-May had asked, but somehow none of that mattered when Violet-May, who had been staring fixedly at the grey screen of the television, turned and smiled at me.

"I'm sorry, Kay," she said.

"Well now, that's settled," said Mrs Duff, "and perhaps, if you have no objection, Mrs Kelly, you would allow Kay to come back with us for an hour or so. Of course I'll drive her home afterwards."

"Can I, Mam, please?" I said. "We need to finish the play today."

"We could finish it here," said Violet-May. "It's not fair for Kay to have to come to my house all the time. We could do it here, couldn't we, Kay?"

I said nothing but the truth was that I did not want to stay to work on the play in our house. In our house there was no possible chance of seeing Robbie Duff. And it was perfectly obvious from the look on Mrs Duff's face that she did not want us to do it at our house either. But as she opened her mouth to say so, Violet-May interrupted.

"Please, Mummy, I want to stay here. I want to, Mummy, I want to!" Her eyes were a little puffy still from crying and the something in her voice that told me another tantrum might not be far off obviously did not go unnoticed by her mother.

"Well, if you really want to," said Mrs Duff, "I suppose you must." Her eyes strayed doubtfully to the window, beyond which I could see a couple of the estate kids circling her car. "But mind, Violet-May, it's only for a couple of hours. I'll be back then to collect you and I expect you to be ready and waiting when I do. And, mind, no playing in the street."

She turned to my mother.

"Mrs Kelly," she said, "I'm sure you'll understand that I would prefer if Violet-May did not play in the street. Her little weakness means that Violet-May needs to take extra care and not expose herself to unnecessary dangers."

Why doesn't she just say kidneys, I remember thinking, and I watched Violet-May's face grow red. Every single person in our class knew about Violet-May's kidneys.

"That's fine," said my mother, "they can play in the back garden. I don't think it's particularly dangerous there – would you like to inspect it?" Her chin was up again and I think Mrs Duff realised she had caused offence.

"Oh no, Mrs Kelly," she said, "I'm sure it's perfectly lovely, perfectly lovely. Violet-May can play in your back garden for a little while, of course she can. As long as she doesn't sit on the grass – you won't sit on the grass, will you, Violet-May?"

She need not have worried; Violet-May had no interest in sitting on the grass in our "perfectly lovely" garden. As soon as Mrs Duff had left, my mother going with her as far as the gate, Violet-May went and stood in front of the television.

"Can we watch it?" she said.

"You mean after we finish the play? Yes, of course."

"No, I mean now, can we watch it now? Why can't we have it on while you – while we're doing the play?"

"Well, I think my mother is watching it now," I explained. "But we could go up to my room and finish the play and then come down and watch the television later. My mother will be baking buns so we can watch whatever you like then."

"Oh alright," said Violet-May. "Come on then and let's hurry and get it done. I wish I never said I'd have a stupid birthday concert – then we could forget about the boring old play and watch the television. I never get to watch television."

"Haven't you got a television?" I asked, trying not to be insulted that she considered my work on the play boring.

"No," she said, "Mummy won't have one in the house."

I looked at her for the first time then with genuine pity in my heart which nonetheless was alloyed with secret joy because we had something the Duffs did not. My mother, against my father's wishes, had rented our television set from the local electrical shop and feasted on *The Love Boat*, *Hart to Hart* and *Cagney and Lacey*. Together we watched *Magnum P.I.*, *Dallas* and *Knight Rider*. My father mocked us mildly but was not above watching the football, the snooker, *Yes, Minister* and *The Streets of San Francisco*.

"Well, you can watch anything you like when the play is finished," I said.

She nodded sulkily, and we went upstairs.

I was sorry that the play and the concert had now been relegated to the ranks of stupid and boring, but thrilled that Violet-May Duff was in my bedroom. And so I threw myself into the play, all the time knowing that she was only waiting for the moment when we could close the copybook and go downstairs and watch television.

But, even so, when I read the finished product to Violet-May she looked at me with gleaming eyes and said, "I told you you'd write the best play ever, Kay."

And in that moment I could have cried with happiness, even knowing as I did that what I had written was not the best play ever but rather a hotchpotch of fairy tales with elements of *Sleeping Beauty*, *Snow White* and *Rumpelstiltskin* all flung in for good measure. Violet-May loved it and that was all that mattered.

"Haven't any of your friends got televisions?" I asked as we went downstairs.

"Some of them have," said Violet-May, "but I don't get to watch them. There isn't time."

"Why isn't there time?"

"Well, there's piano and ballet and horse-riding – you know, that sort of stuff."

I nodded my head to indicate that I knew all about that sort of stuff. In truth, it was unlikely that any of the kids on our estate did piano or ballet or horse-riding. We played kerbs and rounders, and the boys played five-a-side and all of us, every year after Wimbledon infected us, played tennis in the field above the river valley. But at that moment I was puffed up with pride at finding myself with the power to grant Violet-May's wish and I believe I approached a state of perfect happiness as we sat next to one another on the sofa in our sitting room and watched *The A-Team* together.

Mrs Duff came to collect Violet-May at the appointed time and the car had barely driven way before Mrs Nugent was knocking on our door. I heard her talking to my mother in the hall.

"I see you've had Flora Duff here twice today, Mrs Kelly," she said. "What was all that about?"

"Kay seems to have taken a shine to her young one, that's all," my mother told her. "With any luck it won't last."

I remember thinking: Oh I hope it does, I hope it lasts forever and ever.

Somehow or other in that week before our joint birthday, the children in school found out that Violet-May's mother was pregnant. Ken Fitzgerald made a joke about her being "up the Duff" and then he and another boy began vying with one another to come up with ridiculous names for the new baby.

"What about Dandelion-July?" said Ken. "And then the next one can be Primrose-August, unless it's a boy and then they can call it Pansy-August."

Everyone sniggered but, although I thought it was quite funny too, I was careful not to let Violet-May see. I nodded solemnly when she said that the only thing to do with ignorant people was to pity them and ignore them. I already pitied Ken Fitzgerald anyway, because he could not spell. He lived three doors up from our house and he was very annoying and famous for farting in the classroom and blaming others. Ignoring him was a lot harder, however, because like a lot of people with little of any interest to say, he said it loudly and at great length. He kept up this particular joke long after everyone had grown tired of it and, finally, in the yard at lunchtime one day, Violet-May snapped. She screamed at Ken Fitzgerald to leave her alone and then she just kept on screaming. Next she lay down on the ground and began rolling around and all the children stood back and just stared at her and even Ken Fitzgerald stopped laughing and looked at her with his mouth hanging open.

Two teachers came then and shoed us away and between them they lifted Violet-May who had stopped screaming by then and carried her, sobbing, into the school building.

As they passed me, I heard Violet-May saying through her sobs, "I hate that stupid baby, I hate it, hate it, hate it!"

Chapter 5

I have not yet written about the river and yet in many ways it is as much a character in this story as are the people.

On a map its name is given as the Clone. But, just like many people, our river had, still has, different names for the different stages of its life.

The part of our river where we swam in summer was called the Dive. We could stand at the far edges of our estate and look down at it. Set deep in the valley between green banks, in summer its light-dappled waters glittered and winked at us in the sunshine. We swarmed to it – to swim, to paddle, to catch minnows in jam jars. The midges ate us, but we didn't care. My father told me that before mains water had been installed in most of the houses in the town, the Dive was where people sent their children to wash themselves. He himself remembered being sent there by his mother, with a towel and a bar of carbolic soap, and being told not to come home until he was squeaky clean. The Dive was the place where, the previous summer, I had begun to learn how to swim and I longed for next summer to come so I could finish the job.

The place where our river wound itself close by the ruins of the abbey, where the courting boys and girls went to be alone, was called the Stream and there the river was wide and shallow and made a happy sort of gurgling sound as it rippled over the big flat stones.

Further downstream, where the river snaked between the feathered reeds, was the part called the Surly, perhaps because the river was slow-moving there. The water, although not so very deep, was green-black and scummy. It was spanned by a bridge known locally as Bone Bridge, which had got its name from the fact that, when the foundations for the bridge were being laid, human remains had been found in the sediment near the riverbank. The remains were dated to a medieval burial site, the boundaries of which the river had eroded over the centuries, and when the decision was taken to go ahead with building the bridge it had stirred up a good deal of controversy. People argued that the bridge should not be built on what they considered to be sacred ground, but nonetheless it went ahead and from that grew up the superstitious belief that the uneasy dead buried there still walked at midnight. But, whatever about at midnight, in broad daylight we found nothing to fear on Bone Bridge and, although we would never dream of swimming there, it was fun to stand on one side of the bridge and throw something, a stick perhaps, over the wall, then run across and count how long it took for it to emerge on the other side.

Not very far downstream from the Surly, the river narrowed and as a result flowed faster once more. It tumbled past the old mill and through the town park, on the other side of which it became something completely different again in the place we called the Pool. The Pool could only be accessed by foot and by way of a turnstile gate and a narrow path leading off the park. A quiet green place, even the water looked green from the reflected trees, and the light came dappled through the overhanging branches. It was the sort of place one might expect to be popular with couples or for families to eat their picnics, and yet for some reason not many people went there. It had a lonely feel to it. Or perhaps they knew or sensed that the Pool was treacherous. It looked peaceful, innocent even, except for a certain simmering, which was how my father described the tiny movements on the surface of the water. "Don't let that fool you," he told me more than once, because this was where the river was more unpredictable. Those eddies, that simmering movement of the water was a clue to what was happening underneath, and this was the part of the river where you needed to be most careful. Ken Fitzgerald once told me and the other kids a story about a boy who had gone in to swim there and been pulled down by the force of the swirling water and then had become entangled in the reeds on the bed of the river and drowned. When they took him out the reeds were still wrapped around his neck and face like giant green spaghetti. The story gave me nightmares for about a week afterwards. Eventually I asked my father if it were true. He said he could not be certain but that if it were true then the boy had probably made the mistake of kicking and thrashing in an attempt to disentangle himself. Sadly, he said, that would only have made matters worse. The trick was to stay calm when you encountered reeds in water, and to try to float through them using your arms as paddles. I remember comforting myself with the belief that in a similar situation this was what I would have done.

In truth I was nervous of the water and still using armbands in the summer of 1983. My father did all he could to tempt me to try to swim without them. He took me to the Dive from time to time, early in the morning when it was quiet and there were no big lads about to make me nervous with their splashing and horseplay. But I preferred to fish for minnows than swim.

"Never mind," he said. "Come next summer we'll have you swimming like a little fish. Just you wait and see."

Chapter 6

On Saturday the 24th of September my father dropped me to Violet-May's concert on his bicycle. He said it didn't seem right that I should walk there on my birthday, so I sat on the crossbar of his bike, my legs outstretched so as to protect my new birthday shoes from the dust. They were black patent, I could see my face in them, and I wanted to keep it that way. I asked him to drop me off at the Duffs' gate but instead he cycled all the way up the drive and insisted on waiting while I knocked at the front door. The moment I heard footsteps approaching from within the house, I waved to him to let him know that he could go now. I wanted him to go in case it was Robbie Duff who answered the door. I did not want Robbie to know I had come like a baby, on a bike with my daddy. But my father stayed until the door opened and after all it was only Mrs Duff. My father waved at me and I waved back.

Mrs Duff came out onto the wide top step and peered at him as if she had never before in her life seen a man on a bicycle. Then she looked down at me.

"I assume you are here for the concert, Kay, but if so you are very early. It doesn't begin for another two hours. We are only just finishing lunch."

"I asked her to come early," said Violet-May, coming up

behind her mother. "Come on and see what we've done, Kay."

"But you haven't finished your lunch, Violet-May," said Mrs Duff.

Violet-May ignored her. She came out onto the step and took me by the arm. As she led me away, I looked back sadly at the house where most likely Robbie Duff was eating his lunch.

Walking around the side of the house with Violet-May, I was almost afraid to ask the question uppermost on my mind.

"Is Robbie coming to the concert?"

"I don't know. Maybe, if he feels like it."

"Do you think he'll feel like it?" I asked anxiously.

"How would I know?" said Violet-May. "And anyway who cares?"

I cared, I cared so much that I wanted to yell at her that she didn't deserve a brother like Robbie Duff. Instead I said, "Is he still in bad humour about being sent to boarding school?"

"Probably, but today he's in bad humour because Prince didn't come home last night."

"Oh," I said. "Robbie really likes Prince, doesn't he?"

Violet-May nodded her head, "Yes, he does. Sometimes I think he likes him more than anybody else in this house. Stupid dog."

I almost gasped when I saw the second garage. It had been completely transformed with flowers in vases everywhere, and chairs with cushions set out in rows. The stage had a curtain now: a simple dark-green fabric had been draped over a length of curtain wire but somehow it had transformed the makeshift platform, lending it an air of mystery and suspense.

"Did Robbie do that?" I asked.

Violet-May nodded her head happily.

I sat in the front row while she climbed up onto the stage and spoke her lines to me. She was word-perfect and I clapped when she had finished.

Then we went into the house and Violet-May and Rosemary-June were hurried upstairs by Mrs Duff to change and I was told to wait for them in the drawing room. I went and perched on the edge of a pink-and-gold sofa and listened to the sound of a gold clock ticking from its place high up on the white mantelpiece and wondered what it was like to have so many beautiful things in just one room of your house. In my opinion, our house was the nicest house of any I had seen in our estate – but this, this was something else entirely.

They came into the drawing room together, Violet-May and Rosemary-June, the fair and the dark child side by side, and I could only gaze at them in wonder mixed with envy. I was wearing my best dress and my new shoes that day but, as soon as I saw the Duff girls dressed for the party, I felt plain and ordinary. My mother gave birth to me at the age of forty-three and all my childhood she had dressed me in clothes she'd made herself from Simplicity patterns, with matching Alice bands, handknitted jumpers and cardigans with pearl buttons. Next to the Duffs I looked old-fashioned and, that day in particular, I truly knew it. Violet-May's party dress was made of heavy silk, pale violet in colour, and she had a hair slide with a purple flower attached above her right ear. Because it was her birthday, she had been allowed to wear blindingly white, lace-trimmed knee socks instead of the hated tights, and on her feet she wore what looked to me like the same shoes that had caused so much drama a week earlier. Somehow her mother had managed to find a match for the ruined shoe or else she had bought a fresh pair. Rosemary-June was dressed in pale yellow and she had a yellow ribbon tied in a big bow on top of her blonde hair.

"You both look perfectly beautiful," said Mrs Duff, coming in behind them.

"Yes, I do think I look very pretty," said Rosemary-June.

I knew it was true but all the same I was embarrassed for her and wondered what my mother would have to say if I said such a big-headed thing about myself.

The birthday concert was a big success. The audience was

made up of Mr and Mrs Duff, Mrs Riley who came to clean for Mrs Duff, two ladies from Mrs Duff's Bridge club, three girls from our class, one from Violet-May's piano class and three from her ballet class and one from Rosemary-June's violin class who had come with her mother.

Rosemary-June made only two mistakes in her violin recital apparently but it was hard for me to tell where she had gone wrong as it all sounded terrible to me. Violet-May sang beautifully and did an extra song when she got an encore from Mr Duff.

But the play was the highlight of the afternoon, in spite of the fact that it starred Violet-May alone, aside from the occasional fleeting appearance on the stage of Rosemary-June in the roles of (a) a messenger and (b) a drudge/serving woman. It failed in only one aspect: nobody found it remotely sad. I had written a villain who was a sort of amalgam of Rumpelstiltskin and every witch in every fairytale I had ever read, but Violet-May, terrified the character would steal her thunder, had insisted he never actually appear on stage. Instead I stood at the back of the second garage and delivered the villain's lines by shouting them through the small open window. Based on the same reasoning, Violet-May had decreed that I also play the part of the invisible Prince Charming, but I am no actor and my prince and villain were indistinguishable from one another. For some reason this, and the sight of Violet-May talking to a window tickled the audience (all twenty of them) pink, and they laughed when they should have been moved to tears. But everyone applauded boisterously when Violet-May, in solitary splendour, took her final bows. Mr Duff threw a long-stemmed red rose onto the stage and Robbie, who had put in an appearance after all, wolf-whistled through his teeth until Mrs Duff complained he was giving her a headache.

I had come in from my spot under the window and was sitting in a seat in the back when suddenly Robbie yelled,

"*Author, author!*"

Violet-May, who was in the act of stepping down from the stage, turned around and got up again.

"*And the other author!*" yelled Robbie.

Then a hand fell on my shoulder and I was pulled to my feet. I saw it was Robbie and he smiled at me and pushed me gently forward and I found myself walking up the "aisle" with all eyes on me.

Mr Duff came forward and held out his hand. "Indeed, indeed, Miss Kay must join Miss Violet-May in the limelight," he said.

He helped me up onto the stage, where I stood next to Violet-May. I saw her looking at me with a strange expression on her face but then she smiled and took my hand and we took our bows together.

Afterwards we all went into the house for the party. Mrs Duff insisted that the guests go round the front of the house and in through the front door, but Violet-May grabbed my hand and we stayed back until the others had gone. Then she led me across the garden, up the steps to a terrace and in the back door to the huge kitchen.

I was desperately thirsty and she waited while I filled myself a glass of water from the big white stone sink. As I drank I looked about me at the polished wood floor and the timber-beamed ceiling. There were two archways in opposite walls.

"What's in there?" I asked, pointing to one.

"That's the butler's pantry," said Violet-May.

"Have you got a butler?"

"No."

"Then why have you got a butler's pantry?"

"I don't know."

"What's in the other one?" I asked, pointing to the other archway.

"You'll find out if you'll hurry up and come on," said Violet-May.

I put down the glass and she grabbed my hand and led me through the second archway and up a narrow circular iron staircase.

"You have two stairs," I said in wonder.

"This was the one the servants used," said Violet-May.

"Have you any servants?"

"No, just Mrs Riley who cleans, and a man who comes in to cut the grass."

"Where are we going?" I asked, thrilled to the bone.

"Just to my room," said Violet-May.

"Oh," I said, a little disappointed.

We left the stairway on the first-floor landing, where Violet-May's bedroom was, although I would have liked to continue on up and discover where it finally ended. But there was no time for that today and I followed Violet-May to her room where, having shut the door behind us, she let out a loud whooping noise, made a running leap for the bed and hurled herself upon it.

"Did you hear them clapping?" she said. "They clapped and they clapped and they clapped!" She pushed herself to her feet then and began bouncing up and down on the bed. "*That was wonderful, wonderful, wonderful!*" she chanted. "*I'm so happy, so happy, so happy!*" She beckoned to me. "Come and bounce with me, Kay, come and bounce!"

I would have liked to leap up as she had done, but I was afraid of knocking her over, so I walked to the bed and climbed up and Violet-May grinned at me and once again she took my hand and we began bouncing again in rhythm to her chanting.

"*I'm so happy, happy, happy, I'm so happy, happy, happy!*"

And I saw our reflection bouncing in the mirror: me, Kay Kelly, smiling an enormous smile and holding hands with a princess.

The party was held in the dining room, where the most

enormous table I had ever seen had been spread with a white cloth and dressed with pink and white flowers. Everything that Violet-May had promised was there: the soda-stream and the ice-cream cake and much more – wobbling jelly towers in green and red and yellow, biscuits and sandwiches and fancy cakes and buns, and all of it served, not on paper plates like the parties I was used to, but on posh white plates. Like we were all grown-ups, I remember thinking. Violet-May stayed in her princess dress for the party but Rosemary-June shed her drudge's rags in exchange for her yellow dress and ribbon. The only Duff missing from the celebrations was the most important one to me. Robbie failed to put in an appearance at all.

"Isn't your brother coming?" I whispered to Violet-May at one point.

She shrugged her shoulders. "He's probably out looking for the dog again. Well, it will be his fault if there's no ice-cream cake left."

When everyone sang "Happy Birthday" to Violet-May and she blew out the candles on her beautiful ice-cream cake. I remember thinking that not a single person other than my own family had wished me a happy birthday. But then not a single person here knew it was my birthday, except Violet-May, and she said nothing. I wondered if she had forgotten that it was my birthday too.

After we all had eaten as much as we could, Mrs Duff got to her feet and made an announcement that if the children would like to go upstairs to the playroom, there would be games to play and prizes to win.

There was a general scurry and scraping of chairs as we all rushed to get to our feet, then the door of the dining-room burst open and Robbie Duff stood there.

At first he said nothing at all and everyone in the room just stared at him.

I was so happy that he had come after all, and only sorry

that all the cake was gone and he had not had any, that for a moment I didn't notice what he was holding in his arms. Then I saw it was a dog, quite a big dog with a shaggy grey-and-black coat. My next thought was that it was a pity that the first time I saw Prince he should be dead. Because the dog in Robbie Duff's arms was clearly dead: his four legs were sticking out toward us, in a stiff and unnatural pose and his head was hanging down and I could see his eyes, which were open and staring. And when I looked up from the dog to Robbie's face I could see that he had been crying, was still crying really.

Then Mrs Duff said, "What on earth, Robbie? Why have you brought that dog in here? Is he, is he ...?"

Her voice failed her, but Robbie answered the unfinished question anyway.

"He's dead," he said. "Prince is dead. Someone poisoned him and now he's dead."

Chapter 7

If I am honest, I did not really expect to see much of Violet-May after the birthday concert, at least not outside of the schoolroom. Quite aside from my suspicion that I had only been invited because of my writing abilities, the day itself had turned into such a complete fiasco I would not have been surprised if she never wanted to see me again.

The party had ended abruptly with the appearance of Robbie and his dead dog. Mr Duff, moving faster than I had ever seen him do before, hustled boy and dog from the room but not before the little girl from Rosemary-June's violin class began to scream. It was a spectacular scream, high-pitched and with no pause for breath, and it had the effect of setting off some of the other girls too. In an effort to calm things down, the mother of screamer number one said she thought it was best to take her daughter home and then all the other mothers decided it was time to go too. Despite Mrs Duff's best efforts to stay them with promises of games and prizes in the playroom, there was a rush for coats and then quicker than seemed possible everyone had gone, even Mrs Duff who accompanied the guests outside, leaving just me, Rosemary-June and Violet-May in the suddenly silent dining room. I was actually a little afraid to look at Violet-May. I expected her to drop to the floor and begin rolling about and screaming, so I just stared at my shoes and waited.

But there was no tantrum this time and when Violet-May spoke, her voice was perfectly calm.

"Robbie ruined my party," she said.

Her tone was so flat it seemed almost without emotion and I looked up in surprise. Violet-May had a fistful of the gauzy stuff of her princess dress and appeared to be examining a shiny butterfly.

I was so relieved that there was to be no scene, I said what I was thinking. "It wasn't his fault, I mean he didn't do it on purpose. His dog is dead and he thinks somebody poisoned him. But who would poison him? It must have been an accident."

"He probably ate a poisoned rat," said Rosemary-June. "Daddy said he would, if Robbie kept letting him run off into the fields." She looked at her sister. "You said you wished he was dead and now he is."

"But she didn't mean it, did you, Violet-May?" I said.

"I did mean it," said Violet May. "Stupid dog. First he ate my shoe and now he's ruined my party. But now he's dead and I'm glad he's dead."

I was not only shocked, I was outraged, and once again found myself saying exactly what I was thinking. "Well, I'm not glad he's dead, I'm really sorry. And I think it's really mean to say that about your own brother's dog. If I had a brother I wouldn't say things like that."

And then, because I knew I was about to burst into tears and because I had no wish to face Violet-May's anger, I walked out of the room and out of the house. All the way home the tears just kept on coming. I was crying for so many reasons it was hard to count them. I was crying because Prince was dead and because Robbie was sad, and because Violet-May's party had been ruined and because I had stood up to her and she would probably never speak to me again. I was crying because now I would probably never be invited to her house again as long as I lived and because I might never see Robbie ever again. I was even crying because it was my birthday and I was crying.

But Violet-May did want to speak to me again. On Monday, in school, she came up to me at break time and behaved as if nothing had happened. She did not mention the party or the concert or what had happened afterwards. I was longing to ask her if Robbie was alright but I was afraid to remind her of how her party had ended so I said nothing.

And then she said something that put all other things out of my mind: "Do you think I could go and play at your house sometimes?"

"You want to come and play at my house? But why?"

"Because I like it there," said Violet-May. "Because it's fun and I want to."

"OK," I said, trying hard to keep my surprise and delirious joy under wraps. "You can come and play at my house if you like." A dark cloud of doubt passed through my head and I forgot to play it cool as I said anxiously, "But will your mother let you come?"

"I'll make her let me," said Violet-May. "I'll tell her you invited me. You're inviting me, aren't you, Kay?"

I nodded but then a new doubt followed the first. "I'll just have to ask my mam though."

Violet-May, who obviously did not foresee any problems, smiled happily. "OK then," she said. "You ask your mam and I'll tell my mummy."

"What does she want with you, that's what I'd like to know," said my mother.

I had a fairly good idea what Violet-May wanted, but a miracle had occurred in my life and I was happy not to ask any uncomfortable questions.

"She wants to play with me," I said, "and I want to play with her."

"What's so special about this Violet-May, anyway?" said my mother. "And what's wrong with playing with the Nugent twins from next door?"

There was nothing wrong with playing with the Nugent twins, nothing at all. Dolores and Mandy Nugent had been my best friends until now.

"She has two sitting rooms and a library and three bathrooms and six bedrooms and –"

"I'm surprised at you, Kay," said my mother.

But the truth was it had nothing to do with the amount of rooms she had. It was something I could not put into words.

"She's fun," I said lamely, "and she can skip with two ropes."

"That just sounds like showing-off to me," said my mother.

It was actually another two weeks before Violet-May was allowed to come to play at my house. It was a Saturday early in October and the weather was fine if a little chilly but Violet-May showed no inclination to go outside to our "perfectly lovely" back garden. She stood on the step and shivered so much my mother suggested we go inside and watch some television instead. In fact, we watched television for the entire two hours Violet-May was allowed to stay. I thought it a waste of a morning, but Violet-May was obviously in her element, especially when my father went to the shop on his bicycle and brought us back Fat Frogs and Double Dips.

After we had licked the sticks clean of ice-cream and were opening our Double-Dips I found the courage to mention Robbie.

"Is Robbie still going to boarding school after Christmas?" I asked.

"Yes, straight after Christmas," said Violet-May.

"Poor Robbie," I said.

Violet-May, who had just scooped up a heap of fizz on her lollipop, gave me a sharp look.

"I mean because he has to go to school and he doesn't want to," I said.

"Oh, he wants to go now," she said. "He says he's glad to go and he can't wait for Christmas to be over so he can get away from the sick people in our house."

"Who's sick?" I asked.

"Nobody's sick, not that sort of sick. Robbie says 'sick' when he means mad or bad or something. I don't know. He's been acting all weird ever since Prince died."

"How do you mean weird?"

"I don't know, just doing funny things, saying funny things. He still keeps saying that someone poisoned Prince on purpose." She stuck the fizz-covered lolly in her mouth and closed her eyes. "I love your Daddy," she said.

"I do too," I said.

"But you won't tell Mummy about the sweets, will you, Kay? I'm not allowed to have any."

"I won't tell," I promised her.

I forgot about Robbie Duff then, in the pleasure of knowing that Violet-May and I shared a secret, and by the time Mrs Duff came to collect Violet-May there was no sign of the sweets or ice-cream. I had collected up the wrappers and put them carefully in the kitchen bin. Mrs Duff looked fatter than ever, and I couldn't help staring at her stomach. She was really nice to my mother again and praised the house and the garden like she was seeing it for the very first time and she kept thanking her again and again for having Violet-May over.

We all walked out to the car and, just as Mrs Duff was about to get in, Violet-May asked if she could come again next week. Mrs Duff smiled and looked at me and my mother, then looked away again quickly and I knew she was wishing that Violet-May had not asked the question when we were there.

"Well, let's just wait and see, shall we, Violet-May?" she said.

Violet-May stuck out her bottom lip. "I don't want to wait and see, I want to come and play with Kay. I want to, Mummy, I want to!"

I looked at Mrs Duff and I knew we were thinking the same thing: she was going to have a tantrum here in the street.

Mrs Duff said quickly, "Well, perhaps if you girls want to play together it would be nice if Kay came to play at our house next time? What do you think, Mrs Kelly?"

"Fine with me," said my mother. "Take it in turns if that's what Kay wants."

I doubt if that was what Mrs Duff had in mind, but she managed to smile at me when she said, "Would you like to come play with Violet-May at our house, Kay?"

"Yes, please, Mrs Duff," I said. "I'd like to go and play at your house next time."

I deliberately avoided meeting Violet-May's gaze because I knew that was not what she wanted me to say. But fair was fair after all and the truth was we each had something the other wanted. I had a television and Violet-May had a brother and Robbie Duff was going away straight after Christmas.

"Well, that's settled then," said Mrs Duff.

"But we'll take it in turns," said Violet-May, her voice still sulky but not sounding quite so dangerous now and Mrs Duff, after a moment's hesitation, gave the briefest of nods before climbing into the car.

It was only when they had driven away and we turned to go back inside the house that I spotted the Nugent twins. They were standing peering over the hedge which divided their garden from the road, and only their perfectly matching heads were visible. I was fairly certain they'd heard every word we'd said.

"Hi, Dolores, hi, Mandy," I said.

"Hi, Kay," they said together. "Hi, Mrs Kelly."

"Hello, Dolores, hello, Mandy," said my mother. "Kay, why don't you go and play with the girls? You've been cooped up in the house all morning. A bit of fresh air will do you good."

But somehow the idea of playing in the road with the Nugent twins held no appeal.

"After my lunch," I said, and I followed my mother inside the gate.

Dolores and Mandy shifted position so that they were peering now over the hedge that divided our garden from theirs and as I walked up the path I was guiltily conscious of their twin stare following me all the way to our door.

I did go to play at the Duffs' house the following Saturday but I only saw Robbie once and that was from a distance. I had finally made it as far as the playroom, which was on the second floor of the house. Like the drawing room, it proved a disappointment to me. It was nothing more than a big bare-looking room with bars on the bottom half of the two big windows. The walls were lined with shelves which held toys and a great deal of books and board games. In one corner there was an old rocking horse with the straw bursting from a gash in its stomach. In another corner there was a small wooden table, painted blue with white stars, and four small chairs to match. The chairs were too small for any of us to sit in.

Rosemary-June was there that day, sprawled out on the floor making a jigsaw.

Violet-May had gone off to find something in her room and I walked to the window and looked out. That was when I saw Robbie. He was walking across the grass below, then he stopped and bent down. I could not see what he was doing and I climbed up onto the window seat to get a better look.

"He's looking at Prince's grave," said Rosemary-June, coming up behind me. "I bet my kitten wouldn't eat poison."

I turned to her. "Are you getting one?"

"Mummy says no, but perhaps she'll change her mind."

When I turned back to the window Robbie had gone. "Why are there bars on the windows?" I asked.

"So little children won't fall out. Mummy says this used to be the nursery in the old days. Perhaps they should have put bars on all the windows then that girl couldn't have jumped."

"What girl?" I said, Robbie forgotten for the moment and all my attention on Rosemary now.

"Oh, just a girl who worked here a long time ago," said Rosemary. "She was a maid and she slept in the attic room and one day she climbed out onto the window ledge and jumped."

"Was she hurt?"

Rosemary widened her already huge eyes. "Of course she was!" she said. "The attic room is at the very top of the house. I bet she was smashed into little pieces."

"But why did she jump?" I asked. I felt conflicted in the way that I always was by stories of this nature. They horrified me but thrilled me all at once.

"Because of her trouble," said Rosemary-June.

"Are you talking about the scullery maid who jumped out of the attic window?" said Violet-May, appearing in the doorway. "She jumped because she was having a baby and she didn't have a husband. The woman who comes to wash the floors told me so. Now, come on, Kay, I want to play chase."

She ran off then and I hared after her, down the stairs and outside, and I forgot about the poor little scullery maid in the joy of running along the circuitous path that wound its way through the shrubbery.

After that day, for all the talk of taking turns, it was usually Violet-May who got her way and she came to play at our house whenever her mother would allow her to.

From time to time we did actually go out to play in the road, but only because my mother came in and switched off the television and said, "Go out and play and get some fresh

54

air instead of hatching the house." That was one of her favourite expressions: hatching the house.

On those occasions I tried to include the Nugent twins in the games we played but Violet-May made no secret of her disdain for them which made me feel really awkward and uncomfortable.

"I came to play with you," she told me once, "but if you want to play with other people I can go and play with my other friends too."

After that, to my everlasting shame, I avoided the twins when Violet-May came to play and they knew it and I knew they did. My mother saw it too and did not like it and told me so but, to their credit, the twins never once upbraided me for my treachery and whenever Violet-May was not around, which of course was most of the time, the three of us played together as though no such person existed.

But, in truth, when Violet-May came to my house we didn't do much playing – mostly we sat in the sitting room and watched television. Violet-May liked television more than anyone I have ever known – she especially loved cartoons but really it hardly seemed to matter to her what we watched.

Often my father would come in as we sat there, feign surprise at finding Violet-May sitting next to me on the sofa then make a show of shaking his head, sighing loudly and saying, "I suppose you two will be wanting ice-cream and goodness knows what else now?"

"Yes, please, Daddy," I would say.

Violet-May would smile up at him. "Yes, please, Mr Kelly."

Then my father would go off on his bicycle and bring us back Fat Frogs or choc-ices and some sort of sweets – Fizzle Sticks or Sweet Bananas, Milk Bottles or Wham Bars.

When he handed hers to Violet-May he would say, "There you are now, little lady."

Violet-May would give him her biggest, brightest smile

and thank him more politely than I ever had.

In spite of everything my mother said about her, I think my father liked Violet-May and she liked him, which seemed only right to me, because I liked her father too.

Once, while playing hide-and-seek throughout the Duff house, I had burst in on Mr Duff in his library. Once inside the door I had come to a stupefied standstill, just gazing at all the rows and rows of books which lined the length and breadth of two entire walls. Mr Duff himself was sitting before the fire in one of a pair of enormous brown leather chairs, their backs shaped like great shiny brown wings. The light from the fire and a couple of table lamps picked out the gold inscriptions on the spines of some of the books and made them gleam. I thought it the most wonderful room I had ever seen.

Mr Duff, his pipe in his mouth, looked up from the book he was reading and smiled at me. He took his pipe out and said, "Ah, it's little Miss ..." and then he stopped and waggled his ear.

I realised he had forgotten who I was. Ear-waggling, I had come to recognise, was a habit Mr Duff resorted to at times of puzzlement, anxiety, stress and distress.

"Kay," I reminded him. "I'm Miss Kay."

I loved being called Miss Kay so much that whenever I went to play at the Duff house I would play a game with myself in which I was not Kay Kelly at all, but somebody else entirely, somebody called Miss Kay. But for all that he had bestowed the title on me, Mr Duff frequently forgot who I was. In fact, I suspect he often forgot who his own children were. Time and again, I had witnessed him, called on by Violet-May or Rosemary-June to settle a quarrel between them, glance up from whatever book or paper he was reading with a mystified expression on his face and say, "Of what are we speaking?"

"What's he reading?" I asked Violet-May once.

"History and stuff," said Violet-May.

"But does he never go to work?"

"He used to," she said, "but not anymore – he's retired now."

"What did he do before he was retired?"

"He was an accountant," said Violet-May.

"My daddy works in a factory, making glue," I told her. I thought about it for a while and then I asked, "What does an accountant make?"

"They don't make anything," said Violet-May.

"Oh," I said. I said nothing more because I did not want to make Violet-May feel bad, but I could not help but feel sorry for her. I felt that for once I had the upper hand because my daddy made something and her daddy did not.

I was almost a grown woman before I realised that my father, who by nature should have been a farmer or a woodsman, hated every day of the forty years he spent in the glue factory. But how could I have guessed when the only complaint I ever heard him make was about the smells?

If anyone had told me that Violet-May and I would still be friends by Christmas, I would not have believed it. The truth was that I lived in daily expectation of her growing bored with me. But December came and still she wanted to come to our house most Saturday afternoons, to watch our television and eat my father's sweets.

Then two weeks before Christmas, Violet-May got sick and did not come to school and, on the 16th December, Mrs Duff had her baby. My mother heard about it when she was out shopping.

"A little boy," she said, "born early this morning. I hear she had a hard time of it." She was not speaking to me, but to my father.

"Why did she have a hard time?" I piped up.

She looked put out when she realised that I was behind her. "Little pitchers have big ears," she said, "I only mean that Mrs Duff is tired, that's all."

"Violet-May has two brothers now," I said enviously. "I wonder what the baby looks like? I hope Violet-May is better soon and I can go and see him." In my mind I was seeing a sort of infant version of Robbie all nestled up in a Moses basket and covered with a blue blanket.

"Even if she is better," said my mother, "I wouldn't be expecting to see her anytime soon. Her poor mother will have her hands full with a new baby in the house and she won't want you hanging about the place."

It was the first time I had ever heard her refer to Violet-May's mother as "poor". And she was right – I did not see Violet-May at all that week and when school finished for the Christmas holidays without her having come back, I remember a thought worming its way into my head: "She doesn't want to be my friend anymore. She has a little brother now and a little brother is better than a television."

On Christmas Eve, our house was full of the smell of the Christmas tree and the ham that had been boiling all day. But in *Dallas*, Southfork was on fire and JR and Ray had already collapsed from the fumes. I was sick with worry about who would save Sue Ellen and John Ross who were asleep in their smoke-filled bedrooms.

When we heard the knock at the front door, I did not even look away from the screen.

"For God's sake, who's that now?" said my mother, but she did not move.

When the knocking began again, my father said, "I'll get that then, will I?"

But Bobby Ewing had just arrived in his speeding shiny red car, and neither of us answered him. He came back with Violet-May and I was so shocked that I could not move from my chair. She was wearing a new red coat with a hood trimmed with white fur and she looked like a princess in a winter fairy tale.

"I came to give you this," she said. "Happy Christmas, Kay."

I reached out and took the present from her. "I didn't get you anything," I said.

"I don't mind," said Violet-May. "Do you like my new coat? It's for Christmas Day really, but Mummy let me wear it tonight. I think it's beautiful."

She did a twirl and over her shoulders I saw my mother roll her eyes.

The mention of Mrs Duff had reminded me of something. "What's the baby like?" I said.

"He never stops crying and neither does Mummy," said Violet-May. "I have to go now, Daddy's waiting in the car. We're in a hurry because Robbie's going to a party."

The realisation of what she had said suddenly hit me.

"Is Robbie waiting for you in the car?" I asked and, when Violet-May nodded, I followed her out into the hall.

My mother came too and opened the door. "Where do you think you're going?" she said, as I made to follow Violet-May outside.

"I'm just going out to the car to wish Mr Duff a Happy Christmas," I said.

"Well, here, throw on your coat," said my mother, reaching up and taking it down from the hallstand. "It's freezing out there."

She came out with me to the gate and stood there watching. It was very cold and very dark and the sky was spattered with bright sharp stars.

Robbie Duff was sitting in the passenger seat right there close to me, looking straight ahead, and when Violet-May opened the back door and climbed in behind him there was a blast of sound from the radio. She must have said something to her father about me wanting to wish him a Happy Christmas because Mr Duff said something then which I could not hear and Robbie suddenly leaned forward and the music faded to a low hum. He rolled down the window and Mr Duff leaned across and they both peered up at me. All of a sudden I felt too shy to say anything at all, but Mr Duff was smiling at me.

"Happy Christmas, Miss Kay," he said. He leaned a little further across Robbie's body and called out, "Happy Christmas, Mrs Kelly!"

"Happy Christmas, Mr Duff," said my mother.

I found my tongue at last. "Happy Christmas, Mr Duff," I said. "Happy Christmas, Robbie."

"Happy Christmas, Kay," said Robbie and he gave me one flash of a smile. Then he leaned back in his seat and said, "Now can we go? I'm already late."

They drove away then and my mother told me to come in quickly out of the cold. As we walked back to the door, I remembered the package I still held in my hand and in the hall I stood and examined the red-and-gold wrapping. My mother went ahead of me into the kitchen and I heard her talking to my father and mimicking Violet-May's high little voice and doing a particularly good job of it too.

"*Oh, he never stops crying and neither does Mummy,*" she said. In her usual tone she added, "That little *madam*."

"Ah, she's a bright little thing," said my father.

"That's not bright," said my mother. "That's cheeky."

"It isn't cheeky if it's true," I said, coming into the room. "But why can't Mrs Duff stop crying?"

"Never you mind," said my mother. "And don't you go repeating what I said, and anyway isn't it time you had your bath and got ready for bed? It's Christmas Eve, for God's sake."

Violet-May's gift to me was a diary with a blue cover and a silver lock and key, and in my eyes not one of the many more expensive gifts I received for Christmas that year came close. Before I went to sleep that Christmas Eve of 1983, I made my first entry: *Violet-May Duff is my best friend and Robbie Duff knows my name.*

Chapter 8

The beech trees that lined the Duffs' avenue began to sprout, just tight green spearheads at first, then fat buds which in turn burst out into their full glory. The thick green-leaved plants I had thought so little of in September exploded too into great blossoms of showy red and purple and dazzling white. Rhododendrons, my father told me they were called, one spring day when he dropped me to play with Violet-May, on his bicycle. He also told me that they were noxious weeds and would destroy all the plants around them if left to do so. I wondered if that was why I had disliked them from the beginning.

But the garden itself looked beautiful and each time I went there it had grown more and more so. But for all that, in those early months of 1984 it made no difference to me whether I played with Violet-May at her house or mine: Robbie Duff had gone to boarding school so now there was no chance of seeing him anywhere.

But in April everything changed. Easter was coming and Robbie was too, coming home for two whole weeks. And not only that, there was to be a garden party at the Duffs' house on Easter Sunday, not because it was Easter but because it was Robbie's fifteenth birthday. And I was invited and so was my mother and so was my father.

"I don't know if I'll bother," said my mother when the invitation came in the post, but in the end she bothered a great deal. She wore a new blue dress and my father had a new shirt and a blue tie and I had a yellow dress, not made, but bought from Roches Stores, because I had said "Please, Mammy, please can I have a dress from the shops, like Violet-May and Rosemary-June have?"

"Don't you like the things I make for you?" said my mother.

"I like them fine," I said, "but I'd like something really special for – for the Easter party."

I had almost said that it was for Robbie's party I wanted it but I think my mother might not have noticed if I had. She was looking out of the window when she said, "I thought something I made for you would be special. But if you want a bought dress you will have a bought dress."

I have wondered since if that was the first time I wounded my mother's heart.

On Easter Sunday my parents and I walked to the Duff house together. As we turned off the path and in at the gates, I remember seeing a teenage girl with very dark hair standing just inside the gateway. She turned and looked at us and, because I was happy and because I thought she was pretty, I smiled at her. Instead of returning my smile, the girl rushed past us and out through the gates. My mother turned and looked after her, then she nudged my father and leaned in to whisper something in his ear. I was too interested in what lay ahead of me to care about anything else and I skipped ahead of them up the avenue until my mother called after me and told me wait for them.

"Can you hear the music?" I said as they caught me up.

"You'd be hard set to miss it," said my mother. "It sounds like she's hired an entire orchestra. For a fourteen-year-old's birthday party, can you believe that?"

"Robbie isn't fourteen," I said, "he's fifteen."

Then we came out from under the trees and past the blazing rhododendrons and we saw the white tent in the middle of the circular garden before the house.

"Look at that," said my mother. "I told you she'd pull out all the stops – a marquee, the lot. I bet she has caterers."

"How the other half live," said my father.

"It's beautiful," I said, and I ran off ahead of them because I could see Violet-May and I wanted her to see my new dress.

"Oh, you've copied Rosemary-June," she said as soon as she saw me. "It's exactly like the one she wore to my birthday concert."

Looking down at my dress, I said, "It's not – mine is dark yellow, Rosemary-June's was light yellow. It's like a primrose and a daffodil, not the same at all."

"Oh, well, it looks the same to me," said Violet-May. "Do you want to come and see Robbie's cake?"

I wanted to see Robbie, not his cake, but I let her lead me across the grass and into the tent where tables were spread with food. Three girls in white shirts and black skirts were serving drinks on silver trays. The cake was done in the shape of a record player and I said quite truthfully that it looked very nice. Then I asked where Robbie was.

"Who knows?" said Violet-May.

"But it's his party," I said.

Violet-May just shrugged.

Her mother came over then and told her to go check on Alexander. Violet-May pulled a face but she ran off. I would have gone with her but I was too afraid of missing Robbie so I stayed where I was and watched her as she crossed the lawn toward the house. The pram was standing up against the wall of the house right underneath one of the ground-floor windows. I saw Violet-May lean over it, to kiss him perhaps. I thought I heard a wail from the pram, then she straightened up and stood there for a moment. Then she walked away from the pram and disappeared inside the open doorway to the house. I wondered why, if Alexander was awake, she didn't come and tell her mother.

Mrs Duff and Mr Duff came over just then and I forgot about Violet-May and Alexander.

Mr Duff shook hands with my parents. I thought he looked more rusty than ever and hot, very hot – his face was so shiny it looked almost sticky.

Mrs Duff said, "You must try a cocktail, Mrs Kelly." She held up her own glass. "They really are delicious."

"No, thank you, Mrs Duff," said my mother. "Just a cup of tea."

"And perhaps some cake," said Mrs Duff. "There's a rich chocolate sponge or a strawberry and cream –"

"Just some plain sponge will do me fine," said my mother.

"I'll go and get it for you," said Mr Duff and he walked away.

"And have you tried the *vol au vents*?" said Mrs Duff. She did not look fat anymore and she was wearing a pink dress with a pattern of purple roses. Her hair was up and for once she was smiling like she really meant it.

"We only just got here," said my mother. "I haven't tried anything."

"Well, do try them," said Mrs Duff, "There's chicken with mushroom in white wine sauce or prawn cocktail. And there's quiche of course – perhaps you'd rather some quiche?"

"No, thank you," said my mother.

"Later then, perhaps," said Mrs Duff. "And be sure to try something from the hot buffet. Isn't the string quartet divine?"

"Divine," said my mother in the voice she used when she was saying the opposite of what she meant.

A woman tapped Mrs Duff on the shoulder and she turned and then walked away to speak with her.

"Has that man gone to China to get my tea or what?" my

mother whispered. "And whose idea was this whole affair anyway? Not the birthday boy's, that's for sure. Who does that woman think she is?"

"What does it matter who she thinks she is?" said my father. "I don't know why you have to get so worked up about her."

"She's a phony, that's why," said my mother. "That voice, that accent, everything about her, none of it is real."

"I don't know if she's a phoney," said my father. "Maybe this is really who she was meant to be."

But that was too subtle for my mother. She had a go at him for defending Mrs Duff, who, so annoyed was she, she insisted on calling Florence Flynn.

I listened for a while and then I wandered away to look at the food. It all looked very fancy to me although I liked the hedgehog made from tinfoil stuck with cocktails sticks threaded with cubes of cheese and grapes. There was a lot of celery and dishes of things to stick it in, but I did not like celery.

I took some cream buns and left the tent. I ate as I walked in the direction of the pram which was still under the window at the front of the house. Somebody else was standing next to it now and as I came closer she turned and saw me coming and quickly walked away in the other direction. I recognised her as the pretty black-haired girl who had earlier rushed past us at the gates. She looked back once and, when she saw I was still watching her, she broke into a run and kept on running until she rounded the turn in the avenue.

I turned back to the pram. The baby was fast asleep. "Hello, Alexander," I whispered.

He was dressed that day in a sailor top and dark-blue shorts. He had kicked off one white sock and the sole of his little naked foot was wrinkled, like an old man's face. I thought he was a nice baby, Alexander Duff, plump and with a big face like his father and thick pink lips like Mrs Duff. His hair, which had been dark when I had last seen him, had turned fair and he had long fair eyelashes and big round cheeks with a perfect red spot in the middle of each, like a moon. I wondered if he was too hot. But, if he was, wouldn't Violet-May have come and told her mother so?

"Poor little baby," I whispered and I wished again that he was my baby brother. I would not have left him lying there in the heat, that was for sure.

I left him and strolled away around the side of the house. I had not been there alone since the day I had come for the birthday concert. A memory from another day struck me and I kept on going until I came to the place where I had seen Robbie bending down that day when I had stood at the playroom window. There was a little mound with a wooden cross on top, and someone had carved the word *PRINCE* into it.

"What are you doing?"

I jumped up and whirled around.

Robbie Duff was standing there watching me.

"Nothing, I was just looking."

"Who was that girl, the one looking into Alexander's pram?"

"I don't know," I said.

"Are you sure you don't know?" Robbie sounded angry.

"Yes, I'm sure. I never saw her before. Except at the gate when we were coming in today, I saw her then but that was the first time. I don't know who she is."

Robbie said nothing, just stuck out his foot and toed the green mound.

After a while I said quietly, "I'm sorry your dog died."

"He didn't die," said Robbie. "I wish everyone would stop saying that. He was killed."

"Because he ate a poisoned rat," I said, "or my daddy said that maybe he ate poison in one of the fields – the farmers put it down to kill rats."

"Is that what your daddy says?"

Something in the way he said it made me realise what a baby I had sounded. "Well, that's just what my father says," I amended.

I watched as Robbie's foot toed the mound once more.

"I bet you're glad you're home from boarding school," I said.

"Wrong again." Robbie bent down and with a fierce little movement pulled out the cross.

I had no idea what to say then, so I said something stupid just for the sake of saying anything at all. "But you're having a lovely party."

Robbie looked at me. "Wrong again," he said. "Listen to that – does that sound like it's my party?"

I listened. Even from there we could hear the strains of the music.

"You don't like the string quartet," I said. I was proud of myself for remembering what Mrs Duff had called the band. "I don't like it either." I wondered desperately what music he liked. I wondered if he liked Bananarama. I was afraid to ask in case he would think I was a baby again.

While I had been torturing myself, Robbie had been staring down at the cross in his hands,

"Are you going to put that back?" I said.

"No, I'm not." He raised his arm and hurled it from him, so violently that it rose in a great arc in the air and soared across the garden before falling to earth what seemed to me a great distance away, lost among the shrubs. He watched it go. "I was just a dumb kid when I made that." Then he turned to me, "And you're just a silly little girl, Kay Kelly, who knows nothing. Now why don't you run away back to the party you think is so lovely, and leave me alone?"

It was the second party at the Duffs' house where I had felt miserable. After Robbie walked away I almost burst into tears and thought about running home alone. I wondered if my mother would notice I had gone. It would have been a perverse sort of comfort to be able to convince myself that she would not, but I knew the truth was she was probably looking for me right this minute. I decided to go into the house and see if Violet-May was still there. I went in through the kitchen and up the iron staircase, which was a thrill because it always felt to me like a secret staircase even though everyone who lived in the house knew it was there.

As I came out onto the first-floor landing I was just in time to see Robbie on his way up the main staircase to the next floor. There were three other boys with him and they were laughing and all talking at the same time and Robbie was laughing too, almost as if he were a completely different person to the one who had been so cross with me in the garden.

I was still watching them when the door to the bathroom opened and Rosemary-June came out. She looked past me and up the stairs to where now only the feet of the four boys were visible and then they too disappeared, although we could still hear them laughing.

"You were watching Robbie again," she said.

"No, I wasn't," I said, and I felt my face growing hot and knew it was getting red and there was nothing I could do to stop it.

"Yes, you were," said Rosemary-June. "You're always watching him. I suppose he's gone up to his room with his friends to play his tapes and drink beer. I hope he locks his door or Mummy will walk in and catch him."

"Robbie wouldn't drink beer," I said.

"Yes, he would, he already does," said Rosemary-June.

Then from above our heads we heard a sudden burst of music.

Rosemary-June looked up and then she smiled at me. "See, tapes and beer. I have to go now," she said. "Mummy sent me to fetch the baby but I needed the bathroom."

"He's asleep," I said. I was relieved her mind had moved

away from Robbie, although my face was still warm.

"He'll wake up soon," said Rosemary-June, "and he'll start crying again, because he's hungry or wet or something."

"He's only little," I said, "he can't help it."

Rosemary-June put her head to one side as she looked at me. "You like Alexander," she said. "So does Robbie, so do I."

"Of course we like Alexander – he's a baby, everyone loves babies."

"I don't think Mummy loves him," said Rosemary-June. "She says he's difficult. And Violet-May hates him. She pinches him and makes him cry."

"I don't believe that," I said. As I said it I was thinking of how Violet-May had leant over Alexander's pram and the little cry I had heard. A terrible thought came into my mind: had she kissed him or pinched him?

I told Rosemary I needed to use the bathroom too, but as soon as she went downstairs I crept up to the second landing. I stood for a while just listening to the sounds of music drifting along the corridor. A man's voice was singing, "*I want to break free*", and I could hear the sound of laughing and voices although I could not hear what they were saying. Then someone or something fell against a door and I bolted back along the corridor and down the stairs again. My heart was thumping so hard in my chest that it hurt but I didn't care, because I had been almost outside Robbie Duff's room door and I had heard the music he was playing.

At home that evening I told my parents that I was too old for 'Mammy' and 'Daddy' and from now on I would be calling them Mam and Dad.

Chapter 9

There was an earthquake in Dublin in July 1984 and apparently in some of the flats in the tower blocks in Ballymun ornaments fell from the mantelpieces. It did not even register on my personal Richter scale but, even so, apart from going to see *Ghostbusters* in the cinema with my father, it was still the most exciting thing to happen that summer. The Duffs went to France at the beginning of July and did not come back again until the beginning of August. When I first heard that they were going away, I had let myself imagine that Violet-May might invite me to go too. I allowed myself to conjure up vivid and elaborate daydreams in which Robbie and I had wonderful adventures on sunny beaches during which it became clear to Robbie that I was not a silly little girl at all, but quite intelligent, very interesting and incredibly witty. Instead the Duffs sailed to France without me, leaving me to play in the road with the other kids in the estate.

I did not learn to swim like a fish that summer either. In the Deep one of the big boys pushed me and I went under and swallowed a lot of water and almost choked. As a result, I was even more nervous than I had already been. My father had bought our first car, a second-hand Ford Escort, the colour of mustard, and in it he took us to Portmarnock beach a couple of times. On both occasions the wind was high and the waves too strong for my liking. I considered myself too big now for armbands but too frightened to leave the shallows without them, and so I stayed paddling at the sea's edge while my father swam so far out he was just a dot in the distance.

Violet-May came back from France, brown and somehow different, although I could not have put into words what the difference was.

The day her mother's car pulled up outside our house I had been playing in the road for hours and was sitting on the Nugents' wall between the twins. We were dusty and hot, the ice-cream van had just been and my face and hands were sticky from the ice-pops my father had bought for the three of us.

Violet-May got out of the car and came across to us. She was wearing a white skirt and a white top and her hair was done up in a new and fancy way in some kind of plait. She looked beautiful and absolutely, impossibly clean. Maybe that was why Mandy Nugent stuck out her tongue at her or maybe it was because the Nugent twins had got me back and were not about to let me go again without a struggle. I knew in my heart that they resented the time I spent with Violet-May and, although I felt guilty about it, I was also human enough to recognise and be pleased by the compliment.

But right now Mandy Nugent's tongue was purple from her Dracula pop and I felt so embarrassed I wished I could pretend I didn't know her.

Violet-May acted liked nothing had happened.

"Do you want to come into my house?" I said, getting up from the wall.

"I can't," said Violet-May. "Mummy's waiting."

"*Mummy's waiting*," said Mandy, and she sniggered.

"Stop it, Mandy," I said.

"Yeah, stop it, Mandy," said Dolores.

I walked away from them and back toward the car with Violet-May.

"So immature," she said.

I nodded in agreement. "I know."

As we walked, I was watching Violet-May out of the corner of my eye, trying to figure out what was different about her. She had definitely grown taller, but that was the only thing I could pin down, that and the plait.

"I like your hair," I said.

"It's a French plait. Do you want to come over to my house tomorrow? Mummy says it's OK."

"Yes, please."

"OK, well, I'll see you then."

Mrs Duff leaned across and opened the car door. Alexander was crying his heart out inside.

"If you're quite ready, Violet-May," Mrs Duff said. "Mummy needs to get the baby home. Hello, Kay." She was wearing very big sunglasses and I could not see her eyes, but she did not sound one bit pleased to see me.

Violet-May got in and I peered into the back. I had half hoped that Robbie would be there but there was only Alexander, all strapped up in a baby seat. His face was bright red, his mouth was open as he roared and waved his fists at the back of his mother's head. The car door slammed and I could only hear him faintly then.

As I stood watching the car move away, the twins came and stood one on either side of me.

"She's such a snob," said Mandy.

"You're so immature, Mandy Nugent," I said, and I walked away.

I went to play with Violet-May the next day but my only sighting of Robbie was at his bedroom window. It was a lovely day and, after running about the garden for a while, Violet-May and I sat down for a rest on the front steps. They felt warm to the touch and the tiny flecks of what looked like silver in the stone winked in the sunlight. After a while we got bored of sitting and played at chasing one another up and down the avenue.

As we walked back toward the house, I saw that somebody had brought out a striped blue-and-white deckchair to the lawn in front of the house. Then Mrs Duff came out through the open front doorway, pushing the pram ahead of her. She wheeled it to its usual spot under the window, put on the brake then picked up a book which had been inside the pram.

When she turned and saw us, she put a finger to her lips and said in a whisper, "Play quietly now, girls, and no running or squealing please. Mummy has only just got Alexander to sleep and she needs a little time to herself."

We watched her walk across the lawn toward the deckchair where she settled herself with her book in her lap. She slid the sunglasses which had been perched on top of her head down over her eyes then leaned back and raised her face to the sun.

"I want to sunbathe too," said Violet-May. "Let's go and get some more deckchairs."

She raced off and I ran after her to a shed behind the house where an assortment of garden furniture was stored. Violet-May chose one with a faded yellow stripe and I took one in blue-and-white and we carried them around to the front of the house.

Crossing the lawn, I saw that Mrs Duff's book still lay in her lap and the breeze had flipped it open and was riffling through it like an invisible finger. Her head had fallen to one side and her sunglasses had slipped down onto her nose. As we came nearer I could hear a gentle little rumble coming from her open mouth and I remember being a little bit shocked to discover that Mrs Duff snored just like my father did, just like an ordinary person really. I looked at Violet-May and we both began to giggle and then we tip-toed past where her mother was snoozing and found a spot some distance away to pitch our chairs.

I was just about to sit down when there was an explosion of sound which startled me and caused Mrs Duff to jerk awake. I saw her leap to her feet and her sunglasses slid from her nose and landed on the grass. At the same moment Alexander began to screech and Mrs Duff let out a roar which made me jump as the music had not.

"*Robbie Duff!*" she roared at the top of her voice.

I was shocked because I had never before seen her lose her temper or even really raise her voice. But now she was striding across the grass toward the house, roaring, actually roaring.

"*Robbie Duff, show your face this instant. This instant, do you hear?*"

From an open window on the second floor, Robbie's head appeared.

"*What do you want?*" he bellowed.

"*Turn off that music immediately!*" his mother roared back. "*You selfish, thoughtless boy! How dare you play it like that when I expressly asked you not to! You've gone and woken Alexander and now I'll never get him back to sleep!*"

"*Oh, for God's sake!*"

As I watched, Robbie's head disappeared and a moment later the music stopped.

Mrs Duff kept on marching and did not stop until she reached the pram. I saw her touch her foot to the brake, then push it very fast to the base of the steps which led up to the open front door. I watched as she climbed the steps, dragging the pram behind her. Watching it bounce, I remember wondering how it must feel to Alexander – bumpy, I was sure – and as the door slammed behind them I could hear him crying.

"What will she do to Robbie?" I said, turning to Violet-May.

"Who cares?" said Violet. "Give him another lecture about disturbing her when she's trying to take a nap and relax. But so what – she's always taking a nap or going for a lie-down or trying to relax."

And I stared at the window where Robbie had been and hoped very hard that he would not get into too much trouble.

By the time I next went to play at Violet-May's house Robbie had gone to stay with a friend where, Violet-May informed me, he would remain for the rest of the school holidays. It made me sad to think that I might not see him again until the Christmas holidays. Christmas seemed a very long time away. But perhaps, I thought suddenly, he would be allowed to come home for Violet-May's birthday, which reminded me of something else I had been wondering about.

"Will you be having a birthday concert again this year, Violet-May?" I asked anxiously.

"Mummy says not," said Violet-May. She pulled a face. "She says it's too much trouble and she doesn't want any fuss this year. It's all Alexander's fault – his crying is driving her mad."

And then I had an idea. "Why can't we have a party at my house this year?" I said. "Then your mother wouldn't have to fuss and we could invite your friends and my friends too."

"What, have *my* party at your house?" said Violet-May, pulling a face again.

"It would be *our* party, yours as well as mine," I said.

"Oh right, it's your birthday too," said Violet-May as though this was news to her. "But I don't know, I'll have to ask Mummy."

She did ask her mother and I was almost at fever pitch as I awaited the verdict, but I might have known that Violet-May would get her own way. In fact, it was my mother who proved most resistant to the idea of a joint birthday party and I had to enlist the help of my father in my efforts to persuade her that it was indeed a good idea and not just another opportunity for Flora Duff to come and lord it over everyone while at the same time looking down her nose at them. Having once secured her reluctant agreement, I then lived what was left of the summer in that happy state of anticipation of an event, which is almost always better than its realisation, and never more so than on this occasion.

Because our birthdays fell on a Monday that year, the party was originally set to take place on the previous Saturday, the 22nd of September. Then Violet-May discovered that she had a music exam on the Saturday and the party was rescheduled for the 29th of September, the Saturday following our birthdays.

On the day originally set for the party, my father decided that as it was a beautifully sunny day we should make the most of the fine weather and go on our annual family nut-picking expedition. Nut-picking in autumn had become a tradition in our house. My father was a natural-born forager and, even before I could walk, as he often reminded me, he and my mother used to take me along with them on this annual expedition, riding high on my father's shoulders. As I grew older I looked forward very much to the outing and we had never yet missed a year. I shared my father's love of nature and in particular I loved the woods, so dim and shadowy that it made me shiver just a little to be there. My father taught me the names of all the trees. Beside the hazel, there were the giant oak and the ash, and though you did not always see them, you knew that animals lived there – foxes and pheasants and rabbits. It was always September that my father chose for nut-picking because, he said, if you left it too late into the season, the birds and squirrels might beat you to it. He was an expert in the art of gathering nuts and taught me at an early age how to spot the small clusters, often hidden in the bushes, camouflaged by their leafy green shells. He always came armed with a stick which he used to bend back the branches so that my mother and I could get at the nuts.

We dropped our pickings into the wicker baskets which my mother and I carried on our arms and, when they were full, we would find a place to sit and eat the picnic we always brought with us. It usually ended with us helping ourselves to a great many of the hazelnuts we had picked – I loved the incomparable sweetness and crunch of the fresh nuts – and my father would bring along a small silver nutcracker which he used to crack them open. Afterward we would walk slowly home where my mother would store the nuts at the back of the airing cupboard for eating at Halloween.

That Saturday I put on my denim shorts and my red T-shirt. I had to search for the basket I always used for gathering nuts and eventually found it in the cupboard under the stairs. It had once held an Easter egg and I thought it was very pretty with its blue-and-yellow weave.

Then, just as we were leaving the house, my father said he felt a pain in his chest – a tightness he called it – and although he said it was probably nothing to worry about, my mother wanted to call the doctor immediately. My father would not let her do that and to stop her he agreed to postpone the nut-picking and go and lie down. After he had gone upstairs and I had asked my mother, admittedly for possibly the seventh time, if he was going to be alright, she snapped at me and told me to stop "hatching the house" and sent me out to play.

I found my basket in the porch where I had dropped it and I picked it up and went and sat on our front wall and wondered miserably if my father was going to die.

Then Ken Fitzgerald came along and began picking up small pebbles and flinging them in my direction in an attempt, he claimed, to get them into my basket. I told him to stop but he kept on doing it and I finally got up and walked away.

"Where are you going?" he called after me.

"*I don't know!*" I yelled back. "*Anywhere to get away from you, Ken Fitzgerald!*"

Sometimes I have tormented myself with the thought that

had Violet-May not had her music exam that day, or my mother had not sent me out to play, or Ken Fitzgerald had not thrown those stones, the terrible things that happened afterwards might not have.

But they did.

Chapter 10

I walked to the end of our estate and out onto Old Road and then I kept on going. As I passed the Duff house I walked across to the gate and peered up the avenue. I knew, however, that there was no point in going in because Violet-May had a piano exam and so I turned away again and continued walking. Somewhere along the way I had resolved that if I could not feast on nuts today, I could at least gorge myself on blackberries. I knew a spot along the road where every year the hedges grew heavy with the fattest and sweetest of berries. This year was no exception and I spent some time happily enough, alternating between eating the fruit and dropping them into my basket. But it wasn't so much fun to do on my own and I finally grew bored and decided to go home and see if the Nugent twins wanted to play.

Approaching the Duffs' gate once more, I heard the sound of distant voices and then Violet-May appeared around the bend in the avenue. She was pushing a pram and I raised my hand and waved to her. She did not wave back and, as I stood and watched, Rosemary-June appeared behind her. Violet-May turned and said something to her. I could not hear what but it sounded to me as though they were arguing. I stood at the gate and watched them coming closer. Violet-May was pushing the pram very fast and when she suddenly called my name I hurried up the avenue to meet her. I remember that there were fallen leaves on the ground and as I walked the wind whipped more of them from the branches and they sailed down slowly past me. Up close I could see that Violet-May's face was very red and hot-looking. She looked cross too and for once even Rosemary-June who was walking slowly some distance behind her was unsmiling.

I turned and fell into step with Violet-May. We had only gone a short distance when she turned and yelled at her sister, "*I told you to stop following me, didn't I?*" She turned back to me and said, "You're so lucky not to have any sisters." She looked down at the pram. "Or brothers."

As always, I wanted to agree with her but the truth was that all my life I had wished I was not an only child so I did not know what to say and decided to change the subject.

"I thought you had a music exam today."

"I did have a music exam. But Miss O'Connor is sick and it was cancelled. So instead I have to do this." She gave the pram a violent push.

"Where's your mother?" I asked.

"*Mummy needs to rest her eyes,*" Violet-May mimicked her mother's voice so well it made me smile. She spotted my basket then and said, "What's that for?"

"I was picking blackberries," I said. "We were supposed to be going picking hazelnuts and then we were going to have a picnic but my daddy got a pain in his chest and my mammy said he needs to lie down so now we can't go." I bit my lip, hearing how babyish I sounded – I found it hard to remember my resolution to call my parents Mam and Dad. "Do you want some blackberries?"

"I don't like blackberries," said Violet-May. "It's a pity you didn't pick any nuts, I like nuts."

"I like blackberries," said Rosemary-June, coming up behind her.

So I held out the basket and she took two handfuls, which I thought was just greedy.

"Mummy doesn't like picnics," said Rosemary-June. "Flies land on the food and it isn't hygienic – and the grass is always damp and Violet-May isn't allowed –"

"Nobody asked you," interrupted Violet-May, "and I told you to stop following me." She turned to me. "Where do you pick hazelnuts?"

"In the woods – my daddy knows the best places."

"We could go," said Violet-May.

"Picking hazelnuts?" I stared at her in surprise. "I'm not allowed to go into the woods without my daddy, without my dad. I don't even know the way properly."

It was true. My father always led the way on our excursions to the woods, by a labyrinthine route it was impossible to fully remember.

"Well, then, you might as well go home," said Violet-May. "Everything is horrible today."

"I know somewhere else where there are hazelnuts," I said quickly. "It's down at the Surly. It's not as good a place for nuts as the woods, but we should get some."

"Where's the Surly?" said Violet-May and I looked at her in surprise that she did not know.

"It's the part of the river at Bone Bridge – you know Bone Bridge, don't you? It's only down the road from here really?"

Violet-May nodded.

"Right, well, there's a copse there." I said. "It's right in the middle of the field and there are always hazelnuts there – you just need to know where to look."

"What's a copse?" said Rosemary-June.

"That's what my father calls it," I told her. "It's like a little wood really."

"Why is it called Bone Bridge?" said Rosemary-June then and I told her the story of the bones that had been found and the superstition that the spirits of the dead still walked the bridge at midnight. I expected her to show some sign of fear but Rosemary-June hardly blinked.

"Let's go and get some nuts," said Violet-May.

"Mummy said we were not to go any further than the gate," said Rosemary-June.

"*Mummy said, Mummy said!*" said Violet-May. "Don't be such a baby, Rosemary-June. No-one asked you to come anyway – we don't want babies with us, do we, Kay?"

I glanced at the pram and thought that, as there was an actual baby with us, it was hard to answer that question so I said nothing.

"Well, if you're going I'm going too," said Rosemary-June. "I want some hazelnuts too and if you try to stop me I'll tell Mummy."

In an attempt to make peace, I said, "I'll push Alexander if you like."

Violet-May immediately let go of the pram and I took over. The handle was warm from where her hands had been holding it, and I smiled down at Alexander's face which was pinker and hotter-looking than Violet-May's.

We were close to the gates now and I realised there was someone standing half-concealed by one of the pillars, peering round at us.

"Who's that?" I asked Violet-May.

"I don't know," said Violet-May. "But she shouldn't be here – this is private property."

She sounded so like her mother when she said this that I almost smiled. But, in any case, the girl had spun round quickly and disappeared.

"I saw her here before," I said suddenly. "She was here on the day of Robbie's birthday party."

"Maybe she's in love with him," said Rosemary-June. "All the girls are in love with Robbie."

My heart was suddenly swamped by jealousy at the thought of that pretty dark-haired girl loving Robbie Duff.

As we came out onto the path, I looked back to see if she was still around and she was. She had walked some distance back up the road and was standing leaning against the Duffs' wall, apparently inspecting her nails. She was wearing a black top and a skirt of very bright green and as I watched her head came up and I saw her glance in our direction. Then she moved on again, walking slowly in the opposite direction.

"Come on," said Violet-May. "What are you staring at? You have to keep pushing the pram. If you stop, Alexander will start bawling again. He's teething and he's like an anti-Christ, Mummy says."

So I pushed the pram and we all moved off down Old Road and I forgot about the girl for a while. I liked pushing the pram – the road was downhill all the way so it was no bother really. The whole way down only a few cars passed us and one of them, I have no idea why I remember it so clearly but I do, was bright red in colour. Perhaps it was because the windows were open and the radio was playing very loudly so I could distinctly hear the words of the song that was playing. I remember thinking – but rain isn't purple, it isn't really any colour at all. Forever afterward I could not hear "Purple Rain" but I was transported back to that September afternoon, pushing Alexander's pram down Old Road, the silver handles shimmering in the sun, warm beneath my hands.

I do remember that I looked back once, just before we rounded the corner, and the girl was still in sight. She was closer than she had been and I had the impression she had just stopped walking that very moment and it caused my mind briefly to wonder if she had been following us.

To me it seemed no distance to the Surly, I had walked it so many times. But Rosemary-June soon began complaining that it was too far and Violet-May asked twice if we were nearly there. I remember thinking that it was probably because they were driven everywhere and I wondered if now that my father had bought a car I would grow lazy too. Then I thought about him lying in bed and I began to fret once more and hope his pain had gone away.

When we finally got to Bone Bridge, Violet-May leaned against the wall and peered down into the water. "It's horrible," she said, "black and horrible."

"I know," I said, "but it's good fun if you throw a stick or something that floats in, and then watch for it coming out the other side. It takes ages, it does. Have you never been here before?"

She shook her head, looking about her. "I'm going to find something to throw in."

"Where are the hazelnuts?" said Rosemary-June. "I'm hungry."

I suddenly realised that I had no nutcracker with me but shied away from telling them. Hopefully we would be able to break them open with stones? I pointed to a gap in the hedge through which you had to climb in order to get into the field beyond.

"The hazel copse is in there," I said. "But we can't all go through – the pram won't fit so someone will have to stay here with Alexander."

"I'm not going in there," said Violet-May. "I'd tear my dress."

"I'm not going either," said Rosemary-June. "I'm thirsty and I'm hungry and you said there were hazelnuts."

"Yes," said Violet-May, pushing out her lower lip, "you said there were hazelnuts."

"Here, eat these," I said, and I spilled out the rest of the blackberries into Rosemary-June's two hands. "There are hazelnuts," I told Violet-May, "but you have to go through the field to get them."

I pointed at the gap again but Rosemary-June was stuffing blackberries into her mouth and Violet-May was staring at me as though she hated me.

I said quickly, "I'll go on my own and bring back the nuts. You stay here and have a rest."

I left them on the bridge and the last thing I saw as I clambered through the gap in the hedge was Violet-May leaning over the parapet of the bridge, staring down at the river. I wondered if she had tried throwing something in to watch it come out the other side. Rosemary-June had taken over pushing the pram to and fro, one hand on the handle, one hand feeding blackberries into her mouth.

The copse was nothing more than a thicket of overgrown bushes and straggly trees in the middle of the field, a great deal more overgrown than I remembered it. It took me a lot of time to wriggle myself in to where the hazelnuts were and I caught my shorts on a sharp thorny bush, got my hair caught a couple of times and scraped the back of my hand quite badly too. And, after all that, the squirrels must have got there before me because I could only manage to pick a handful of them. I remember looking sadly into my basket as I came out into the bright sunshine of the field again and thinking that Violet-May and Rosemary-June would not be pleased. For that reason I did not hurry back to them as quickly as I could – in fact I strayed a little from the middle of the field toward the river and gazed at it for a little while. The water was moving here – not fast but you could see it flowing. It was only at that place under the bridge that it seemed to stop, as though, I thought, it had suddenly got tired and decided to have a good rest before it moved on again. I shielded my eyes against the sun and tried to see the girls on the bridge but there was no sign of them from where I was and I moved away again and began making my way back toward the gap in the hedge.

I heard the first scream quite clearly. It was high and very shrill and it came from a single voice. At the sound of it I stopped and stood quite still. It stopped and then it started again, only this time I knew it was more than one person doing the screaming and I also knew without doubt that it was Violet-May and Rosemary-June I was hearing. The hysteria in their voices infected me and I began to run. All the time I ran the screaming never stopped and I ran so fast that I caught my foot in something and I fell. I hurt my foot but I got up again and kept on running until I reached the hedge at the boundary with the road. My heart was bounding in my chest and in my confusion I could not find the gap. What was so clearly identifiable on the road side of the hedge was not so easily found on the field side and, peering desperately into the tangle of hawthorn, I darted first left then right, trying to find the opening I knew was there.

I had done this a couple of times when I saw a flash of blue and knew I was seeing Violet-May's dress. In the same moment I realised that the screaming had stopped and I remember thinking that perhaps everything was alright. Perhaps Violet-May had had a tantrum but it was all over now or maybe Rosemary-June had been stung by a bee – there were still some around because the weather was so good. As I peered through the hedge I could not see Rosemary-June at all. And it was Violet-May's voice that I could hear, not screaming now, but still high-pitched and hysterical. But for all that, I knew for certain then that something bad had happened after all. At the same moment I spotted the gap in the hedge and I flung myself through it, not caring if I ripped my clothes or my hair got pulled out or if I tore my skin to pieces. As I burst through, it was Rosemary-June I saw first: she was standing facing me, staring right at me, her eyes wide with an expression in them that I had never seen there before. Behind her Violet-May was running from one end of the bridge to the other, all the time making horrible little whimpering sounds. Every few seconds she would stop to lean over the wall as though looking for something in the water and then off she would go again.

"What's she doing?" I pleaded with Rosemary-June. "What's wrong, why were you screaming?"

"Alexander," said Rosemary-June.

That was all she said and her voice was barely a whisper and her eyes stayed fixed on my face and something about them made me suddenly very afraid.

"What's wrong with him?" I said but she still didn't answer me.

I ran across the road to where the pram stood, its hood still up, the yellow-and-white blanket spilling out over the side, one corner touching the ground. And, although I somehow knew before I looked inside that there would be no red-faced baby in his bright-red romper suit lying there, seeing his blue rattle and the empty space where he should have been made me so afraid that I began to tremble.

I looked at Violet-May and she was still running up and down and making that terrible whimpering sound.

"Where is he?" I called. "Violet-May, where's Alexander?"

When she did not answer me, I called her name again, and this time it was a scream.

"Violet-May! Tell me what's happened to Alexander!"

She stopped running then and when she looked at me I saw the terror in her wild, wet eyes.

"He's in the river," she said. And then, as though she was realising for the first time not just who I was but that I was there at all, she said, "It was an accident, Kay – Alexander fell in the river, but it was an accident. I can't find him, Kay – he's in the river but I can't find him. Please help me find him, Kay, please help me find Alexander."

And that was when Rosemary-June began to scream again.

Chapter 11

They found Alexander's body snagged in the branches of a tree. The current had swept him downriver for almost three hundred yards. The guards who found him tried to resuscitate him but failed and he was taken to the nearest hospital where he was pronounced dead on arrival. I found out about all of this in the days afterwards from listening to what people were saying and also from the television.

"What's a post-mortem?" I asked once and my mother, who had not realised that I was standing in the doorway watching the news because she was too busy crying, jumped in her chair then shot to her feet and turned the television off.

"You shouldn't be listening to that, Kay," she told me.

From the beginning her coping mechanism was one of denial. Not that it had happened – because Alexander was dead and she could not get away from that fact – but denial that any of it had anything to do with me. Unlike the police who had asked me and Violet-May and Rosemary-June a lot of questions over and over again, my mother asked me only once if I had seen what had happened to Alexander. When I told her I had not, that I had been in the field looking for nuts and come back to find the pram empty, she never questioned me again about what had happened that day.

She was there of course, the day Alexander died, when we were taken to the local police station and questioned, and she sat with my father and Mr Duff all in a row against the wall. I remember thinking that Mr Duff looked older somehow. Mrs Duff was not there and I heard Mr Duff tell my mother that she had been sedated. I did not know what sedated meant.

My mother told Mr Duff that my father should be in his bed as he'd had a scare to which my father said, "Never mind that now, Liz."

We were questioned by a policewoman who was wearing a uniform and a man who was not. They sat on one side of the table and Violet-May and I sat facing them on the other side with Rosemary-June in the middle. There was a box of paper hankies on the table and I wondered if they were going to make us cry. I already wanted to cry anyway, every time I thought about the empty pram. But they were very kind to us, right from the beginning, and the policewoman smiled at us and told us we were not in trouble. She put a can of Fanta Orange down in front of each of us and said that her name was Fidelma. I remember thinking that I liked the name Fidelma, that it would have been nice to put it on my list of names. But I knew I never would now because it would always remind me of Alexander. Rosemary-June opened her can straight away and I remember the rasping sound of the ring-pull and the noise in her throat as she drank.

Fidelma sat down and opened her notebook and picked up a pen. She told us the man was a detective and that they would need to ask us a lot of questions because it was very important that they be clear about what had happened. She said that all we had to do was tell the truth and then our parents could take us home. I looked over my shoulder at my mother and she was smiling at me. Fidelma said that the first thing they needed to know was what we were doing on the bridge in the first place and why we had the baby with us.

I told her how the plan to pick hazelnuts had been cancelled because of my father feeling sick, how I had gone for a walk past Violet-May's house and met her and Rosemary-June.

"They were minding Alexander," I said, "because Mrs Duff needed a lie-down."

Talking about Alexander made me feel upset and I began to cry. Fidelma gave me a paper hanky and asked me if I needed to take a break. I said I was alright and she asked if I would like to have a drink of my orange, and when I nodded she opened the can for me and I drank some.

After a while she asked me if I was alright to tell her some more now and I said I was. So I carried on telling her what I remembered.

"Violet-May said why couldn't we go for hazelnuts ourselves but I'm not allowed to go in the woods by myself so I told her about the copse at Bone Bridge."

When I said that, I saw my father lean forward in his chair and put his head into his hands.

I continued, "I thought we'd find some nuts there but when I got there I could hardly find any – the squirrels must have eaten them."

"So you walked along Old Road to Bone Bridge?" Fidelma prompted me.

"Yes. Rosemary-June wanted to come too so we all walked down together."

"Did many cars pass as you were walking down Old Road?"

"A few, I think, but I only remember a red car."

"Alright, so what happened when you got to the bridge then, Kay?"

"Kay wasn't on the bridge when the accident happened," said my mother. "I've already told you that a few times now. She was in the field looking for hazelnuts just like she said."

"Mrs Kelly," said the detective, "if you could let Kay tell us in her own words what happened, please."

"Tell them where you were, Kay," said my mother. "Tell them you were in the field."

"I was in the field," I said.

"*Mrs Kelly*," said the detective.

"Liz," said my father and my mother made a sound in her nose and tossed her head not unlike the way I had seen horses do.

"Tell us about what happened before you went into the field to get the nuts, Kay," said Fidelma.

"Nothing happened," I said. "Rosemary-June was hungry so I gave her my blackberries. Then I went to get the nuts in the field."

"And what did Violet-May and Rosemary-June do?"

"They stayed on the bridge,." I said.

"And where was Alexander?"

"In his pram. Rosemary-June was pushing him so he wouldn't start crying again."

"Where was Violet-May?"

"She was leaning over the bridge looking at something in the water."

Fidelma looked at Violet-May, "What was in the water, Violet-May?"

"A stick," said Violet-May, her voice sulky. "I threw in a stick to see how long it took to go under the bridge."

"OK," said Fidelma. "So you went into the field, you say, Kay. Which field is that?"

"The field with the hazelnut copse," I said. "It's beside the river and you get in through a gap in the hedge."

I looked down at the scrapes on my hands. There was one big scape on my left hand and two small ones – the right hand had two middle-sized scrapes.

"The pram wouldn't fit and anyway Violet-May didn't want to tear her dress so she stayed on the bridge with Rosemary-June and … and Alexander."

"How long were you gone looking for the nuts, Kay?" said Fidelma.

"I don't know."

"She was gone ages," said Violet-May suddenly.

Her voice sounded sulky and I turned to look at her, but she was looking down at her arm and fiddling with the beads of a white-and-yellow bracelet. I sat back thinking with a shock that she had made it sound somehow like what had happened had been my fault. The idea made me feel a little bit sick.

"I ran back when I heard the screaming," I gasped, "but I couldn't find the gap in the hedge, I couldn't find it for ages and ages. And then I found it and I climbed through but the pram was empty and Alexander was gone."

When Fidelma spoke again I didn't hear what she said, and she had to repeat her question. She was asking if I had heard anything or seen anything while I was in the field.

I didn't answer at once. I looked from Fidelma to Violet-May and this time she was looking right at me.

"Kay?" said my father gently.

I glanced at him. He was watching me and trying to smile.

I looked down at my can of Fanta Orange on the table.

"Only the screaming," I said. "I didn't hear anything only the screaming."

My mother said, "You see, it had nothing to do with Kay, she wasn't even there."

"But were you there on the bridge, Kay, when the Dempsey family came by in their car and stopped?" asked Fidelma.

The Dempseys, I remember thinking – was that who they were – that fat man with the red hair who had stopped his car on the bridge, stuck his red face out of the window and looked at us suspiciously? That woman who had got out so quickly and knelt down and put her hands on Rosemary-June's shoulders and tried to make her stop screaming so she could understand what we were saying? Her kind worried

92

face had changed when she realised what we were telling her and her hand had gone to her mouth as Violet-May wailed, "My brother fell into the river! Alexander fell into the river and I can't see him, I can't see him anymore!"

The woman had stared at the empty pram and said, "Oh sweet Jesus, oh sweet Jesus!" Then she too was screaming, screaming at the man in the car to come and help, "*Oh sweet Jesus, Peadar, hurry up, there's a baby in the river!*"

And the fat man had cursed and climbed out of the car and leaned over the parapet of the bridge and rubbed the back of his balding head and said he couldn't see him, Jesus Christ he couldn't see him, and were we absolutely sure he went in there?

And Violet-May said, "Yes, I'm sure and please, please, will you get him out?"

And the fat man said, "How the fuck am I supposed to get down there?"

And the woman, crying now, said, "I don't know, Peadar, can you jump or something? I don't know, I don't know ... but you have to do something, you have to, Holy Mother of God, Peadar, you have to do something!"

And the fat man cried, "*Christ Almighty, I can't jump in there, ah fuck me, fuck me!*" and he put his hand to the back of his head again and paced the length of the wall, peering down into the river.

And all the time the small boy and girl in the back seat were watching us through the car window from big, stricken, terrified eyes.

Fidelma said gently, "Kay? Were you there when the Dempseys came?"

I came back to the present moment with a start.

"Yes, I was there then," I said. "The car came and the woman got out and Violet-May told her about Alexander and then the fat man got out to look, but he couldn't see Alexander in the water. So I showed him how to get to the

93

river by way of the gap in the hedge. I went with him and I watched him take off his shoes and socks and get into the water in his clothes. Then he went under the bridge and I stayed on the bank and I couldn't see him anymore. And when I went back up onto the road two more cars had stopped and somebody went to phone the police and somebody asked us our names and a man who knew Mr Duff went to get him and then ... and then ...."

I wasn't sure quite what happened then. I remembered a small crowd of people had gathered on the bridge. I remembered standing staring into the river, watching the fat man flounder about as he waded downstream, his head down, staring into the water, looking I knew for Alexander. I watched him until he reached the curve of the river and then disappeared. I remembered Mr Duff arriving in his big car and the door opening and Mrs Duff almost falling out onto the road and I remembered hearing her screaming. I remembered the police coming and somewhere, at some point, the three of us being put in a car to be taken to the police station.

And finally, I remembered looking back as the car drove us away and seeing the faces of the people staring after us: a woman with a small dog sitting at her feet, his tongue hanging out, a man in a silly-looking straw hat leaning on a walking stick, and a dark-haired girl in a bright green skirt.

I remembered what happened when we arrived at the police station clearly and in detail though. I still do. We all three sat in a room and said nothing and did not look at one another and waited. After a while the door opened and my mother and father came in and my father knelt down and put his arms around me and told me not to worry because everything was going to be alright. My mother stood looking down at us and said nothing at all and I saw that she had a hanky in her hand and that she had been crying. After a long time Mr Duff came into the room too and Rosemary-June got up and ran to him but Violet-May stayed where she was sitting and just looked at them. Over the top of Rosemary's head, I saw Mr Duff looking at my father and shaking his head and my mother began to cry again.

It was Violet-May's turn next.

"Why did you take Alexander from his pram?" Fidelma wanted to know.

"He wouldn't stop crying," said Violet-May. "I kept pushing the pram but he wouldn't stop. So I took him out and I sat him on the wall. I thought if he could see the water it might make him stop – he likes shiny things. And I think he did like the water because he stopped crying and he waved his arms."

When Violet-May said that, my mother opened her bag and took out her hanky and blew her nose.

Mr Duff got up and walked to the door and stood there with his back to us and waggled his ear furiously. Fidelma waited until he sat down again before she asked the next question.

"And what happened then, Violet-May?"

"Alexander slipped," said Violet-May, "he just slipped. I was holding him, I was, but he sort of jumped and I couldn't catch him and he slipped and he fell in the river. I could see him in the water but I couldn't get down to him. There wasn't any way down from the bridge. He wasn't moving, he was just lying there with his face in the water, but it wasn't my fault, it wasn't, *it was an accident, it was just an accident!*"

I remember thinking that she was going to become hysterical and I wondered what Fidelma and the detective would make of her rolling about on the police-station floor. But while I was thinking that I was also thinking something else, that if I had been there when Alexander fell I would have known the way down from the bridge. I would have gone through the gap, I would have got into the river. So what if the river was black and scummy and smelled bad? So what if I couldn't really swim? I would have waded in. I wouldn't even have waited to take off my shoes. I would have found Alexander and saved him, I would, I would ... if only I had been there on the bridge instead of in the field.

"Nobody is saying it was your fault, Violet-May," said Mr Duff, and I saw his hand stray to his ear once more.

Fidelma nodded. "That's right, nobody is accusing anyone here – we are just trying to establish what happened."

Then she turned to Rosemary-June.

"Rosemary-June, could you tell us now what you remember, please?"

I turned to look at Rosemary-June. She was running her finger around the rim of her Fanta can but she lifted her head and smiled at Fidelma before turning to look at Violet-May. Violet-May turned to her too and I saw the quick smile she flashed at her sister.

Then Fidelma said, "In your own words, please, Rosemary-June."

Rosemary-June turned back to face her. "Alexander was crying," she said. "Violet-May said maybe he'd like to look at the river, maybe it would make him stop. The sun was shining and it made the water sparkly and Alexander likes sparkly things."

She smiled when she said that and Mr Duff cleared his throat and I remember thinking, she's younger than us, she's only eight and she doesn't understand that Alexander is really dead.

I glanced at my mother and her eyes were fixed on my face. She smiled at me and I tried to smile back so she would know I was alright, but my mouth would not make a smile because Alexander was really dead.

"Violet-May took him out of his pram," said Rosemary-June. "She put him on the wall."

"Sitting or standing on the wall?" asked Fidelma.

"Sitting," said Rosemary-June. "She put him sitting on the wall."

"Did she hold him? Did Violet-May hold Alexander while he was sitting on the wall?"

Rosemary-June turned her head and glanced at Violet-May once more. "Yes, she had her arms around him."

"Look at me, please, Rosemary-June," said Fidelma. "Around him how? Where on his body was Violet-May holding Alexander?"

"Is this necessary?" said Mr Duff.

I remember glancing at him and, child that I was, suddenly realising that he was as I had never seen him before – close to anger. Even then, as incapable of being rude as he was of being pale, his voice was still polite. "I mean to say," he said, "what is to be gained by these questions? After all, the child is ..."

He did not finish the sentence and my mother put her handkerchief to her face once more.

"I'm afraid it is necessary, Mr Duff," said the detective.

"Around his waist," said Rosemary-June, "she was holding him around his waist."

"And what was Alexander doing while Violet-May was holding him around his waist?"

"Kicking," said Rosemary-June, "kicking and waving his arms."

"Was he still crying?"

"No, he stopped crying when Violet-May put him on the wall."

"But you say that Alexander was kicking and waving his arms, Rosemary-June. So would you say that he was moving about a good deal?"

Rosemary-June turned to Violet-May once more.

"He wouldn't stop jumping about," said Violet-May.

"Wriggling," said Rosemary-June. "He was wriggling around."

I got the feeling she was pleased with her choice of word.

She turned back to Fidelma. "And then he fell. He fell into

the river and I screamed." Her eyes went back to Violet-May once more. "I screamed. I screamed and screamed because I could see Alexander in the water. He wasn't moving and after a while he just floated away."

For a while there was silence in the room.

Then Violet-May said, "Daddy, I want to go home now. Please can we go home?"

Mr Duff got to his feet, "I think perhaps my daughters have been sufficiently traumatised for one day, don't you?" he said. "Might it be possible for me to take them home? Beside anything else, my wife is in need of me."

"And I'd like to take Kay home," said my mother, getting up. "She's had enough too."

"Just one more thing," said Fidelma. "At any point while you, Violet-May, and you, Rosemary-June, were on the bridge with your brother, did you see anybody else about? Anyone who might have witnessed what happened?"

Violet-May shook her head.

"You saw nobody?" said Fidelma.

"Nobody," said Violet-May.

"Rosemary-June?"

"Somebody went past," said Rosemary-June and I saw the surprise in Violet-May's eyes as she turned and stared at her sister.

"When? I didn't see anybody," she said.

"It was when you were watching for the sticks in the river," said Rosemary-June.

"Who was it, Rosemary-June, do you know?" said Fidelma.

"I don't know," said Rosemary-June. "Just a girl, a woman, I don't know who she was."

"Was it a girl or was it a woman? Can you remember, Rosemary-June?"

"I don't know," said Rosemary-June. "I can't remember and I didn't really look at her."

"And you didn't see this girl, this woman, Violet-May?"

"I didn't see anyone," said Violet-May.

At that moment I remembered the girl with the black hair and the bright green skirt lurking behind the pillar of the Duff gate, the flash of green as we were driven away from Bone Bridge.

I waited to be asked about her but then Violet-May said once more, "Please, can I go home now?"

Fidelma looked at the detective and I saw him nod his head and Fidelma said yes, we could all go home, and she told Mr Duff she was very, very sorry about his little boy. And Mr Duff bowed his head but said nothing.

Outside the police station I remember noticing that Violet-May had her can of Fanta in her hand and I realised that I had left mine behind. I didn't even care.

The doorbell rang just after I went to bed that night. For some reason I got it into my head that it might be Violet-May and I jumped out of bed and went out onto the landing. But it was only Mrs Nugent and she did not get past the doorstep. I heard my mother tell her firmly that now was not a good time and we were all off to bed.

"But isn't it a shocking thing to happen, Mrs Kelly? Shocking, just shocking, and that's the second child she's lost too – well, so to speak. Of course, the first one was different but ..."

"The first one was very different," said my mother. "Not the same thing at all."

"Oh, I know that, but even so, it's very sad, very sad. I don't know how you'd get over something like that, I just don't."

"You never would," said my mother and then I heard the sound of the door shutting and I hurried back to my room for fear I would be caught out of bed.

The following day I had to go back to the police station. I knew that it wasn't just me, that Violet-May and Rosemary went too, because although I didn't see them at the police station, I was standing in our hallway when the call came through.

I heard my mother asking whoever was on the other end whether the Duff girls were being brought in for further questioning too. "Because I won't stand for any distinction being made between Kay and those other two children," she said.

"I don't want to go to the police station on my own," I said, after she had hung up the phone.

"You won't be on your own," my mother told me. "I'll be with you and your daddy too. They just want to speak to each of you without the others being there.

I remember it was raining this time when my father drove us into the car park behind the police station and I remember crying because I didn't want to get out of the car.

"But all you have to do is exactly what you did the last time," my mother said. "And then that will be that and we can all go home and try to forget about this."

And my father said gently, "Your mother's right, Kay. Just tell them what you told them yesterday. As long as you tell them the truth, you have nothing to be frightened of."

And I remember wishing that I could make him, make them understand, that the truth was exactly what I was afraid of.

But in the end it wasn't so very bad. There was no Fanta Orange this time, just water if I wanted it, but Fidelma was there, and the same quiet detective and they were both as kind as before and asked me all the same questions to which I gave all the same answers. I remember as we walked through the doors out into the rain which was still falling, looking back over my shoulder, half expecting someone to come running out after me, calling my name, forcing me to go back in again, but there was nobody to see and nothing to hear, except my father smiling reassuringly down at me and my mother saying firmly, "And that, as far as we're concerned, is that."

Chapter 12

The Monday of my birthday was grey, showery and dismal. I woke to it from a night punctuated by nightmares in one of which I had been dandling Alexander from the wall of Bone Bridge when he slipped from my hands. The moment he hit the water his red romper suit swelled and became bloated and I watched in horror as he suddenly rolled over and looked up at me. His arms were outstretched as though he were beseeching me to save him. I reached down as far as I could but my arms were too short and I watched as he floated away, his romper suit getting bigger and bigger until it resembled some kind of giant red paddling pool. I suddenly became aware that somebody was watching me and when I looked round a strange man was standing there and I knew it was the ghost of one of those unquiet dead my father had told me about, who had been buried next to Bone Bridge.

I woke up screaming and struggling in my mother's arms, convinced that her grip was Alexander's and that he was trying to pull me into the river with him.

"Now now, it was only a bad dream," she soothed, "only a bad dream and it's over now and I'm here, chicken, I'm here."

My mother only called me chicken when I was hurt or sick

and that night as I lay shaking in her arms I felt myself to be both. She stayed with me until I fell asleep again to another variation of the same dream. This time when I woke I was alone in my room. My mother had left my bedside lamp on and I got out of bed with the intention of waking her. On the landing I heard the sound of my father snoring and I was struck with the fear that by waking my mother I would disturb him too. At the back of mind, beneath the horror of what had happened to Alexander, was the terror that something bad would happen to my father too.

I kept hearing my mother's words: *"This can't be good for your heart, Jim."*

In the end I went back to my room, switched on the light and turned off the lamp and lay on my back staring at the white ceiling. I willed my eyes to stay open and I think they did for quite some time but eventually sleep did overtake me and I woke to the light still on overhead and the thought that today I was eleven years old.

My mother had already decided that I should stay home from school – "On account of all the excitement," was how she had put it. She never mentioned Alexander's name to me then or ever afterwards, unless I brought it up myself. And because I felt she did not want me to bring it up I never mentioned his name either.

When I went downstairs there were cards on the mat in the hall for me, one from my granny and one from my Auntie May. I carried them into the kitchen and my mother looked up and said "Happy Birthday! I was just about to go and see if you were awake. Sit down and open your cards and I'll put an egg on to boil for you."

My father was sitting at the table drinking tea from his favourite mug. It was blue with white stripes and it had a crack in it, but he would never let my mother throw it out because he said it made tea taste better than any other mug he'd ever had.

He smiled at me over the rim, then he put it down and said, "Happy Birthday, chicken."

"Why aren't you in work, Daddy?" I said. It was unusual to see him at the breakfast table – usually he would have left for work by the time I came down.

"I just took a couple of days off work," he said, and I immediately began to worry that it was because of his heart.

After breakfast he went down to the shed and brought back the bicycle he and my mother had bought for me. It was red and silver and it had a basket and a bell and as I thanked them I wished with all my heart that I could feel the way such a bicycle should have made me feel.

"If the weather picks up this afternoon," said my father, "you can take it for a ride and see how it goes. I might need to adjust the saddle for you."

In fact, the weather picked up by mid-morning and I did take the bike out for a short while and it was grand, but I hadn't the heart to go far.

After lunch my father went out, wearing his good suit. I asked my mother where he was going and she said she wasn't sure. When he came back much later he asked me how my birthday was going but I thought he looked very sad and my mother nagged him until he agreed to go upstairs for a little lie-down. There was no party of course, as my mother said, under the circumstances – so I blew out my candles with only my parents to watch me. I wondered what Violet-May was doing for her birthday – perhaps she didn't even have a cake, under the circumstances ...

And so, despite the best efforts of my parents, my eleventh birthday was a dismal day with none of the excitement usually associated with the event. All day long, I could not help thinking about what had happened to Alexander and, when I managed to put him from my mind for a moment, I would find myself instead remembering last year's birthday when I had leapt from bed excited to begin getting ready for

Violet-May's birthday concert. And that only served to remind me that last year Alexander Duff had not yet been born and now he was dead and so I would land right back where I had started again, thinking about what had happened to Alexander.

After dinner I went upstairs to my room. I told my mother that I wanted to look at the new books she had given me. I did look at them for a while but somehow I could not concentrate so I put them away on the bookshelf and then I got down on my knees and pulled my vanity case out from under the bed. It was red and round in shape and it was lined with red satin and it was the place where I kept my treasures: postcards and photographs and shells, my autograph book, dried leaves and flowers, the blue and broken shell of a bird's egg wrapped in tissue paper and tucked into a ring box my mother had given me for the purpose. It was also the place where I kept the diary that Violet-May had given me last Christmas. I had started well in January until I forgot, then picked up again in February and kept it up for a while but after that the entries had dropped off and now I only wrote in it when I remembered, which was not very often. I took it from the case and sat on my bed and opened it and began to write.

Later I came downstairs for a drink of orange. I was in my stocking feet and my parents who were in the sitting room with the door closed did not hear me. I didn't mean to listen but their voices were raised, or my mother's voice was anyway. I heard my father use a word I had never heard before – *coroner*. At first I thought he had said "corner", but that didn't make sense because corners cannot speak so I listened hard and realised the word was "coroner". I didn't know what a coroner was.

They were talking about this coroner saying that children shouldn't have been left in charge of a baby while its mother was sleeping. Then my father talked about a doctor "testifying" about some kind of depression. I knew the word "testifying" and realised my father had been in court that day.

"I'm not saying I don't feel sorry for the woman," said my mother, "but that won't bring back that poor infant and it won't stop Kay's nightmares."

"God love them all," said my father. "Whatever way you look at it, it's a bloody high price to pay for a few hours' kip."

I knew he was talking about Mrs Duff and I slipped away then before they saw me, and went back upstairs to my room.

It seems to me my life narrowed after the day on Bone Bridge. There was no wandering off to play at will, no going down the river with the other children from our estate. I was still allowed to play in the street but only if I went no farther than the corner where my mother could keep an eye on me. I thought about Alexander Duff all the time. Sometimes when I was doing something ordinary, like working out a sum in school or eating my lunch or tidying my room he would come into my mind.

Sometimes when the thought of him became too much I took out my diary and wrote down what I was thinking. It seemed to help to put the thoughts down in words and see them on the page. My mother came across me writing a few times and once she asked me about it.

"It's nothing," I told her, "just stuff."

"What kind of stuff?"

"Just stuff that I think about."

My mother looked at me for a while before she spoke again. "Would it not be better to talk about it, you know, instead of writing it down?"

I shook my head. "It's easier writing it down," I said.

My mother nodded but I could tell by the look on her face that she was not happy. She wanted to know what I was thinking, I knew she did, and that being so, I was suddenly certain that given the chance she would read my diary.

105

After she had left me alone, I looked about my room trying to think of a safe place in which to hide it – if I left it in the usual place she might find it. But there was a place. All the bedrooms in our house had a vent, high up in the wall; I could reach the one in my room if I stood on my chair. That night, for the first time, I hid my diary inside it. I put the key there too, wrapped up separately in a cotton handkerchief.

My nightmares about Alexander continued. I grew ultra-sensitive, bursting into tears at the slightest provocation and prone to feelings of exaggerated guilt over minor offences. I remember one day, when I was helping my mother by doing the dusting, knocking an ornament off the mantelpiece, a little white bird of no particular value but which my mother liked. Initially, when my mother asked what had happened to the ornament I denied all knowledge of it only to confess later on that same day. My mother, who was going gently with me in all things at this point in time, made nothing of the damage to the bird itself only mildly reprimanding me for having lied about it in the first place. And I remember how bewildered she looked when I burst into great heartbroken sobs and ran upstairs to my room where I continued to cry myself into a state of near-hysteria.

I also developed a series of nervous ticks which began with throat-clearing and moved through compulsive humming, hand-flapping, squinting and crossing my eyes. No sooner would I overcome one habit than another took its place. It culminated in a bout of sleepwalking, the most spectacular of which was the night I let myself out of the house and walked in my pyjamas and bare feet as far as the end of the estate. Mr O'Toole from two doors down was coming home from working late in the glue factory and when he saw me in my pyjamas he took me home. I had no memory then or ever of having spoken to him but Mr O'Toole told my father that when he asked me where I was off to in the middle of the night I told him: "I'm going to the Surly for hazelnuts."

My father carried me upstairs and put me back in my bed and my mother slept next to me that night. In the morning she took me to see the doctor. I remember having to stay in the waiting room while my mother went in alone first to talk to the doctor. Then I was called in and the doctor was very gentle and kind to me and he examined me and assured her that I had come to no physical damage. Nightmares and sleepwalking, he said, were not unusual under the circumstances and I knew then that my mother had told him about Alexander Duff. When he told my mother, in my hearing, that if the problem continued it might be a good idea for me to see somebody else, I instinctively knew that he was not talking about just another doctor. It would, I felt certain, be someone who would ask me questions about what had happened that day on Bone Bridge. My dread of that happening was so intense that I remember going to sleep that night willing myself not to sleepwalk or wake up screaming and, whether as a result of willpower or chance, the sleep-walking was never repeated. My nightmares too lost some of their intensity, taking the form of mere bad dreams which I made sure disturbed nobody but myself.

I was allowed to go back to school after a fortnight, but neither Violet-May nor Rosemary-June put in an appearance then or at any point that term. I was, of course, a focus of curiosity and there was some staring and whispering at first, but only Ken Fitzgerald actually dared ask me what had happened and immediately Dolores and Mandy Nugent with one voice told him to shut up and leave me alone. Mandy went even further and kicked him in both shins. After that, the subject was never mentioned again, not in school, not at home, not anywhere, and although I did not forget that it had happened I thought about it less and less until my memories of that day blurred and faded like an aging snapshot fallen to the bottom of a box of photographs, lost under the weight of fresher happier memories. Just one of many old forgotten things.

And then, after the Christmas holidays, Violet-May and Rosemary-June still did not come back to school and the next news of the Duffs was that Robbie had run away from boarding school. We heard that he had been found in Kerry and had only agreed to go home again on condition that he be allowed to leave boarding school. It was not so very long after that we heard the news that the Duffs had let the house and moved away to England. For a while the house was empty and then a Swedish family rented it and lived in it for four years before eventually buying it from the Duffs.

"They'll play at being squires for a while," said my father, "but no doubt they'll get bored." But in fact they lived in the house for eight years before they sold up and went back to Sweden.

Chapter 13

During the summer of 1990 everybody in the entire country went a little bit crazy. "Put 'Em under Pressure" was number one in the charts. The kids in our estate sported giant blow-up green hammers and almost every house had a tricolour hanging from a window. Some had them in every window and they billowed green, white and gold in the breeze. But while it seemed that every other living soul was fixated on Italia 90 I was swotting for my Leaving Certificate exam. My head was crammed with a jumble of historical dates, mathematical formulae and quotes from WB Yeats and *Silas Marner*. I remember waking one night in a sweat reciting aloud like a mantra the major themes from Othello, "Jealousy, Revenge, Power, Good vs Evil, Appearance vs Reality ..."

I also remember spending hours drawing up a complex colour-coded study timetable which I stuck to my bedroom wall over my desk and which my father beheld with seemingly genuine awe in his eyes. I was disgusted when it failed to similarly impress my mother whose only comment on seeing it was, "In the time it took you to do that you could have been doing the real thing". She never said it in so many words but she managed to impress upon me her belief that the Leaving Certificate was desperately important, and that upon its results hung any future hopes of success and indeed happiness.

On the morning of my first exam she got up early to make a pot of porridge. She made it with milk and took care to ensure that it was entirely smooth and lump-free which was the only way I could ever abide it. Even so I turned up my nose at it and told her the smell of it made me sick and without a word she disposed of it in the outside bin and made me eat a bowl of cornflakes and two slices of toast.

My first exam was an Irish paper and I remember comforting myself that never again in all of my life would I need to think about that hideous woman, Peig Sayers. That same evening my father insisted I take time off from studying and sit with him and my mother to watch Ireland play England. I did it, if only to please him, but when eight minutes into the game England scored, his agony infected me and when Kevin Sheedy eventually equalised, I roared as loudly as he did. Two weeks later, when Ireland played Romania, and with all but two of my exams behind me, I did not need to be coaxed to sit down with my parents to watch the match. When Packie Bonner saved the penalty, over the sounds of our own roars we could hear the roars from the Nugents on one side and Taylors on the other. And when David O'Leary stepped forward to take the penalty for Ireland, my father did what he rarely did, he cursed.

And then there was silence in our sitting room while O'Leary took what seemed liked forever to place the ball.

"The nation holds its breath," said the commentator and I realised that I had in fact stopped breathing.

But then O'Leary took his shot and we were through to the quarter final and my father and I leapt to our feet and jigged around the sitting room for joy. My father reached out an arm then and beckoned my mother to join us and she got up, smiling a little sheepishly, and let herself be pulled into our embrace. For a while we danced together as a threesome and then without anyone saying anything, without even looking at one another, we moved as though we were one body for the hall and the front door. And as the door opened on the bright night we saw that everyone had done the same, because almost all the doors to all the houses were open and people were flooding into the street. And everybody was singing the same song and I joined in too, yelling at the top of my voice the endless choruses of '*Olé, Olé, Olé, Olé!*'.

Long after we had gone inside, the cars continued to honk in the road outside. And somehow that feeling seemed to carry on after the match, like something had changed, like we had changed, so that when a week or so later Ireland lost to Italy in Rome, it did not seem to matter very much at all. I remember watching as the final whistle blew and Jack Charlton did a lap of the stadium carrying an Irish flag. Hearing the roar of the Irish crowd, I remember thinking that we could not have cheered any louder if we had won, and in a way it felt like we had won. That was the 30th of June and, proud as I was for Ireland, by then Robbie Duff had come back into my life and left it again and my world had shifted on its axis.

I was walking up Old Road on my way home from school and feeling very sorry for myself. As I approached the gate to what I still thought of as the Duffs' house, a silver car passed me, slowed and indicated to turn. I watched as it turned in and stopped before the Duffs' gates, which were always shut now. As I drew level with the car I glanced toward it. The driver's window was partially open and the person behind the wheel, who had been staring straight ahead, turned suddenly and looked straight at me. He had dark-blonde hair and brown eyes and I knew him straight away.

Without being aware I was doing it, I said his name aloud: "Robbie Duff."

I saw him frown a little, then his eyes narrowed and I knew

he did not have a clue who I was.

"It's Kay," I said, "Kay Kelly."

"Kay Kelly," he repeated still frowning and then he was smiling and opening the car door and getting out. "No way, not little Kay Kelly!"

And then he was standing in front of me and smiling down at me. He was taller than I remembered but not so thin, and he was older of course, but in every other way he was the Robbie Duff I remembered.

"Look at you," he was saying, "practically all grown up."

I was not thrilled at the use of the word *practically* and I wished with all my heart that I had not been wearing my school uniform, but I was too happy at seeing him again to care much about anything else. I tried hard to be cool and not to say something stupid or childish but in any event the butterflies in my stomach rendered me so speechless that all I could do was smile at him.

"So how are you doing, Kay?" said Robbie. "What are you up to these days?"

"Oh, you know," I waved my hand vaguely as though a myriad projects required my attention.

"Still at school, I see," said Robbie.

"Actually no, I'm finished school. I'm starting university soon, or at least I think I am, if I don't fail the rotten exam I did today."

"*Ouch!* What was it?"

"Double Dutch," I said ruefully, "otherwise known as chemistry. I hate science."

"So what do you like?" said Robbie

"Words," I said.

Robbie nodded. "Of course," he said. "The little playwright."

I looked at him in surprise. "You remember that?" I said eagerly.

He was no longer smiling and I had a sudden memory of

112

him walking into the Duffs' dining room, his dead dog in his arms. Of course he remembered it. I stared at him in dismay, then looked away and mentally kicked myself.

"Well, at least you won't need chemistry for that," said Robbie. "So what will you study in college?"

"I don't know if I want to go to college," I said. "Did you go to college?"

"I did," said Robbie. "I studied ancient history and archaeology. Actually I've just finished my degree."

"What are you going to do now?"

"Keep on studying archaeology and get some practice in."

"How did you know?" I asked. "How did you know you wanted to be an archaeologist and not anything else?"

Robbie put his head to one side as he considered, "Well, I've always known I love history and I want to travel. And I care about the past. No, I more than care about it, I'm curious about it, about the people who lived in it and how they lived. So archaeology seemed like an obvious choice." He smiled at me. "I suppose that makes me sound like an awful nerd."

I shook my head. "I think it sounds really exciting."

"Most of it isn't exciting at all – most of it is about being patient and waiting for things to reveal themselves to you, give up their mysteries if you like, in their own good time."

"I'm not very patient," I said.

Robbie smiled. "Aren't you, Kay?" He shook his head a little then. "Little Kay Kelly, fancy running into you here!"

"So why are you here anyway?" I was wishing he wouldn't keep calling me *little* Kay Kelly.

"If you mean why I am back in Ireland, just for a bit of a holiday. I've been staying with a guy I went to school with. As for why I'm right here, I don't know really. I suppose I just took a notion today to take a stroll down Memory Lane."

He turned and looked at the gate and the driveway beyond it and I followed his gaze.

"Are you going to go in?" I said. "The Swedes would

probably let you look around, you know, if you told them you used to live here."

"No, I don't think so," said Robbie quickly. "It's not my home anymore."

"But you wish it still was," I said and, although he didn't reply, the look in Robbie's eyes made me certain I was right. "I would too. I mean if it was me. If this was my house, I'd never want to live anywhere else."

"I didn't want to live anywhere else," said Robbie. "But as it happened nobody asked my opinion on that."

The way he said it didn't sound sad or angry, it just sounded flat, as though it had been something that made him feel helpless, which I supposed it had.

"Maybe someday you can buy it back," I said. I was serious though I half expected him to laugh at me, but when I looked at him his face was stern.

"I intend to," he said.

I was glad because the Duff house without the Duffs just didn't make sense.

But then he did laugh at me. "No need to look so serious," he said.

And then because I sensed he wanted me to, I changed the subject. "How long have you been back?"

"Almost a week. I'm going back tomorrow then I'm off to Greece for the summer."

"It's well for some," I said brightly to counteract the pang I had just suffered.

"It's not a holiday," said Robbie. "I'm heading out to an excavation as a student volunteer. There's a crowd of us going."

Girls, I was thinking, I bet there's a bunch of girls in the crowd, and I had a vision of him, suntanned, his golden hair dulled by the Greek dust, surrounded by tanned girls in skimpy tops and very short shorts.

"It sounds like a holiday to me," I said more glumly than I had intended.

"Well, don't be too jealous," said Robbie and he gave me a wry little smile and I was horrified, convinced for a moment that he had read my mind. "There'll be plenty of hard work and it's not much fun slaving away in the dirt with the sun beating down on top of you. But I'm looking forward to getting some experience and a chance to dig." He stared at me again and shook his head as though in disbelief. "So you've finished school?"

I nodded.

And then he said it again, "Little Kay Kelly – it's hard to believe."

"Why are you calling me that?" I blurted out. "*Little* Kay Kelly? I'm five foot five and a half – that's not particularly little."

Robbie stopped smiling. "No," he said, looking perfectly serious. "I don't suppose it is really. I'm sorry, Kay, you're perfectly right – it's a long time since you've been Little Kay. Forgive me, it's just the way I've always thought of you."

"It doesn't matter," I said, and I silently, joyfully, hugged the idea that he had thought of me at all.

"So anyway, how are your parents?" said Robbie. "Both keeping well, I hope?"

"My mother is very well," I said. "My father's heart isn't very strong but he's doing OK."

"Good – it's good that he's doing OK," said Robbie.

And then I asked the question I both wanted but did not want to ask. "How is Violet-May?"

"She's very well, running rings around everyone same as always. She says she wants to be an actress and is intent on going to some school for the performing arts. You can imagine how that's going down with Mother. But, knowing Violet-May, she'll get her own way."

"Yes," I said. "She probably will." Once again my thoughts went back to the day of the birthday concert and Violet-May standing on the makeshift stage in the second garage, her face beatific as she took bow after bow to the sound of the cheering audience. "And Rosemary-June and your mother and father, how are they doing?"

"Rosemary-June is Rosemary-June," said Robbie. "And the folks – the folks are doing OK, I suppose."

Then we were quiet for a moment and I felt certain that both of us were thinking of Alexander. I scrabbled about in my mind for something to lighten the tone.

"Robbie?"

"Yes?"

"Did you really run away from boarding school?"

"Now how on earth could you know about that?"

"I don't know, I suppose I just heard. So it's true?"

"Yes, it is," said Robbie. "I hitched a lift to Kerry – it took me seven lifts to get there. I ended up in Kenmare." His face widened in a genuine smile. "You know, I haven't thought about that in a very long time." Suddenly he glanced down at his watch. "I'd better get going. Can I drop you home, Kay?"

"OK," I said, "but only if you have time." I knew I sounded as if I didn't care either way whether he dropped me home or not, but inside the butterflies were doing a céilí at the thought of climbing into his car and sitting next to him.

We got into the car and he waited while I wrestled with the seat belt.

"I'm assuming the address hasn't changed?" he asked.

"It hasn't changed," I said.

"Not like you," said Robbie. "Here, let me help you with that."

He leaned over and I let go of the belt but not before his fingers grazed mine. I caught the warm smell of his skin and could hardly breathe as he fixed the belt.

"What do you mean, not like me?" I said then as he sat back and reached for the ignition.

"Just that you have changed since I saw you last," said Robbie. "I didn't even recognise you you've changed so much."

"Have I changed in a good way or a bad way?"

Robbie turned and grinned at me. "Oh, I'd say it was in a good way, wouldn't you?"

I held his gaze. "It was seven years ago you saw me last," I said. "Of course I've changed. I was a little girl then but I'm not a little girl now." *Kiss me, I was thinking, please oh please oh please, will you kiss me?*

Perhaps something in my voice had betrayed me. When Robbie smiled this time, it was a different sort of smile and when he spoke his voice was very gentle. "You know, you're quite right," he said. "You're not Little Kay any more – you're almost all grown up."

Almost grown up, I thought. I glanced down at my pleated skirt and wished again that I'd been wearing something else, today of all days.

I attempted a nonchalant smile. "I'm only wearing this uniform for the exams," I said. "After today I'll never wear it again in my life. Actually, I'm planning to build a fire in the garden tonight and burn it." I had only just made that decision but I meant it.

Robbie laughed. "I remember that feeling," he said. "OK, Kay Kelly, let's get you home."

He started the car and we drove away and though he chatted to me about various things for the short drive to my home, all I could think about was that I didn't want that journey to end, because when it did Robbie Duff would be gone again and I'd probably never see him again in my whole life. And even if I did, he'd most likely be married to one of those girls he would meet in Greece.

We parked outside my house and Robbie said something about hoping he would see me again soon and how he was sure I would do really well in my exams but I didn't hear half of what he was saying because my heart was too busy breaking.

I did hear one thing, however – Robbie saying with obvious

amusement in his voice, "I see you have an admirer."

I followed his gaze to where Ken Fitzgerald was busily pretending to be doing something with their gate while all the time watching us.

"Ken Fitzgerald?" I said contemptuously. "I can't stand him and anyway he doesn't like me. He never stops teasing me."

"In that case he definitely doesn't like you," said Robbie.

"Now you're teasing me," I said and I jumped out of the car.

But Robbie was quick and he caught me up before I reached our gate and pushed it open for me. Then he leaned in and gave me the barest peck on my right cheek and he was gone back to his car.

As I watched him drive away to his future full of Greece and sunshine and rich girls in shorts, the anguish and the unfairness of it all moved me to sudden anger. I took it out on Ken Fitzgerald who was still watching me.

"*Put your eyes back in your head, Kenneth!*" I yelled at him, then I banged the gate behind me and stalked up the path to the door which opened suspiciously fast before I had even knocked.

"Who was that in the car?" said my mother.

"Robbie Duff," I told her as I made for the stairs.

"Robbie Duff? What ... why is he ...?"

"Stop worrying, Mam," I said. "He's going to Greece and he's probably going to be a famous archaeologist and I'll probably never see him again."

As I thumped up to my room, through the open door to the kitchen I could hear the radio playing Sinéad O'Connor and "Nothing Compares to You" and I felt like I had lost Robbie Duff all over again.

That night I built a fire in our back garden and burned my school skirt. It was the single rebellious act of my teenage life so far and even then it was a half-hearted one because I had a second skirt and wore it the next day for my Geography exam. But it felt good all the same watching the terrible blue-and-green checked fabric begin to scorch then burn.

A week later, Ken Fitzgerald asked me to go with him to his Debs' dance and I said yes, because, after all, what did it matter. What did anything matter?

Book 2

Chapter 14

I still don't fully understand why I decided to move to London.
I never really wanted to; it was just something that sort of
happened. It was 1995, I was twenty-one and two years into an
arts degree in English and History. I entered a competition run
by a London publishing company – I had to write a novella for
young adults – and somehow I managed to win first prize. Part
of the prize was having my novella published and although it
made me only a very little money, it did earn me a couple of
good reviews, one of which referred glowingly to my future
potential as a writer. Then somebody I met at a college party, I
cannot even remember who it was anymore, suggested that if I
meant to take my writing seriously I should get out of Ireland.
And I suddenly decided, why not? The Nugent twins had gone
to England straight from school and were nursing in
Manchester now – half my sixth-year class were there, in fact,
including Ken Fitzgerald. Why shouldn't I go?

"Oh, you wouldn't want to go to London," my father said
when I first mooted the idea at home. "It's very big, is
London. You wouldn't like it, Kay."

When I told him I didn't mind that it was big, I quite liked
the idea of it being big, he tried to put me off by telling me the
Irish were hated in London.

"They think that all we do is blow things up," he said.

"Well, in fairness, some of us did a bit," I said, "but I'm not planning on blowing anything up. And I don't suppose they all hate us."

I knew my mother did not want me to go either and perhaps if she had said outright, "Kay, I don't want you to go," I might not have done so. But she said nothing, only banged plates and did a lot of sniffing. Besides, I had ridiculously romantic notions of what it would be like to live in London. Whenever I imagined myself there I saw myself living in a beautiful apartment overlooking a leafy park where I would sit in the window and write my next book, the one that would make the world sit up and take notice.

My father was right. London was very big and made me feel very small. I arrived in Victoria Coach station with no accommodation booked. I walked around a bit and found a B&B close to Pimlico. The following day I saw an ad in a shop window and that evening I had moved into my first London home, a pokey basement bedsit with precious little natural light. The landlord was a horrible little goblin of a man with a great bulbous nose, a permanent bubble of spittle at the side of his mouth and a penchant for eating pears. He seemed to be always slobbering on one when he knocked on my door to collect the rent and forever afterwards I have had a disgust for the smell of the things.

Not alone did London make me feel small, it made me feel almost invisible, which in a way, at least in the beginning, was a point in its favour. Nobody stared at me on the Tube, nobody cared what I wore, or if I smoked, nobody was judging me, or that was how it seemed to me. People dressed as they liked and there seemed to be no "norm" and as a result I felt less self-conscious than I had at home. And, horrible as the flat was, the location suited me. Pimlico felt sort of safe and I enjoyed the mix of nationalities that we didn't get in Ireland back then. It was great too to be able to hop on the Tube and be in the very centre of the city in next to no time. One stop on the Tube or a short bus ride took me to Victoria or, as I loved to do, I could walk along the river bank. One direction brought me to Westminster Cathedral, which appeared so massive to me, and had a different feel to it than any church I had known before, the other direction took me to Battersea Park where I spent many hours walking or sitting on the grass reading.

I loved passing the Apollo Victoria Theatre too and stopping to read the billboards for *Cats* and whatever other shows were on. I never went to see any of them but it gave me a sense of excitement just to be there, me, Kay Kelly, making it on her own in the city.

In truth I wasn't making very much at all. I spent days on end walking around Victoria, registering with job agencies. I had a notion I would get a job in a publishing house, a prestigious one of course where I would rub shoulders with established writers but in reality the first job I got was in an estate agency typing up letting agreements and promotional brochures. I was also supposed, as part of my role, to promote sales but I was hopeless at it. I told myself it was only for now and my real work would take place in the evenings with my writing, but somehow it never quite happened that way. I produced some short stories but somehow the book I had dreamed of writing happened only in my mind. In fact, I lived mostly in my mind that first year. I was very aware of being Irish, of being immediately identifiable by my accent but that anti-Irish feeling my father had feared on my behalf never really manifested itself to me. Perhaps I had arrived at the right time – certainly, when I heard things on the news about Ireland, it was mostly positive stuff, about how well the economy was doing and how business was booming there.

I met Dominic in 1997 on the day of Princess Diana's funeral.

I had stayed in all day, only venturing out around nine o'clock for a drink in my local bar. I had made friends with one of the girls who worked behind the bar but she wasn't working that night as it turned out. I ordered a drink and was just paying for it when a drunk next to me looked me over and informed me "We could be lovers!".

I gave him a dirty look, picked up my drink and turned to walk away. The dirty look must still have been on my face because the guy who was standing just behind me raised one eyebrow and said, "If wit were shit ..."

"He'd be constipated!" I finished for him and I remember being delighted because he was the first English person I had ever heard using that expression.

He was older than me by ten years, very articulate and quite good-looking. To me, he seemed very cool, by which I mean that he never got over-excited about anything. He was also very sarcastic in a clever sort of way, or so I thought, and I was going through a phase where I considered sarcasm the highest form of wit. His irreverent take on the outpouring of grief at the death of Princess Diana impressed me too, in spite of the fact that I had watched hours of the state funeral on the television earlier that day. I had even sobbed uncontrollably, a little because of those two little boys but mostly I suspect for reasons totally unconnected to Diana or her sons and more to do with my own sense of loneliness. My mother phoned me and knew by my voice that I had been crying so she had a go, mostly because she was outraged that the death of an English princess had overshadowed that of a living saint, which was how she saw Mother Teresa, who'd had the misfortune to die on the same day.

In his turn, Dominic seemed impressed that I'd had a book published which I found very flattering.

We began seeing each other and 'saw each other' – Dominic did not date – for the next two years. It did not hurt that, when we first slept together, it was obvious that he knew what he was doing, unlike me with my one and only previous sexual partner.

On the downside he was very unforthcoming about himself. He told me almost nothing about his past or his family and I learned not to ask. Occasionally, usually after he had been drinking and when we were in bed having made love, he would grant me morsels of information, unsolicited verbal snapshots of his life, passed to me under cover of darkness. I told myself it was a little bit mysterious. I also told myself he would be a great subject to write about.

Dominic had an analytical and scientific mind at complete variance with my own. His gods were logic and physics; they were, he once told me, the only tools necessary to beat one's way through the thickets of life. Physics, he said, cut right through the mumbo-jumbo and exposed the universe for what it was, fascinating but rational and casual.

"But doesn't it strip away all the beauty?" I asked him once.

"Rubbish. Clarity in itself is beautiful."

"But the world is not logical," I said.

"It can best be understood logically."

"Not by me," I said obstinately. "Not everything can be explained in terms of maths and science. Science has its limitations. And most of the greatest mathematicians were mad anyway."

"All greatness is perceived as madness," said Dominic.

Sometimes he would try to explain things to me with drawings, inscrutable diagrams and incomprehensible formulae and he would grow impatient when I failed to understand.

And then I would get annoyed. "You don't understand – I don't want to decipher the universe," I told him once. "It is not a code I need to break, I just want to be at peace in it. You can keep your thermonuclear reactors. I like my stars twinkling and unknowable."

He laughed at me. "Twinkle, twinkle, little thermonuclear reactor," he said.

The way his mind worked intrigued me, the way mine worked bemused him. It snowed that first winter we were together, quietly in the night and made ugly and imperfect things clean and white. When I woke to it and the wonder of it brought tears to my eyes, Dominic found what he considered my overreaction almost inconceivable, so I put my tears down to the dazzle-effect. But this, apparently, had nothing to do with snow itself and everything to do with the molecular structure of the individual ice crystals and how they reflect sunlight, or so said Dominic. I remember it only made me laugh. I think I even thought it was cute and was a little bit proud that my boyfriend was so clever in a way that I could never be clever.

My parents came to London to visit me and while there they met Dominic. It was clear from the start that my mother did not warm to him; she also thought he was too old for me. Although he made a real effort, I am fairly sure my father was not Dominic's greatest fan either.

We moved in together in the winter of 1999. I gave up the lease on my bedsit and went to live in his apartment. Dominic did not believe in marriage and, in fairness to him, I knew that the first week I met him; he was always unambiguous on the subject. So coming from him, an invitation to cohabit, in my mind at least, equated with commitment. In truth, though, he did not so much invite me as suggest it as something that "might make sense".

When I told my mother she said nothing but I knew she wasn't happy about it. I heard her as she was handing over the phone to my father saying, "She's moving in with that fella."

"She doesn't approve, does she?" I said when my father came on the line.

"She's only worried about you, that's all," said my father. "If you're happy she'll get used to the idea. I've a bit of news for you anyway – the Swedes have sold up. Some arts crowd have bought the Duff house and I hear they're going to turn it into some sort of writers' retreat. Good luck to them."

I remember lying in bed next to Dominic that night thinking about the Duff house and the day when I had sat in Robbie's car wishing he would kiss me. I wondered where he was right that minute. The truth is, I thought about them all from time to time through those London years. I even saw Violet-May on television once. I was flicking channels and there she was, playing the part of a sort of vampy nurse in an American soap opera. I was almost certain it was her, but I waited for the credits to make sure. Her name was there although she had dropped her surname and was calling herself simply Violet May. I did an internet search on her after that and it seemed she had done a bit of work in American theatre and appeared in a couple of daytime television shows. Good for her, I thought – at least she had pursued her dream and made some sort of success of it. At the time I had two half-written plays, a smorgasbord of stalled short stories and two half-hearted attempts at novels on the go. Somehow I could never seem to finish anything.

Of course, I did a search for Robbie Duff's name too then and found numerous references to him, all in the context of archaeology. There was one long article about the discovery of a Mycenaean hoard and with it an image of Robbie bent over something or other that he was in the act of unearthing. There were other images too, outdoor shots mostly, showing him squinting into the sun or examining some find. In one shot, taken with him sitting behind a desk in a blue shirt which intensified the colour of his eyes, he was staring directly into the camera. Meeting that head-on gaze I experienced something like a pulse of energy and for a moment I was aware of myself as a living being, by which I mean that I was conscious of being completely and unequivocally alive, the way you occasionally know yourself to be after a close shave such as a bus missing you by a fraction of an inch or when you wake from a dream of dying to find that you are not only alive but the sun is shining.

I thought it would make me happy to live with Dominic. His apartment was in Purley, which was a nice area really and it was not Purley's fault that I was not as happy as I had expected to be. It was not the fault of Dominic's apartment either – that was spacious and full of leather and chrome and pale shining wood and in every way modern, but the truth was I preferred things with a past, things with a history. I told myself I was crazy. I had moved on from the awful damp basement with the creepy goblin landlord but my second home was nothing to write home about either – compared to it, Dominic's apartment was a palace. But perhaps that was the problem; it always seemed to me like Dominic's apartment, Dominic's home, not mine, not ours.

It was not until I was actually living with him that I fully realised how different Dominic and I were. That sarcasm I had so admired wore thin quite quickly while I found his views on the world and almost everything in it increasingly cynical. I discovered too that there were only two things he really feared: one was being suspected of showing enthusiasm for any earthly thing, the other was losing his hair. He was absolutely terrified of losing his hair and constantly asked me if I thought it was thinning.

He was also pessimistic, although he disagreed.

"I'm not a pessimist," he told me once. "I'm a stoic."

And then there were the little things like Christmas, except that to me Christmas was not a little thing. In our house Christmas had always been a big thing. But Dominic didn't "do" Christmas. He looked at me askance when I asked him where he kept the decorations. "Surely you don't go in for that nonsense?" he said.

"But we can at least get a tree," I said. "Everyone has a tree."

In the end I did buy a tree, albeit a sad synthetic dwarf thing in its own pot. It was less than three feet high but still, it was a Christmas tree, and I put it on a corner of a bookshelf. I switched off the lamps and in the darkness the tree's tiny LED bulbs glowed silvery soft. It smelled of nothing of course but I had thought of that and bought a scented candle. When I lit it the room slowly filled with the scent of pines and I sat in the darkness and gazed at it. I discovered that if I narrowed my eyes the lights blurred and the smell of pine flooded my brain with memories so that I was no longer standing in Dominic's sterile flat but in the middle of the sitting room at home, gazing up at one of the giant real trees of Christmas past. I could pretend that my father had just hauled it in, fresh from the woods, dragging it the short length of the hall, my mother groaning anxiously as its wider branches scraped her beautifully papered walls.

Dominic clocked the tree as soon as he walked through the door and pulled a face. I reassured him that it wasn't real and so could not shed.

"That pong seems pretty real," he said.

"It's not a pong," I told him. "It's pine – pine and cedar actually. I bought a scented candle. You don't really mind, do you?"

Dominic shrugged. "Knock yourself out," he said drily. "I'm off to take a shower."

And that was the thing: he never tried to stop me doing or having the things I wanted, he just chose not to share them with me and over time that made me feel lonely, as lonely if not lonelier than if I were actually living on my own.

But there were positives to being with Dominic too – how else would I have stayed with him as long as I did? Unlike me, he was practical, so after years of listening to me moaning about hating my job and regretting not finishing my degree, he finally stopped sympathising and he told me to either shut up or do something about it. There was, he said, nothing to stop me finishing my degree here in London. Egged on by him, I looked into my options and eventually found a way of working as an intern on a magazine while accumulating credits in a local college. In essence I was nothing more than a general dogsbody – I did the coffee run and proofread other people's articles and, although I got to attend the editorial meetings, it was only to take minutes and, when the time was right, to go out and wheel in the sandwich trolley. It took another three years, but eventually I did graduate with my degree. In the meantime, because I was paid only a pittance, Dominic without demur covered the lion's share of the bills. I made a point of letting my mother know that he did, but she had taken against him and was not for turning. In one of her letters to me she even informed me that if he were ever to cheat on me, I was not to think twice but to pack my things and come home. "If there is one thing I cannot abide," she wrote, "then it's a philandering man." And, because I had never entertained fears of that nature, I remember laughing it off despite an underlying feeling of annoyance that she could even contemplate a scenario in which a man would find another woman preferable to her own daughter.

My father, in his own very different way, must have sensed that all was not right either. He never said so directly. Just once on the phone, he said to me, "You know you can come back any time you want to, love? You know that, don't you?"

I said I knew that, but that I was fine.

And he then said, "You know I say a prayer for you every night, don't you, Kay?"

That I had not known, and it moved me almost unbearably to think of those nightly prayers rising into the empty darkness, my name borne aloft by the force of his will for my wellness. "Thanks, Dad," I said, "please don't ever stop saying them."

Chapter 15

One of the worst times of my life began in the early hours of the 9th November 2011. My mother, having shown no prior symptoms, died in her sleep of sudden cardiac arrest. My father rang me with the news and within a couple of hours I was on a plane back to Ireland. I arrived home to find my father, more dazed than distraught, or so it seemed to me. He stayed that way through the days before and immediately after the funeral, mechanically doing and saying what was expected of him at such a time. I did not worry overly at first. I was shell-shocked myself and not a little disbelieving – a world which did not contain my mother seemed to me not just inconceivable but unimaginable. But when the mourners went home and we sat together, just the two of us in that silent house, the full magnitude of his loss hit him in a tidal wave of grief. Before my eyes he sank into a visible depression. Always a quiet man, he withdrew now more than ever into himself. He suffered from insomnia and lost his appetite and the weight fell away from him, ageing him in a way I found frightening to watch. I decided that I could not in good conscience return to London, leaving him on his own, so I decided to stay on for a while. Dominic said I was doing the only thing I could. I took a leave of absence, initially for one

month, but I was still unhappy to leave him by late December.
Dominic said he would not come for Christmas – with it being
our first Christmas without my mother he thought my father
and I would want to be alone together. He said he would try
to make it for New Year's Eve but in the end he caught a flu
and said he felt too miserable to fly. In January his job became
so busy that he was, he said "pulling nighters as well as
working weekends" and the promised weekend in Ireland was
put off once more. I remember, near the end of that month,
watching television with my father and seeing a clip of the
Taoiseach, Enda Kenny, telling the audience at some economic
Forum that the Irish people "went mad with borrowing"
during the boom.

"Would you listen to that chinless wonder!" said my father
contemptuously and I saw it as a sign that there was light at
the end of the tunnel of his grief.

But still I was reluctant to leave him alone for too long. In
the end, one Friday early in February, it was I who caught a
flight to London to spend the weekend with my partner.

We made love that night – I instigated it.

On the Saturday morning I woke up to find that Dominic
had already risen. From the living room I could see him on the
balcony: he was standing with his hands on the rails gazing
down and I had to say his name before he became aware of
me. I came out and stood next to him, glancing down to see
what had grabbed his attention.

I caught a flash of kingfisher blue and turned with a grin to
Dominic, "Are you ogling our neighbour?"

"No, but I'm thinking that that's what we should be
doing," said Dominic.

I laughed aloud. "Running – us?"

"It's not like we couldn't both do with losing a bit of
weight," he said, his eyes still on our neighbour pounding the
pavement below.

We, or rather I, had christened her Thin Lizzy, but in my

defence only after I had taken against her on account of being snubbed. She had moved into the apartment right opposite ours a couple of months earlier. I first met her in our hallway when we came out of our apartments at the same time one morning. I had never met her face to face before although I had caught glimpses of her back as she hurried out ahead of me in the mornings, trailing expensive scent, all spiky black heels and briefcase. To me she looked like the sort of woman who would know how to do clever things with scarves; and she was thin, enviably thin. Once or twice she had run past me as I dragged myself wearily home in the evenings, a flash of black and kingfisher-blue lycra, her blonde ponytail flying behind her as she moved – she had a tiny bum and the skinniest thighs I had ever seen. That morning when we met in our hallway, she rewarded my smile with a blank look, just long enough for me to notice that her lips were thin and her eyes slightly prominent before she turned her back on me and made herself busy locking her door. Nope, I definitely was not her type.

Now, on the balcony with Dominic, I looked down at my body, more surprised than put out. I could always afford to lose a bit of weight, but in all our years together he had never said so before.

"It's just Christmas fat," I said and I smiled at him.

"Which Christmas?" he said, and he was not smiling.

On the Sunday evening, Dominic dropped me to the airport and I remember reassuring him that this situation, me in Dublin and him in London, would not last forever – it was just until my father showed signs of feeling a bit better. Dominic told me not to worry, to do what I had to do and for as long as it took. I remember thinking how understanding and unselfish he was being and wondered if I had been selling him short all this time.

Not long after I returned to Dublin, my father had a fall at home and fractured his hip. He was taken to hospital in an ambulance, spent the night in a corridor on a trolley and was operated on the next day. I spent anxious hours awaiting the outcome of his surgery. I was terrified he would not survive the operation and that I would lose him too within months of losing my mother. He came through the operation without any complications and bore up under the obvious pain like the Spartan he was, and I spent large amounts of each day in the hospital at his bedside. I was then informed that when he was finally discharged it would not be to his own house but to a nursing home. I was extremely resistant to the idea, but the surgeon who had operated on him persuaded me it would be in his best interest and absolutely essential to his rehabilitation. I capitulated, hired a car as my father had given up driving at that stage, then spent the next week sourcing and visiting places where I would feel comfortable leaving him. His surgeon had estimated he would need to stay there for at least eight weeks and so I was anxious to find a nursing home as close to home as possible. It was easier said than done but I decided on one and stayed in Ireland for another ten days, until my father was ready to be discharged and I could get him settled into the home. Once that was done, the pressure was on for me to return to work and my father was adamant I go too.

"Get back to your work and don't worry about me," he told me. "I'm like a pig in clover here – they're looking after me better than a hotel would."

I was still unhappy about leaving him. Not even my determination to return to Dublin every Friday evening and stay the weekend could assuage my sense of guilt but there was nothing for it but to go back to my life in London.

The day I was leaving I had a visit from Mrs Nugent who told me that the Duff house had been sold again. It made me wonder at the hold that house still had, even after all these years, on my imagination. It made me wonder too, as I had wondered so many times over the years, where Robbie Duff was now.

On my return to London I found Dominic a bit distant but I had so many other things on my mind that I didn't pay it much heed. Nor did I think a whole lot of it when, shortly after my return, he came home from work one evening with a couple of bags that bore the logo of a sportswear store.

"I thought I'd take up running, try to get fit," he said.

"These are serious running shoes," I said, opening the box and peering inside. I could see from the price tag that they were seriously expensive too. "Talk about jumping in at the deep end."

"You're mixing your sporting metaphors," he said, and I thought he sounded a bit huffy. "If I'm going to do it, I might as well do it right. I actually started doing a bit while you were in Ireland, turns out I like it. It's good for the head."

"Fair enough," I said. "I just never thought running was your thing. You must have caught the bug from Thin Lizzy across the hall."

"Actually her name is Megan," he said.

"Oh! How did you find that out?"

"We got talking one evening when we came in at the same time. She introduced herself to me."

"Wow, that's more than she ever did to me. All I ever got was a cold fish-eye. So not Thin Lizzy after all then, more like Matchstick Meg."

Dominic had his back to me at the time but I had the distinct impression his back stiffened. All he said was, "She's not so bad."

His phone rang then and the subject was dropped and, in my case, forgotten. I really did have more important things on my mind. Working five days a week, then commuting forward and back to Dublin to spend time with my father each weekend took its toll on my health. I felt rundown and tired all the time but under the circumstances that seemed natural enough.

I only found out I was pregnant the day I miscarried.

Dominic did not understand my grief. "How can you miss something you didn't know you had?" he said.

I could not explain to him that to me it seemed a double loss: for a while, I had been a mother and I had not even known it. Now there was nothing where I had never even known there was something. I felt that I had in some way betrayed my child by not being aware of his or her short but remarkable existence. I think I might have been better able to make him understand if I had not suspected that he was relieved. He had never expressed any interest in children, in fact I sometimes wondered if he actually disliked them. But I was certain, like many women before me I am sure, that all that would change when he had one of his own. I remember one particular night when I began crying as we lay in bed together, our backs to one another. I knew he knew I was crying but for a long time he ignored me, hoping, I knew, that I would stop. He hated women crying and so I had rarely done it. But now, let him lump it, I thought, he owes me that at least: the loan of his ear, the crook of his arm, the semblance of tenderness. And in the end he did turn over and his arm came down and encircled my body. He said nothing and I said nothing and, in spite of the warmth of his body, I felt cold.

In the weeks after my miscarriage, I admit I fell into a pit of inertia in which even the simple mechanics of daily living seemed too much to ask of my mind or body. All those showers to take and teeth to brush and food to choose and cook and eat, and bins to empty and work to go to – how many times, how many times must I do it all – wash, dress, eat, make up, make ready, rush, race, go, why, where, what for?

I continued commuting back to Ireland to visit my father and I did my best to hide my grief from him. He knew nothing about the pregnancy of course but he remonstrated with me for "wearing yourself out with travelling" when, he insisted, he was doing fine. He actually was doing fine but I had been told that his recuperation would take even longer than had at first been envisaged, which only added to my worries and general sense of gloom.

In the end Dominic told me straight that I needed to buck myself up. He actually used the words "buck yourself up".

When I asked him how he suggested I might do the bucking, he said I should go see somebody. I was so miserable being miserable that I agreed and so I went to "see somebody" called Elaine. On each visit I would sit in one of the two armchairs next to the window. The window had a wooden blind and if my appointment was early in the day sunlight fell across my lap in slats. In the evenings the only light in the room came from the tall lamp behind my chair which spotted us in a soft yellow gold, leaving the spaces beyond dim.

Even on my first visit, I knew straightaway which chair was for me and which for Elaine. A small table had been pulled up closer to the chair on the left than the one on the right. At its centre there was a cardboard box of paper tissues, one tissue standing proud, ready for use. We talked about how grief was a process and how everything I was feeling was natural and valid. Elaine was very fond of the word *valid*. Talking about my parents did help me, I think, but it did not lift the general sense of sadness with which I was consumed. I remember on one occasion staring at the box of tissues on the table and wondering if my visits made Elaine want to cry too. I asked her if perhaps I should stop coming.

"Would you like to end the sessions, Kay?"

"I don't know – I thought maybe you might be tired of listening to me."

"Do you find the sessions tiring, Kay? Because I am happy to continue for as long as you like, for as long as you find it useful. Do you find the sessions useful at all?" Elaine's expression looked pained. She had classic English Rose good looks, very fair hair and very blue eyes and the palest gold eyebrows I had ever seen. I had to think about her question. Was it useful to sit for long periods of time in a room with a stranger, sometimes talking about everything and sometimes talking about nothing much at all? The quiet was restful it was true, soothing; beyond the slatted blind the sounds of the traffic were audible but only just. The clock on the wall ticked the seconds away, the seconds I paid for, 3,600 of them a week. I remember thinking I might as well sit here as anywhere else?

In fine clichéd fashion, I came home early from work feeling unwell one day and caught Dominic letting himself out of our bug-eyed neighbour's apartment. He did not even have the grace to look sheepish.

"These things have a life expectancy, you know that, Kay," he told me later that day as he packed some things into a holdall – I had told him to get out. "No use in being naive about it."

But, as it turned out, I was also naive enough not to even consider that he would move in with Matchstick Meg, which was exactly what he did, while I went on living right across the hall in what had been our home. I remember holing up there, unable to face work, trying to sound bright and normal on the phone when I spoke to my father. At night I imagined I could hear them, Dominic and Matchstick Meg going at it like gym bunnies or running bunnies or whatever the correct analogy was. I wondered how long it had been going on, I did not believe Dominic's assurances that it had started only recently. I imagined them laughing at me and I felt such a fool. I wondered if it was because I had put on weight or if in some other way it was my fault – after all, I had left Dominic alone for a long period of time, not just once but over and over again. But then I beat myself up for blaming myself when he was the one who had cheated and lied and no doubt would have gone on doing so if he had not been found out. We were not even married – I had a vague notion that if I pushed for it I might be able to claim rights to the apartment and more as a common-law wife, but, legalities aside, I somehow knew right away that I would not do so. In fact, I had no idea what I would do, so I just did nothing except sleep and eat and cry. I even lied to my father and for the first time since he had gone into the nursing home did not go home that weekend, citing Dominic's old excuse – pressure of work.

When I also missed two appointments with Elaine, she phoned me and I agreed to go and see her, more I think out of concern for her than for myself – she'd sounded so genuinely worried about me when she called.

When I told her all about the latest development in my life, Elaine's response was to ask me how that made me feel.

"How do I feel about the fact that my relationship of fifteen years is over? I feel like absolute shit, that's how I feel," I told her. I remember expecting Elaine to be shocked at this but I think she was only surprised. It was the most vigorous expression of emotion she had managed to yank from me over all our sessions.

"And perhaps it would help to examine the underpinning emotions to what you have just said, Kay – name them individually perhaps?"

I knew what she meant – she was talking about rage and jealousy and grief and shock and disbelief, the whole can of worms – but in that moment I realised that I felt just one thing when I thought about the entirety of my life with Dominic.

"The waste," I said out loud like a revelation, which in a way it was to me. "The awful bloody waste."

"Why do you say it was a waste, Kay?" asked Elaine. She leaned slightly forward, real interest on her earnest face.

"Because it was," I told her, "and I've always known it in my heart. Because always, right from the beginning, I haven't been able to shake the feeling ..."

"What was that feeling, Kay?"

"The feeling that I'm still waiting for my life to begin."

I never saw Elaine again. Walking home, I passed an old man sitting on a bench. He was painstakingly peeling an orange and instantly the sharp, bitter-sweet scent of the fruit transported me to our kitchen at home and my mother making marmalade. And in spite of what I had just told Elaine, a feeling of terrible sadness overwhelmed me. Even now, after all that has happened since, I can truly say that I have never felt so sorry for myself in my life as I did in that moment in a London park. I had also never felt so completely alone but that was the moment too when I knew that I was going home.

Chapter 16

It did not take me very long to wrap up my life in London and move it back to Dublin. I gave in my notice at work, pleading my father's health as the reason for my decision. As for my possessions, what I could not take on the plane I packed into two crates which I had collected for shipping on to Dublin. Other than a couple of lamps, some pictures, a silver candelabra I had bought at a jumble sale, a couple of favourite bowls and the miniscule Christmas tree which I refused to leave to the mercy of Dominic, it was mainly clothes and shoes, records, CDs and DVDs. It all only served to reinforce the sense I'd always had that I had been living in Dominic's home, not ours. The morning I flew home, I watered my collection of plants particularly well, then left one at each door to the other apartments on our floor, all that is, except Matchstick Meg's. Dominic did not do plants. The keys to his apartment I put in an envelope with his name on the front, which I posted through his new girlfriend's letterbox in the foyer of the building. I did not trouble to leave a note.

I moved back into my parents' home, back into my old bedroom. It felt strange and lonely living there alone but also safe. I picked up a second-hand car but went out only when it was absolutely necessary, to visit the nursing home or to shop. I did not answer the door when Mrs Nugent came knocking and once when she called to me over the hedge as I made a dash for the car I pretended not to hear her. I made a point of visiting my father every day, sometimes going twice in one day. It was, I think, partly in an effort to make up for the times I had not been able to visit him at all – but mostly, if I am honest, because I needed to see him to remind myself that I still belonged to someone because the truth was I was feeling unutterably alone. All my life I had taken it for granted that I had people who loved me; a world in which that was not so was more than I could contemplate.

The only positive thing about that whole time was that I began writing again; I was not sure why exactly. Out of nowhere the urge struck me and it became my one source of pleasure apart from the times I spent with my father. I considered the possibility that I was one of those people on whom unhappiness acts as a creative charm. But I had been unhappy enough many times during my time in London but had still found myself unable to produce anything I considered worth finishing. It was a long time before I came to understand that it was not a question of happiness or unhappiness, but rather for me a question of place. I should never have gone to London, I had never felt that I fit in there, and so, happy or unhappy, I would never have been able to write anything worth writing there. I was quite simply a home-bird. My father had known it but I'd had to find it out the hard way.

And so I wrote and went for walks and visited him at the nursing home and then went home and wrote some more and, if I was dissatisfied with my life and completely uncertain about my future, I at least had the satisfaction of knowing that I was in a place where I belonged.

I was back two weeks when, walking through the town with an unwrapped plunger in my hand, I met Robbie Duff.

The kitchen sink was blocked and, in my efforts to unblock it, the wooden handle of the old plunger had snapped.

This time it was he who noticed me first. My mind was on the renovation work due to start at the house and what an almighty mess that had escalated into, and as a result I did not even see him until he stopped right in front of me and said my name, a little tentatively.

"Kay, is it Kay? Kay Kelly?"

His hair was darker than I remembered with strands running it through it of silver and old gold, his face was brown, not so much sun as weather-tanned, and his eyes were as blue as I remembered them but now when he smiled the skin around them crinkled into a tracery of tiny lines.

"Robbie," I said, "Robbie Duff."

He hugged me then, really hugged me as though he was genuinely pleased to see me.

"You look great," he said, "really great."

"Oh, I don't know," I said. I was fairly certain that I looked anything but great. I have always been one of those people who eat when they are happy and stuff themselves when miserable and I had put on at least a stone in the past month.

"Well, I do, so take my word for it," said Robbie. "It really is great to see you. Are you still living around here or are you just visiting?"

"I just moved back recently from London," I told him and before he could ask anything further I said quickly, "But what has you back here?"

"I live here now," said Robbie.

I shook my head in disbelief. "Really? Where?"

"I bought back the family home a few months ago," said Robbie. "It needed some work done but it's ready now. I moved in a fortnight ago."

I was stunned. "That's wonderful," I said. "I heard that it had been sold but I had no idea. So you're actually planning to live there permanently?"

"That's my plan," said Robbie and I noticed again his use of the first person singular. "Well, at least as much as my work allows. I have to be away a fair bit lecturing but, yes, that's the plan, it's always been the plan. And, to be honest, it's not like I could afford to keep another place going. Everything I have went into buying back the old place. Dad's will made it possible – he died three years ago. Well, that and the recession – I'd never have been able to afford it even a few years ago."

I liked him more than ever for that admission. "I'm sorry about your father," I said, "but I'm very happy for you about the house. I remember you told me once that you would buy it back some day and now you have."

"Would that be the same time you lectured me about calling you *little* Kay Kelly? As I recall it, you gave me a good telling-off."

"Yes, well, I was sixteen and I had no manners, what can I say?" As I said it, I was thinking of that day when he had kissed me at our front gate. Which made me rush to change the subject without really thinking about what I was saying. "And your mother, will she move back in too or are you, is there ..." I stopped just as quickly, realising that if I went on I could rightly be suspected of fishing to find out if he was married or not. But of course he was married, why wouldn't he be married? Though he had used that first person singular ...

"My mother died," said Robbie, "just over a month ago."

"Oh no, I'm really sorry to hear that," I said. "Had she been ill?"

"Well, she had heart problems and other issues too, but to be honest it came as a surprise, even to her doctor. She died in her sleep."

He asked after my parents then and I told him about my mother's death and about my father's accident.

He said then, very gently, "Then you've been having a tough time, Kay."

"No more than you," I said, then quickly changed the subject. "But I hope that Violet-May and Rosemary-June are well?"

"Honestly? They've both been better. I'm sorry to say Violet-May has left her husband and come back from the States, chasing after some English actor she's fallen for. She was talking divorce but I get the impression this guy has cooled it now she's actually left Calvin. As for Rosemary, she lost her husband in a car crash."

"Oh my God," I said. "Poor Rosemary-June! Does she have any children?"

"Two, a little girl of three and a boy of almost eighteen months. Actually they're all arriving back this evening, the two girls and the kids. Violet-May's been staying with Rosemary since she got back from the States and I've managed to talk them both into spending a month here at the house with me."

"Well, that's good," I said. *Me*, he had said *me*, not *us*. "Especially for Rosemary-June – she'll be surrounded by family."

"That's what I thought," said Robbie. "But it's hard to know what to do for the best sometimes, isn't it?"

I watched as he took a swipe at his hair. I thought he seemed distracted, uncertain even, and it made me wonder if he was thinking about the memories the house might stir for both his sisters, the memories that were already stirring in my own mind.

But then his face lightened. "You'll have to come over and see them, Kay, and the house too of course. In fact, why not come now?"

"What – right now?"

"Yes, why not? Unless you have somewhere else to be of course?"

"No, at least not until later this evening when I go to visit my father."

"Then let's go," said Robbie. "The car's just over there, or are you driving yourself?"

"No, I walked."

"To buy a plunger, I take it?"

And I looked down with something like wonder at what I held in my hand. I had completely forgotten the plunger.

There are only two details I can recall about the Duff house that day. The rhododendrons were running riot and the front door had been painted royal blue instead of the yellow I remembered. Aside from that, all my other recollections of that visit are of the emotions and sensations it evoked in me. Even the smart new blue paint of the front door brought me back to that first time when I had stood on the step and knocked and Mr Duff had welcomed me inside.

"Did it need a lot of work?" I said. "The house?"

"A lot of painting, certainly," said Robbie, "but structurally it was all still sound."

"And all that lovely furniture, what happened to that when you moved?"

"That was all shipped to England lock, stock and barrel when the house was sold. A fair bit of it has come back now though."

There was a quiet satisfaction in Robbie's voice which was impossible to miss.

"Do you want to go in and have a look around inside now?" he said. "Or would you rather walk around the garden first? I have to admit there's been little or no work done on the outside yet – the shrubbery is completely overgrown, especially up close to the house. But all in good time."

"Walk, please," I said and we set off on a tour of the grounds, covering almost every part of it and in every corner memories big or small were triggered. Perhaps it was the same for Robbie because he was very quiet but that suited me fine.

At one point he said, "I've been trying to find Prince's

grave. I have a feeling it was somewhere round here but I can't remember where exactly."

"You shouldn't have thrown away the cross," I said.

"No, I shouldn't," he said, turning to me with a rueful smile. "You know, I seem to remember I was quite rude to you that day."

"I was being a nuisance," I said. The fact that he had remembered I was there at all that day was not only surprising but gratifying.

"Not a nuisance," said Robbie. "You were being what you always were – kind little Kay Kelly. You know you're different every time I see you? You're like some sort of creature that sheds its skin every few years."

"You do know you've effectively just called me a reptile?" I said.

Robbie laughed. "Not quite what I had intended," he said.

"I forgive you," I said. "But what do you expect? You first met me when I was ten, and again when I was sixteen. I'm thirty-nine now – of course I'm different every time you see me."

"I didn't mean the way you look," said Robbie.

He didn't say what he had meant.

"Yes, well, losing people will do that," I said.

"Has there been a lot of loss, Kay?" he said. "And do you mind my asking?"

"No, I don't mind." The way he phrased the question reminded me of his father, that gentle old-world courtesy at which it was hard to take offence.

"My mother you know about, and there was a long-term relationship that came to an abrupt end – not a marriage, we were never married."

I did not mention that other loss but I was thinking about it.

He watched me thoughtfully before saying gently, "You're right, Kay, losing the people we love does change us."

It was then, looking into his eyes, that for the first time in a long while, Alexander Duff's small face came into my mind. I saw him clearly, the plump feverish cheeks with a red moon on each, the fine blonde hair and long fair eyelashes. A sense of loss and grief descended on me, so strong I had to turn away pretending to inspect something in a nearby flower bed, for fear Robbie would see it.

"If you don't mind, I'll leave seeing the house for another day," I said.

"Of course," said Robbie. "Are you alright, Kay? Can I get you something, some water or a coffee or something?"

"No, I'm fine thanks. I just need to go home."

"Then I'll drop you there?"

"You don't have to, I'm fine to walk."

"I insist," said Robbie. "I'm assuming home is where it used to be?"

I nodded. Yes, I was thinking, I'm right back where I began and with nothing to show for it: no husband, no child, no book, not much of anything at all really. My mood took a further nosedive and perhaps Robbie sensed it because as we drove home he tried to keep things light.

"Do you still have an interest in writing?" he asked.

It pleased and surprised me that he remembered that about me, but then I had to tell him about my first little foray into publishing and my miserable failures since. He, however, did not appear to see it that way and urged me not to give up.

"Actually," I admitted, "I have been writing again, but only since I came back to Ireland. I've started on a new book."

"But that's wonderful, really wonderful. Maybe you needed to come home to find your voice again. I find it hard to even try to visualise you in a London setting. But now you've come home you need to be what you were obviously meant to be – be a writer, Kay!"

We had pulled up outside my front gate by then and, while

I was fumbling with my seatbelt, Robbie got out of the car and I realised that he was planning to open my door for me. I remember thinking with a pleased little shock: he's looking out for me, the way he's looking out for his sisters, because we are women. And I thought I recognised it for what it was: chivalry, out of date and un-politically correct, but as natural to Robbie Duff as it had been to his father before him. There was nothing disrespectful or patronising about it – the opposite in fact – and it made me like him all the more. But I was already pushing open the door myself by the time he got there. He held it open though as I stepped out and walked with me to the gate. I wondered if he was expecting to be asked in and the thought came to me that somewhere the ghosts of my ten and sixteen-year-old selves were probably hugging themselves with delight. But I realised that I did not want him to come in just then. Just then I wanted to be alone.

But Robbie made no attempt to go beyond the gate. He stood and looked up at the house, "You're on your own then," he said, "while your father is in the nursing home? That must be hard."

It was so exactly what I had recently been thinking that I was startled and it was all I could do to stop my eyes filling with tears. But Robbie's eyes were on the house.

"Are you having some work done?" he asked, seeing the bags of cement and other supplies the builders had left there that morning. "I can't imagine that will be very conducive to your writing – all that knocking and hammering – you won't get much peace."

"You have no idea," I said. "It was just supposed to be a downstairs bathroom being put in because Dad had his fall on the stairs but, when the builders came out to take a look so they could give me a quote, they spotted signs of dry rot in the roof."

"Dry rot? That's going to be a messy and expensive business, Kay."

"Don't I know it," I said. "All the infected timber will have to be removed, destroyed and replaced. And apparently the timber close by will need to be treated with some sort of fungicide. It's a complete disaster." I put my hands to my face at the mere thought of the scale of the disaster. "But it has to be done. I want it all finished by the time Dad comes home again."

"But what will you do while the work is being done?" said Robbie. "You can't stay here in the middle of all of that."

"No," I agreed, "I can't. Find somewhere to rent short-term maybe – more expense. To be honest, I don't know what I'll do. I've only just found out and I haven't quite got my head around it. Anyway, look, I'd better not delay you further. Bye, Robbie."

"Bye, Kay."

As I walked away he called my name and I turned back, overcome by a sudden hope that he was about to ask for my phone number.

"Don't forget your plunger." And, raising it in the air, he waved it at me.

Chapter 17

Robbie came back four days later although Mrs Nugent had beaten him to it. I was amazed it had taken her so long, but it turned out she had been away for a couple of weeks visiting the twins. She chose the day the builders came back to finally call and interrogate me, taking advantage of the front door being left wide open to accommodate them traipsing in and out. She just walked right in and bearded me if not in my den then in the kitchen. I had no choice but to ask her to sit down and make her some tea.

She went right to the heart of the matter.

"You're home on your own again," she said. "Been here a few weeks, I'm told, and himself not with you. Busy with work, is he?"

"There is no himself, Mrs Nugent – it's just me now."

She surprised me. "Probably better off," she said. "Your mother wouldn't be sorry, she never took to that fella at all."

I smiled in spite of myself. "No, she didn't," I admitted.

"And is it right what I hear, that Robbie Duff has been to see you?" said Mrs Nugent.

There was no point in denying it – she knew – and, before very much longer, I was in full possession of all known facts and rumours concerning him. He was not married, had never

153

been married though not for the want of trying – the women went mad for him, had no children and had bought back the Duff house which he had got for a bargain. But he was spending a small fortune now, it seemed, doing it up and he must be mad to want to come back and live in Ireland – did I not think he must be mad?

"It's his money," I said. "And he must want to come back."

And then I spent the next half hour trying to evade all Mrs Nugent's best blatant, as well as devious tactics, to elicit further information from me on the subject of Robbie Duff's finances and intentions, what exactly the builders were going to be doing to the house, and why he had brought me home and from where.

The day that Robbie arrived, the builders had just left to go to their lunch and I had just made myself a cheese-and-onion sandwich for my own lunch and had eaten half of it when the doorbell went and there he was standing in the porch, smiling a little uncertainly at me.

"I'd have rung if I had your number," he said, "but I didn't, so I've come instead."

"Come in," I said.

I wished with all my heart that I settled for cheese and tomato or cheese and anything other than onion; I was sure I reeked of it. But, when I offered to make him a sandwich of his choosing, he insisted on having what I was having and then we sat down at the kitchen table and ate our first meal together. We chatted about all sorts of things but I couldn't help feeling that something was on his mind. I asked if the two girls had arrived and he said they had. I was conscious of the fact that, technically, I should have called them "women" but they were still girls to me.

"How are they settling in?" I asked. "Are they as happy to be back in the house as you obviously are. It must feel strange for them, for all of you actually?"

Actually, I thought that he looked far from happy that day. "They're settling in," was all he said. "It's just unfortunate that I have to go away again almost immediately."

"Oh, how come?"

He told me that an archaeologist colleague who had been due to speak at a conference and then go on to oversee a field trip, had been involved in a road traffic accident. Robbie had been asked to take his place.

"The timing couldn't be worse," he said, "with Rosemary and the children there."

"It's unfortunate," I said, "but you won't be away for very long, will you?"

"I'll be gone for seven days in all," said Robbie.

"Well, that's not so long," I said, "and it's not as though she's there alone. She has Violet-May too."

Robbie made a sound in the back of his throat; it was hard to know whether it was derision or something else.

"You haven't seen Violet-May in some time, have you?" he said.

"Not since I was ten." I didn't like to think about the last occasion I had seen Violet-May. I had never liked to think about it. We had all left the police station together, a cluster of silent, glum, downward-looking people.

"Right," said Robbie. "Well, let's just say she's not exactly great with small children." He darted me a quick glance then looked away again. "And Rosemary needs all the help she can get right now."

"I can imagine."

He told me then that his mother had died while staying with Rosemary-June. "It was particularly unfortunate coming on top of her losing her husband Justin. He died while she was pregnant with Oliver. It's all taken a toll on Rosemary and as a result I believe she's very fragile right now. She needs peace and quiet and stability. Most of all she needs to be around somebody calm and kind and practical."

He looked at me again then, and this time his gaze was direct and searching.

"She needs to be around somebody like you, Kay," he said.

"Someone like me?" I repeated, not at all pleased at the description.

"Have you found somewhere to rent yet?"

The change of subject threw me and I shook my head, slightly mystified. "Not yet, no."

"Good. Because I've been thinking about this and I've come up with an idea that could help us both. As I said, I have those work trips coming up. And, to put it bluntly, I don't like the idea of leaving Rosemary to the tender mercies of Violet-May."

I was a little shocked at his frankness but I tried not to show it.

"And meanwhile," he went on, "here you are being forced to move out and find somewhere to rent. So it occurred to me, why not just move into my place?"

"Move in?"

"Yes."

"Live there, you mean?"

"Yes – while this place is being fixed up. That way you'd have rent-free accommodation."

"In return for what?" I asked, smiling, not taking him very seriously.

"Well, you'd be doing me a favour – keeping Rosemary-June company – but I suppose you could help out with the kids. Violet-May is next to useless and there's Grace but she's got other things to attend to."

"Who's Grace?"

"I hired her to help out in the house, that sort of thing. And now the children are here, she's sort of a nanny too, I suppose. Look, just think about it, Kay. You want a place to write in peace and you can have that at the house – lots of space and quiet, exactly what you need."

"And what would Violet-May and Rosemary-June think of that arrangement?" I said.

"Why would they think anything other than that it makes practical sense?" said Robbie. "And, besides, you're an old friend."

"Hang on a second," I said. "Is this you taking pity on me, because I was moaning about the cost of renting and doing this place up?"

"Not at all. But you can't deny you're in a bit of a fix and I genuinely do need someone to keep an eye on things."

"Keep an eye on what exactly?"

"The girls. Keep an eye on the girls. I'd like to know they have someone like you there."

"Ah yes, someone – what was it again? Calm and kind and practical," I said and I laughed a little to show I was taking that lightly.

But Robbie was not laughing, he was not even smiling, and I stopped laughing too.

"You do know they're not 'girls' anymore, don't you, Robbie?" I said. "They're grown women, grown women I haven't set eyes on for over twenty-five years. You call me an old friend but I don't know the first thing about Violet-May or Rosemary anymore. And so what if Violet-May isn't mad about kids? She's still Rosemary-June's sister. I'm not, I'm nothing to her. She and I were never even friends and I'm practically a stranger to her at this stage. You say I can help out with the kids, but you've just told me you already have a sort of nanny in this Grace. I know you're concerned about Rosemary, Robbie, but it's a ridiculous idea."

"It may be a ridiculous idea," said Robbie, "but it's the only one I have. I honestly don't think Violet-May is the best person for Rosemary-June at present."

I watched as he got up from his chair at the table and stood at the kitchen window with his back to me.

"That year," he said, "the year Alexander died, I hated my mother with a passion. I don't mean afterwards, I mean before."

"Well, I don't suppose that's so unusual," I said. "You were fifteen and there was all that boarding school stuff and ..."

"No, you don't understand," said Robbie, wheeling round. "It wasn't about being fifteen or school or any of that sort of thing. It was something else entirely. The year before that, I got into a fight with a guy at school. I can't remember what it was about, only that he came out the worst for it and as a result he kindly informed that I had a sister who had been born before my mother was married to my father – 'your little bastard sister', he called her." Robbie's eyes narrowed. "I don't know if this is news to you, Kay. I suspect not."

I tried to look noncommittal. "I think I might have heard something over the years, but just a rumour, none of the details ... I had no idea if it was even true."

Robbie gave a short laugh and turned back to the window. "I thought as much," he said. "No doubt everybody heard something, some version of the truth. Even I had suspected that there was some secret about my mother – there was some sniggering, that kind of thing – but until that day nobody had come right out and said it. Of course I called that boy a liar. Then I saw the expression on the face of another boy, a friend of mine this time, and I knew it was the truth."

He turned again and came and sat down and I waited while he sipped the dregs of his tea which I knew must be cold by now but I could not bring myself to speak and offer him a fresh cup.

"I never told my mother what I had discovered," said Robbie. "I wish I had, I wish I'd given her the opportunity to tell her side of the story. Instead I was a judgemental little fool and I was ashamed of her and so angry with her that, like I said, it felt like I hated her. I did find the courage though to ask my father about her."

"What did he say?" I asked.

"He admitted that there had been a little girl," said Robbie. "Other than that, all he would say was that the only thing I needed to know about my lady mother was that she was indeed just that – a lady."

I smiled. "That sounds exactly the sort of thing your father would say."

"I only really found out more about it all after Alexander died." He smiled bleakly. "Even then it was only by listening to what was not intended for my ears. I had been taken out of school for the funeral and I overheard my parents talking one night. My mother was very upset, she was reliving the past and the way my grandmother had reacted to the pregnancy: it seems she saw it as my mother having shamed the family. So when my father asked her to marry him, Mum expected her mother to be relieved, instead of which it seems she was almost angry. Apparently she saw it as Mum being rewarded with a wealthy husband and a fine house, instead of being punished for her sin as my grandmother thought she ought to be."

"Her sin!" I said. "For God's sake!"

"She went further than that," said Robbie. "She warned my mother that sooner or later she would be punished and told her that married or not she would always be 'a dirty little slut'."

"Talk about harsh!" I said involuntarily.

"Yes, indeed," said Robbie absently, and I knew that his mind was still in the past, listening to his mother unknowingly revealing herself to him.

"My father said all the right things of course but I don't believe Mum even heard him – I'm pretty sure she was speaking more to herself than to him. She said something about how marrying him had seemed like a second chance, a fresh start. And that she had tried to make it more so by turning herself into somebody else entirely – 'somebody respectable' was how she put it."

I felt a rush of sympathy for the dead woman and moved uneasily in my chair, but again I doubt if Robbie noticed.

"But she said that in spite of how hard she'd tried, she'd always known that people saw through her. 'I hear them laughing at me,' she said. 'I know they talk about me behind my back – some of the women are barely even civil to my face.' She said she saw it and heard it every day but she had made a conscious decision to ignore it by telling herself that it was Florence Flynn they were talking about, not Flora Duff."

"Your poor mother," I said. "I'm so sorry she had to endure that."

Robbie bowed his head and put his cup down on the table. "My father tried to convince her that she was wrong, of course. He told her she imagined all of this but, as I say, she wasn't really speaking to him, she was just thinking out loud."

He got up, pushed the chair under the table and, leaning on it, looked at me. "I don't recall all of what she said that night," he said. "But I do remember she talked about herself as she had been when she was a child. How hard she had tried to please her mother, how she had done what she was told, minded her manners, kept herself clean and how it hadn't made any difference. Her mother had found fault with her, accused her of slyness, of vanity, of 'putting herself forward'." He grimaced. "Putting herself forward. What a horrible expression."

"Your grandmother sounds like a pretty horrible woman," I said.

"I never met her." He took his hands from the chair. "Would you mind if I opened the door? I could do with some fresh air."

"Of course." I made to get up to do it myself but he got there first and I sat back down and watched him standing in the bright square of sunlight that flooded in from the garden.

"Both my grandmothers cut themselves off from my parents for different but equally misguided reasons," he said. "My paternal grandmother thawed slightly when I and my sisters came along, but she never forgave my mother for the breach the marriage had caused between her and my father. I don't know if my mother ever saw her own mother again but, in any event, that night, the night of Alexander's funeral, I remember Mum saying that her mother had been right all along. She was being punished for her sin and would go on being punished."

"But that's terrible!" I said.

I was feeling a little sick, remembering the many unkind things I had heard and thought about Mrs Duff, the things my mother had repeated, had said herself, and the things she had not said but insinuated. Although, in her defence, I was fairly certain that it was not the change in Florence Flynn's fortunes my mother held against her, as much as the unforgiveable crime of forgetting where she came from. And so, she, like many others, made a point of remembering and reminding each other regularly in case they ever forgot.

"My father told her not to torment herself with superstitious nonsense, that she had done the right thing by her first child and that Alexander's death had been a terrible accident and not her fault. I don't know if she believed him or, as I've said, if she was even listening to him. But I do know I stopped hating my mother that night. She had a nervous breakdown shortly after that. It was one of the reasons we sold the house and moved away. And I also know that having to leave this house almost broke my father's heart."

"And did you find out what happened to your sister?"

"I found out," said Robbie shortly.

161

I was silent for a while but when he didn't elaborate I said very gently, "Well, I'm glad you stopped hating your mother. That must have been a great relief to you."

Robbie nodded. "That was exactly how it felt, Kay, a relief, like an enormous weight being lifted from me. And not long after that night, before I went back to school, my father took me aside and told me very solemnly that one day it would be my job to protect my mother and my sisters and he asked me to promise I would do that to the best of my ability."

"And you promised." It was not a question.

"And I promised," said Robbie.

"And now, you think that Rosemary needs your protection."

I thought about the word he had used when she spoke about her: 'fragile'. I thought about how she had lost her husband and, very soon afterwards, her mother. It was, now I came to think about it, not unlike my own situation – was that why Robbie thought I was the right person to help her? But, in Rosemary's case, there were two small children to be taken into account. Was that it? Was Rosemary struggling so badly with grief and depression that she was unable to cope? I stole a sidewise glance at Robbie who was leaning against the doorjamb. One hand hung down by his side – the skin was very brown and I could see the short golden hairs glinting.

Without consciously forming a decision, I asked, "When do you have to leave?"

"In two days. That's the first trip and I'll be away for seven days, as I said. The second trip is shorter, five days in Crete, but it's likely that for part of it I'll be out of phone coverage which means it won't be possible to phone home."

"OK," I said. "And you honestly think I could be of some use while you're away?"

"I do, I truly do, Kay."

"Then I will," I said.

"Do you mean it, Kay?" Robbie's face lit up.

"Yes. I'm not going to pretend it won't be wonderful to have somewhere to live while this place is being pulled asunder and put back together again. But I'll only go if you're absolutely sure that Violet-May and Rosemary-June wouldn't mind. And I'll be happy to help out with the kids. But you do realise I'll need to visit my father every day? And then there's my writing – I prefer to do that in the mornings but it means I won't be around the whole time – you do realise that, don't you?"

"I know all of that, Kay," said Robbie. "To be honest I'll be happy just knowing you'll be there in the house and will spend a little time with Rosemary when you can, and with the children. Do you like children, Kay?"

"I love children," I said quietly.

"I had the feeling you would," said Robbie.

He said nothing more and I was grateful once again that he would never be crass enough to enquire any further into my personal life. And then it occurred to me that it was more than probable he just wasn't interested enough to want to know.

Robbie came over then and laid his hand on mine.

"Thank you, Kay," he said. "And take it from me, we do need you, you have no idea how much."

Chapter 18

I have never really been able to understand how people can say they love autumn better than any other season. Yes, the crisp cool mornings can be stunning and the leaves changing colours is a beautiful thing, but fundamentally all any of that really means is that things are dying. No, autumn has always made me feel just a little bit sad. And that autumn when I half-reluctantly agreed to move into the Duff house was particularly beautiful.

I arrived on a Saturday in early September and, while I was parking, Robbie came round the side of the house, holding a small girl by the hand. I got out of the car and walked to meet them.

"Hello!" He was smiling broadly as though he were really glad to see me. "We've been in the garden." He glanced down at the child. "Somebody wanted to give you a present to welcome you."

The little girl stuck out her hand and I saw that she was clutching a small bunch of flowers. I dropped to my hunkers and smiled at her. "Hello," I said, "my name is Kay. Are those for me?"

She nodded and I took the small bouquet, still warm from her grasp. "They're beautiful, and so are you. What's your name?"

"Caroline," said the child and smiled at me shyly. She was a frail-looking, beautiful little thing with very pale skin, remarkably blue eyes very much like her mother's, and a fuzz of blonde hair that looked like a dandelion-puff in the sun.

I smiled up at Robbie. "She has to be Rosemary's daughter, she's the spit of her. Did you say there was a little boy too?"

Robbie, who had been smiling fondly at his small niece, nodded and the smile flitted away as though a thought had troubled him. It was back almost instantly, however.

"I presume you have some bags and things?" he said.

"Just the one," I said, straightening up once more. I did not add that I had packed lightly as I was not at all sure how long I would actually stay. I was more than curious to see how his sisters would receive me.

We walked back to the car to fetch my bag, Caroline still holding Robbie's hand. When she reached up and slipped her free hand into mine I felt a warm feeling spread through my physical being. I smiled down at her but she was looking ahead and seemed entirely unconscious of the effect of her action. I adjusted my expression to what I hoped was one of nonchalance, but I was careful to hold the small hand as gently as I could, terrified lest I crush her fingers.

"I wasn't sure where to park," I said. "Is it alright there?"

"Sure," said Robbie. "You can stick it in the second garage later if you like."

He took my bag from me and we walked back to the house, accommodating ourselves to the child's short stride. As we walked up the steps to the open front door, I caught the glint of mica in the granite, picked up by the sunlight, and a memory assailed me of sitting there on the sun-warmed stone with Violet-May on the day that Robbie played his records so loudly he woke his brother, Alexander.

In the hall I gazed about me. Everything looked almost exactly as I remembered it, even to the paintings on the wall.

I turned to Robbie and found him watching me.

"It's like you never moved out," I said.

"I suppose it is," said Robbie, looking around him. "It's a protected building of course so the Swedes and the people who came after them weren't able to change the structure of the house. As I told you, the original furniture has come back with me too – not all – some of it has gone to the girls, some of it I just didn't like, frankly. But as much as possible I've tried to have everything put back where it was."

He turned to me suddenly, a troubled look in his eyes.

"You probably think all this is weird or unhealthy or something, do you, Kay? Like I'm living in the past or trying to recreate something or –"

"I don't think anything at all," I said, "except that this house was supposed to be yours and now you've come home and it is."

Robbie's face cleared. "That's exactly how I feel – like I've come home." He smiled broadly. "You see, you're already making things better around here. Come on, let's go find the girls."

As I followed him I could not help wondering just why things needed to be made better.

Violet-May and Rosemary-June were in the drawing room. Here too everything seemed the same, only the people had changed somewhat.

"Look who's here," said Robbie, a little too brightly, I thought.

Violet-May, who had been flicking through the pages of a magazine, gave a small theatrical squeal, dropped the magazine and got up from the sofa where she had been sprawled. She came toward me in a graceful sashaying movement.

"Kay," she said, "how lovely to see you. Look, Rosemary-June, it's Kay." Her accent sounded English now, but with a slight American drawl.

She was dressed casually in a sleeveless white top and

loose-fitting pale-grey trousers in some silky material –
somehow she managed to make them look slinky and
glamorous. As she kissed me on both cheeks I caught the
floral notes of her perfume. She seemed to me even more
beautiful as a woman than I remembered her as a child. The
cloud of dark hair was sleeker now and streaked with
expensive-looking highlights. She was tall and, to my mind,
just a little too thin but that, I told myself, was splitting hairs.
We would both turn forty that year but she did not look a day
over twenty-eight. Being human, I could not help but sigh a
little at all that perfection. I turned to the other woman in the
room. "Hello, Rosemary-June," I said.

She had been half-sitting, half-lying in a chair by the
window, but she got up now with a languorous cat-like
stretch and came toward me slowly.

"It's just Rosemary these days," she said. "With Justin's
double-barrelled family name – Palmer-Jones – it was all
getting a bit too ridiculous so I dropped the June."

Like Violet-May she had acquired a plummy sort of
English accent but without the American twang of her sister.

She kissed me too but on one cheek only. She was taller
than Violet-May, considerably taller than me too, and
painfully thin – in her scooped-neck top I could see her
clavicle bones sharply defined. Her eyes were just as wide and
blue as ever, but she had none of her sister's glamour and in
comparison her fair prettiness appeared a little washed-out. I
reminded myself what she had been through, the death of her
husband followed by that of her mother, and on top of that
she was the mother of two young children. It was hardly any
wonder she wasn't exactly glowing.

"Please sit down, Kay," said Robbie.

I crossed to an armchair and perched on its edge. I felt self-
conscious and ill at ease and, when nobody spoke for what
seemed like an eternity, I rushed into speaking without really
thinking.

"I was very sorry to hear about your husband, Rosemary," I said.

Rosemary bowed her head and said nothing and I wished I had just stayed quiet.

"Your little girl is beautiful," I said quickly, and I smiled at Caroline who had climbed onto the sofa next to her mother.

Rosemary turned to the child and brushed aside the frizz of hair that had fallen over her eyes.

"Yes, isn't she?" she said.

"And Robbie said you had a little boy too."

"I do," said Rosemary, her eyes still on Caroline.

"Where is Oliver?" said Robbie.

"I put him down for a little nap," said Violet-May. "He's so fretful today I thought Rosemary could do with a break."

"What she means is he was giving his aunt a headache," said Rosemary lightly but I sensed an undertone.

"OK then," said Robbie. "I'll go and make us some coffee and then perhaps, Violet-May, you'll show Kay upstairs and she can get herself settled in."

Violet-May, who had gone back to her seat and resumed reading, looked up and gave me a fleeting smile.

"Anytime you like," she said languidly then went back to her magazine.

Robbie left the room and there was silence. Violet-May was engrossed in her magazine. I glanced at Rosemary. The half-smile was back on her lips and she was examining the rings on her left hand. I wondered if I was just imagining an atmosphere and, if not, whether it had something to do with my coming to the house. I decided I would sound Violet-May out as soon as I had an opportunity to speak to her alone.

The silence was lengthening. In desperation, I addressed a couple of remarks to Caroline, admiring her dress and her shoes. The child answered me with smiles and nods and the odd shy short sentence and then there was silence once again.

I was flailing about for something else to say when

Rosemary suddenly glanced up from her rings and said abruptly, "How long do you plan to stay?"

Violet-May's head jerked upwards and the magazine slid from her silken lap.

"I'm not exactly –" I began.

"As long as she needs to, I expect," said Violet May. "Isn't that right, Kay?"

"Well, perhaps – I wouldn't want to put anybody out," I said.

"Dry rot," said Rosemary musingly, her eyes on her rings once more.

I waited for more – clearly Robbie had explained the situation at my father's house – but it appeared that was all she had to say on the subject. Was she doubting the story? I glanced at Violet-May who was also looking at her sister, a peculiar expression on her face. She said nothing, however, but bent down and retrieved the magazine from the floor.

"I've finished with this, Kay," she said. "Would you like to read it?"

I didn't but I nodded anyway and she came across and handed me the copy of *Vogue*, glossy and almost as fat as a phone book. She wandered over to one of the big windows and stood with her back to me and I gave up on any further attempt at conversation, as even Caroline had turned away from me and was snuggled into her mother's side, her face hidden by a fall of downy hair. So I opened the magazine and turned the pages and then pretended to read while all the time wondering just how much longer it would take Robbie to make that flaming coffee.

He arrived back carrying a tray.

"Oliver's awake," he said.

Rosemary looked up from her hand. "You checked on him," she said, making it sound like an accusation.

"No, I heard him warbling as I came through the hall," said Robbie lightly.

"I'll go and bring him down, shall I?" said Violet-May, turning away from the window.

Rosemary glanced at Robbie again, then got to her feet quickly. "No, I'll do it," she said.

Robbie gave his attention to pouring out coffee and pressing biscuits on me. I relaxed a little then and looked about me at the drawing room, which although it had obviously had a facelift was still very much as I remembered it. Glancing at a photograph on the table next to my chair, I recognised a younger Robbie, dressed in his Master's conferral gown and cap. Behind him I recognised Mr Duff, an older, frailer-looking Mr Duff than the one I remembered. He had the same ferocious eyebrows that had so awed me as a child and his skin looked as rubicund as ever – I smiled as I recalled that I used to think of him as rusty. By his side was Mrs Duff, thinner than I remembered and, despite the occasion, wearing only the merest whisper of a smile. Looking at her, I recognised the signs of suffering in the downward lines of her face but in spite of everything she was still a very good-looking woman, a fact I had not appreciated as a child. Gone was that up-tilted chin, gone I realised too was whatever that quality had been which made her seem at all times so very alive. Life, I thought a little sadly, had certainly done its best to make her humble.

It was Violet-May who offered to show me to my "rooms".

"Rooms?" I repeated. "Surely I don't have more than one?"

"You have two: one for sleeping, one for writing," said Violet-May as she went ahead of me up the staircase. "Robbie said you want to write." She glanced over her shoulder at me. "Do you really think you'll get much done here? With the children about and everything, I mean?"

"Well, I hope so," I said. "I imagine I'll be able to write here as well as anywhere else. As Robbie has obviously told you, I'm having to have a lot of work done on the house." I plunged into a lot of unnecessary detail then about my father's fall and the need for downstairs plumbing and the dry rot.

When I was finished talking, Violet-May gave me another look over her shoulder, unreadable this time, and neither of us said anything more until she threw open a door off the first landing.

"This is your bedroom," she said and stood aside for me to pass.

The room was large, bright and airy, with cheery yellow walls and twin bay windows letting in the afternoon sunlight. There was an enormous bed, an oak wardrobe with matching dressing table, as well as a desk and easy chair. The period fireplace was still there but it contained a simulated coal fire which I assumed could spring to blazing life at the flick of a switch. I even had a television.

I could not fault it.

"It's great," I said, but I stood where I was, just inside the door, feeling slightly ill at ease, like a guest being shown to her room in a guesthouse. What was I doing here?

"There's a bathroom through that door," said Violet-May. "You're right next door to Caroline and Oliver. I don't know what Robbie was thinking putting you next to them – but, don't worry, you won't hear much – these rooms are practically soundproof. Robbie's had the heating updated too, you'll be relieved to hear – it's not such an ice-box as it used to be when we were little."

I looked at her and asked another question that had been on my mind.

"It must be strange being back here, after all these years, Violet-May. How did you feel about Robbie buying the house back?"

Violet-May shrugged. "He didn't tell me, he didn't tell anyone, not until it was done and dusted. I've no idea why he'd want to, but it makes no difference to me, I won't be living here. I wouldn't be here now if it wasn't for ... if it wasn't for Robbie."

I had a feeling she had been about to say something else but she turned from me and went and stood at one of the windows, her back to me.

"And Rosemary-June," I said, "how does she feel about being back here?"

"You'd have to ask her," said Violet-May. "Nobody has ever been able to guess what Rosemary-June thinks about anything, and I doubt they ever will."

"I gather she's been through a difficult time," I said. "Her husband and your mother. I was very sorry to hear about your mother. Robbie said it was very sudden. I know how that feels – my own mother died very unexpectedly in her sleep."

"Mummy died in her sleep too," said Violet-May. "Poor Mummy. Oh well."

That strange response silenced me. I sat down on the stool in front of the dressing table and waited for her to turn around.

After a moment she said, "Do you ever get the feeling that you're being watched?"

I was completely unprepared for the question and unsure how to answer it. Eventually I said, "Being watched? Do you mean like God or something? Isn't that all part of being brought up Catholic? Long after you think you've shaken off the shackles, there He is still watching."

"That's not what I meant," said Violet-May. "I meant somebody literally watching you."

"Why would they be?" I said quietly.

Violet-May turned and looked me straight in the eye. "I have no idea," she said. "So you don't believe in God then, Kay?"

"I don't know what I believe." I also had no idea where she was going with all of this. Was she deliberately trying to make me feel uncomfortable, unwelcome?

"I'm surprised to hear you say that," said Violet-May. "I don't know why, but somehow I would have expected that these things would be simpler for you."

"Why would you think that?" I said, feeling slightly insulted.

Violet-May turned back to the window.

"If there is a God," she said, "it raises the question of why he would have created people. But then again I think he'd have had to, don't you? Otherwise, without us, without our small lives to meddle in, how would he know he was God?"

I hesitated for a moment before saying, "Is anything wrong, Violet-May?"

"Wrong? Oh, I suppose Robbie told you about the divorce."

"He just mentioned it in passing, not the details. I was sorry to hear about it but that's not what I meant, I –"

"Don't be sorry," Violet-May interrupted. "I didn't like being married. I don't mean to Calvin in particular – I don't think I'd like being married to anyone. It's like being the queen instead of the princess and I have only ever really wanted to be the princess. Even as a child." She turned suddenly and gave me a wry smile, then she went and sat down on the edge of the enormous bed. "But you probably remember that, don't you, Kay? No, I always wanted to be the princess because, even then, I somehow knew instinctively that once you became the queen all the fun was over. I mean all the best fairy tales end at the point where the princess marries the prince and there's a very good reason for that. No, marriage is going from being the princess to being the queen and that isn't so much fun at all."

"You two look very serious – what are you talking about?"

I turned. Rosemary was standing in the doorway.

"Kay was just asking about Mummy," said Violet-May, "and my boring marital problems and all that dreary stuff. Where's Oliver?"

"He's downstairs with Robbie and Caroline."

"OK. In that case why don't you take over now, Rosemary, and show Kay her where her writing room is? I have things to do." She yawned ostentatiously then got up and left, leaving me with a suspicion that she considered me one of those dreary problems she found so boring.

My writing room, as Violet-May called it, was the attic at the very top of the house. I had never been any further than the second landing before and, as I followed Rosemary up the stairs, I was suddenly reminded of the day I had stood there ear-wigging while Robbie and his friends listened to Queen. It struck me as somewhat remarkable that this house, where, when you added it all up, I had spent very little time, should be capable of triggering so many and such vivid memories.

It was a small but cosy room with a beautiful vaulted ceiling ribbed with thick dark wooden beams. There was a single sash window, oak floorboards polished and buffed to a high sheen, and a large faded but still very beautiful rug in hues of blue and yellow. I looked about me with pleasure at the carved love seat and the satinwood rocker and best of all the antique writing desk which had been placed so that it faced the window with its wonderful view over the meadow behind the house. There was also a comfortable-looking swivel chair in black leather for me to sit in as I wrote, an angled reading lamp and even a printer with a stack of paper still in its red-and-white wrapper stacked high next to it. It seemed to me that everything had been supplied for my comfort and convenience and I knew it was Robbie I had to thank for this.

I turned to Rosemary. "This is wonderful," I said. "I've never been up in this room before."

I looked at her uncomfortably, realising that I had inadvertently referred back to when I was there as a child, a time I imagined she would much prefer to forget.

But Rosemary had dropped down into the rocking chair and, looking completely unperturbed, was gently rocking herself to and fro. "Mummy used to keep it locked back then. This is the room where that maid or whatever she was did herself in."

174

"Oh," I said, my eyes going to the window. "Of course. She must have been so lonely and unhappy to do that."

"I suppose so," said Rosemary and then, as though by a process of thought association, she said. "Do you think that Violet-May is alright?"

The suddenness of the question threw me. "Violet-May, yes, I think so. Why do you ask?"

"Oh, it's just that thinking about the day that Mummy died always upsets her. None of us will ever forget it."

"No, of course not," I said.

I was thinking that nobody could ever forget the day their mother died and a wave of sadness crept over me, when Rosemary suddenly stood up, picked up a small silver box from a side-table and examined it. Then, turning, she surveyed me with an odd look on her face. She looked down at the box, opened the hinged lid and shut it again.

"Yes, well, it was upsetting for everyone," she said, "but I think for Violet-May especially. But of course she'll have told you about what happened with Oliver."

I shook my head. "What happened to Oliver?"

"Didn't Violet-May tell you about it?" said Rosemary. "Or Robbie? I was sure one of them would have. Oliver almost drowned that day."

She said it in what I thought was a curiously flat tone of voice, as though she were telling me that we had run out of milk or that it was starting to rain, but all the time her eyes were fixed firmly on mine. It had the effect of giving me the impression of some powerful emotion only barely contained.

"My God," I said. "What happened?"

"Well, nobody really knows for sure but somehow Oliver managed to get out of the house and into the garden. This was at our house, mine and Justin's, and there was a pond at the back of the house, an ornamental pond, not very deep as it happens but deep enough to ... Anyway, Oliver was playing with his yellow ball. It must have rolled into the pond and he went in after it or he slipped or … well, it doesn't bear thinking about and so I try not to. But, anyway, I saw him from the window, actually in the water I mean, and so I screamed and screamed and I rushed downstairs like a crazy thing."

I was experiencing a sick sensation in the pit of my stomach which had come into being while I listened to how a baby had come close to losing his life by drowning.

"By the time I got to him, Violet-May was already there. She'd heard me screaming and had gone running too and got him out. And by some miracle he was fine – he must have only just hit the water when I looked out. But you know …" her voice trailed off into silence.

"What was Violet-May doing there?" I said abruptly.

"What was she doing at our house? Well, she was staying there at the time actually. It was after Justin died and Violet-May had decided I needed looking after. So Mummy was there – and Grace too."

"Grace was there? You mean the same Grace who's here now?"

"Yes, the same Grace," said Rosemary. "Why are you surprised?"

"Oh, it was just that with her working for Robbie now, I assumed that Grace came from round here."

"Perhaps – actually I believe she did," said Rosemary. "But she worked for Justin before she worked for Robbie, so I suppose she must have lived in London then. But don't ask me, it was Mummy and Violet-May who found her and talked Justin into hiring her, nothing to do with me. She was supposed to be helping to look after Caroline and Oliver." She laughed and I thought I detected a bitter ring to the sound. "And then Mummy died that very same day, that night to be really accurate. She'd come to stay with me too. A nightmare, the whole thing was, a complete and absolute nightmare."

"Yes, I can only imagine," I said. "But at least your mother

176

died peacefully."

I was flailing around for platitudes and I knew I was.

"Is that what Violet-May told you, that Mummy died peacefully?" Rosemary's question sliced through my thoughts and I looked at her in surprise.

"I thought so. Yes, I'm almost sure that's what she said – that your mother died in her sleep. Was that not what happened?"

"Well yes, I suppose technically that is true," said Rosemary. "Mummy did die in her sleep but I wouldn't exactly say she was peaceful that night, not for that whole afternoon she wasn't. She took some sort of turn in the afternoon – actually it was me who found her and she was barely able to breathe. You see nobody had checked on her because of what had happened with Oliver, but she must have got out of bed, because when I found her she was slumped in her chair beside the window. She looked so awful that it frightened me and she was very agitated – it was hard to know what about exactly because she was having trouble breathing. Then Violet-May came into the room and Mummy got even more agitated. In the end we had to get the doctor back to look at her. He'd been out to the house to check Oliver over in case there had been any damage to his lungs or whatever, which luckily there wasn't."

"What did the doctor say about your mother?" I said.

"He said she'd taken a little turn and he gave her a sedative and she did sleep then. Only she never woke up again."

"I'm so sorry," I said.

"Yes, poor Mummy, it was all so sudden. Even the doctor was surprised because in spite of her weak heart he hadn't expected her to go so soon."

"And did you find out what had upset her? Had she seen what had happened to Oliver?"

"We're not sure," said Rosemary. "That was what everybody assumed, but I've always thought it had something to do with Violet-May."

"Why do you think that?" I said sharply.

"Because Violet-May's name was the last thing that Mummy said before she slipped off to sleep."

"Just her name, nothing more?"

"Her name and Oliver's name too," said Rosemary. "She said them over and over again: Violet-May, Oliver – Violet-May, Oliver – just like that, almost as though she were trying to tell us something. Or that was how it seemed to me at the time but Violet-May thought that Mummy must just have wanted to see Oliver. But I don't think that was it. But really so much happened that day, it isn't easy to remember it all."

"I'm sorry I reminded you of it," I said. "I had no business to."

"Oh, but it is your business, Kay," said Rosemary, smiling. "After all, isn't that why you're here?"

"How do you mean?" I said, feeling a little confused by the tone of her voice which seemed at variance with the serenity of her smile.

"Only that you're here in this house because you're an old friend, Kay," said Rosemary. "I mean, isn't that why Robbie asked you to stay with us? And as an old friend you have every right to ask about anything you wish, wouldn't you say?"

"Yes, I suppose you're right," I said, still a little uncertainly. "Was Robbie there when all this happened?"

"Robbie? No, he came the following day when we, well, you know, when we found Mummy." Rosemary leaned her head back again and closed her eyes. "It was a difficult time for all of us, but at least Violet-May had the comfort of knowing that her name was on Mummy's tongue at the very end: Violet-May and Alexander."

She means Oliver, I thought. Oliver not Alexander.

But Rosemary's eyes were still closed, so I did not point out her mistake.

"Violet-May and Oliver," said Rosemary, her voice still dreamy. "They were both on Mummy's mind at the last. I suppose it was because she loved them best. I imagine people think about the people they love best at the very end, don't you, Kay?"

"I don't know," I said. "But I'm sure your mother loved you and Robbie and Caroline just as much." I said it to comfort Rosemary but my mind was elsewhere. The truth was that hearing Rosemary's youngest brother's name spoken aloud after so many years had given me a small but sharp and sudden shock.

After leading me back downstairs to my bedroom, Rosemary left me alone with the suggestion that I might like to rest until it was time to prepare for dinner. She glided away then, leaving me feeling like some character in a grand period-piece drama and wondering if I should begin hunting out my best blouse and cameo brooch. While I stood there looking about me, I heard my mother's mocking tone sound in my ears: *Prepare for dinner indeed!*

As it transpired, we did eat in the big dining room but thankfully nobody had changed their clothes. The meal was simple enough too, a beautifully cooked fish dish with steamed baby potatoes, minted peas and salad, all of which it appeared Robbie had cooked himself. As we sat down at the long table I had a flashback to the day of Violet-May's birthday concert, all of us sitting down to eat jelly and cake off fine china plates. Today there was fresh fruit salad and cream for dessert and afterwards we all sat in the drawing room again.

I soon excused myself and went upstairs to my new study to begin work on my book. Because the time for excuses was over and, after all, the book was part of the reason I was here.

I had been working for some time when there was a gentle tap on my door and Robbie said my name.

179

"Come in!" I called, swivelling round in my chair, but he merely put his head around the door.

"I don't want to disturb you," he said. "I just want to make sure that you're comfortable up here, that you have all you need."

"Please come in," I said with a smile. "You're not disturbing me."

He came in then and flung himself down in the rocking chair. "So you think you'll be able to work here then?" he said.

"Are you kidding me?" I said, looking about me. "It's perfect. Everything is perfect. The room, the chair, the view. There's nothing more I could possibly want."

Robbie smiled and got up again and came around behind my desk. I swivelled in my chair to keep him in my sights and watched as he began to fiddle with the catch on the sash window. "It can get a bit stuffy in here when the sun shines," he said. "This window opens but it's stiff so you have to pull it up quite firmly."

"I'm sure I'll manage it," I said.

He turned and smiled at me, "Right, good. But don't hesitate to say if there's anything that needs fixing, anything more you need, or want for that matter."

"There's nothing," I said.

"Good."

Robbie folded his arms then and said he should probably go and leave me to get on with my work, but he showed no sign of doing so. I was more than happy to have him stay but I had a sense that there was something on his mind and, while I was wondering what it was, he turned back to the window and stood there with his back to me.

"So how did you find the girls?" he said.

"They both seem well," I said. "They both look well anyway, Violet-May in particular – she's unbelievably glamorous."

180

"And Rosemary?"

"Well, I thought she looked a bit ..." I hesitated.

"Ragged around the edges?" offered Robbie and he cast a swift look at me over his shoulder.

"I was going to say, tired," I said. "But that's only to be expected with two small children to look after, not to mention all she's been through."

"Yes, indeed," said Robbie. "Did you get a chance to talk to either of them alone?"

"Yes, I talked to each of them alone."

He turned then and looked at me once more.

"I was just wondering how they seemed to you, Kay," he said. "Women talk to women, don't they, about what's going on in their heads? You know, feelings, that kind of thing?"

"Ah yes, feelings," I said with mock sarcasm and he smiled. "I haven't had time to look into their souls if that's what you mean, but from what I can gather both girls as you might expect are distressed by the sudden death of your mother. Rosemary-June of course had the double shock that day of what almost happened to Oliver so –"

"She told you about that?" Robbie was looking at me intently now. "What did she say about that exactly?"

"Exactly?" I frowned as I tried to recall what I had been told. "Well, she told me that Oliver's ball must have rolled into the pond and he'd gone in after it. She saw him from the window, so she screamed and ran downstairs but Violet-May got there first and got him out and luckily there was no harm done. Actually, Rosemary-June was feeling sorry for Violet-May, I think, because of how it had happened and –"

"But it shouldn't have happened," said Robbie. His voice sounded harder and there was a look in his eyes I had not seen there since the day of Violet-May's birthday concert when he burst into the dining room and announced that Prince had been poisoned.

"No, of course it shouldn't have happened," I said gently.

It certainly shouldn't have, was what I was thinking, not with all those people around who were supposed to be looking after that little boy. "But it did and the main thing is that no harm came to Oliver."

For a moment the hard looked held, then Robbie's face softened.

"Yes," he said. "That, as you say, is the main thing. And you see now why we need you around here, Kay, because you always see things the right way up."

"Do you think so?" I said. "I'm not so sure your sisters would agree."

Robbie frowned. "What makes you think so? Has someone said something to you?"

"No, no," I said quickly. "Nobody said anything, at least not in the way I think you mean. It was just an impression I got from a comment Violet-May made. It made me wonder if she might think I'd come here to … look, it was nothing. I was tempted to tell her that you'd asked me here so I could help look out for Rosemary-June, but I thought it was best to say nothing. After all, Violet-May is Rosemary's sister and I didn't want to imply for a second that she's not capable of being a support to her."

"No, best to say nothing," said Robbie. "In fact, please don't say anything, Kay. You're quite right, it might only lead to misunderstandings." He smiled at me again, "OK. And now I'm going to go away and leave you in peace to create."

After he had gone I sat in that quiet room at the top of the house, but instead of writing I found myself wondering why it was that none of the Duff siblings seemed capable of talking to one another. And that night, for the first time in many, many years I dreamed of Alexander Duff.

Chapter 19

I woke early the next morning and had to mentally pinch myself to realise that I was waking up in a room in the Duff house. I also had to contend with the three unanswered calls on my mobile. Dominic had phoned at 1.55 and again at 2.10. I had not felt comfortable putting my phone on silent in case the nursing home needed to contact me about my father but I had put it on vibrate after the second call. The third call had come through at 2.45 but nothing after that.

As I showered I see-sawed between calling him back now that he would be sober once more – I was assuming that the calls had been made while he was drunk. But, either way, did I want to hear what he had to say? What did he have to say? Did I care? I decided not to decide and got on with dressing.

As I stepped out onto the landing I heard the sound of a child crying. This was followed by Caroline's high sweet little voice which was followed in turn by Robbie's deeper tone. The door to the next room was ajar and I put my head around. Robbie was kneeling on the floor wrestling a little boy into a pair of dungarees, while the child wriggled and rolled for all he was worth. I had not seen Oliver the previous evening as he was in bed by the time I came down for dinner. Now I was struck with his likeness to another child. Pink-skinned and blonde-haired, with the same eyes, the same long fair eyelashes, this was the toddler that Alexander might have become.

"Good morning," I said brightly, pushing the dark thoughts away.

Oliver stopped wriggling and gave me a toothy smile. "Hi," he said.

"Hi, yourself."

"Hi," said Oliver again.

"This is his week for 'hi'," said Robbie, releasing the little boy who clambered to his feet faster than I would have thought possible. "Last week it was all about 'bye'."

"Bye," said Oliver. "Bye."

He toddled across the room to where the bottom drawer in a large chest of drawers gaped open and promptly climbed in.

Meanwhile, Caroline, who had been sitting on the floor attempting to jam on a blue shoe, had abandoned it, got up and run at me full tilt. I knelt and opened my arms to her and her fuzzy blonde hair tickled my chin like a brush of feathers.

Over the top of her head I saw Robbie grinning at me.

"Someone has a fan," he said.

I gently released the little girl and got to my feet and then felt an enormous rush of pleasure and gratification as Caroline slipped her hand into mine.

"Are you in charge this morning?" I asked Robbie.

"I was up and I heard them, so why not?" said Robbie.

"I'm impressed," I said. Was there anything this man could not do?

"Good to see we have another early riser in the house," said Robbie. "Fancy some breakfast?"

"Yes, please."

"Great. Then if you wouldn't mind grabbing Caroline's other shoe, I'll fetch Oliver from his drawer and we can all go down and have breakfast together."

"*Wasins!*" Oliver piped up suddenly and Robbie laughed.

"Raisins are Oliver's greatest joy in life," he told me as he went and lifted the little boy from the drawer. "Next to balls and cars, that is, and if you let him he'd eat raisins all day long. No raisins for breakfast, Oliver, but perhaps later, if you're a very good boy."

In the end I carried Caroline down while Robbie followed with Oliver in his arms.

I will never forget that first breakfast I shared with Robbie and his small niece and nephew in the big kitchen of the Duff house. Robbie was wonderful with the children and they obviously adored him and it was a joy to me to watch him with them. Milk was spilt and a box of cereal upended itself on the kitchen floor and scrambled egg worked its way somehow into people's hair, including mine, but not since the family breakfasts of my childhood in that cramped little kitchen at home had I enjoyed the first meal of the day so much.

Rosemary put in an appearance at some point. She took in the sight of the three of us still sitting at the table, Robbie with Oliver on his lap.

"I went to get him up and he wasn't there," she said. "You've changed him – I would have done it."

"I was up and I heard him," said Robbie. "I thought I'd take him down and let you have a lie-in. Actually, I caught him just as he was climbing out of his cot – he has it down to a fine art."

"He's always climbing," said Rosemary, eyeing her son wearily. "If he isn't climbing out of his cot, he's climbing on the furniture."

"Going to be a mountain climber when you grow up, are you, Oliver?" said Robbie, as Rosemary went to make coffee.

Robbie asked if I would mind taking Oliver and I willingly took him onto my lap. He felt warm and solid and he smelled of the eggs and yogurt he had been eating. I closed my eyes for a moment and thought about what could have been mine and, when I opened them again, I found Rosemary watching me over the top of her steaming cup.

"He's a lovely little boy," I said.

She smiled but said nothing and I wondered if she was sleeping these nights – she looked tired and had dark circles under her eyes. No doubt Oliver was keeping her up with his teething – his molars apparently – the tough ones. And she really was much too thin to my mind. No wonder Robbie was concerned about her.

"It must be a great help having Robbie and Violet-May around to share the load," I said and Rosemary raised one fair eyebrow.

"Surely you remember, Kay? Violet-May doesn't do sharing."

"Well, no, but I'm sure ..." I realised that I was not sure of anything really and I fell silent.

"But, as you say, Robbie is wonderful with them," said Rosemary, smiling once more. "It's good to know I can always count on Robbie to be there."

I still thought she sounded a little off and, just as I was wondering about that, the kitchen door opened and a woman came in.

"Morning!" she called, her voice quiet but cheerful.

"Morning, Grace," said Robbie. "Come and meet Kay – Kay Kelly."

Grace crossed the room, smiling at me, and held out her hand.

I shook it. 'Hi, Grace," I said.

"I hope you'll be very comfortable here, Kay," said Grace and she said it like she meant it.

She was, I guessed, not much older than me, tall, big-boned, with black hair and brown eyes. She had a local accent and I remembered Rosemary saying she had originally been from round here. Grace had by now turned her attention to Oliver who, from the moment he saw her in the doorway, had been straining to go to her. She held out her arms now and I released the little boy and she swung him high and kissed him and tickled him until he roared with joy.

While I had been talking to Grace, I had noticed Robbie leaving the kitchen. He came back in again now, briefcase in hand.

"I need to get going – I've papers to pick up for the conference tomorrow." He smiled at me, "I'll see you later, Kay. I hope you get some writing done. And remember, if there's anything you need be sure to let Grace know. I'll check in with you when I get back."

"There's nothing," I said quickly.

I could not help but notice that he had not suggested I let his sisters know of my needs and I wondered again just how much they resented my presence in the midst of a family gathering and just how aware Robbie was of the fact. It made me feel uncomfortable and I suspected Robbie read something in my face as he dithered for a while in the doorway, looking at me a little uncertainly. But then he was gone and soon after I went upstairs to begin writing. Caroline tried to follow me but Grace called her back and as I walked away I heard the little girl asking why she wasn't allowed to go with Auntie Kay. It made me smile.

My study was the perfect place to write, but at first I was distracted by its view of the meadow behind the house. There the dog daisies had run rampant and their long, lanky stalks swayed in the wind with here and there a gash of poppy red, startling against the sea of white. I sat down to write and found the words willing to flow, so much so that I lost track of time and suddenly realised that it was just after one and I had done nothing to help with the children.

There was no sign of anybody about as I went downstairs but I found Grace at the kitchen table with Caroline on one side busily colouring and Oliver on the other in a highchair which had been pulled to the table.

Grace looked up as I came in and smiled. "Have you come down for a bit of lunch after all your hard work? I hear you're a writer."

"I'm trying to be," I said and smiled at Oliver who had a peeled banana in his hand. The ripe sweet smell of the fruit was pungent and the absorption and concentration in the little boy's face as he sucked on it fascinated me. He glanced up and caught me watching him and immediately he opened his mouth in a great wide grin which displayed the pale-yellow mess on his tongue.

"Hi," he said.

"Hi, Oliver – is that a good banana?"

"Nana!" said Oliver and waved the fruit at me.

And I remember thinking that, despite the tragedy of losing her husband, Rosemary-June was lucky to have such enchanting and good-natured children.

"Are you on your own with them?" I asked Grace. "Where's their mother?"

"Lunching," said Grace, "followed by a spot of shopping, no doubt."

I wondered if I was imagining an edge to her tone, but the next moment she was smiling warmly and inviting me to sit down while she made some tea.

"There's soup and freshly made sandwiches if you'd fancy that too," she said. "But if you'd rather something else, just say."

"Oh, I hope you didn't go to a lot of bother on my account, Grace," I said worriedly. "I'm more than happy to make my own lunch and look after myself. You have the children to take care of ."

"It wasn't any bother," said Grace. "I do a bit of this and that around the house, and it's all the same to me whether it's cooking or cleaning or child-minding, at least while Robbie's sisters are here. Robbie's asked me to come in most days as long as they're here. The children's mother isn't up to much at the moment what with being made a widow so young and apparently Violet-May can't boil an egg."

Somehow I was not surprised to hear that. "So you don't live in," I said.

Grace, who was ladling soup from a saucepan into a bowl, looked up and said a little sharply, "I could – if I wanted to, I could."

"Oh absolutely, I'm sure," I said hastily, worried that I had somehow inadvertently offended her. I didn't ask her anything else of a personal nature though I was curious about her and would have liked to know where exactly she lived and with whom.

She busied herself with serving me lunch and sat down at the table with me while I ate the delicious soup and the sandwich she had prepared.

Watching her with the children, I could not help thinking that she had in abundance all the qualities Robbie had ascribed to me: she was placid and kind and calm and obviously very sensible, so with her around just what need was there for me?

But I forgot all about that when Caroline offered to let me help her colour and, sitting there with a ham-salad sandwich in one hand and a purple crayon in the other, I realised that this was the second time in a single day that I had sat down to eat almost as part of a family.

Afterwards, we all had a good laugh watching Oliver's antics as he tried to reach the tin where the raisins were kept. Grace had put it out of his reach on a worktop but Oliver tried an assault on it by means of an attempted climb using the drawer handles on the units below. Failing at this, he then proceeded to push a kitchen chair, slowly but surely, across the floor until it was next to the unit. He then climbed up on the chair and with a triumphant whoop reached out with both hands to grab the tin, losing his balance in the process. Both

Grace and I, foreseeing the danger, had sprung up and it was she who caught him just before he would have fallen.

"That's so dangerous," I said as Oliver roared, more I am sure at the failure of his mission to reclaim the raisins than the fright of the near-fall.

"Olber is naughty," said Caroline and I smiled at her take on her brother's Christian name.

"Don't I know it?" said Grace. "You little rascal!" she scolded Oliver. "Don't do that again!"

But the only punishment he received was a particularly loud smattering of kisses on his outraged face, which was quickly followed up with a handful of raisins.

With peace once again restored, I returned to my colouring, all the time thinking how comfortable it felt to be there in that big kitchen which, except for the addition of a new electric cooker and some fitted cupboards, was almost exactly as I remembered it. The same polished wood was underfoot, above was the same timber-beamed ceiling. The Belfast sink was there too and the two archways, one leading to the butler's pantry, the other to the back staircase. Looking at them, I remembered Violet-May, ecstatic at the success of her concert, leading me by that staircase to her bedroom that long-ago day to bounce out her joy on top of her bed.

After my lunch, while Grace went to put the children down for their naps, I went for a walk in the gardens. When I came back in they were still asleep and I decided to go upstairs to write some more.

And once again it was Robbie who tapped gently on my door to alert me to the fact that dinner would soon be ready. I picked up my phone to check and was astonished to discover that it was a quarter to seven.

"My God," I said, "is it that time? I had no idea. Thank you. I'll just shut down my laptop and go and tidy myself up a bit."

Robbie smiled. "Well, I imagine that's a good thing, isn't it, losing time because you're lost in your art? And I like to think that being in this house has something to do with it."

"My art?" I said derisively. "I wish."

But Robbie said quite seriously, "You shouldn't belittle your talents in that way, Kay."

"I suppose I shouldn't," I agreed. "And I think you're right that this house is agreeing with me as far as writing goes."

"Then perhaps this is the right time to give you this," said Robbie. "So you can come and go as you wish."

I looked at the key in his outstretched hand and then I looked back to Robbie's gently smiling eyes.

"Thank you," I said and as I took it I remember telling myself to get a grip – it was only a key. But it was more than that and I could not pretend otherwise, despite the fact that I was no longer ten years old. I was holding the key to the Duff house and it still symbolised something for me, even if right then I was not quite certain what.

"And Grace looked after you as regards lunch and all that, I hope?" said Robbie and I was recalled to the moment.

"She looked after me beautifully," I said. "But I feel like a fraud – I barely saw Rosemary today. She went out to lunch with Violet-May and to do some shopping, Grace said. I intended to go down much earlier than this and spend some time with the kids but I just got stuck in and forgot about everything else. I suppose they're both in bed now?"

"They are, but that's OK," said Robbie. "The girls are back now. Actually we'll be having a drink before dinner in half an hour or so – if you'd like to join us?"

I said I would and Robbie went away just as my phone began to ring. It was Dominic again and I decided to get it over with and see what he had to say.

"Kay?"

"What do you want, Dominic?"

"Why haven't you been answering my calls?"

191

"Maybe I have nothing to say to you. Why are you calling me?"

"Where are you, Kay?"

"I'm at my dad's. What's it to you?"

The door to the study opened and Robbie put his head round the door.

"Sorry, Dominic, I have to go," I said and hung up.

"I beg your pardon, I didn't realise you were on the phone," said Robbie.

"It doesn't matter, it wasn't anyone important."

"OK. I only wanted to give you my mobile number and, if you don't mind, perhaps get yours. I have to leave for the airport early tomorrow morning and, as you know, I'll be away for five days. If you don't mind I'll check in with you just to make sure all is well here."

I said I didn't mind and we exchanged numbers. Shortly after Robbie left, Dominic phoned once more but I let it ring out and he did not leave a voicemail.

Dinner was more relaxed than on the previous evening, or perhaps it was that I felt more relaxed. I was happy with the work I had done that day and, perhaps as a result of their long lunch and shopping expedition, Violet-May and Rosemary-June seemed in better spirits too.

Before I went up to bed, Robbie drew me aside and said goodbye. Then he kissed me lightly on the cheek and said, "I'll see you when I get back, Kay. It will make me a lot happier to know you'll be here."

And I went upstairs feeling happy that I was the cause of making him happy.

Chapter 20

After Robbie left that first time, life in the Duff house settled into a kind of rhythm. Every evening just before the children's bedtime, he would ring the house and, by prior arrangement, Caroline was allowed to answer. Hearing Robbie's voice her eyes would light up and I enjoyed watching her listening attentively to whatever it was her uncle was saying and hearing her whispered responses. Afterwards, the phone was held up to Oliver's ear and we all urged him with one voice to say hello to his Uncle Robbie. I think he may have obliged once but mostly he just grabbed at the phone and proceeded to strike at the air with it as though it was a hammer.

Robbie then spoke to whichever of his sisters happened to be there at the time. He would then presumably ask after me in some casual way because Rosemary or Violet-May would pass on a "Robbie says hello, Kay". But later each evening he would ring me on my mobile, check if I could talk, by which I assumed he was asking if I was alone. As soon as I confirmed that I could indeed talk he would ask, a little anxiously it always seemed to me, if I was still comfortable with being at the house, then he would ask how my writing was going and only then, almost as though it were an afterthought, enquire casually, "So, everything OK there? Kids alright?"

As soon as I had reassured him that everything was OK and the kids were absolutely fine he would audibly relax and begin to tell me about his day, making me laugh at some small thing that someone had done or said and I would lose track of time listening to him and always feel surprised and sorry when he finally said, "Well, I suppose I had better go, then, Kay."

I always wished he wouldn't let me go.

And it was not quite true that I was entirely comfortable at the Duff house. I cannot pretend that it did not feel a little odd to suddenly find myself living there with Violet-May and Rosemary. The truth was that I hardly knew them and, although Violet-May did make some attempt at friendliness, I sensed a weariness about her, as though she were making an effort to be bright and vivacious. I thought too that I detected a guardedness in her manner to me and, once or twice as we sat there catching up, I caught her watching me with an inscrutable expression in her eyes.

But that aside, I found that I liked the feeling of being surrounded by people. I also enjoyed the children very much. I had never lived in a house with small children before and I delighted in the slightly chaotic nature of life with them around. I would have liked to do more with them but it seemed to me that Grace almost resented allowing me to share in their care. Robbie had apparently arranged for her to come in each morning to give them their breakfast, with the idea of allowing Rosemary the option of a lie-in when the mood took her and it appeared the mood took her every morning. I offered to take over this morning duty but Grace wouldn't hear of it. But, quite aside from the children, there was a pleasing thrill to living at the Duff house. I had always loved it and finding myself alone there one day, having seen Violet-May and Rosemary drive off, followed shortly afterward by Grace and the two children setting out for a walk, I gave in to my essentially nosy nature and allowed myself a tour. I wandered the corridors at my ease and peeped into remembered rooms like bathrooms and what had once been Mr Duff's study. Opening the door to the playroom, I saw that it too had been spruced up; there were bright rugs on the floor and new paint on the walls. The bars were still on the windows but although I looked about me for the old rocking horse, it was no longer there – no doubt it had been binned many years ago. In fact there were few toys about, only some beautiful old children's classics on a large but half-empty bookshelf. I reminded myself that Caroline and Oliver did not live in this house, were here simply on a brief stay. But looking about me, I could not help feeling that this was a room waiting for children to bring it back to life. I knew I was being fanciful but I could not help hoping it would not have to wait too long, until it suddenly dawned on me that those children would be Robbie's children and then I turned my back quickly and closed the door on the silent, waiting room.

It was that same evening I witnessed a scene which made me realise it was not only the Duff house which hadn't changed a lot since I had last seen it. Some of the people hadn't changed a great deal either. Grace had taken the children to a playground and when she returned Oliver was out of sorts, hot and fractious. She tried to put him down in his cot but, she told me, he had clung to her and would not let go, so in the end she brought him back down and settled him on one of the big sofas in the drawing room, where he fell asleep with her next to him. Eventually, admitting she had things to do elsewhere in the house, she accepted my offer to stay with Oliver and I was left alone with the sleeping child and his sister. I remember the peace of that big bright room, flooded with the September sunshine, and how I sat next to Oliver and watched him sleep. I remember the small nasal sounds he made and the quiet chatter of Caroline as she alternately scolded and praised her dolls. I remember too how rudely the quiet was shattered by the whoosh of tyres on pebbles, the double slam of doors, the crunching of feet and the banging of the heavy hall door.

I walked to the window and saw that it was Rosemary's car that had just pulled up.

Then behind me the sisters erupted into the drawing room, Violet-May first, face flushed, oversized sunglasses riding on top of her head. Something about the glazed expression in her eyes and her brittle smile made me think she had been drinking.

She crossed the room to the sofa where Oliver was sleeping, curled up in a corner. Its back was to the door and so she was in the act of throwing herself down before she saw him there.

"Is this the nursery now?" she said, rather nastily I thought.

"He's not well," I said, and then as I noticed Oliver stir, I automatically put my finger to my lips. "Do you want to sit somewhere else?"

"No, I want to sit here," said Violet-May with the petulance of a little girl. And she sat.

She dropped her phone noisily onto the coffee table then plumped her handbag down on the sofa next to Oliver with what I thought was unnecessary force. The bag fell open and I saw Oliver give a little jerk and raise his head slightly.

"Hello, sleepy guy," said Violet May, none too sweetly, as Oliver pushed himself into a sitting position. "Shouldn't you be in your own bed?"

Oliver gazed at her, rubbed both hands over his eyes and then looked around the room in sleepy bewilderment. At the sight of his mother, who had settled herself on the far sofa and was smiling down at Caroline sprawled on the floor with her dolls, he gave a watery smile and stuck out his arms.

"*Mammma!*" he said plaintively and pathetically, and I waited for Rosemary to go to him.

She did look up briefly. "In a moment, Oliver," she said, then she went back to smiling at Caroline.

"Can't somebody put him to bed?" said Violet-May. "And where is Ms Primark when we need her?"

I remember I flinched at the small and unnecessary spite. I glanced at Rosemary for her reaction but, although it was impossible she hadn't heard, she was still smiling serenely at her daughter. At that moment the door opened and Grace came in. I felt mortified at the idea that she might have overheard.

Violet-May turned, saw her standing just inside the door and said sharply, "So there you are, you're needed here."

"Oliver's awake," I said quietly to Grace. I glanced at the little boy who had got himself to his knees and was toying with the bright gold charm which dangled from a strap of Violet-May's bag. His face was very pink, and he was still making the little snuffling sounds he had made in his sleep. "I still don't think he's very –" I began, but Violet-May cut across me.

"He needs to be put down in his own room, which is where he should have been in the first place," she said.

I waited for Grace to defend herself but all she said was, "I'll take him."

"He's here because he was too upset to be left alone upstairs." I was too annoyed at the way she had spoken to and about Grace to keep my mouth shut. "Grace did right to put him down where we could all keep an eye on him."

"Who are you, her lawyer?" said Violet-May.

She was not looking at me when she said it, she was watching Grace who had come around in front of the sofa, arms outstretched to take the little boy. I saw the unguarded look in Violet-May's eyes and I remember thinking with a stab of surprise – oh, she really doesn't like Grace. But at that moment, Oliver suddenly lowered his head and was sick into the open handbag. Violet-May leapt up with a shriek.

"Olber is sick," said Caroline calmly.

That and the look of pure horror on Violet-May's face made me want to laugh. But then she began yelling at Oliver.

"Oh no, look what you've done, look what you've done to my bag! You absolute little wretch!"

As he gazed at her, eyes huge and terrified, she turned her fury on Grace, *"Just look what he's done to my bag!"*

She picked up the bag by one strap between a finger and thumb as though it might infect her and held it up for inspection. It was a mid-sized tote of dark navy blue, the leather soft and buttery-looking, and I could well believe it had been expensive.

Then Oliver wailed and Grace leaned in and swiped the child up and held him to her, making softly muttered comforting little noises into his hair.

"He couldn't help it," she said. "Poor little mite, he's been poorly all day and it's only a handbag at the end of the day."

"Only a handbag, only a handbag?" shrilled Violet May. "Do you have any idea how much this cost? Do you? Actually scrap that, of course you don't, how could you?"

"Violet-May," I said, "do you have to be so bloody rude?"

After all, as Grace had rightly said, it was still just a bag and we were talking about a sick little child who also happened to be Violet-May's own nephew.

Violet-May rounded on me. "Oh, that's right, everybody turn on me! I have an extremely expensive bag I happened to love, ruined, absolutely ruined, and I'm the one who gets told off!"

"I'm sure the bag can be cleaned," I said in an attempt to appease her.

"Oh great," said Violet-May, turning once more on Grace. "And have it stink for ever more of vomit! I don't want it cleaned. And my things are in there, my wallet, my phone –"

"Your phone is on the table," I said. "And I'm sure the bag can be properly cleaned."

"I'll pay to have it done," said Grace quietly.

"*I said I don't want it cleaned!*" Violet-May all but screamed. "*Can't you see it's ruined, you stupid, stupid, woman? It's fit for nothing but the bin!*"

I watched in something like disbelief then, as she flung the bag on the floor, deliberately stood on it with both feet and began jumping on it. Her face was red with anger and I could almost swear I saw tears of temper in her eyes.

"*Ruined, ruined, ruined!*" she chanted furiously as she pounded the bag underfoot. Her hands which were bunched into fists moved up and down in synch with her feet. Watching her I had a sudden strange and unsettling feeling that I was looking not at Violet-May the woman but Violet-May the child.

Then Oliver began to scream and behind me I heard Caroline say plaintively, "Mummy?"

"Rosemary," I appealed, turning to her.

She was sitting there with all the appearance of someone who thought it had nothing in the world to do with her. She sighed, got up slowly, took Caroline by the hand and walked across to Grace.

"Give him to me," she said.

In response Grace appeared to clutch the child tighter and for a moment I thought she was going to refuse to let him go, but then she handed him to his mother who took him and left the room without another word, followed by a visibly upset Caroline.

Grace followed Rosemary from the room almost immediately and I was left with just Violet-May. As soon as the door shut behind her, she stopped her ridiculous dance, glanced up and around the room, saw that I was her only audience and burst into tears.

"For God's sake, Violet-May," I said helplessly.

"Don't talk to me," sobbed Violet-May. "Don't, just don't."

I shut up and watched as she bent down, picked up the bag and carried it once again between finger and thumb to the door. "It's fit for the bin!" she sobbed. "It's fit for the bin and that's where it's going!"

After she had gone I sank down on the window seat and pressed my head against the glass. I felt drained and bewildered and almost tearful myself. I thought about ringing Robbie – was this the kind of thing he wanted to be told about? Then I thought about just packing my things and going and telling nobody. But going where? I had no home that was available to me right then and nobody was waiting for me. At that thought I actually did cry a little.

"You're still here," said Rosemary.

It was some time later, I wasn't sure exactly how long. I had moved from the window seat to an armchair and was almost dozing when she came in and startled me with her comment.

"I've been sent down to get her phone," she said.

I saw that she was grinning and I felt annoyed that she was making light of that disgraceful scene.

"Have you?" I said drily. "Well, if Violet-May wants her wallet you'll have to rummage in the bin for it. Last time I saw her, she was heading that way with the polluted handbag."

Rosemary laughed. "I think you'll find that Grace has already fished it out and done the needful there."

"Then more fool her," I said.

Rosemary put her head on one side. "You don't like scenes very much, do you, Kay?"

"No, I don't. I don't imagine most people do," I said coolly. I straightened up in the chair and realised that I was stiff from sitting there so long in a strained position.

"And I don't like rudeness either," I said. "Yes, it was a pity about the bag but the way she spoke to Grace, there's no excuse for it."

"You don't really think it was about the bag?" said

200

Rosemary incredulously as she picked up Violet-May's phone from the coffee table.

"Then what was it about?"

Rosemary waved the phone at me. "He won't take her calls," she said. "Violet-May's boyfriend. She'd been trying to reach him all through lunch and afterwards. She isn't getting what she wants. Surely you remember, Kay, what happens when Violet May doesn't get what she wants?"

After a moment she turned and went out and I was alone in the room once more. I thought about what she had just said and how, watching Violet-May dancing on her handbag, I had felt I was witnessing not a woman fast approaching forty but a spoiled out-of-control and spiteful brat raging because a dog had eaten her party shoe.

I said aloud, "They're all mad, they're all stark staring mad."

Chapter 21

The day Oliver went missing it had rained heavily all morning. It was two days after the incident with the handbag, which apparently we were all to pretend had never happened. Certainly that was how Violet-May and Rosemary had behaved the following day and it seemed Grace was in agreement with this strategy. I had begun telling her how badly I felt on her behalf but she had stopped me with a frown, and said that it was all forgotten now.

"But she shouldn't have spoken to you that way!" I said.

"Some people set more store on their belongings than others," said Grace evenly. "And that's their prerogative."

I felt almost reprimanded and said no more. If she chose to defend Violet-May's behaviour then let her, I thought. But I had made a point since, whenever I had the chance, of being cool with Violet-May.

That afternoon, I was at my desk writing when the door to the study opened and Violet-May came in.

"Is Oliver here?"

"Oliver? No, he isn't," I said shortly.

Then I turned and saw the expression on her face.

"What's up?" I said.

"He's missing," said Violet-May.

202

"Missing? For how long?" I closed down my document and got to my feet.

"I don't know exactly." Violet-May ran a hand through her hair distractedly.

"Doesn't Rosemary?" I asked as I followed her from the room.

"No, Rosemary had a bad headache and Oliver was making it worse – he's been grizzly all morning. So I offered to look after him while she went for a nap. Grace hasn't been here this afternoon."

"Yes, he's been unwell for a while, hasn't he?" It struck me that she might be finally feeling guilty for her behaviour over her precious bag. Then I realised that Oliver must have gone missing on her watch. "So what happened then?"

"Well, but he got worse and worse so I gave him a spoonful of Calpol and put him down in his cot," she said as we made our way down the narrow staircase to the second-floor landing. "I checked on him after an hour or so and he was fast asleep so I left him sleeping. But he's not there now."

"You mean he got out of his cot? Well, don't panic, he'll be somewhere in the house. Have you checked with Rosemary? Maybe she heard him and took him in with her?"

"Rosemary was the one who told me he wasn't in his cot," said Violet-May impatiently. "She came down while I was on the phone to Calvin. I told her I'd put Oliver down but when she went up to get him, he wasn't there."

"How long were you on the phone to Calvin?" Her rich, if the internet was to be believed, and soon-to-be ex-husband.

"I'm not sure." She glanced over her shoulder and grimaced. "When Calvin calls me he's inclined to go on and on and on, trying to wear me down so I'll give in and go back to him. I'd say it was at least twenty minutes anyway."

"Right, well, we'll just have to search the house – he has to be somewhere."

"What do you think we've been doing?" said Violet-May.

"We've already checked every room on the first floor. Rosemary is downstairs now, checking the rooms on the ground floor. I suddenly thought of you and hoped maybe Oliver had climbed up here."

"In a house this size there are plenty of places for a little boy to hide – we'll find him."

"I know that," said Violet-May but I was aware of her unease and I found it infecting me too.

We had reached the first-floor landing and I glanced through a window as we passed. Rain slanted in the wind and the garden was a green blur behind the wet glass.

"There's no way he could have got out, is there?" I said.

Violet-May turned and looked at me. "No, no, I don't see how he could have," she said but there was nothing reassuring about the way she said it.

"No," I said quickly. "It's unlikely – he's probably –"

I broke off as Rosemary came rushing toward us.

"Have you found him?" said Violet-May.

"You mean you haven't either?"

I read mounting fear and anxiety in her eyes and in the taut set of her mouth.

"Then where is he?" she said.

"He'll be hiding somewhere in the house, Rosemary, thinking it's a game," I said quickly. "We'll just have to go through every one of the rooms with a fine-tooth comb. Why don't we start on the second floor, all three of us together and work our way down?"

"Thanks, Kay," said Rosemary absently. She brushed past us, back toward the second landing, calling to her son as she went. *"Oliver! Where are you, Oliver? Don't hide from Mummy now! Oliver! Oliver!"*

I looked at Violet-May. "She could do without this," I said.

Violet-May said nothing. She was staring after her sister, an unreadable expression in her eyes.

I hurried after Rosemary, then glancing back saw Violet-

204

May standing where I had left her.

"Aren't you coming?" I said, and she moved then, as though I had woken her from a trance, and hurried after me.

Between us we searched every room on the second floor, calling out the little boy's name repeatedly as we went.

At one point, I heard Violet-May's voice calling enticingly, *"Oliver, Oliver, come and get some sweetie raisins!"*

Remembering how he loved the treat, I followed suit.

"Look what I have for Oliver!" I cooed. *"I hope I find him soon or I'll have to give all the sweetie raisins to Caroline."*

But there was no responding cry, no little boy came running to grab his sweetie raisins and, as we moved through the house from top to bottom, I felt a rising sense of panic.

Finally, as we all came together once more in the hallway, Rosemary said urgently, "He's not here, we've looked everywhere but he's not here. So where is he, Violet-May, where's my baby? You said you'd watch him but you didn't. You didn't and now he's gone. Where is he, Violet-May, where's Alexander, where is he?"

At the sound of her dead brother's name, I felt a sickening lurch in my stomach. I stole a glance at Violet-May. She was staring at her sister but I couldn't read her expression.

"Look," I said, partly to break the awful tension of the moment but also because it was what I believed now, "unlikely as it seems, *Oliver* may have got outside." I deliberately laid stress on the little boy's name. "So I think we should start searching the gardens."

"How could he have?" said Rosemary. "All the doors are shut. He can't reach the lock on the front door even climbing up on something. And it's the same with the back door."

"No, but he can reach the one on the side door, through the butler's pantry," said Violet-May quietly. "I've seen him try to open it before."

"Yes, standing on something," I said. "But if he'd got out that way there'd be a chair or something pushed up against it

205

and there isn't, is there? The only way he could have got out that way would be if the door had been left ajar. Does anyone remember leaving it ajar?"

"Did you?" said Violet-May. "I know I didn't."

"No, I didn't," I said. "I've never gone in or out that way."

"This is wasting time," said Rosemary. "For all we know, it was Grace who left it ajar."

"I wouldn't put it past her," said Violet-May sourly. "I've seen her use that door a couple of times."

"Well, I'm going to search at the front of the house," said Rosemary. "Can you two please do the back?"

Without waiting for a reply, she ran to the front door, wrenched it open and ran out into the rain, leaving it open behind her.

"She hasn't even got a jacket on, she'll be drowned."

I knew even as I said it that it was an inane remark to have made.

Violet-May said, "I don't suppose she'll notice. We'd better get started. I'll begin with the garages and outhouses, you can search the garden."

She hurried away along the hallway toward the back of the house and I ran upstairs to grab a jacket. In the time it took me to run back down again and out on the terrace, the rain had slackened to a thin drizzle. I stood for a moment and asked myself where a toddler like Oliver would go, finding himself on the loose out here? The most obvious place was one of the sheds or outhouses and so I decided to join Violet-May in her search of them. I found her coming out of the main garage.

"No luck?" I said and she did not even bother to answer.

She had not bothered with a coat either and she looked soaked and dishevelled; it was the only time in my life I had ever seen her appear anything but perfectly turned out. We moved on together to the second garage, working our way from there through every shed and outhouse, leaving no nook, corner, ledge or box unsearched. We then moved on to the rest of the garden and had just decided to search the portion of the shrubbery which ran along the side of the house when Rosemary emerged through the bank of rhododendrons.

I had never seen her so wild-eyed or unkempt. She had clearly been searching like a crazed thing, her hair straggly and pulled about, with even some pieces of greenery poking through.

"We were just about to start searching the shrubbery," I said. "But I'm guessing you've already done that."

"Yes, and he isn't there!" said Rosemary shrilly. "He isn't anywhere and there isn't anywhere else to look."

I made a decision. "There is a chance he's left the grounds," I said.

"You mean he may have gone outside the gates onto the road?" said Rosemary.

"Yes, I do." Then seeing the fresh alarm in her eyes, I said, "It's just a possibility. More than likely he's still here in the gardens or the house somewhere. I know we've looked everywhere we can think of but we could have missed him. All the same, I'm going to get my car and go take a look."

"No," said Rosemary. "I'll go. My car is out front. You stay here, Kay, with Violet-May and keep on searching, please."

"Are you sure?" I said, doubting she was in any fit state to drive.

"Yes, I'm sure. I have to. I want to." She was already running across the grass.

"Why don't I come too?" I called after her. "I can drive in one direction and you the other. Violet-May can stay here, in case he turns up."

"No, I'd rather you stayed!" Rosemary called over her shoulder. "Please, Kay, I really would rather you stay and keep on looking."

"I will!" I called.

I turned to Violet-May. "Where do we start this time?" I

said. She gave a helpless shrug which infuriated me. "Well, we have to start somewhere!" I snapped at her.

"Fine!" she barked back. "Then I'll go over the back garden and you do the front and then we'll start on the house again. Will that satisfy you?"

"What will satisfy me is finding Oliver safe and well," I said and for a moment we held one another's gaze, then she stalked off toward the back of the house and I raced after Rosemary.

I came around the side of the house in time to see her drive off in a spatter of flying pebbles and my heart went after her. As I stood for a moment surveying the vast garden that lay before me, I became aware that it had stopped raining. For Oliver's sake I was happy about that at least, although if he was anywhere in the grounds he would by now be soaked through in any event. The portion of the garden in front of the house had really few places where a small child could be unseen and presumably Rosemary had already searched all that. That left the shrubbery which she had also searched and, beyond that the stretch of driveway as far as the gates. There were also, aside from the double line of trees, a great deal of shrubs and hedges which had been planted beyond the beeches on either side. No doubt Rosemary had searched there already too but I would do so again. In her state of anxiety I imagined her search had been more frantic than careful and she might well have missed the little boy if he had fallen asleep curled up somewhere amid all those trees and shrubs. Unlikely in that heavy rain, but we could rule nothing out.

I determined to go over every inch again, peer behind every tree trunk, every bush, leave quite literally no stone unturned. And if I did not find Oliver there, then I too would search the shrubbery, beginning at the point where the trees ended and working my way up to the side of the house.

I decided to begin at the gate, moving from right to left.

With that plan in mind I set off at a jog, past the banks of rhododendrons and round the turn of the drive. Once at the gate I was about to begin my search on the right-hand side, when I heard what I was sure was a child's voice.

I halted and listened. Hearing the voice again, I realised it was coming from the direction of the road outside. It might not be Oliver, I told myself as I ran to the gate, it could be any passing child talking to its mother. But it could be Oliver, it could be Oliver.

I went flying through the open gates and stood staring along the road where it sloped toward the town, but I turned sharply to the left as I heard a voice call my name.

Grace was walking toward me, holding Oliver in her arms.

"Thank God!" I said. "Thank God!" I ran to her and almost fell on her, my arms out to take the child.

But she did not relinquish him, and I was aware of her eyes on me, narrowed in suspicion.

"I was on my way here and I found him wandering along the side of the road, not even on the footpath. What the hell was he doing out here on his own? He could have been killed!"

"He's not hurt, is he?" I said. "Please tell me he's not hurt?"

"I don't think so. As far as I can tell he's OK."

She then reluctantly, it seemed to me, relinquished Oliver and I took him and inspected him for any signs of injury. Other than looking a bit dusty, he seemed none the worse for wear. His cheeks were very pink and he did seem a little groggy but that I put down to the Calpol.

I realised that Grace was watching me.

"So how did he get out here?" she asked again.

"We don't know, we presume he climbed out of his cot and then somehow got out of the house."

"And where were his mother and Violet-May when that happened?"

"Rosemary was lying down, Violet-May had given him

Calpol and put him in his cot. We've all been all over the house and gardens searching for him. And Rosemary just went off in the car to see if he'd got out onto the road. She's only just left – she must have gone in the other direction. Where did you find him?"

"Just up there," she said, pointing back up the road. "He hadn't got far, thank God. But it's lucky I came along when I did."

"Thank God you did," I said. The thought of any harm having come to the little boy whose head was heavy on my shoulder made me feel a little sick.

Then I suddenly thought of Rosemary driving about still believing her son to be in danger. I wished I had her number so I could call her and put her out of her misery. God only knew what terrors were in her mind right this moment.

I dropped a kiss on the little boy's head. In some chamber of my brain I registered the fact that his hair was quite dry – in fact, he was dry all over. But I did not dwell on that puzzling fact. Violet-May would have Rosemary's number and she too was waiting anxiously for news of him. I needed to put them both out of their misery without any more delay.

"Let's get him inside, Grace," I said. "Put everybody out of their misery."

Violet-May must have been watching from the window. The door opened as we emerged from under the beech trees and began walking toward the house. She came out to meet us and, as she drew near, held out her arms to take the child from me. I watched as she took him and hid her face in his hair.

"Thank goodness!" she said. "Where did you find him, Kay?"

"I didn't. It was Grace who found him. He was wandering along at the side of the road up there. But what I don't understand is ..."

I stopped as Rosemary-June's car swept up the drive,

spitting pebbles as it came. It drew to a sharp stop next to mine, the driver's door flew open and Rosemary leapt out and ran to where her sister stood. I watched as she almost wrenched Oliver from Violet-May's arms and, without a word to either of us, turned and marched with him toward the house. As she went I could see Oliver's dusty, dazed little face as his chin bounced against his mother's shoulder.

I turned and looked at the two women and found that both were staring after Rosemary, each with a different but equally inscrutable expression in their eyes.

Chapter 22

There is something wrong in this house. I was lying in bed on
the night of Oliver's disappearance, exhausted but unable to
sleep, puzzling over what had happened, when the thought
crossed my mind like a shadow. It took me by surprise and I
sat up quickly, reaching for the lamp next to my bed. Just
what, I asked myself, did I mean by wrong? I had been living
in the Duffs' house for just over a week and although I now
tried to relive in memory every single one of those days, I was
unable to put my finger on what was bothering me. Even so,
the sense that something was amiss refused to dissipate and I
recognised that it had begun that first afternoon I arrived.
What was it that Violet-May had asked me that day? *Do you
ever get the feeling that you're being watched?*

That was it, I realised, that was how it felt – in this house,
everybody was watching everybody else. Robbie was
watching the two girls, the girls were watching one another,
Violet-May was watching Grace and me. And what of me? It
came to me with a small shock that I too was watching.
Wasn't that the reason I had been brought here in the first
place? To – how was it Robbie had put it – "to keep an eye
on things"?

But what things? And did that mean that Robbie too had

felt that something was wrong? Was that why he had wanted me here, so I too could watch? But if so, what was I was watching for? I told myself I was being ridiculous. I was overtired and as a result my imagination was working overtime. But all the same, before I went back to sleep I had made up my mind to talk to Robbie on his return. I could do it when I told him about Oliver's adventure.

But it seemed that Robbie was not to be told about Oliver's adventure.

"It would only worry him," said Rosemary. "Violet-May thinks so too. Actually it was her idea not to say anything to him, and I think she's right. Robbie is such a fusspot when it comes to the children – he'll blame himself for not child-proofing the doors or something."

I didn't think that sounded very like Violet-May but I said nothing. We were alone in the kitchen. It was the first time since I had moved in that I had known Rosemary to get up early. Robbie was due back on an early flight and I could not help wondering if she had got up early on purpose to catch me before he arrived home.

"But I will speak to Grace about being sure to lock the doors in future whenever she goes in or out," said Rosemary.

"It's not just Grace," I said. "There's no reason to think it was she who left the door ajar. It might have been anybody."

"Of course not," said Rosemary. "Nobody is blaming her, nobody is blaming anybody, which is all the more reason why it's best that nobody should mention anything to Robbie. And I've already spoken to Violet-May about being more careful too."

"You might mention the gates too," I said. "The gates are always left open, and as we saw today it's dangerous with small children in the house. They need to be kept shut – that way if Oliver ever does manage to get out again, at least he won't be able to leave the grounds."

"Absolutely," said Rosemary. "I'll mention that to Robbie

and Grace and Violet-May. But I think it's probably best if we leave it at that. Don't you, Kay?"

I said nothing but I nodded. Rosemary smiled then, picked up her coffee and glided from the kitchen. And if I was left with a sense of unease about what I had tacitly agreed to, I dismissed the feeling and told myself that Rosemary was Oliver's mother. If she was satisfied to leave it at that, then so be it; it really was none of my business.

I was up in the attic room when Robbie returned and the first I knew of his being back was when he knocked on the door and called my name softly. I told him to come in and I got to my feet as he did. I tried not to look flustered when he came across and kissed me on the cheek. I thought he looked tired for all he had got some sun, but he smelled good.

He dropped into the rocking chair and we chatted for a while. He asked me how I had been, how my writing was going and then he asked how things had been while he was away.

I found I could not meet his eyes while I lied.

"Fine," I said, and I made a production of shutting down my document.

Perhaps he picked up on something because he apologised then for having disturbed me at my work. "But maybe when you've finished for the morning, you'd let me take you out to lunch. Would that be alright, Kay?"

I said it would be alright and he went away and I put aside my sense of unease at having kept Oliver's adventure from him by telling myself that I had not in fact lied. Mostly things had been absolutely fine while he was gone, and Oliver was fine too now, wasn't he? And, if I had not quite convinced myself, I refused to dwell on the fact and gave myself up to the pleasure of getting ready for lunch with Robbie Duff.

He drove us out to Malahide. The weather was glorious, sunny but with a wonderful sea breeze, and as we strolled from the car to the restaurant the boat masts in the marina clinked and chimed. Robbie had phoned ahead and booked a table on the outside deck overlooking the water and I remember there was a boat out on the horizon, its sail making a sharp bright triangle against the blue of the sea and sky. Robbie drew out my chair for me and when a waitress came to take our drinks order, he encouraged me to have a glass of wine. I was happy to oblige and, as I sipped it, a feeling of freedom slipped over me. Freedom from what, I wondered briefly, but I was too relaxed and hungry to think about it too deeply just then. I ordered the seafood linguini and when Robbie said he would have the same, I felt an almost childish sense of pleasure that our tastes should be in agreement. And then, not for the first time it struck me that I reacted to Robbie Duff more like a teenager with a crush than an adult woman fast approaching forty. But once again I pushed the thought aside in favour of food. It really was delicious and I was happily tucking in when a girl came into view, jogging along the walkway below. She had a long blonde ponytail and other than the colour of her lycra shorts, which were black and pink rather than black and blue, she was almost a mirror image of Matchstick Meg. I had a sudden vivid memory of that day on the balcony of the flat in London when I had caught Dominic watching our bug-eyed neighbour running on the path below us.

I glanced at Robbie. His eyes were on his food but he happened to look up just at that moment. "What?" he said. "Is there something wrong with the food?"

"No, no, the food is perfect." I glanced back at the girl. She had stopped jogging and was standing with her back to us now, facing the sea, engaging in a series of star jumps. "I was just thinking that that's what I should be doing."

Robbie followed my gaze. "You could, I suppose," he said. "Or you could sit here eating pasta and prawns. And I know which I'd prefer."

"Me too," I said and Robbie smiled at me before going back to his food.

But I just sat there looking at his lovely mouth and thought of Dominic and wondered how I could ever have fallen for a man with thin lips. And I knew then that this was no teenage crush, that I loved Robbie Duff and always had, and the thought filled me with a painful, hopeless joy that almost stole away my appetite. Robbie looked up again and caught me watching him and I hurried into speech to cover my confusion.

"So it must be an interesting life, being an archaeologist?" I said. "I mean, besides the work itself you get to travel to these incredible places, discover wonderful things."

"It's interesting to me," said Robbie. "And, yes, the travelling is part of that. Nowadays, I'm involved in a lot of field schools and this lecturing I've been pulled into now. But, yes, I have been lucky enough to be part of digs where wonderful things have been discovered."

"Treasure? You mean gold and silver and stuff like that?" Once again I sounded to myself like a breathless adolescent, but the truth was I did find the idea fascinating.

Robbie was smiling at me again. "Yes, gold and silver and stuff," he said. "But honestly, for me it's the everyday ordinary things I find most poignant. You know, things like a bowl or a broken pot or cup, things that ordinary people used. When you hold something like that in your hand, something that hasn't seen the light of day for thousands of years, it brings it home to you that the people who used them were real. That despite all that time between us, fundamentally they were just like you and me, just living their everyday lives. And somehow it links you to them in a way nothing else can, not all the books you've read or the lectures you've sat through. It's very special."

"It must be," I agreed.

"But look at me boring you about my job. Never mind all that. What about you, Kay?"

"What about me?"

I wanted to tell him that he could never bore me, that I could sit here with him in the warm September sun for the rest of my life just listening to him speak, just looking at him in fact.

"Has your life so far been an interesting one?"

"Not so much," I said. "I went to London and I've come back. Back where I started you might say, with nothing to show for it."

No book, no husband, no child, I was thinking and perhaps it showed on my face because I saw how intently Robbie was watching me – a little too intently for comfort.

"I read a book a bit like that once," I said with a deliberate change of tone. "It was by Anne Tyler and it was about a woman who left her old life and began a brand-new one. I don't know if it was a very good book, but the premise fascinated me. She was with her family on a beach – I think they were on holiday and, anyway, she just walked away from them, with nothing only the clothes she was wearing on the day."

"What happened to her?"

"She had adventures, got a job, found another man, became part of another family, or at least she had the opportunity of becoming part of it. I remember the ending made me furious."

"Why so?" said Robbie.

"Because she let herself be sucked back into her old life," I said. "The life she left because she was dissatisfied with it – she literally went back to the husband who had not appreciated her and her kids who were selfish and took her for granted. The ending of the book brought her right back to the beginning. It seemed to me like such a waste of time."

"Her whole journey, you mean?"

"No," I said. "I mean it seemed like a waste of time reading it."

Robbie laughed and picked up his glass of water and, as he sipped, his eyes stayed on my face.

"So you never married, Kay?" he said and his voice was very gentle. "Or would you rather not talk about that? Please tell me if so."

"I don't mind," I said. "No, I never married. There was someone and we lived together for – for quite a long time. Then he left me for a woman who lived across the hall from us."

Robbie's eyes narrowed and he put his glass down slowly. "If you don't mind me saying so," he said, "he sounds like a bit of a dick."

I laughed out loud. "I don't mind you saying so. So what about you, Robbie? Were you, are you married?" I believed I knew the answer to the question already, courtesy of Mrs Nugent but I wanted to hear it from him.

Robbie shook his head. "No and no," he said. "So you see there are two of us in it, Kay. Now, what about dessert, I know I'm having some."

And so we had dessert and a change of subject, and after we left the restaurant we went for a stroll on the beach before heading home. A small child, not much older than Oliver, broke away from a man who had been holding his hand, and came careering toward us. He ran almost blindly into Robbie, head-butting him in the shins. Laughing, Robbie immediately bent down and engaged the child long enough for the man to catch him up and, watching the small incident, I was reminded guiltily of what I had concealed from him and made up my mind to unburden my conscience.

I waited until we had left the man and the child behind us on the sand before I spoke up.

"Robbie, there's something I haven't told you," I said. "There didn't seem any point in worrying you while you were away, and Oliver was perfectly alright so I didn't think it was necessary."

Robbie, who was still smiling after the encounter with the toddler, stopped walking and turned to me swiftly.

I watched his face harden into alertness.

"What didn't you tell me, Kay? What happened to Oliver?"

"Nothing happened to him – he just went missing for a while, but we found him and he was absolutely fine."

"How long was he missing, where did you find him?" His voice had risen. "For Christ sake, Kay, why didn't you tell me about this before?"

"I'm sorry, I should have told you, I knew I should." I felt angry with myself and resentful toward Violet-May and Rosemary-June for persuading me to keep quiet against my better judgement.

"Well, tell me now." His voice was as hard his face.

So I told him all about Oliver's adventure, about Grace finding him along the road. I told him how we had come to the conclusion that the door from the butler's pantry must have been left ajar. I was careful not to speculate by whom.

"And he was fine," I finished, "absolutely fine. I'm sorry, Robbie, of course you should have been told, but you weren't there when it happened and we thought why worry you with –"

"Who's we?" said Robbie sharply.

"Violet-May, Rosemary, all of us really. We decided that there wasn't any point in worrying you. But that's no excuse and I should have known better."

"It's not your fault, Kay," he said then. "The girls should have told me."

That was true of course but I could not help feeling that it was I who had let him down.

"Grace should have told me," said Robbie.

"You can't blame Grace," I said robustly. "It wasn't down to her to tell you, if your own sisters decided to keep it from you."

"You don't understand," said Robbie.

"What don't I understand?"

He seemed to hesitate. "Oh, never mind – but you have to

promise me, Kay, that if anything remotely like this happens again or if anything worries you, anything at all, you must tell me. Tell me, or, if I'm away at the time, ring me. Promise me you'll do that, Kay."

"Of course," I promised. "Of course I will." But as I did I asked myself why he would think anything like that might happen again, and why would he think that something might worry me?

We were walking toward the carpark now and, although Robbie was thanking me and his face had relaxed, I had a sense that his mind was anything but.

I kept quiet until we were in the car and driving toward home. Then, looking at his set profile, I found myself unable to stay silent.

"Robbie, is there something you're not telling me?" I asked. "Because I can't help feeling that there is."

"What do you mean, Kay?" He glanced at me quickly then looked back to the road.

"I don't know exactly, I can't put my finger on it. It just seems to me that everybody is uneasy, at the house I mean. And you seem so anxious all the time. And I don't know, but just now when I told you about Oliver going missing, the way you acted, the way you seemed, it just made me wonder."

Robbie threw me another glance. "What?" he said. "It made you wonder what, Kay? Spit it out."

He had never spoken so brusquely to me before, not since the day when, as a child, I had interrupted him at Prince's grave.

It fired me up and so I spat it out. "It made me wonder why you really asked me to come and stay at the house."

"Why? Is there something you're not telling me, Kay?" he said evenly. "Perhaps there's something that happened, something you saw or suspect?"

It was my turn to stare fixedly at the road ahead.

"Is there, Kay?" said Robbie. "Is there something, because

220

if there is I hope you know that you can tell me."

Still without looking at him, I said quietly, "There's nothing."

"Well, that's alright then," said Robbie. "And for my part, the reason I invited you to move into the house was because you clearly needed somewhere to live, and because I thought it would be good for the girls to have you there. And also, of course, because I thought it might be convenient for your writing."

I sneaked a glance at him then and his head turned and our eyes met.

"But you're right, I haven't been entirely honest with you. There is something, and I had thought about telling you a couple of times, but in a sense it isn't my secret to tell. It still isn't but I trust you to keep it to yourself. And, for all I know, it may not come as a great surprise to you."

"Yes?"

"It's about Grace, Kay. The truth is that Grace is my half-sister."

"You don't seem surprised," said Robbie.

He had pulled into a lay-by and stopped the car before unbuckling his seatbelt and turning to me.

"I am. This is honestly news to me."

But I was not as surprised as I might have been. It sort of made sense of some things that had been puzzling me – Grace living locally now, but having been in London and working as Rosemary's nanny, not to mention the way Violet-May behaved around her.

"Violet-May and Rosemary know, don't they?" I said.

"Violet-May does, but she only found out a short time before my mother died. She's still struggling with it to be honest."

An involuntary sound escaped my throat.

"What is it, Kay?"

"It's just … let's just say I sensed a bit of tension between Violet-May and Grace."

"Yes, well, Violet-May made the discovery in an unfortunate manner," said Robbie. "She overheard a conversation between my mother and Grace. I don't know exactly what she heard but I gather it was enough for her to grasp the situation and also convince her that our mother cared a lot about Grace."

"And Rosemary doesn't know?"

Robbie shook his head. "We decided to wait a while before breaking the news to her. It just seemed that she had enough to contend with. Grace agreed it was for the best to hold off on telling her for now."

"Right," I said absently, because a vivid memory had just sprung into my head. "She was there on the day of your fifteenth birthday party, wasn't she?"

"Yes, Grace was there," he said.

"I remember I saw a dark-haired girl first at the gate, when I arrived with my parents, and later on I saw her standing next to Alexander's pram. I noticed her because she behaved so oddly – guiltily. And you were angry about it, I remember that too. You asked me if I knew who she was and, when I said I'd never seen her before, it was as though you didn't quite believe me."

"I probably didn't," said Robbie. "But that was because I knew who she was by then and I was sure that everybody in the town knew it too. I kept imagining them all whispering and sniggering behind my back."

"Not everyone knew," I said. "I certainly didn't, although I think some people may have known." I had a sudden memory of my mother nudging my father as Grace rushed past us on the Duffs' avenue.

"I have no doubt they did," said Robbie. He eyed me uncertainly. "So you've never actually heard anything about Grace then?"

"I heard there was a child, but not what happened to her.

I remembered our neighbour, Mrs Nugent, talking about Mrs Duff having lost another child but I suppose I thought that the child had died."

"It was Grace," said Robbie.

"So what happened to her? Did your mother give her up, was that it?"

"Something like that," said Robbie. "When my mother fell pregnant with Grace she was packed off to one of those mother-and-baby homes but under the pretence of having gone away to work. After Grace was born, my grandmother made it a condition of my mother returning home that the child be left behind. It seems my mother refused and stayed on at the home where she was farmed out as a domestic help. Eventually she was sent to work for my grandmother, but the role was a live-in one. While she was there, her child, Grace, was placed in a foster home without my mother's permission."

"But surely they couldn't do that?" I protested.

"I think we all know they could pretty much do anything they pleased back then," said Robbie dryly. "Anyway, whatever happened between my mother and father happened and they were married. And it seems that the decision was made to leave Grace where she was."

The decision was made, I thought bitterly, but who had made it? I had a sudden memory of smiling, avuncular, absent-minded Mr Duff waggling his ear in perplexity and I wondered.

"But surely they could have ... I mean why didn't they ...?"

"I don't know, Kay," said Robbie. "I don't know why things were done the way they were. Most of what I do know, I heard from Grace herself. My mother was never fully comfortable discussing that part of her life with me, or with anyone else either. I believe that for her it would always be something she would think of as shameful. I only know that Grace was sixteen when she discovered the identity of her

223

birth mother. She came looking for her, took to hanging around the grounds of the house – you saw her there yourself. She went as far as to get a job in the town so she could be close to my mother, and at some point she approached my mother and told her who she was."

"And how did your mother take it?"

"Not particularly well at first, I gather. But over time things improved and they began to meet up and so got to know one another a little better, all of it in secret of course. But then Alexander died and that changed everything."

"Yes," I said quietly. I stared through the windscreen of the car, through the bars of the gate ahead and into the field beyond. "That changed everything."

"I'm sorry, Kay," said Robbie, very gently. "That has to be a painful memory for you as much as for any of us."

I shook my head as though I could shake off the shadow of that day on Bone Bridge, before turning back to him.

"So what happened?" I said. "How did Grace end up working for Rosemary?"

"Well, as you know we packed up and moved away, but unfortunately in the process Grace was entirely forgotten. No forwarding address was left and so she had no way of knowing where we had gone and no way of contacting my mother. Frankly my mother was too ill and depressed to have cared. The only thing she cared about for a long time after that was her lost baby boy. But time passed and it seems she began to think about her other lost child. She began to ... well, pine is the word that springs to mind, she began to pine for Grace."

Robbie fell silent and I waited until he was ready to continue with his story.

After a while he turned to me and said, "Have you ever seen a person pine, Kay?"

"I don't know, I don't think so."

"You'd know if you had," said Robbie. "Kay, remember

that day when we met at the gates of the house when you were still at school?"

"Yes?"

"Well, one of the reasons I had come back to Ireland was to find Grace and deliver a letter to her, from my mother."

"Ah, I see."

"Yes," said Robbie. "Well, it wasn't difficult to find her as she was still living and working in the town. I gave her the letter and she wrote to my mother and it all started again. At first it was just letters but then it was arranged between them for Grace to fly over – and so ..."

"And so they came together again?" I said. "I'm glad your mother had that."

Robbie smiled at me. "Yes, she had that. Not for very long as it transpired, but I like to think it gave her some comfort, and from the way she kept Grace near, I think that it did."

"I'm sure of it," I said. "So what then? When Rosemary-June needed someone to help with the children, your mother recommended Grace, was that it?"

"She went further than that," said Robbie. "My mother provided Grace with fictitious references lauding her skills. She sold her to Violet-May as the perfect fit for Rosemary, Violet-May sold it to Justin and after that it was all settled very quickly. Grace moved in with Justin and Rosemary."

"But under false pretences," I said.

"Yes, I know. It was a bad idea but, I like to think, done for all the right reasons. And in fairness to my mother, she always intended to come clean at some point. It was just unfortunate that before she could do that Violet-May found out in the worst way possible. And then the cat was truly among the pigeons. She confronted Grace. She had got it into her head that my mother favoured Grace over her, the first-born child, all that sort of thing. She was extremely jealous and resented Grace fiercely. There were a lot of nasty accusations and tears and tantrums and what have you."

I bet there were, I thought, and was tempted to ask if Violet-May had danced on her handbag.

But another part of me could understand how Violet-May must have felt at the deception that had been practised on her, at least to begin with.

"It's a wonder Grace stuck around," I said, "if Violet-May was that nasty to her."

"Maybe she thought it was worth it to be near her mother and her family," said Robbie. "But she left shortly after my mother died and came back to Ireland.

"Of course, she was there when your mother died," I said.

"Yes, Grace was there, and I think losing my mother again was a big blow to her."

"It must have been," I said. "And so, when you bought back the house, you asked Grace to come work for you?"

"Absolutely not," said Robbie shortly. "That was Grace's idea, after I'd told her that the girls were coming to stay with me for a time and bringing the children with them. Frankly I felt quite uncomfortable about it. Somehow the idea of having my sister come in to cook and clean for me ... well, it just felt wrong. No, I invited her to make her home here. Let's face it, the place is big enough."

"But she refused?"

"She refused. She said she preferred to keep things on a business-like basis for the time being."

"I see," I said, although I didn't really.

Robbie sighed. "It's not exactly an ideal situation, is it?"

"No, it's not. Not with Grace in a position where Violet-May can take every opportunity to take a swipe at her."

Robbie turned to me, his eyes narrowing. "Has there been some unpleasantness you haven't told me about, Kay?"

"No, no," I said quickly. "But, Robbie, knowing how badly Violet-May took being deceived about Grace's real identity, has it occurred to you that leaving Rosemary in the dark about it is just storing up more of the same trouble in the long run?"

"Of course it has," said Robbie. "But right now that's how it has to be. It's just best that Rosemary doesn't know for the moment."

His worried gaze held mine and I said gently, "I understand that you think it's for the best, Robbie."

"But you don't. OK, I respect your being honest with me, Kay, but I have my reasons for wanting to wait to tell Rosemary about Grace. Can I ask you respect that?"

"She won't hear it from me," I said.

"Thank you, Kay." He smiled but almost immediately sighed. "I wish I didn't have to go away again so soon, but you have no idea how good it will be to know there's someone like you at the house, someone down-to-earth and ordinary and uncomplicated."

He was smiling again now and I smiled too and so I could hardly blame him if he was completely oblivious to the effect of his words upon me. *Ordinary*. The word hit me like the flick of a whip and I was silent all the way back to the house while I nursed my wound.

Chapter 23

If there was a row about Oliver's adventure, I did not hear it, but I had deliberately taken myself up to the attic room so that Robbie and his sisters could feel free to shout to their hearts' content. But perhaps they did not shout at one another ever – after all, what did I know about how siblings interacted? What did I know about anything? I was still feeling sorry for myself and I took it out on my keyboard, banging out the words furiously and telling myself that if Violet-May had a go at me for telling Robbie about what had happened to Oliver, I would just pack my bags and move out. Why I had ever agreed to move in in the first place was beyond me. What good was I doing? I hardly ever saw Rosemary, though I spent time with the children, yes, and I loved every minute of that time. But they had Grace, Grace who belonged to them by blood while I, when you came down to it, was just some stranger. It was true that I had peace and quiet up here at the top of the house to write and I got to see Robbie. Robbie who thought I was ordinary.

And what if he did, I asked myself? What, after all, was Robbie Duff to me? I reminded myself that I hardly knew him. I had developed a childish crush on him when I was ten years old, seen him for all of an hour as a moony-eyed adolescent and, if I had now allowed those feelings to reignite, then more fool me. It could only be because I had happened to meet him again at a time in my life when I was particularly unhappy and vulnerable. And when all was said and done, nothing at all had happened between us – we had gone on one date, which was not even a date. And so what if that day in Malahide had been one of the happiest I remembered for a very long time? So what if he made me laugh, if being with him made me feel good about myself, made me want to reach out and touch his face and wonder how it might feel to have him touch me?

I stopped typing, jumped up and hurried down to my room. I grabbed my jacket and keys and went down the stairs and out into the afternoon sunshine. I needed to see my father, I needed to be with someone who valued me and loved me, who thought I was anything but ordinary.

Arriving back at the house, after visiting my father, Robbie himself met me in the hall. He apologised for how he had been earlier about my not telling him about Oliver. I made light of it, but he was adamant that he had been out of order.

"Aside from everything else," he said, "Grace has been telling me how much time you've been spending with the children. I think she's half jealous of how attached they've become to you. I appreciate it very much, Kay. Oliver is at that age where he's starting to get into everything and it's nice to know there's an extra pair of eyes looking out for him, especially as I'm going away again."

"It's not exactly a chore," I said, more spicily than I intended. "I do it because I enjoy spending time with the children."

"I know you do," said Robbie. "I've watched you with them."

The expression in his eyes was gentle and, as always, I felt the charm of him. He thinks I'm ordinary, I reminded myself, and the thought acted like a cup of cold water thrown in my face.

"So how long did you say you'll be away this time?" I said in my best matter-of-fact tone.

"Five days," said Robbie, with what I thought was a rather rueful smile, considering where he was going.

"You could look happier about it," I told him. "Five days in Crete is not exactly a punishment, you know. Think of all that Greek sunshine and those wonderful blue seas."

"There is that, of course," said Robbie, his smile returning. "But I will actually be working, and for part of the time we'll be away from the coast in the mountains. As I mentioned before, we may run into problems with phone signals for a while – there are some local dead spots in the more mountainous areas of Crete."

"And that worries you," I said more gently.

"I like to think I'm contactable, that's all."

"I understand that," I said. "But everything will be fine here, Robbie. Rosemary has Grace as well as me now to help her with the children." Realising I had left somebody out I added as a hasty afterthought. "As well as Violet-May of course."

"Of course," said Robbie.

He still did not look particularly happy and I considered telling him about the decision I had made to do my writing in the evenings in future, after the children had gone to bed. But that, I thought, might imply that I was discommoding myself in some way, and so give him something else to fret about. Besides, if Robbie were to ask me why, I was not at all sure I would know how to explain my motives. I only knew that on some level I had satisfied myself that it made sense to spend my days with the children, who at least seemed to enjoy my company, then write in the evenings instead of sitting in the drawing room watching Violet-May knocking back wine and Rosemary sitting almost trancelike smiling at the television screen. They barely spoke to one another let alone to me.

"So you just concentrate on your trip," I said.

"I'll try," said Robbie. "You know, I think you'd enjoy

coming along, Kay. Not on this sort of thing, this is just a field trip, but on a real dig. Perhaps one day you might think of ..."

He stopped as my phone rang. Glancing down I saw that it was Dominic again. I looked up quickly, intending to tell Robbie that I didn't need to take the call but he was already turning away and motioning to me to carry on.

I set off up the stairs in a temper. I was almost certain that Robbie had been about to invite me along on one of his trips. The phone in my hand kept on ringing and out of pure frustration I answered it.

"What, Dominic, what do you want?"

"Kay?"

"Yes, it's Kay, who else would it be? Why do you keep on ringing me, Dominic? Can you not take a hint? I don't want to talk to you. I never want to talk to you again."

"I know you don't mean that, Kay. Where are you anyway? And don't tell me you're at your dad's, because I know you're not."

"How can you know?" I said.

"Because I'm here and you're not. Nobody is, and nobody was here last night either. So where are you, Kay?"

"Here?" I asked, alarmed. "You mean at my father's house? What are you doing there?"

"Kay, are you going to stop asking idiotic questions and tell me where you are?"

"I'm staying at an old friend's place, not that it's any of your business."

"What old friend?"

"Why do you want to know? His name wouldn't mean anything to you in any case."

"*His* name – it's a guy? So who is he?"

"I just told you that you don't know him, Dominic."

"So what's the big deal about telling me then?"

"There is no big deal, Dominic. I just don't feel like it, that's all. Are you happy now?"

"No, I'm not happy, Kay. So you're staying with this guy instead of at your folks' house? Come on, Kay, what's going on? I know I screwed up, but don't pretend you don't miss me."

Did I miss him? I had certainly thought about him a good deal since we split up, mostly at night. But if I was really honest, I had to admit that it was not so much Dominic himself I missed, so much as the comfortable rhythm of our shared lives, the familiarity of his warm, clean-smelling body, the comfort of his breathing as he lay next to me in bed at night.

"Kay? Kay, are you there?"

"I'm here, Dominic."

"I miss you, Kay, I miss you more than I thought I would."

"Ever the flatterer. So what's happened to Matchstick Meg then?"

"Oh, that! That was just a minor peccadillo, but it's over now. But you, Kay, you're the light to my shade."

I believe I actually gurgled into the phone at that point. Peccadillo, the light to my shade – how had I put up with this fool as long as I had?

Dominic misinterpreted my mirth. "It's good to hear you laugh again, Kay," he said. By the tone of his voice I knew he was grinning, pleased with himself and smugly sure that he had clicked his fingers and I was ready now to come running. "Tell me where you are and I'll come and get you and take you home."

"You know what, Dominic," I said. "Don't bother. I'm already home, and if you have any sense at all you'll get on the next plane back to London, and I hope that you and your peccadillo will be very happy together. Oh, and by the way – "

"What?"

"That last time when you asked me if I thought you were losing your hair?"

"What about it?" said Dominic and I could hear the fear in his voice.

"I lied. Give it another two years and you'll be as bald as a bald eagle's egg."

Then I hung up, and I knew that I was not just hanging up on Dominic, but on that entire part of my life, forever.

In bed that night I found it hard to get to sleep. I kept replaying the day over and over, but of all the various incidents the thought that kept coming uppermost in my mind was Grace and her story. I thought about the day I had first seen her, the day of Robbie's party, lurking by the gate, then hanging around Alexander's pram. I tried to imagine how she must have felt. Looking at that baby who was her own flesh and blood. How she must have felt looking at that great house and those beautiful gardens and all the lavish show of that party which had been thrown to celebrate the birthday of yet another of her unacknowledged siblings. She would have known that Violet-May and Rosemary-June in their pretty party dresses, their hair ribbons and shiny shoes, were her own half-sisters. I wondered if she had resented them at all, all those Duff children who had what she had been denied? I wondered if she resented them still. Natural if she did, I told myself, but she hid it well if so. And she chose to stay close to them so that must mean something. Yes, she stayed very close to them. I was drowsy now, my thoughts falling from my mind like dropped stitches, but I could not quite surrender to sleep. Something was niggling at me, keeping me just this side of rest. I was on the very edge of sleep when it struck me what it was. That flash of colour, that fleeting but unmistakable flash of a vivid green skirt.

"She was there," I said aloud. "Grace was there."

There on Bone Bridge that day, one of the small crowd that had gathered and who watched as we were driven away to the police station. And there again on the day when Oliver followed his yellow ball into the garden pond and almost drowned, the same day Mrs Duff had died. And more recently still, there when Oliver got out of the house and out of the grounds to wander alone by the side of the road.

Grace was there.

Chapter 24

The second incident involving Oliver happened four days into Robbie's trip to Greece. As with his previous absence, he had made a point of phoning the house each evening at a pre-arranged time just before the children's bedtime. And again it was Caroline who was allowed to answer the phone before it was passed in turn to Oliver, Rosemary and Violet-May. Again there were the separate calls to me, later in the evenings, when I had been happy to report that I, and indeed all, was well. Aside from the calls, on this trip Robbie had also sent me a couple of texts. The first was a picture message of a blue sea and a brilliant sun, with a message assuring me he was hard at work and not taking advantage of either. The second, on the morning of the day in question, was to let me know he was heading into the mountains.

I had, as I had promised myself, made a special effort to spend most of each day with the children. If, as Robbie had suspected, Grace resented my doing so, then that was just too bad. After all, I also told myself one of the reasons I was here was to help out with Caroline and Oliver. As for those uncomfortable thoughts I had entertained concerning Grace, those were the product of an overtired and over-imaginative mind, which when examined in the light of day appeared too ridiculous to contemplate.

But, on this particular morning, I woke very early with lines of dialogue and strands of plot floating through my mind. I knew from experience that the only way to prevent them floating right out again was to pin them down, and I had got up, thrown on some clothes and gone upstairs to the attic room. I remember wrestling with what at the time I considered something of a dilemma. One of the characters in my book was a little girl, and I suddenly realised that without being conscious of it happening, Caroline had become the model for my fictional character. Perhaps it was because I had been spending so much time with her, but her small quirks had somehow made their way onto my pages, things like the way, when she was very tired, she would bunch her hands into fists and vigorously knuckle her eyebrows, how she always leaned her head to the right and never to the left when she was considering something. That day I remember worrying about what Robbie would think, were he ever to read my book and recognise his niece. But little did I know that before very long I would have something a whole lot bigger to worry about.

Once I began writing, I found myself on such a roll that I forgot about everything else until I was retuned to an awareness of the real world by hunger and a consciousness of cramping limbs. I went downstairs for food. I was just in time to catch Rosemary heading out and discovered that Grace had taken the children out for some fresh air earlier. I asked where they had gone but Rosemary was vague. After she had gone I made myself a sandwich and once I had eaten set off myself to stretch my legs in a long walk. I struck out through the meadow behind the house, revelling in the windy but sunny day and enjoying the sway of the long grass as I moved through it. I kept on going until I came to a field where the blackberries were ripening nicely and was immediately reminded of the day that Alexander died. I found myself thinking, as I had so often thought before, that had I stayed at home that day after the nut-gathering expedition had been abandoned, instead of going to pick blackberries, things would have been different and the nightmare on Bone Bridge would never had happened. And, as I had also done many times before, I pushed the thought from me, knowing that that way lay, if not madness, then pointless, painful regret.

I turned and began making my way back toward the house. By the time I arrived there, I felt tired from both my physical and mental exertions and decided to go and lie down for a short while. I popped my head into the kitchen first but nobody was around, and I headed upstairs. As I passed the door to the playroom, I heard the sound of children's voices. The door was ajar and, looking in, I was surprised to see Violet-May down on her knees next to Caroline, who was sprawled on her stomach on the floor. Before them was an exquisite wooden Victorian-style doll's house which I had never seen before. Oliver was there too, sitting on a rug engrossed in play with a large red-and-yellow truck.

"Where did all this come from?" I asked, going in for a closer look.

Violet-May glanced at me over her shoulder. "I ordered them online," she said. "They arrived today."

"What a beautiful doll's house!" I said. "You're a very lucky little girl, Caroline."

"Olber got a truck," she said.

"I see that," I said and would have duly admired the truck too, if Oliver could have been parted from it for even a second.

"This was very nice of you, Violet-May," I said and, for no reason I could clearly identify, this display of unexpected thoughtfulness toward the children filled me with a sense of light-heartedness.

"Has Grace gone home?" I asked and Violet-May, distracted by Caroline's dilemma of which chest of drawers should go in which room, nodded absent-mindedly.

I left them then saying that I was going for a short nap, and headed to my bedroom. It was only afterwards, when I really thought about it, that I realised I had assumed Rosemary had come back and was in the house somewhere near at hand.

In my room, I took off my jacket and shoes and lay down on the bed. I intended only to close my eyes for a short time but the next thing I knew I was starting awake to the sound of tapping on the door.

What happened next seemed like some awful recurring dream.

The door opened and Violet-May came in.

"Is Oliver here?"

"But he was just with you," I said, sitting up and swinging my feet to the floor. "In the playroom, only minutes ago. He was there with you and Caroline."

"That was over an hour ago," said Violet-May. "He isn't there now."

"And you've checked with Rosemary?"

"Rosemary is out," said Violet-May. "She's been out all day."

I stared at her. "Then you were there with them all by yourself?"

"Yes, I was, what of it?"

I got to my feet, "Oliver's gone missing again, that's what of it," I said, because by then I did not care what she thought of me. "So what happened? Who were you on the phone to this time, Violet-May?"

"I wasn't on the phone. I just left him for a few minutes, that's all, and when I came back he was gone."

"You left him on his own?" I repeated. "Why, Violet-May, *why* would you do that? After what happened last time, tell me why in God's name would you do that? *What's wrong with you, Violet-May, what the hell is wrong with you?*"

The colour flooded her face then, and she came back at me with another small show of spirit. "Caroline needed the bathroom, that's why. But Oliver wouldn't leave his truck. He kicked up a fuss and then Caroline started whining that she couldn't hold it any longer. I tried to pick him up, but I couldn't manage him and her and the damn truck at the same time, so I left him playing on the rug. Two minutes I was gone, less than that, and I shut the door behind me. But when I came back the door was open and Oliver was gone. But I know I shut the door after me, I swear on my own life I did. And there's no way he could reach the lock on that door, it's too high up, even if he tried climbing up on something. And anyway, there really wasn't time, I swear, Kay. It doesn't make any sense."

"No, it doesn't make any sense. And yet once again Oliver is missing."

I said nothing more then. The truth was I was afraid that if I once began to speak, I would say things I did not want to put into words, things I could never unsay. Instead I took a steadying breath and pushed past her.

"Where have you looked?" I asked brusquely.

"Here on the landing and on the stairs, then I came in to you. You'd said you were going to lie down and I thought perhaps he'd come looking for you."

"Right, then the first thing is to make sure he hasn't got out again."

I ran to the playroom door where I found Caroline, still sprawled on the floor before the doll's house. When I scooped her up without warning she not surprisingly protested loudly but I ignored her and carried her squirming from the room and down the stairs. I was aware of Violet-May hurrying behind me.

As we reached the hall and I set Caroline down, Violet-May said a little breathlessly, "How should we do this? Do you want to do the back and I'll search out front?"

"No," I said sharply. "This time we don't split up, we search together."

"Fine with me," said Violet-May evenly.

"We'll check the driveway first in case he's making for the road again ..."

"You're forgetting that the gates are kept shut now," said Violet-May. "Not to mention that there wouldn't have been time for him to get that far this time. He was only on his own for –"

"Less than two minutes, so you keep saying. Even so, that's where I think we should check first."

I forced a smile as I glanced down at Caroline. "Come on, Caroline, let's go look for your little brother."

"But I want to play with my house!" said Caroline.

"And so you can, as soon as we find Oliver."

"Olber is naughty," said Caroline and I felt my false smile growing ever more crooked.

"Well, yes, if he's really run off again, I suppose he is a little bit naughty. But we still need to look for him, because he's very little, you know. Will you help us, Caroline, and when we find Oliver we'll have a housewarming party for your beautiful new doll's house? Would you like that?"

Caroline nodded in hearty agreement and allowed herself to be picked up once more. I carried her outside and down the steps, followed by Violet-May, then cut diagonally across the garden the quicker to reach the driveway. Even from the turn of the avenue, I could see that the gate was in fact closed and I felt myself breathe a little easier. Even so, I felt the need to reassure myself that the bars were too narrow for Oliver to climb through. And, having done that, I left Caroline with Violet-May while I unbolted them and went out onto the road. I looked to the right and to the left, but there was no Oliver in sight, and I went back inside the gates and bolted them behind me.

We set off back toward the house. This time Violet-May carried Caroline and I walked ahead, calling Oliver's name and scanning the avenue to left and right as I went.

"I told you there wasn't time for him to get this far," said Violet-May.

"I wanted to be sure," I said shortly. "And now we can go

back and search the house. I just hope to God we find him before Rosemary comes back."

Violet-May said nothing and I glanced at her, but her chin was buried in Caroline's hair, and her eyes were downcast.

As we approached the house once more, I said, "You go on in and start searching inside. I want to just run round the back and make sure he's not there somewhere."

She went without demur and I hurried round the side of the house and did a quick scan of the garden. I crossed to the middle of the lawn where I stood for a moment considering whether I should do a quick search of the garages and sheds and outhouses, or just go in and help with the search of the house. I decided on the latter course.

Then, just as I turned back toward the house, it occurred to me that it might be worth calling Oliver's name a couple of times on the off-chance that he had managed to get out here after all. I opened my mouth to do just that, and as I did I glanced up. To this day I still don't know what made me. Even then, all I saw at first was a flash of colour and it was another moment before my brain processed what my eyes were telling it. But when it did, when I realised what I was looking at, it was as though the machine that worked my heart, my lungs, my very breath, had momentarily stalled, leaving me in a state of absolute physical paralysis. In fact it felt to me as though no part of me was working as normal. Only my brain continued to function like some awful soulless computer remorselessly registering the facts.

Fact: the window to the attic room was open.

Fact: there was somebody crouching on the outside window ledge.

Fact: this was the window from which the broken-hearted scullery maid had jumped all those hundreds of years ago.

Fact: this was no unhappy young woman now, but a very small boy dressed in bright blue.

And I stood there staring in horror at Oliver perched three floors up on that narrow window ledge.

Chapter 25

Even now, there is a gap in my memory that has never been fully filled – the space of time between realising it was Oliver up there on the ledge of the attic window and finding myself inside the house again. I can clearly remember standing rooted to the ground, eyes fixed in a sort of petrified fascination on that small figure on the window ledge. I can also remember the moment when the machine finally kicked in once more, restoring my power of movement: it was the same moment that Oliver, who had remained until then in his crouched stance, suddenly straightened up. As he did, there was a flash of something red and yellow, which some part of my brain recognised as his new truck. He was clearly attempting to lift it, which even under the best of conditions looked impossible: the truck appeared far too big and unwieldy for a child of his size to be able to hold. But somehow he did, and even managed to hug it to himself before he gave a little drunken stagger and I knew with certainty that he was about to topple forward and plunge to the ground below. That was the moment when I opened my mouth to scream his name. How I stopped myself, I do not know, but somehow I did, and the scream exploded silently in my throat. It left me feeling sick and dizzy at the thought of what I had almost done – Oliver, already in terrible danger on that window ledge was at least blithely unaware of the fact – all it took was something to startle him in any way, or cause him to jolt or wave or …

As I say, I have no real memory of getting from the garden to the house, but somehow I did end up there with Violet-May coming toward me down the staircase.

"I can't find –" she began and then jumped back as I pushed past her.

"*He's in the attic room. Window. Outside.*"

I was too breathless for coherence, but I heard the gasp she gave and was aware of her hurrying up the stairs behind me.

"What do you mean, outside? You don't mean he's climbed out onto the window ledge?"

Ignoring her, I breathed over my shoulder, "Caroline, where is she?"

"In the playroom with her doll's house."

"You're supposed to be with her. Keep her there. Make sure – don't let her see."

"She's fine, I'm coming with you," said Violet-May.

There was no time for arguing so I didn't.

At the foot of the stairs to the attic room, I turned to Violet-May and put a finger to my lips. She nodded and I bent down and whipped off my shoes and motioned to Violet-May to do the same. On tiptoe, I darted up the short flight of stairs and stood for a second at the door before reaching out and gripping the knob with both hands. I turned it as slowly as I could, but even then it emitted a rusty little whine and I held my breath before gently pushing the door inward.

The open window was straight ahead and I saw Oliver at once. He was almost dead-centre on the window ledge, crouched again now, head bent and from the small jerking movements of his body, I deduced that he was wheeling his truck to and fro on the ledge. From the sound behind me, I knew that Violet-May had seen him too, but when she reached out and touched me on the shoulder I started in shock and spun angrily to face her.

"Let me," she mouthed.

I hesitated. She, after all was Oliver's aunt, while he was in no way related to me. But my hesitation lasted all of a split second and I made my decision. As I shook my head, I remember instinctively putting out both arms as if to physically bar her entry into the room, should she try to push past me. And for a moment, as we stood there eyes locked, I thought she would challenge me. But her eyes dropped first and I turned from her and focused my attention on Oliver. There were, I had realised, two ways of doing it. I could draw attention to myself and try to talk him in, or I could creep up behind him as soundlessly as possible so as not to in any way startle him, then quite literally fling myself forward and grab him backward through the open window. The risk with the former was that at the sound of my voice Oliver might start or worse still, move to come toward me or away from me. With the latter, despite all my efforts, he might hear me coming and jump, or turn to me and in so doing slip or ... or ...

Every new possibility made me want to vomit just thinking about it but there was no time to think any longer and so I made my decision. I took one deep breath and set a foot down as far inside the room as the length of my legs would allow, then I lifted the other foot and brought them both together. And that was how I crossed to him, loping slowly and soundlessly as possible, like an adult playing a child's game of Giant Steps, until I was level with the desk where I wrote each day. I remember putting my hand down on its edge in an attempt to steady myself, because I was trembling from head to foot and I needed steady hands for what I had to do. I remember that the wood felt solid under my fingers. I also remember that somehow, although I would have sworn that every part of me was focused on the little boy framed in the window, my brain registered that the chair had been moved.

Ordinarily it was right there before the desk, but now it had been pulled up close to the window seat. I had a fleeting memory of watching with Grace as Oliver pushed a kitchen chair across the floor, to enable him to climb up and reach the can of raisins. I remember how we had laughed at his ingenuity. While all of this was going through my head, my eyes and conscious mind were fixed on Oliver. I was so close to him now that I could hear him babbling to himself as he played. I was so close that I could see how his little blue sweatshirt had rucked up in the back exposing a stretch of his pinky-white skin and the top of his disposable nappy which rose above the waistband of his trousers. From this angle, his position on the ledge looked even more perilous. All I could see below him was the distance between him and the ground.

If he falls, I was thinking, *if he falls*.

I took another step toward him and poised myself to spring. In the same moment, Oliver, just as he had done as I watched him from the garden below, attempted to lift the toy and it fell from his hands and plummeted and Oliver let out a disconcerted growl. Everything after that appeared to me to happen in slow motion. Oliver's arms came up once more, this time in a pummelling motion as he beat the air that had robbed him of his toy. Then, as though to follow the course the truck had taken, his head went down and he leaned forward from the waist. I have no actual memory of moving – one moment I was watching as Oliver canted forward and the next I was dragging him backward through the open window, aware that somewhere behind me somebody was screaming.

"We should have thought of looking in the attic room," said Violet-May. "Why didn't we? But you were in your bedroom and it just didn't occur to me that he might have crawled up there. And then we had to make sure he hadn't got outside again."

I was not sure if she was talking to me or to herself but in any case I did not answer her. I was sitting in the armchair by the window of my bedroom, where I had been since I carried Oliver down from the attic room. Violet-May had followed me there and I was aware of her watching me as I sat still holding Oliver. I was aware too that my whole body was trembling – so much so, that when the little boy made a sudden lunge, he almost toppled from my lap, so unsteady was my hold on him.

"It's probably best if I take him," said Violet-May and, although I wanted to protest, I could not seem to muster the necessary energy to speak, so I let her take him from me and sit him down on the bed next to her.

"Hi!" said Oliver, but nobody answered him.

I am not sure how long we stayed that way, me on the chair, she on the bed amusing Oliver with a string of beads which she had taken from her neck to appease him after he had tugged at them a couple of times.

After a while she asked me if I would be alright to stay with Oliver while she went and got us some coffee with a dash of brandy. For the shock, she said, and I wanted to tell her that I did not like brandy, but again I found myself unable to turn my thoughts into words. Before she went, Violet-May sat Oliver down on the floor at my feet and I remember looking down at him and how he waved the beads at me and grinned and that was when I burst into tears.

I was still sobbing when Violet-May came back with a tray that held two cups and Caroline tagging behind her, a doll in one hand and a clutch of biscuits in the other.

Violet-May glanced at me quite calmly. "This is why we need brandy," she said. "Now drink this."

She held out the tray and I took the mug nearest me. There was, I suspected, a great deal of brandy in it and I wrinkled my nose at the smell.

"Drink it all," said Violet-May, and I did what I was told.

246

"And blow your nose."

She handed me a cotton handkerchief that smelled of the perfume she used, and once again I obeyed her. And that was where we remained, me in the chair, now no longer shaking, Violet-May on my bed, leaning back against the pillows, with both Oliver and Caroline playing together at her feet. She had retrieved her beads from Oliver, having gone out again and returned with books and toys from the playroom. It had made me think of the truck again. I couldn't help myself picturing it on the ground where it had fallen. I pushed the thought from me but perhaps Violet-May's thoughts had taken the same path, because she reached out and stroked Oliver's head.

When she spoke again it was absently, and once again as though she was thinking aloud.

"He must have climbed up onto the window seat." She looked at me. "The chair, did you see the chair? It was pulled right up to the window seat."

I did not answer her.

"He does that," said Violet-May. "Oliver does that when he wants to climb up onto something he can't reach – you must have seen him do it, Kay?"

Still I did not answer her.

"He uses a chair or whatever he can find and does it that way. That's what must have happened; don't you think so, Kay? And, of course, the window was open – it wouldn't have mattered if the window hadn't been open."

"The window wasn't open when I left the room this morning," I said.

"Are you sure?" said Violet-May, her eyes fixed on mine. "I mean it must have been. Perhaps you opened it and then forgot about it? But that's not to say it was your fault, Kay, please don't think I'm saying it was. Of course it wasn't. He's incorrigible, Oliver is incorrigible. He climbs on everything. That's what happened – he climbed up on the chair and onto the window seat and then out onto the ledge."

"The window wasn't open when I left the room," I said.

"Then perhaps Grace ..."

"Don't!" I snapped. "Don't try to bring Grace into this. Grace isn't here. And I know for certain that I didn't leave that window open. I've only opened it once since I've been here, because it's quite stiff and it doesn't open easily."

"Well, then who?" said Violet-May.

She got up from the bed and walked around it and round to the window where she stood for a moment with her back to me. Then she turned around again and looked at me.

"If you didn't open it and Grace didn't, then who did?"

I was just about to answer when the door opened and Rosemary came in. Her eyes were bright and her skin had that healthy outdoor glow and I remember wishing I had anything to tell her but what I must.

"Rosemary," I began, "I don't want you getting upset because everything is fine now, and Oliver is safe ... but he somehow got himself up to the attic room. The window was open and he climbed out onto the sill and ..."

Rosemary's hand went to her heart and then she was loping across the room to where Oliver sat. He had heard her voice and was looking up at her with his beacon smile, but when she swooped down on him and seized him, the car he was holding slipped from his fingers and he let out a protesting howl. Rosemary ignored him and stood with her back to us, so all we could see was Oliver's face suffused with the colour of outrage. She must have been holding him too tightly, for which I did not blame her, because Oliver squirmed and wriggled to be free.

Then Rosemary spun round. "How did this happen?" she said. "Where was Grace?"

I remember noticing that her question was directed not at Violet-May but at me. And although her voice was unexpectedly toneless, there was a quality to it which told me she was holding some strong emotion in check.

"Grace wasn't watching him," said Violet-May very quietly. "I was."

Rosemary turned on her sister. "*You!*" she said and the single word was like a slap.

"Grace said she wasn't feeling well and went home," said Violet-May. "Though I have to say she looked perfectly well to me."

"Oh, please don't start ..." I said wearily but Rosemary cut across me.

"And you," she said, "were you there, Kay?"

I shook my head. "I went for lie-down." It seemed suddenly a shameful thing to admit to.

"It was just me," said Violet-May. "And I had to take Caroline to the bathroom, so I left Oliver in the playroom playing with his new toy. I shut the door after me, but somehow he got out, I don't know how. I don't believe I was gone long enough for him to get up to the attic room, and yet somehow he did that too. Kay says she didn't open the attic-room window."

"Kay?" Rosemary turned to me.

"I didn't," I said.

"And yet somehow," said Violet-May, "again I don't know how, the window was open and Oliver ended up out on the ledge."

She said it, I remember, like a piece of prose she had been forced to learn by heart, with no variation of tone, no nuance, and no discernible emotion, but as soon as she had finished she dashed from the room.

"Bye!" said Oliver.

Then Caroline piped up. "Olber is naughty and Mummy made Auntie Vilemay sad."

Rosemary's face seemed to unset then. She smiled sadly at her daughter, kissed Oliver on his head and, putting him back down on the bed among his toys, turned to me.

"I suppose I'm to blame," she said. "They're my children

and I leave them alone too much, I know I do. But I find it all so very ... and I feel tired almost all the time. And there's the noise, so much noise, and sometimes I just need to be alone to think about Justin and Mummy, or just to be quiet and not think about any of it at all."

"You don't have to explain, Rosemary," I said.

I had never seen her look so forlorn, so sad, and it made me almost furious on her behalf that she felt the need to justify herself in this way.

"You've been through so much, so very much," I said. "And you don't leave them alone, Rosemary, you leave them in the care of other adults. You left them with Grace today, you couldn't know ..." I stopped mid-sentence.

"No, I couldn't know," she said. "But even so, in future I need to ... well, I just need to be more careful."

And then she smiled at me and I watched as she lowered herself to the bed and lay down on her back next to her children.

"I'll stay with them now, Kay," she said, and she closed her eyes.

I stood for a moment looking at her still form, her wet lashes dark against the skin of her cheeks, no longer ruddy from her time outdoors, but pale once more. I did not have the heart to remind her that this was my room, that it was my bed she was lying on. I crept away and closed the door behind me and went to find a place where I too could lie down and be quiet and think as I needed to.

Chapter 26

I had taken refuge in the library and I was still there, slumped in one of the chairs which I imagined were the same ones in which Mr Duff once sat and read his books and took refuge in the past. I lost track of time but was recalled to the present by the sound of footsteps in the hall beyond. I wondered if it was Rosemary, in which case I could reclaim my room so I got up to investigate. I looked into the drawing room but it was empty, then I made my way to the kitchen.

I opened the door on the sound of humming and running water. Grace standing over the sink, her back to me.

"Oh," I said. "Grace?"

She turned, a colander of lettuce in her hands and I realised I had startled her.

"I'm sorry," I said. "I thought you were Rosemary. But what are you doing here?"

"I'm getting the dinner ready," said Grace. She put the colander down on the draining-board and turned off the tap.

"But I thought you'd gone home feeling unwell, Violet-May said?"

"I had cramps," said Grace abruptly. "All I needed was some painkillers and a sit-down, but she sent me home."

"Violet-May sent you home?"

"Yes, she did, but I'm fine now so I've come back to do my work."

This was so patently not what Violet-May had earlier implied that for a moment I was silent.

"Well, if you're sure you're alright," I said.

"Like I said, I'm fine now. But if you don't mind me saying so, you don't look too hot yourself today. Is anything up?"

I thought about telling her – after all, Oliver was her – what exactly was he to her – was there such a thing as a half-nephew? But I decided to leave that to Rosemary or Violet-May.

"Nothing's up," I said. "I'm just going to get myself some water."

"Help yourself," said Grace. "Where is everybody anyway? This house is like a morgue this afternoon."

I remember I shuddered at her choice of expression.

That evening I tried to call Robbie but unsuccessfully. All I got was a recorded message telling me that the person I was calling was not available and asking me to try again later. I did, repeatedly, but with the same result. I had known it was probably a waste of time trying to reach him – he had warned me the previous evening that for the next while he would be out of range of phone signals – but I'd had to try. I thought about sending him a text anyway, but decided to wait until the following morning and try calling him again. A text would hardly cut it anyway – what exactly would I say?

Oliver climbed out on 3rd floor window ledge to play with truck. Truck in bits. Oliver in one piece. Kay.

Perhaps I could add a smiley-face to take the edge off.

The following morning I got up early, and the first thing I did was to try Robbie once more, again without any success.

I decided to make myself useful and got the children up and gave them their breakfast before Grace put in an appearance.

252

Rosemary came into their room as I was getting them dressed, but she looked so awful that I urged her to go back to bed, saying I was happy to look after the children until Grace arrived. She admitted that she had slept very poorly and had another bad headache. After our conversation the previous day, it did cross my mind that in her case "headache" might well be a euphemism for depression brought on by grief and I felt very sorry for her.

I found Oliver, who was still cutting those difficult molars, a real handful and I wasn't sorry when Grace showed up. Violet-May, whom I had not seen since she had rushed off the previous evening, did not put in an appearance at all, and I had lunch with Grace and the children and then left her in charge while I did a little writing.

Later, on my way downstairs to get the car out to go visit my father, I had a sudden thought and ran back up to lock the attic door. The key had always been in the keyhole but I had never before felt there was any need to use it. Oliver, I knew, had been put down for his afternoon nap. Having grown increasingly fractious during the course of the morning, he had eventually worn himself out and was likely to sleep for some time. But better safe than sorry from now on, I thought, as I dropped the key into my pocket. I had also checked that the window was securely shut. The truth was, during the night, I had found myself wondering if it was possible after all that, lost in the world of my book, I could somehow have opened the window without consciously being aware of doing so. I did lose track of time when I wrote, I forgot to eat, I forgot to get up and move about – as a result I had often come up for air to find that hours had passed and I had cramped muscles or a stiff neck. But for all that, in my heart of hearts I knew I had not opened the window.

I had also casually enquired of Grace whether by any chance she had done so. She seemed to take umbrage at the very idea, and I was afraid she thought I was suggesting she had been snooping. I then felt I had to mention Oliver's latest adventure, as it was clear that nobody else had, although I was afraid that she would take even greater offence at my question now, implying as it might seem to, that she was in any way responsible. But her reaction seemed purely one of horror at what might have happened to Oliver and gratitude at what had not.

Coming down from my room now, I met her coming out of Oliver's room and we started downstairs together.

"Are you off to see your da?" she said, and I nodded. "You're very good to him, the amount of time you spend with him."

"He's always been very good to me," I said. "And I love spending time with him."

"You're very lucky to have him," said Grace.

"Yes, I am very lucky," I said more gently this time. I had been reminded suddenly of her own situation – did she even know who her father was?

There was a sound behind me and turning I saw Rosemary coming toward us, pulling on a jacket.

"How's your headache?" I asked.

"Better," she said. "I thought I might just go out and get some air. I thought I'd take Oliver with me but ..."

"Oh, you can't do that now," said Grace. "He's sleeping tight and that's the best thing for him today after all that terrible business yesterday."

"I know he is, I just looked in on him," said Rosemary.

I thought she sounded a bit sharp but Grace, if she noticed, said nothing. But it made me wonder again if perhaps Rosemary resented Grace's involvement in her children's lives – mine too for that matter. And I wondered too if in fact Robbie's efforts to lighten her load were actually making her feel undermined. Because concern was one thing but interference was quite another. I made a mental note to raise the subject with him, if not by phone then certainly on his return. And then there was the elephant in the room – Rosemary's complete ignorance of her real relationship to Grace. On that issue at least I was certain that Robbie was making the wrong decision.

The three of us parted company in the hall, Rosemary letting herself out through the front door, while I walked with Grace as far as the kitchen where I left her to go and get my car. It was sunny when I came out onto the terrace at the back of the house and I remember thinking that Rosemary had chosen a fine afternoon for her walk and I hoped it would do her some good. I have no real memory of walking to the second garage or reversing and turning the car. I must have lowered the window on account of the lovely afternoon but I don't actually recall doing so. I do remember thinking, as I drove slowly around the side of the house, that Robbie was right about the rhododendrons being overgrown – they badly needed cutting back if they were not to encroach even more on the space available for driving between the shrubbery and the wall of the house. Clearing that space I picked up speed just a little and the next thing I remember is seeing a sudden movement and something moved into my path. I say *something*, but I knew at once that it was a somebody. I caught a glimpse of blonde hair and the blur of his features in profile. I braked violently and screamed his name, "*Oliver!*"

At first I could not move, I could not even let go of the steering wheel. All I could do was repeat the same thing over and over again: "*Please God don't let me have hit him! Please don't let me have hit him! Oh please God, don't let me have hit him!*"

If I had not been so paralysed by shock, it would have been perfectly obvious that I had not in fact hit Oliver. For one thing he was standing right there in front of me, very red in the face and looking cross and generally outraged. He was expressing this outrage in some very loud bawling, but was otherwise clearly unharmed. Then I heard another voice and somebody raced past the open window of my car. I caught Violet-May's scent and saw her swoop down on Oliver. My powers of movement returned then and I unbuckled my seatbelt, noticing as I did that my hands were shaking. I opened the door and climbed out. I half expected my legs to buckle when I tried to stand up, but somehow they managed to bear my weight and I walked to where Violet May, inches from the car's bumper, was on her knees clutching a bawling Oliver. She looked at me accusingly over the top of his head.

"*You almost hit him!*" she shrieked. "*You could have killed him!*"

"I know," I said. "Is he alright? Please tell me he isn't hurt?"

"I don't know."

She held Oliver away from her for a moment and studied his face and his body. He suddenly stopped crying and gazed at her from great, tear-blurred sleepy eyes.

"I think he's alright – he looks fine, but you almost hit him. How the hell did it happen?"

"He came out of nowhere," I said. "One minute there was nothing and then he came running out from the shrubbery."

"I saw him," said Violet-May. "But what the hell was he doing in the shrubbery? What was he doing outside at all and where the fuck is Rosemary?"

I had never heard her swear before, not even when she was really angry.

"She went out for a walk, I just saw her go. She'd just been in to check on Oliver and he was asleep. Grace said so too – she'd given him Calpol for his teeth because they were driving him crazy all morning. I don't understand it – how could he be fast asleep one minute and out here in the shrubbery the next? I mean, look at him, he's practically asleep in your arms now. It doesn't make any sense, you know it doesn't, Violet-May."

"Yes, well, I'm taking him inside now," said Violet-May,

getting to her feet with Oliver in her arms. "And then I'm going to have a word with Grace."

I was watching her walking away, Oliver perfectly quiescent in her arms now, when I suddenly called after her. "You saw it, did you, Violet-May? So where were you when it happened?"

She stopped and turned to look at me. "I was coming round from the back of the house. Now, do you think I might be allowed to take Oliver inside, please?"

I let her go and after a moment I turned back and stared at the massed-up rhododendrons. There was a clearly discernible gap in one spot and I was fairly sure it was from there that Oliver had emerged. On an impulse I crossed to it, lowered my head, plunged into the depths of the dark-green leathery leaves and pushed my way through them to the path beyond. It was, I knew, the same path that wound its way the entire length of the shrubbery and once there I was able to straighten up and look about me. It was cool and dim and shady, just as I remembered it from the days when Violet-May and I used to play our games of chase or hide and seek here. But since then the rhododendrons had run wild and the sinuous path along which we used to run had become overgrown. Standing there, I asked myself just what exactly I hoped to find here now. Some sort of answer was the answer, but I failed to find it.

I retraced my steps, plunging back amid the rhododendrons again.

It was as I was stooping to climb through the gap once more that I spotted the red cardboard box. It was lying on the ground and, even before I picked it up, I knew exactly what it was. I picked it up and turned it over, satisfying myself that it was in fact one of the miniscule boxes from the multi-pack that was kept in the kitchen cupboard as snacks for the children. Emerging from the shrubbery I climbed into my car, pulled the door closed and, leaning back against the headrest,

I stared at the little cardboard box once more and asked myself what it meant.

"Are you alright?" said Grace. "You look like you're about to pass out. And I'm not a bit surprised. Violet-May told me what happened." She had been drying her hands on a towel but dropped it as soon as she saw me and came toward me, her face a study of concern.

"No, I'm not alright," I said. "I almost killed him, Grace."

"You didn't kill him and that's what counts," she said.

"Where is she?" I said. "Where is Violet-May? Is Oliver alright?"

"Violet-May took him upstairs, he's fine. The car didn't even touch him."

"Go up to her, would you, Grace," I said urgently. "Make sure he's OK."

Grace looked at me in obvious surprise. "I was going to make you a cup of tea," she said. "The kettle's already on."

"I don't want tea. I need to go and see my father."

"You're not going anywhere until you've had a cup of tea," said Grace. "You need time to get over the shock you've had. Now sit down, that's an order."

"OK," I said, pulling out a chair and sitting down at the table. "I'll have the bloody tea if you go and check on Oliver. But only because I should wait and talk to Rosemary. I need to explain to her what happened."

Grace, her back to me, clattered some dishes and muttered something I only half heard to the effect that if Rosemary was around a bit more often, she'd know herself what had happened.

"She only went for a walk," I said. "As far as she knew, Oliver was asleep in his room. That's what you said, isn't it, Grace? That you'd given him some Calpol and he was fast asleep?"

"That's right," she said.

258

"So what I don't understand is how in God's name he ended up outside running in front of cars!" I looked up as a thought struck me. "You said the car didn't touch him, Grace. How did you know that? Did you see it happen?"

"No, I didn't. Violet-May mentioned it," said Grace, her back still to me. She turned and came toward me, carrying a small tray which held a pot of tea large enough to serve a family of seven, a jug of milk, a bowl of sugar and a single mug. "Drink that," she said. "And be sure to stir some sugar into it – you need it for the shock."

"I don't like sugar," I said. Last night it was brandy, now it was sugar being pressed on me. It occurred to me I should be used to the feeling of shock by now.

"Have some anyway," said Grace. "And I'll go look in on the little fella."

She left me and I stared after her and then I sat alone in the silence of the big kitchen. After a while I pulled the little red box from my pocket and turned it over in my hands. I was thinking and while I did my tea grew cold.

When later that evening I returned from the nursing home, I went in search of Rosemary. I had waited over an hour earlier for her to return from her walk before giving up. I found her in the drawing room where she was lying on the sofa watching *The Vicar of Dibley*. I remember being a bit disconcerted to hear her laughing then decided this could only be a good sign for me. It was only when I came further into the room that I realised she was not alone. Violet-May was lying on the sofa opposite and at first I thought she was asleep. Then I realised that her lids were just lowered.

Rosemary saw me first and she stopped laughing, lowered her feet and raised herself to a sitting position. She did not, however, lower the volume of the TV.

"Hi, Kay," she said and immediately Violet-May's neck craned and her eyes turned to me.

"Hi, Rosemary," I said and I crossed the room and sat down on the far end of the sofa on which she sat.

"You heard about what happened?" I said and she nodded.

"Right, well, I just wanted to tell you how sorry I am. And I know there isn't any point in saying I didn't see Oliver, that I don't know where he came from. But that's the truth, I didn't and I don't. I swear to you, Rosemary, one minute the drive was empty and the next he ran out right in front of me. And I don't think I was going faster than I should have, at least I'm fairly sure I wasn't. But none of that would count for anything if I'd hit him, if I'd hurt him, if –"

"But you didn't," said Rosemary. "You didn't hit him and you didn't hurt him one little bit."

Her voice held no hint of blame or anger and, although logically I knew I could not be held responsible for what had happened or what might have happened to Oliver, this was his mother after all – the very least I expected was some mild show of reproach.

I looked helplessly at Violet-May.

"You heard Rosemary," she said. "It's fine."

"Yes, everything is perfectly fine," said Rosemary in the same lacklustre tone of voice. "Let's all just forget about it."

But nothing was fine. I knew it and I knew they had to know it too.

"I don't suppose either of you have heard from Robbie today?" I said abruptly.

Violet-May did not respond but Rosemary looked up quickly. "Robbie? No, I haven't spoken to him today. Why, have you, Kay?"

I shook my head. "I can't reach him."

Violet-May was surveying me coolly. "No need to worry. He did say he'd be out of range for a day or two."

I met her gaze straight on. "It's not Robbie I'm worried about," I said, then I turned on my heel and left them there.

Back on my room, lying on top of my bed, I remember

feeling for all the world like someone who has unwittingly walked onstage in the middle of a play. Not only did I not know my lines, I didn't even know if I was taking part in a tragedy or a farce.

This time it was not a dream, how could it be, when I was awake? Although perhaps it had started out as one, because I had started up distressed and disorientated, unsure of where I was for a moment. Then realising that I was in my bedroom at the Duff house, I lay back against the pillows and tried to remember what it was that had unsettled me. But the dream, if dream it had been, had evaded my grasp as is their wont and I had no choice but to let it go wherever it is that dreams go in the daytime. But it wasn't quite daytime yet and I lay there for a while wondering just what time it was but too drowsy to make the effort to check. I had the sense that it was just before the dawn and for a while I stayed where I was on my back, just staring at the faint outline of the ceiling-rose above my head. That was when it happened, like a reel of film unfolding before my eyes.

I saw them as I had seen them that day, through the gap in the hedge, Violet-May and Rosemary-June on Bone Bridge. Not all of them, I could not see all of them, just pieces of them, like a jigsaw puzzle, but I could hear them, I could hear them very clearly just as I had that day. Not them, her. It was only Violet-May who was speaking, urgent, her breath coming in little sobbing gasps. Not speaking so much as shouting really, shouting at Rosemary-June, telling her, urging her, ordering her what to do.

Chapter 27

Unlikely as it seems I did get back to sleep that morning. I even dreamed, about Alexander again of course. I had that sense of picking up from where I had left off that sometimes happens with recurring dreams. This time while he was falling I was sitting watching him from the wall of Bone Bridge, but instead of trying to help save him, I wrote about what was happening in my diary. Then Fidelma, the policewoman who had interviewed us all those years ago suddenly appeared by my side.

"Why didn't you help him?" she said. "Why didn't you help Alexander?"

"I had to write it down," I told her, and it seemed to me a perfectly legitimate reason.

Then Fidelma was gone and so was Bone Bridge and I found myself in our sitting room at home. My father was there and he was shaking his head at me as he used to do when he was disappointed at something I had done.

"But it's my diary," I explained. "I have to write it down so I won't forget."

My father shook his head sadly and when I spoke again I was no longer asleep.

"My diary," I said out loud to the silent room. "I need to

find my diary."

But in the end it was well into the evening before I managed to get away to search for the diary. Grace was busy with a humungous batch of baking and, although Violet-May was home all morning, Rosemary was again conspicuous by her absence and I decided to stick around. After lunch, Grace had to go shopping for food and so it was four before I set out to visit my father and after six before I pulled up outside my parents' house.

As I put the key in the door, Mrs Nugent came out and accosted me over the top of the hedge.

"You're back?" she said.

"Just back to get some bits and pieces, Mrs Nugent," I said.

"Is that it?" said Mrs Duff. "You know, you won't believe this, but somebody tried to tell me you'd moved into the Duff house, imagine that?"

"Imagine that indeed," I said and I shut the door firmly behind me.

She clearly knew exactly what I'd been doing but I had no patience with her nosiness right then or her obvious hunger for gossip.

Inside, the hallway was an obstacle course and I had to step over floorboards and even dodge a wheelbarrow in order to get to the stairs. I let myself into the room where I had slept as a child, the room I had come back to as an adult.

I climbed up onto the bed. And when I reached my hand into the narrow vent-opening I was still telling myself that the chances of the diary being there were less than slim. But after all it was there, exactly where I had left it all those years ago, pushed back behind the scrunched-up newspapers my father had stuffed in there to keep the draughts out. I drew it out and looked at it with a sort of fearful reverence, at the blue cloth cover, faded now and slightly damp to the touch and spotted in places with mildew. The little lock, once a bright silver, was tarnished now and I had to think for a while about what I had done with the key. Then I remembered and with a further short rummage inside the vent I pulled out the rolled-up hanky in which I had always wrapped it. The key was only slightly tarnished and when I sat down on the bed and inserted it in the lock it turned quite easily. Inside, the pages had browned and thinned a little with age, but otherwise it was surprisingly unharmed by the years it had spent inside the vent.

On the inside cover I had written my name, address and age and underneath, in large capitals the words:

THIS IS MY DIARY THAT VIOLET-MAY DUFF GAVE TO ME FOR CHRISTMAS

The pride behind the words seemed to me to sing off the page and in spite of myself I smiled. The first few pages of the diary were given over to the last week in December 1983 and I started from the first entry which I had made on Christmas Eve.

24 December
Today I am very happy because it is Christmas eve. But most of all I am happy because Violet-May Duff is my best friend and Robbie Duff knows my name.

26 December
I made popcorn with my new popcorn maker that I got for Christmas. Some of it got burnt but not too much.

1 January
We had a turkey and Christmas pudding again. I don't even like Christmas pudding so I had jelly and ice cream instead. I am going to write in my diary every single day for the whole year. That is my new year resolution.

2 January
Violet-May got a hairdryer for Christmas. I have no hairdryer. Robbie Duff went back to boarding school so I will not see him for ages and ages. I wish he didn't go to boarding school. I wish I was older and that I had a hairdryer.

3 January
Ken Fitzgerald got in trouble in school again. He is so stupid. Violet-May is coming to my house on Saturday. Nothing else happened.

4 January
Nothing happened today.

5 January
Ken Fitzgerald pulled my hair again. I wish my hair was like Violet-May's.

6 January
Nothing happened today.

12 January
I am writing a story about a girl with a pet fox but nobody can see the fox except her. He is really a magic fox but nobody knows that except the girl. The girl's name is Violet-May.

13 January
My teacher said my story was the best in the whole class. I am going to be a writer when I grow up and I am going to live in a big house like Violet-May. Robbie Duff will probably live next door.

14 January
Nothing happened today.

14 Feburary
Violet-May got 3 Valentine cards but I got none. I wonder if Robbie Duff sent any Valentine cards. I hope not.

9 March.
I got my sums all wrong again but I don't care. Sums are stupid and I hate them. You don't need to know sums if you are going to be a writer anyway.

2 April
Ken Fitzgerald played an April Fool joke on the teacher even though yesterday was April's Fool Day. Violet-May said it was a stupid joke but I thought it was kind of funny. Violet-May said stupid people don't know they are stupid because they are too stupid to know they are stupid. I think that means that Ken Fitzgerald does not know that he is stupid even though everybody tells him all the time.

22 April
I got two Easter eggs. Robbie Duff said I am a silly little girl.

21August
Violet-May came back from her holidays. She is very brown. We are having our birthday party in my house. It is her party and my party too and I am getting a new pink dress from a shop. I am very happy.

10 September
Mrs Duff is ordering the birthday cake. Mam said Flora Duff is a busybody. I don't care because the cake is my cake too and it is an ice-cream cake.

24 September
It is my birthday and I am sad because there is no party

and because Alexander fell in the river. Mam said it is not my fault. It was an accident and I am not to think about it anymore. I got a bike for my birthday and four books and money and cards. It is hard not to think about Alexander. I wish he was not dead. I went to the police station two times. The policewoman is called Fidelma and she is kind but I hope I don't have to go anymore.

26 September
There is sausage and mash for dinner but my tummy hurts. I think it is because I am sad about Alexander. I think about Alexander all the time and I dream about him too. Mam says stop but I don't know how to stop.

29 September:
The twins want me to go to the pictures with them and Mrs Nugent. My mam said go and have a nice time but I don't want to go to the pictures and have a nice time. I want to have our party, me and Violet-May. But we can't have a party because Alexander fell in the river and now he is dead and everybody is too sad.

5 October
I am afraid Mam will read my diary. I think I found a good hiding place. Violet-May gave me this diary but now I think she is not my friend. I don't know because I never see her any more and she does not come to school. I wish I had a sister to talk to like she has a sister. If I had a sister I would tell her my secret.

6 October
I woke the whole house again. When Mam asked what did you dream about, Kay, I told her I don't remember. That was a lie. I dreamed about Alexander falling into the river. I always dream about Alexander.

7 October

I broke the bird ornament on the mantelpiece. Mam said it does not matter that I broke it because it is no use crying over spilled milk and Daddy can fix it with the glue from work. She said she only minds because I told a lie. She said you should always tell the truth and you will feel better. I want to tell the truth but I can't. Violet-May did not tell the truth. She said it was an accident when Alexander fell in the river. But an accident is when you did not mean to do something and Violet-May did mean it. I heard her and I know she did it on purpose.

Memory dilutes and refines the past but I had never realised just how much until that day when I sat on the edge of my bed in our old house, reading that damp-spotted little diary in which I had recorded in all its freshness, the great and small pains and joys of childhood. Children see things in terms of black and white and that was how I had written it, all those years ago. The writing itself had faded but not the impact of what was recorded there first-hand. There it was – no equivocation, no ifs or buts or maybe's – Violet-May had done it on purpose.

The diary did not end there and I read it to the final entry, but nothing else had the impact of those five words: *she did it on purpose.* Seeing that in my childish hand made it all so much more real, so much more chilling than last night's memory of the conversation between Violet-May and Rosemary-June on Bone Bridge that terrible day.

I sat there for a long time, feeling chilled in the silent house, the diary, closed now, in my lap while I struggled to come to terms with things. How, I had to ask myself, had I allowed myself to become part of that terrible lie?

Violet-May did it on purpose; it was not an accident. Alexander had not slipped, she had dropped him into the water off Bone Bridge that day and I had known she had. I might not have seen it with my own eyes as Rosemary-June had, but I had known it in my heart, otherwise I would not have written about it in such unequivocal terms. Violet-May did it on purpose.

Why had I kept quiet? Whatever about Rosemary who was Violet-May's sister, why had I not spoken up? And how could I have forgotten what I knew – and had I ever really forgotten or had it simply been more comfortable to allow myself to believe I had? Because wasn't it the case that, despite what everyone had sought to instil in me, despite all the assurances that it was best to forget, somehow I had always known better?

Those nightmares, those awful nightmares that had culminated in that sleepwalking episode, hadn't all of that been because in my heart of hearts I had known what Violet-May had done? So what then? My mind, unable to deal with the burden of that knowledge, had found a way to block out an unbearable memory, an unbearable truth, was that it?

There were so many questions and I had almost no answers. But of one thing I was certain: as soon as I got back to the Duff house I would confront Rosemary with what I knew and insist that she too confront the truth which we had both for whatever reason chosen to bury – which was that Violet-May had deliberately caused the death of her baby brother. But I also needed her to confront what I also now firmly believed – Oliver was in danger from Violet-May, just as Alexander was. The incident with the pond, his being found on the roadside, the attic-room window ledge and finally the near-miss with my car – it was impossible to pretend anymore that all of these things were not linked, particularly now that I had finally accepted what I knew to be true. Rosemary herself, who knew as much as I did, knew more in fact, might not want to confront the reality of the situation, and as for Robbie – I did not know about Robbie but, regardless, my obligation now was not to Rosemary or Robbie but to Rosemary's innocent children. One more dead child on my conscience was not something I could even contemplate.

Chapter 28

"I need to talk to you, Rosemary."

"What's up?"

She was at the kitchen sink drying her hands on a towel and she turned and smiled at me. I have never known anyone with a sweeter smile than Rosemary Duff and as I looked at her that day I was overwhelmed with sudden doubt. How was I to say what I needed to say to her, ask her what I needed to ask? Did she actually already know or had she blocked it out the same way that I did? After all, she was two years younger than I was, so only nine at the time of Alexander's death. And what if I had got it all wrong, what if it was all just one terrible big mistake? She had been through so much already – this could very well be the final straw that broke her. But then I told myself what I had told myself in my parents' house: this was not about Rosemary or me or Violet-May or Robbie, this was about Oliver and Caroline. Rather I should be wrong, rather I should embarrass myself beyond all redemption, than risk their safety for one second more. I wished with all my heart that Robbie was here, that I could abdicate the responsibility I now felt to him, but Robbie was not here and my conscience would not allow me to waste any more time.

"I'm sorry, but it's about the kids," I said, apologising

before I had even begun.

"What is it?" said Rosemary, still smiling. "Is Caroline being a nuisance? I know she's taken to following you about like a little shadow. Is she getting in the way of your writing?"

I shook my head. If only it were something so trivial.

"Caroline could never be a nuisance," I said. "I love spending time with her. Look, Rosemary, there's no easy way to broach this, but I have something on my mind and I won't rest easy until I talk to you about it. The truth is I'm worried about the children."

Rosemary, who had begun folding the tea towel, looked at me, startled. "What do you mean you're worried about them?"

I hesitated as I tried to put into words what I needed to say. In the end I blurted it out.

"I think Oliver may be in danger, Caroline too for all I know. But mostly it's Oliver I'm afraid for."

"Afraid for Oliver?" said Rosemary. Her eyes had widened and were fixed on my face.

"Yes, Rosemary, I'm afraid for Oliver. All these accidents, his going missing and turning up outside the grounds where he might have wandered into the road and been killed, that nightmare the other day with him up on that window ledge? Didn't it make you wonder, Rosemary? And what about yesterday, when he ran out in front of my car? One minute he's tucked up in his cot, the next he's in the shrubbery. It doesn't make sense, Rosemary, you must know it doesn't. And I may be wrong, I really hope I am wrong, but all I can think about is what happened to Alexander and that's why I know that this time around I can't and I won't keep quiet."

"This time?" said Rosemary. Her voice was a low flat echo. "What do you mean by 'this time', Kay?"

"I'm talking about what happened to Alexander, Rosemary. I'm saying that what happened to him can't be allowed to happen to Oliver. And I'm saying that I don't think

Violet-May is the right person to be around ... to be around small children."

"Violet-May," said Rosemary, and again her voice was completely expressionless, devoid of surprise or outrage, denial or any of the reactions I had expected. She was staring down at the towel in her hand which, while I had been speaking, she had folded into a neat square. Then she looked up and our eyes met, and hers were huge and haunted, so much so that I almost caught my breath at the naked emotion I saw there. Perhaps it was because, used as I was to her smiles, her dreamy, sometimes vacant gazes, I had never yet seen her in real distress.

"I thought I was going mad," she said. "I thought it was only me who saw it."

She reached out toward a kitchen chair, fumbled at it like a blind person and I hurried to help her sit down. I got her a glass of water and slipped into a chair opposite and waited while she drank.

"Are you OK?" I asked, as she put the glass down on the table.

"I'm fine, thanks, Kay," she said and she flashed me her smile but it was a mere ghost of itself. "It's just that I've never said it out loud before. And the really strange thing is that it's almost a relief."

I bowed my head in acknowledgement of what she meant. "I understand better than you know," I said.

"You see, I meant it, Kay, when I said just now that I thought I was going mad. I kept telling myself that I was imagining things, seeing things that weren't there, that I had to be. And I kept worrying all the time that something terrible was going to happen."

"You mean to Oliver?" I said.

Rosemary nodded. "But I can't be going mad, can I, not if you see it too? Oh my God, you see it too, Kay." On the table top her two hands had found each other and I could see that the fingers were shaking.

I reached out and put my hand on hers.

"It's OK," I said. "I do see it too, so from now on you don't have to deal with this on your own. Between us all, we'll make sure that nothing bad happens to Oliver, or to Caroline either. We just need to decide what to do for the best, you and me and Robbie."

Rosemary looked up. "Robbie? Robbie knows too?"

"No, I don't know what Robbie knows. I'm pretty sure he suspects something is wrong though."

"I think so too," said Rosemary. She looked at me uncertainly. "So you haven't mentioned this to Robbie at all, these things you've been thinking?"

"Not yet I haven't, but haven't you ever spoken to him about your own suspicions, Rosemary?"

Rosemary shook her head. "Not in so many words."

"But why not?"

Rosemary hung her head very much like a child might. "I don't know," she said. "I mean, where would I start?"

"Perhaps," I said gently, "you could start with what happened that day on Bone Bridge."

Rosemary's head came up and her eyes met mine. "Sometimes I wonder if he knows," she said. "If he's guessed. I mean I've sensed he's worried about Oliver, the way he fusses about him so much. But the truth is we've never talked about what happened to Alexander, not really. He did speak to Violet-May about Oliver, about being more careful of him. That was after he'd found out about Oliver going missing and Grace finding him out on the road. It was you who told him about that, wasn't it, Kay? I knew it had to be, although we had agreed not to." She sounded mildly reproachful.

"Yes, it was me who told him," I said stoutly. "We never should have kept it from him in the first place."

"I agree," said Rosemary. "I always thought we should have told him really. It was Violet-May who thought otherwise and I let her talk me into saying nothing. I was glad when you told Robbie." She shot me a questioning glance. "I suppose you've already told him all that's happened recently too?"

I shook my head. "I would have but his phone must be out of range, because I can't reach him."

"Even if you had reached him," said Rosemary, "what could he do? All that would happen is he'd worry himself sick and what good would that do to anybody? It's best to wait until he gets back. But I don't mind admitting I'm very glad you're here, Kay. And I'm glad we've been honest with one another. I just wonder why Robbie didn't say anything to me – I mean, if he suspects something is wrong, as you say. Perhaps it's because he can't bring himself to believe it. I can hardly believe it myself, it's too fantastic, like something you'd read in a book not something that could happen in real life … but …"

"But still you know it's true," I finished her sentence for her.

Rosemary nodded slowly. "I do now," she said. "But what about you, Kay? Robbie asked you to come here so he must have told you something when he did that? I mean that's why you're here, isn't it, because Robbie thinks something is wrong? But what does he think you can do, Kay? What did he tell you about Violet-May?"

"He hasn't told me anything about Violet-May," I said. "At least, like you said yourself, he hasn't said anything in so many words."

I read disbelief in Rosemary's watching eyes.

"It's true, Rosemary. When Robbie first asked me here, as far as I was concerned it was because he didn't like going away and leaving you on your own with the kids. He told me he didn't think Violet-May would be much use when it came to the kids and he'd be happier if he knew I was here keeping an eye on things, looking out for you …"

"For me?"

"For you and the kids. That was what he told me, I just wish he'd been straight with me and told me what he suspected was really going on. I suppose, like you said, he doesn't really want to believe it himself."

"So he told you nothing about Violet-May at all?"

"No, just that he was worried about you ..."

"Me, he said he was worried about me? Why so?"

"Well, because of all you'd had to deal with, you know, losing your husband and then your mother. He was worried you might be a little fragile."

"Fragile."

"Yes, I think that was the word he used. But of course I now know why he really wanted me to come here. Actually, I guessed almost at once that something was up, you all seemed so ... so pent up, like there was an enormous elephant in the room that everyone was trying desperately not to think about. And you all seemed so odd about Oliver ..."

I fell silent as the enormity of what we were still not saying hit me all over again. Rosemary-June was staring at me intently. I leaned across the table and put my hand on hers once more. "Please don't worry, Rosemary – the main thing is that we're facing up to things now, not just to what's happening now but to what really happened on the bridge that day. As soon as I read the diary I realised that the time for pretending is over. We were kids then but we're adults now and we'll do the right thing to keep your children safe."

"What diary?"

"Oh right, I didn't tell you. I used to keep a diary – actually it was one that Violet-May gave me for Christmas, that year before Alexander ... before Alexander died. I'd forgotten all about it, but then when all these things started happening – Oliver going missing, then almost getting run over, well, I don't know, but it just came back to me. You see, I'd written about it in the diary, after what happened to Alexander. I couldn't talk about it – let's face it, nobody wanted us to talk about it. At least, I don't know how it was for you, but I know my mother thought it should be put behind us, like it had never happened. She meant it for the best, I know she did, but you can't just turn your thoughts off, can you?"

Rosemary shook her head.

"And you can't just unhear what you've heard either," I said, "but I wasn't allowed to talk about it."

"So you wrote about it instead," said Rosemary. "And you've still got the diary, after all this time?"

"I didn't know I still had it. I used to hide it, you see, because I was afraid my mother would find it and read it. She worried about me – you know, after what happened. I think she thought I wasn't getting over it or something, and so I used to hide my diary in an air vent in my bedroom. I only just remembered about it and so I went to see if it was still there. And unbelievably it was."

"After all those years! Incredible! And had you written down everything that happened?"

"Well, they were only brief little entries – and, remember, I wasn't on the bridge when – when it happened. But I did hear some things. Only somehow I'd forgotten." I ran my hands through my hair in my frustration at myself. "Jesus, Rosemary, how the hell could I have forgotten?"

"Perhaps you wanted to forget," said Rosemary quietly.

"Yes, maybe I did – and, because I wanted to so badly, somehow found a way to do it."

"But now you think you were wrong?"

I reached out again and touched her hand. "I was wrong. We were both wrong – wrong to lie and wrong to cover up and wrong to think that we could ever pretend that what had happened did not. And now we have to do something about that, Rosemary. Because it's clear that Violet-May needs help. She's sick, I mean really, really sick, because how else can you explain it?"

Rosemary-June gently withdrew her hand and I was

276

reminded that, in spite of everything, it was her sister I was talking about.

"I'm sorry," I said. "This must be a nightmare for you and the last thing I want to do is add to your distress."

She pushed back her chair and got up and walked to the window. "No, it's alright. I know that what you're saying is only the truth. The lies do have to stop."

She turned to face me again and I saw with surprise that she was actually smiling once more.

"Robbie was right to bring you here," she said. "And I can see why he did now. It's because you have something none of us have, not me, not Violet-May, not even Robbie. You have common sense, Kay."

"I wouldn't be so sure about that," I said a little bleakly. "If I really had any sense I'd have acted on my uneasiness long before now. But the main thing is that we do act now."

"But what are we supposed to do? If Robbie were here but he's not … I wouldn't be comfortable making any big decisions without him knowing what's going on. It wouldn't feel right."

"Alright, but he'll be back soon – the day after tomorrow isn't it? And in spite of what you say, Rosemary, I think he needs to know what's going on."

"And we'll tell him," said Rosemary. "As soon as he gets back we'll tell him. But this isn't something that can be talked about on the phone, Kay, don't you agree?"

"Fine," I said. But I was thinking about the promise I had made to Robbie and, although I didn't argue any further, I knew in my own mind that if I did manage to contact her brother I would have to say something. "But in the meantime we must make sure never to take our eyes off Oliver for a second. And it goes without saying that we need to watch Violet-May like hawks. And I think we should –"

I stopped short at a sound from the hallway then the door swung open and Violet-May sashayed in. She was wearing a floor-length silk dressing gown the colour of cherries which was hanging open to show a matching baby-doll nightie which barely reached mid-thigh. It was impossible not to notice her nipples poking through the silk. I noticed too that she was barefoot and I wondered just when she had approached the door, if she had been standing outside and just how much if any of our conversation she had overheard. But, if she had been listening, she had certainly chosen the right profession because her face showed no trace of anything amiss.

"What are the long faces for?" she said. "Anyone want a coffee?"

"It's a bit too late for me," said Rosemary.

"And me, thanks," I said. "I was just going up to my room."

I flashed a questioning look at Rosemary who came and picked up her mobile phone from the table. "You'd better give me your mobile number then, Kay," she said. "So I can text you the number for that hair salon."

"Oh right," I said and I called out the digits and Rosemary tapped them in.

"Got it. I'll text you that as soon as I find their card."

I muttered my thanks and then I left them without another word and hurried off to my room.

Before I went to bed that night I decided to try Robbie one more time. This time it went to voicemail and I left him a message.

"Hi, Robbie, it's Kay. I've been trying to reach you." I hesitated, wondering what exactly I should say. Rosemary was right – what could he do from where he was? And what was the point of worrying him, when he'd be home soon and would know all there was to know? But he had made me promise to tell him if anything, anything at all made me feel uneasy.

"Look, don't worry," I continued. "Everyone is safe. I

mean fine, everyone is fine. We just need to talk, that's all. The thing is, you asked me if there was something I hadn't told you, and well, there was. So, like I say, we really do need to talk, you and me and Rosemary. OK – well, bye then, Robbie. Bye."

I hung up feeling I had said nothing of any sense and that I had no way of knowing when he would get my message but, even so, I somehow felt better.

Chapter 29

I slept badly and woke later than usual with a tension headache and sense of impending unpleasantness hanging over the day like a storm cloud. There was still no word from Robbie and I decided there was no point in trying to call him again – he would get my message and call me as soon as he could. In the meantime, I knew that there was no point in even attempting to write. I do remember thinking, however, that were I to put down on paper what was actually happening in real life just then I would most likely be accused of being unrealistic. In any event, until I spoke to Rosemary again I could not settle down to fiction. Instead I reread the exchange of texts which had taken place between us shortly after our conversation in the kitchen the previous evening.

Rosemary: Meet this pm away from house 4 obvious reasons.

Me: OK. Where? Somewhere kids can play but quiet.

Rosemary: Town park? U leave first. Pick u up along old road 2.30

She was right of course to suggest meeting away from the house and my setting off first on foot meant there was no risk of Violet-May seeing us together. I wondered again if she had overheard anything of consequence the previous evening. She did not put in an appearance that morning at all but then again, neither did Rosemary, and once again it was left to Grace and me to dress and feed the two children. I felt bad now about the thoughts I had been entertaining about Grace, and I was extra nice to her that morning. It was a beautiful sunny morning and while Grace got on with her housework I made the most of it by taking the children out into the garden. At some point I found myself agreeing to a teddy bear's picnic – Caroline's idea – but the very last thing I had the heart for that day. I did my best however to enter into the spirit of the thing, helping Caroline position her collection of bears and set out her little bright plastic cups and saucers and pots and things along with two small wooden chairs for the children to sit on. We enlisted the help of Grace who supplied us with miniature banana sandwiches and *fromage frais* and even came out to join us for half an hour. I remember at one point, as Caroline was pouring juice from her little teapot, her face almost fierce with concentration, I glanced at Oliver who was sitting next to me nibbling on the inevitable raisins while simultaneously waving his sippy cup in the air, and I wished with all my heart that things could be other than they were. I wondered too what sort of sick heart would feel the urge to harm this beautiful little person, or could do what had been done to poor little Alexander? Only a sick person, I told myself, because otherwise that would make them a monster. A wave of anger mixed with sadness overcame me. I was close to tears, a combination, I imagine, of a bad night's sleep and what I knew was ahead no doubt, but in any event I made an excuse to go back to the house and made my way to my room for a few minutes of silence.

After I had pulled myself together I went into the bathroom to freshen up. While I was drying my hands, I thought I heard a noise in the bedroom.

"Hi!" I called out. *"Is there someone there? Hang on, I'm just coming!"*

I opened the bathroom door. As I did so I heard the door to the bedroom click shut. Assuming that whoever it was had been looking for me and had not heard me call out, I hurried to the door, opened it and stuck my head around. The corridor was empty. I closed the door again, shaking my head. Then I noticed the drawers of the dressing table. Two of them had been pulled out and I was absolutely certain that I had not left them that way. I went across and inspected the two opened drawers. In the top drawer there was nothing but a couple of jumpers and my hair dryer but in the second drawer where I had put my underwear and socks, my things looked pulled about. But who would have done it and why?

I dressed quickly and went downstairs and outside once more.

"You weren't in my room just now, looking for me, were you, Grace?" I asked.

"In your room?" Grace looked up and I read genuine surprise in her face. "No, I've been here with these two, why?"

"No matter," I said. "I just thought I heard somebody while I was in the shower, that's all, I must have imagined it."

But I knew I had not imagined the open drawer or the click of the door as it shut to. Somebody had been in my room going through my things.

I set off on foot just after ten past two that afternoon. There had been a lot of changes to the town in the time I had been away but Old Road seemed to me just as it had always been, almost as though there time had stood still. Granted the traffic was not quite as light as it had been when I was a child but it was still a relatively quiet road, as narrow as it had ever been and lined on both sides with hedges white with cow parsley. I knew I had left the house much too early but the incident in my room had spooked me and I wanted to get away well in advance of Rosemary. As a result I had to dawdle about on the roadside killing time for a good twenty minutes. I remember being surprised at how the weather had deteriorated. A wind, chilly for September, had started up and the sky was beginning to cloud over and I was glad I had brought along a little jacket. Finally Rosemary's car came along and as I climbed in next to her I glanced into the back and was surprised to see two empty child seats.

"You haven't got the kids with you?" I said.

"No, I thought we could better talk without them around."

"But who's looking after them?" I said anxiously. "You haven't left them with ...?"

"No, I haven't," said Rosemary curtly. "Violet-May is picking some friends up from the airport this afternoon and driving them to their hotel in Ballsbridge. She was busy getting dolled up when I left. I left them with Grace with strict instructions not to let them out of her sight for a second."

"I suppose that's alright then," I said, although I was actually thinking that under the circumstances if they were my children I'd have taken them with me. But I wish we'd known that Violet-May was going out. "We could have just stayed and talked at the house then. But never mind, the children will be safe with Grace."

"Yes, good old Grace O'Dreary," said Rosemary and I turned and stared at her in reproach.

"Oh, but she's so kind," I said. "And she's wonderful with the children." Not to mention the fact that she's actually your sister, I was thinking. All these secrets, all these pointless secrets.

"So have you spoken to Robbie?" said Rosemary as though she had not heard me.

"No, no, I didn't." It was not, I told myself, really a lie. Technically I had not spoken to Robbie and as Rosemary seemed to have a bee in her bonnet about worrying him while he was away, I saw no point in mentioning that I had left him a voicemail. She was already clearly tense and on edge, so there was no point in making her worse.

"So, where do you want to go to talk then?" I said. "Now that the kids are not with us, we could just park and talk in the car, or would you like to go somewhere quiet for a cup of coffee maybe?"

Rosemary glanced at me. "Oh, I don't think so," she said. "Let's just stick to the original plan and go to the park – that way there's no chance of being overheard and besides I could do with some fresh air."

"Yes, of course," I said. "The park will be perfect. If it doesn't rain."

"Speaking of being overheard," said Rosemary, "that diary that you told me about, I hope you've put it somewhere safe?"

"I pushed it down between the headboard and the mattress," I said. "You think Violet-May overheard us talking, and will try to find it?"

And then I remembered the sounds I had heard from my bathroom, the open drawer and the door closing as I stepped back in from the bathroom.

"What?" said Rosemary.

"Nothing," I said. "I was just thinking about what you said. If she heard us, she heard us and there's no point in worrying about it." There was no point in worrying her either, I had decided.

"I suppose not," said Rosemary.

She drove in silence for a while until a song came on the radio which she must have liked because she turned up the volume and began to hum along and I remember finding it a little disconcerting just as I had as I listened to her laughing at *The Vicar of Dibley* the day Oliver ran out in front of my car. But then I reminded myself that this was Rosemary, that hers was an essentially sunny personality and no doubt she believed we would find a way through this awful mess. The thought comforted me and I relaxed a little as a result.

We parked and walked the short distance to the big gates.

I looked up at the sky and saw that the rain was now definitely on its way. I glanced at Rosemary and thought about once more suggesting a café instead of a walk but she seemed oblivious to the weather and was setting a brisk pace across the grass toward the river which bounded the park on one side. There was a pathway running alongside the riverbank from one end of the park to the other and it was for this that Rosemary made. It was certainly a pleasant place to walk and, aside from the occasional runner or those busy walking dogs or children, we had it to ourselves. The change in the weather had presumably sent people hurrying for their cars.

"Is that me or you?" said Rosemary, as a phone beeped.

"Me, I think." I pulled my phone from my bag – another text from Dominic – I shoved it back in. "Nobody important," I said.

"Damn," said Rosemary, who had been rummaging in the recesses of her own bag. "I've forgotten my phone. I must have left it on the table in the kitchen when I was talking to Grace."

"Well, don't worry," I said. "The kids are with Grace and Violet-May will have gone by now. Though if it will make you feel better, I can call the house and make sure everything is alright?"

"No, it's fine," said Rosemary. "We won't stay long."

But, as it turned out, she proved reluctant to broach the subject we had come there to talk about. She seemed more interested in our surroundings than anything else. At one point, I tried to lead into it but just then a runner came up behind us on silent soles and it seemed to make Rosemary jumpy. I decided it was best to let her take the lead. It was her family we were concerned with and if she needed to work up to talking about what was happening then that was her right and who was I to rush her?

We were nearing the end of the footpath and I expected

that we would turn back or strike out across the grass toward the ruined castle which bounded the park on the far side, but Rosemary surprised me.

"Let's keep on going," she said. "You can, you know – there's a quiet spot beyond that turnstile thing with a bench where we can sit and talk in privacy."

"You know about the Pool?" I had not expected that she would – the Duffs had left the town when she was only nine and the Duff girls had never been let wander freely as most of the children from our estate had back then in the eighties.

"Robbie brought us all here to the park the week we arrived," said Rosemary. "Caroline spotted the turnstile and wanted to go through the 'twirly gate' as she called it and so Robbie showed us the way."

"You're right, it is peaceful there, and I doubt we'll be disturbed." I cast another look at the sky. "But, you know, I'm fairly sure it's going to start raining any minute."

"I don't mind," said Rosemary, "I like rain." She beamed at me and once again I saw her as she had been as a little girl who conversed with fairies. "Besides, your jacket has a hood," she said. "And the sooner we start talking the better. You know, about stuff."

And so I agreed and we passed through the turnstile in single file. It had been a wet enough summer and the grass here was overgrown. With no sunlight spilling through the overhanging tree branches it was quite dim there too that day, a dim and gloomy place to talk about terrible things, I remember thinking – not at all the sort of place I would have thought would appeal to sunny Rosemary. But I supposed the sun had been shining when they had come here and I smiled inwardly at the sudden vision I had of Oliver riding high on Robbie's shoulders, and Caroline chattering excitedly no doubt as she negotiated the "twirly gate". But there was no sunshine today, no dappled light through the branches and no excited children either. I made straight for the bench which, although wooden, weather-bleached and very much the worse for wear, was still sturdy enough.

We sat down next to one another and for a moment we were silent. It was as quiet there as I remembered it being when I was a child. The Pool had always been curiously quiet. Probably, I decided, something to do with the way the trees enclosed it, nothing more. I gazed at the water. Since I had last been there, the trees had become even more entwined and the river threw back their reflection in watery green. The wind had lessened now and the water looked quite still, but that was the thing about the Pool, the water always looked still at first glance, then you noticed those tiny movements on the surface. And suddenly I had a mental picture of my father sitting on this very bench next to me as he told me about the simmering and how deep the water of the Pool was and how treacherous. And I remembered too Ken Fitzgerald telling me about the drowning boy and how the reeds had wrapped themselves about his face and neck like giant green spaghetti – and I shivered.

Rosemary noticed the shiver because she turned to me suddenly with a thoughtful expression on her face. "You don't like it here, do you, Kay?"

"Not particularly," I said.

"I do. It's pretty and it's peaceful – even the water looks peaceful. A good place to swim, I think."

"I don't swim," I said.

"Yes, I know – you told us about your father's attempts to teach you. Silly girl! It's so easy."

I glanced at her, feeling that was unkind – my cowardice about swimming was a sore point with me. But she was gazing at the water, smiling her usual serene smile.

"And even if I could," I said, "I wouldn't swim here. It might look peaceful but it isn't safe."

"Is it not?" said Rosemary. "What a shame, when it looks so pretty. The children loved it here, that day we came here with Robbie. You thought I should have brought them with me today, didn't you, Kay? I could see it in your eyes."

I had been so far away in my mind that I was taken completely by surprise and I am sure my face showed it.

"No," I said quickly. "It wasn't that. I was just expecting them to be in the car, that was all. But it's fine, they're perfectly safe with Grace, of course they are. Please don't think I'm judging you, Rosemary. I wasn't and I have no right to."

"Yes, perfectly safe," said Rosemary. "Alexander was fast asleep when I left. At least he seemed to be asleep but you never can tell with him."

I felt a small chill creep over me; it was the third time she had made that mistake in my hearing. I had let it go before but for no reason I could put into words I could not let it go again.

"Not Alexander," I said gently. "Oliver."

"What?" Rosemary, who had been staring at the water, turned and looked at me.

"You said 'Alexander', Rosemary. But it was Oliver who was asleep when you left, not Alexander."

Slowly, Rosemary's eyes widened and when she spoke it was a whisper.

"You've seen it too," she said. "I thought it was only me, but you've seen it too, Kay."

I found her stare unsettling. "What have I seen, Rosemary? I don't know what you mean."

"But you do know, Kay, you do. You've seen it just like I have. Alexander and Oliver – they're the same."

"Oh, you mean the resemblance," I said, and I remember feeling uncomfortable because I had of course noticed the likeness between Rosemary's son and her dead brother.

"No," said Rosemary, frowning. "I don't mean a resemblance, it's much more than that. He's come back. I know it and you know it too.

"Who's come back, Rosemary?" I asked but certain now that I already knew what her answer would be.

"Alexander of course," said Rosemary. "Alexander's come back."

"What do you mean, Rosemary? How could Alexander have come back?" My voice surprised me in its evenness because in reality the chill I had felt had become a shiver that snaked the length of my spine.

"Oh, but he has," said Rosemary. "I saw it in his eyes the day he was born, the very first moment they handed him to me."

"You saw what in his eyes?"

"That it was Alexander of course." Rosemary looked at me as though she thought I was perhaps a little slow. "The truth of course is that I never wanted babies. That was all Justin's idea. Justin wanted a son so badly. I shouldn't have had any and I did hold out for as long as I could but in the end I gave in. But instead of a son we got Caroline and Justin loved her and, after all, everything was fine. Because I won't lie, Kay, I'd been worried."

"Why were you worried, Rosemary?"

"Well, it doesn't matter," said Rosemary. "Because Caroline was such a pretty baby and she hardly ever cried. I wouldn't even have minded taking care of her myself, really I wouldn't. But Justin said we should have a nanny so we did. Grace came even before the baby did. I knew it was really Violet-May's idea, I heard her talking to Justin, telling him I should have some help with the baby. She told Mummy the same thing – she just wouldn't mind her own business. Inviting herself to stay at our house even before Caroline was born and then afterwards refusing to go away. She stayed for ages and ages, until she was sure that it was alright, I think."

"Until she was sure that what was alright?"

"Well, she was watching me of course, and she kept on watching me until she was sure that Caroline was safe."

"Why wouldn't Caroline be safe, Rosemary?" I heard the

small tremor in my voice but in any event Rosemary was not listening.

"But it was different with the boy," she said. "It was quite different and that was how I guessed even before he was born. I couldn't be sure but then Justin had that terrible accident and then I knew I was right. He made Justin die, the boy did. I suppose it was because Justin was the only person who would never believe anything bad of me, who would always protect me. And so I knew then that I had to get ready. Violet-May had come to stay again and Mummy too. I told them I didn't need them, I had Grace to help me, but Violet-May just said that I was in shock and didn't know what I needed. But I knew what she was up to, and then the boy was born and I saw his eyes watching me and it was him, the other one, come back to torment me, to trick me and punish me."

"Oh Rosemary," I said gently, "don't you see that you've got things a bit mixed up? Why would Alexander want to punish you?"

"Don't you know?" Rosemary turned her gaze on me and her eyes narrowed. "Violet-May knew and Robbie too. He wanted to punish me for what I'd done to him, of course. And so it all began again, everyone watching me, trying to trick me and catch me out. 'Isn't he beautiful?' they said, and 'What will you call him?' they said. But I was too clever for them. 'Oliver,' I said. 'His name is Oliver after Justin's father.' And so we called him Oliver but I knew who he was really."

"You say that Alexander wanted to punish you because of what you'd done to him," I said slowly. "What did you do to Alexander, Rosemary?"

"Oh, come on, Kay," said Rosemary. "Don't pretend you don't understand." She smiled at me but it was a sly sort of smile and I instinctively drew myself back a little, increasing the space between us on the bench.

"But I don't understand, Rosemary. What had you done to Alexander?"

Rosemary stopped smiling. "You know, Kay, you're really not a good liar, are you? And all this playing dumb doesn't suit you."

"I'm not playing dumb, Rosemary," I said. "I have no idea what you're talking about and, if you don't mind, it's starting to rain and I'd much rather ..."

The truth was that I had an awful suspicion I did know what she was talking about, and while I was speaking I had made a move to get up.

Rosemary took me by surprise, reaching out suddenly and pulling me down roughly onto the bench once more, so roughly that, startled as I was, I was really surprised that anyone so frail-looking could have so much strength.

"What do you think you're doing?" I said angrily.

I tried to push her off, but she had somehow pinned me in, her body leaning across mine, both arms forcing me back against the bench. "Let me go, you're hurting me, Rosemary!"

"But we need to talk, Kay. You said so yourself, you said we needed to talk about what happened on the bridge that day. That was what you wanted, wasn't it?"

"I don't want to talk about anything like this," I said and I struggled against the weight of her arms.

"Then don't try to run away again," said Rosemary.

"I wasn't trying to run away," I said.

"Well, that's alright then," said Rosemary. She took her hands from my shoulders and sat back on the bench next to me, but I sensed that she was primed to spring should I try again to leave.

"Why should I want to run away?" I asked.

"Why indeed, when it was you who said we need to talk about what happened? Except that we already know what happened, don't we, Kay? I know and you know and Violet-May knows." She eyed me speculatively, "And Robbie? Robbie could never be sure before, although I think he suspected, because of the dog ..."

"What about the dog? " I said, bewildered now. "What dog?"

"Oh didn't you know?" said Rosemary. "Robbie's dog, Prince. I was sure Robbie would have told you. He died. I put rat poison in his dish and he died. Robbie guessed it was me who did it." She smiled at me. "It wasn't hard, you know. The worst part was getting hold of the rat poison. I knew where Dad kept it on the top shelf in one of the sheds but I couldn't reach it. I had to get the little stepladder from one of the other outhouses and to drag it across to the shed where the rat poison was kept. It wasn't heavy, but I was afraid that someone would see me. But nobody did. And then I didn't know how much to use, how much would be enough. So I used a lot and, well, it was enough. But Robbie knew it was me. He never told me outright that he knew, but he let me know in other ways. And I'd catch him looking at me, watching me with a look in his eyes. It was the same look you have right now, Kay."

She was smiling at me, a terrifying smile, and I was torn between the urge to get up and run and the compulsion to hear her out.

"But why?" I said.

"Why did I poison Robbie's dog?" Rosemary frowned. "Because I wanted a kitten, that's why," she said in a tone of sweet reasonableness which even if I live to be two hundred years old, I will never be able to forget. "And besides, Violet-May was always saying she wished the dog was dead. But you can't trust Violet-May, because as soon as I made him die, she went and changed her mind and acted all sad about it. You know, Kay, I really was sure that Robbie would have told you all this. But perhaps he knew that no one would believe him." She turned her dazzling smile on me again, "I mean, would you believe that I could poison a poor helpless dog? But Robbie believed it and I suppose that's why he guessed about

Alexander too."

"Alexander?" I echoed and discovered that my mouth was almost dry. "What did Robbie guess about Alexander?"

"You know," said Rosemary. "What I did to him on the bridge that day, Bone Bridge. Do you remember, Kay, how you told us all about how the bridge got its name? How they found a big grave with the bones of all those people – "

"What did you do on the bridge that day, Rosemary?" I demanded and she stopped smiling.

"Why are you still pretending, Kay?" she said. "You know exactly what I did to Alexander, you've always known."

"No," I said. "No, that was Violet-May. You know it was, Rosemary, and I know too because I was there and I ..." I stopped, conscious that I had almost blurted out what I had kept inside for so very long.

I saw Rosemary's eyes which were fixed on my face flash in triumph.

"I knew you knew," she said. "I could see it on your face. Afterwards I kept waiting for you to tell someone, your mother or that policewoman who pretended she was so kind when all she wanted to do was trick us. I could never understand why you kept it to yourself when you knew all the time that it was me." Her eyes narrowed and she said, much quieter now, "You know, you really should have told someone what you saw, Kay."

I shivered as though a shadow had crossed the invisible sun. "I didn't see anything," I said. "I just heard, that's all, and even then I didn't know anything for sure. Or at least if I did, I put it out of my mind."

"No, no, no, no, no, Kay." Rosemary, still smiling, was wagging her finger like some awful parody of a disapproving nanny. "Now we both know that isn't true, don't we?"

"But I heard her. I heard Violet-May and she was pleading with you, begging you to say it was an accident. And I knew then whatever she'd done she'd done it on purpose. It was

Violet-May, it had to be, it had to be ..."

"Stop it," said Rosemary, her voice suddenly hard and peremptory. "It was me and you know it was me. You've always known it, just like you've always known that it wasn't an accident, that I did it on purpose."

For a moment I stared at her in silence. I knew there wasn't any point in arguing with her anymore just as I knew now that what she was telling me was true.

"Why, Rosemary?" I said. "Why would you do that to that beautiful little boy?"

"I told you, I wanted a kitten," said Rosemary, sullen now. "I thought after the dog died I could have one, but that didn't work out because of the baby. But nobody wanted the baby, even Mummy said so once, I heard her ..."

"*But that was before he came!*" I was almost screaming now and I was crying, I knew I was crying, tears making Rosemary's face blur before my eyes. "*And whatever she said, she didn't mean it. How could you believe she meant it?*"

"People shouldn't say things if they don't mean it," said Rosemary petulantly. "Violet-May was just as bad. She said she wished the baby was dead too – you heard her, Kay, she said she wished the baby was dead."

"She didn't mean it, she didn't mean it," I moaned. I had wrapped my arms about my body in a fruitless effort to ward off the horror I was hearing.

Rosemary, still sitting there next to me, frowned down at me disapprovingly. "I don't know why you're getting so upset," she said accusingly. "You have to have known most of this already. After all that's why Robbie brought you here to watch me. Because he guessed about Alexander – and Oliver too."

I stopped rocking. "What about Oliver?" I said.

Immediately I had that awful feeling that comes when you have asked a question to which you do not want to know the answer, when the truth is you already do.

And before Rosemary could speak I said with absolute certainty, "It was you, wasn't it? It was you making those things happen to him, all those near accidents, all the time it was you. Jesus Christ, Rosemary – Oliver, your own son. I can't believe this, I won't, I can't."

"But you do believe it, Kay," said Rosemary. "Otherwise why agree to come and spy on me? You believe it, just like Violet-May does and Robbie. Even Mummy could believe it. But then she actually saw me throw Oliver's ball into the pond that day." She frowned. "She must have been looking out the window. I was sure nobody was around but I didn't think about that upstairs window – that was stupid of me. I suppose it was that that caused her to take a turn, seeing me throw the ball and watch as Oliver went in after it. It was lucky for me she did take a turn, because otherwise she'd have told Violet-May what happened."

"She tried to, though, didn't she?" I said. "You told me yourself that she kept repeating Violet-May's name over and over, Violet-May and Oliver's name – she was trying to warn her."

"Yes, she was, but luckily nobody understood what she was trying to say."

"And so she died in her sleep," I said, "before she could tell anyone what she'd seen."

"Oh Kay!" Rosemary looked at me as though I was a thing to be greatly pitied. "Don't you know yet that nothing in life is ever that simple? Things don't just happen, not the things you really want to happen, not unless you help them happen."

"I don't know what you mean." I was thinking about poor Mrs Duff desperately trying to make herself understood, how helpless she must have felt, how afraid and powerless.

"Don't you really know, Kay? Just think about it, why don't you? Mummy knew what I'd done and she'd already tried to warn Violet-May and Robbie that Oliver was in danger. Well, I could hardly let that happen, could I? So I did what I had to do. I always do what I have to do."

"You killed your own mother," I said.

There was no surprise in my voice. I think I had moved beyond surprise and even for a moment horror, at least that was how it felt to me at that moment.

"You make it sound so dramatic," said Rosemary. "But I expect that's the writer in you, Kay. In fact I hardly had to do anything at all, just a little gentle pressure and then her breath stopped, that's all it was, I made her breath stop. I had thought about using a pillow, but instead I used a rubber glove. I got the idea from a detective programme I watched on TV – PD James I think it was. I thought that was quite clever of me actually."

She looked at me, her eyes shining. She's pleased at herself, I remember thinking, she's actually proud of herself. I wanted very badly to get up then and step away from her, get as far away from her as I could, but the horror had returned and I was afraid my legs would fail me, that if I tried to stand I would sag at the knees.

"You see, I'd gone to her room much later that night," said Rosemary. "Mummy was still sleeping and she looked so peaceful it was hard to believe she was any danger to me. Perhaps if I had gone away then ... but in any case, I didn't. I sat down in her armchair and I waited. I waited for a long time and, while I did, I watched her sleeping. She looked quite beautiful lying there. When she was awake she always seemed so sad and worn, but asleep she looked quite different, young and sort of content. Perhaps she was dreaming of Alexander, I never realised how much she cared about Alexander."

"Of course she cared about him," I whispered. "He was her son, her baby."

Rosemary frowned. "Yes, I suppose she must have but she never seemed to when he was alive."

I said nothing more because there was nothing more I could find to say, and Rosemary continued with her story.

"I fell asleep and then when I woke up Mummy was awake too, and this time it was she who was watching me. And as soon as I saw the look in her eyes I knew that she knew what I'd done. I pretended not to, of course. I went to her and asked her how she was feeling. I told her how she'd given us all a scare, that kind of thing. But when I put my hand out to touch her, she drew away from me as though I were a serpent or something ... something vile or unclean. That was how it seemed to me, and I knew for sure then that she'd seen me throw Oliver's ball into the pond. But it was worse than that, she'd guessed that it was I who let Alexander fall too, and of course seeing what she had that day she knew it hadn't been an accident. And so ..."

"You're mad." I could not help myself.

"Do you think so?" said Rosemary, sounding almost intrigued. "You know, I find that quite interesting. Violet-May thinks I'm sick and Robbie just thinks that I'm bad but you see it as madness. I don't see it in any of those ways but I suppose I wouldn't, would I?"

"Do they know?" I said. "Do either of them know or suspect what you did to their mother?"

Rosemary shook her head. "Nobody has ever known about that. Not until now, not until you, Kay." Her eyes took on a new expression and she shifted her body so that her leg which had been just grazing mine pushed against me. My instinct was to shift away from her, but I fought it. Without actually admitting it to myself I was beginning now to actively play for time.

"Tell me about Oliver," I said. "How you managed it all. How you made it look like an accident every time. That time in the car, for instance, when I almost ran over Oliver, that was you too, right?"

"Well, I didn't plan it, if that's what you mean," said Rosemary. "I was on my way out for a walk when I heard you on the stairs tell Grace you were going to visit your father. I knew you'd hang about chattering in the kitchen with Grace, so after you had both seen me going out through the front door, I just let myself in again by the side door through the butler's pantry. Then all I had to do was run up by the back stairs to Oliver's room and lift him from his cot and carry him down the back stairs and out through the side door again and into the shrubbery. He was asleep so he didn't make a sound and if anyone had seen me all I had to say was that I'd heard him crying and was taking him downstairs. And then, well, I just waited."

"You mean you waited for me to drive past," I said.

"Yes, but he'd woken up by then though and he was so crotchety I was afraid he'd start mewling and I had to give him something to shut him up."

"Raisins," I said, "you gave him raisins."

Rosemary's eyes rounded. "Yes, I did actually. How did you know? I found a box with some still in it in the pocket of my jacket. I usually keep some on me – they're the only thing that shuts him up."

"I found the box where Oliver dropped it," I said automatically while in my head I was picturing her skulking in the cool dimness of the shrubbery watching and waiting while she fed raisins to her groggy little son.

"You pushed him out in front of me, didn't you?" I said.

"Well, I might just have helped him along," said Rosemary. "But first I told him to run to Auntie Kay, Auntie Kay who had lots more sweetie raisins. Auntie Kay, you like the sound of that, don't you?"

I said nothing and I saw Rosemary's smile twist a little.

"I think you do," she said. "I think you'd like it if you could really be their Auntie Kay. Or perhaps you'd like to be even more than that. I'm right, aren't I, Kay? You'd like them to belong to you, to be your children. I see the way you watch them, and they like you too, Kay. Everybody does, everybody likes kind little Kay Kelly. The boy didn't need to be told twice to run to his Auntie Kay."

She was goading me and I knew it, but what might have hurt me another time was washed away in the bigger realisation.

"So you pushed him out in front of my car," I said. "You did that, knowing that he might be killed or badly injured."

Rosemary shrugged. "An accident, a sad accident, but accidents happen."

"And if he had been hurt or killed, I'd have been responsible."

"Well, in a way, yes," said Rosemary. "And of course that would have been a pity for you but after all people could really hardly have blamed you."

Her tone was so sweetly reasonable it was hard to keep my train of thought.

"And of course it was you," I said, thinking out loud now in an effort to keep my calm, "it was you who was responsible for Oliver ending up wandering alone on Old Road. So how did you manage it?"

"He was in my car all along," said Rosemary. "Asleep on the back seat, I put him there when I carried him down from his cot. Of course there was the small risk that he might wake up – but I didn't think he would – he was in a deep sleep. Violet-May was on the phone to Calvin and my car was out front and I guessed nobody would think of looking there. But, just to be certain, I made sure to be the one who searched the front of the house."

"That was why he didn't get wet then," I said. "It was raining that day but Oliver was bone dry. I noticed but I didn't think any more about it."

"Did you, wasn't that clever?" said Rosemary. "I did have a bad moment you know when you volunteered to go searching for him along the road. You see, I'd always intended to be the one to do that."

"So what, you drove off with him in the back of the car and what then? You left him on the side of the road, is that what you're telling me?"

"Pretty much," said Rosemary. "I stopped the car outside the gates, lifted him out, carried him a little way up the road, left him there, ran back to the car and drove off in the opposite direction."

"You drove off and left him there – you left him alone on the side of the road where anything might have happened to him."

She shrugged and I wanted to look away but I needed to know it all now.

"And the attic-room window?" I said.

"Of course that was me," said Rosemary. "I'd been out all day and when I came back I went straight upstairs to change. I was passing the playroom and I heard you all in there. I was about to go away again when I heard Violet-May tell you that Grace had gone home. Then I heard you say you were about to go for a nap. I didn't fancy having to spend time with the children so I hurried off to my room so that nobody would realise I'd come back. Then after I'd changed I decided to go down and make myself a cup of coffee. I heard them in the playroom again – this time Caroline was whining that she needed the bathroom and he, he was screaming. I figured out that Violet-May had been trying to pick him up but he wasn't about to leave his truck behind. She was trying to calm him down and I heard her tell him to be a good boy and she'd be right back and I knew she was planning to leave him there alone. I went back to my room and waited until they passed me on their way to the bathroom, Violet-May and Caroline. Then I ran to the playroom and he was there on his own sitting on the rug playing with that truck. He looked at me in that way he does when he wants me to know who he really is. So I picked him up, him and his truck, and I carried him up to the attic room. I opened the window and I put a chair against it and then I took his truck from him and I put it out on the windowsill outside. You should have heard him roar. I was sure someone would hear him and spoil my lovely plan. But he shut up when I told him it was a climbing game, when I told him to climb up quickly and go get his lovely new truck. I helped him up onto the windowsill, then I left him there and ran downstairs and hid in Daddy's study. It all only took a few minutes, nothing could have been simpler. But, after all, it didn't work that time either."

That was when I snapped.

"Your lovely plan?" I said, jumping up so suddenly that I took her by surprise. "You leave an eighteen-month-old baby on a windowsill in a third-floor room, and you sit there and call it your 'lovely plan'. You crazy fucking bitch!"

I had at least the brief satisfaction of seeing Rosemary flinch and then she too was on her feet and we stood there face to face.

"You can't actually say that I harmed him," said Rosemary. "After all, he's still perfectly fine, isn't he? All I did was try to exploit situations."

"*Don't!*" I put my hand up as though it could block her from my sight. It was a visceral reaction because just looking at her right then made me feel sick to the pit of my stomach. "*Don't you dare split hairs!*"

Rosemary just stared at me, her face inscrutable, and suddenly my rage dissipated and I was left feeling physically shaken. I walked slowly back to the bench and lowered myself down.

For a while, Rosemary stayed where she was, just looking at me and then she came across and sat down next to me once more, not close this time but at the far end of the bench. For a while we just sat there quite still and silent and when I glanced at her again she was staring straight ahead at the water, looking thoughtful, and I could not help myself trying once more.

"Why are you doing all of this, Rosemary?" I said. "Can't you see yourself how craz– how it doesn't make sense?"

"You know why, Kay," said Rosemary, without turning her head to look at me. "He's come back, he's come back and he's trying to catch me out. I see him watching me, watching me and waiting. They're all watching me, waiting for me to make a mistake."

"Nobody wants to trick you, Rosemary," I said gently. "You've got things mixed up, that's all. You're confused or traumatised or something, I don't know what exactly, but you have to try to understand. Alexander was your brother, but he died a very long time ago. This little boy now is your son, your little baby son, Oliver. Not Alexander – Oliver."

Rosemary had turned now and was staring at me so intently that for a moment I almost believed I was getting through to her. Then she shook her head slowly.

"I know that's what they'd like me to think," she said. "Violet-May and Robbie and now you too, Kay, because I know you're one of them. You told me yourself that Robbie asked you to spy on me ..."

"Not to spy!" I said desperately. "He asked me to keep an *eye* on you, that was all. And that was only because he was concerned about you, after all you'd been through."

But even as I was denying it I knew that Rosemary was at least right about this much: Robbie had invited me to the Duff house effectively to watch Rosemary. Just one more pair of eyes, that was all I had been, because he had known, or at the very least suspected that Rosemary was a danger to Oliver, just as she had been to Alexander. And I felt anger rise up inside of me. Why hadn't he told me, why hadn't Robbie just told me?

"It isn't any good, Kay," said Rosemary. "I knew what Robbie was up to as soon as he first suggested we all come back to Ireland to stay at the old house. Robbie might have loved that house but nobody else did, except perhaps Daddy. I certainly didn't, it meant nothing to me, and Violet-May doesn't give a toss about it either. And if she had been alive, nothing and nobody could have persuaded Mummy to come back here, not even for a visit. She told Robbie so when he told her he'd bought it. It just reminded her of what happened to Alexander."

"Then why did you come?" I said. "You didn't have to, you could have refused and stayed in England."

"I wanted to see what they had planned," said Rosemary. "They thought they had me fooled, you see. Robbie trying to make me believe he wanted me to see what he'd done with the house and Violet-May going on about how nice it would be to have us all here together again. I knew exactly what was going on and so I decided to let them set their traps. I knew I could outsmart them all, I always could. And anyway, none of it matters now. The only question now is what to do next?"

Her head was to one side now and she was eying me speculatively and I knew then with absolute certainty that she meant to kill me. But how could she? Yes, she was taller than me but I was bigger-boned – there was nothing to be afraid of physically. But even as I reassured myself I saw something in her eyes that told me I was wrong, something that made me certain that Rosemary Duff was not a woman just like me – Rosemary-June Duff was almost certainly insane. And I was afraid.

I was afraid, but I was also determined not to let her see that. Somehow I knew that the only way was to bluff it, to act like I had no fear for my own safety, no consciousness even of being in any danger. With that in mind I picked up my bag from the bench and got to my feet. I opened my mouth with the intention of saying casually that we should probably get back to the car.

But before I could get a word out Rosemary had made a lunge for me, pulling me down again with a force that shocked me and made me drop my bag.

"Stay there while I think," she said and once again she was pinning me to the seat with the force of her arms.

My instinct was to struggle but I remembered the force of

the way she had dragged me down and I decided not to test her just yet. I did not want to remove any doubt she might have that she could actually hold me physically there. So I made a great effort to force myself to relax.

"What do you think you're doing, Rosemary?" I remember that my own voice sounded remarkably unworried. I even managed a smile of mock surprise.

"Be quiet please," said Rosemary sharply. "I'm trying to think."

She was staring down at me, but I was almost certain that she was not really seeing me. Her face was fixed and intent as though she were working out some complex puzzle. Perhaps I should have stayed quiet at that point, but I didn't.

"Why don't we go somewhere else?" I said. "Somewhere where we can –"

"*I said shut up!*" Rosemary screamed. "*Shut up, shut up, shut up! I need to think!*"

I struggled then but her grip on me tightened. Her face was too close to mine now, contorted and almost unrecognisable, and I saw the rage in those normally mild and smiling eyes.

"Why are you doing this, Rosemary?" I said. "You can't really want to harm me. And even if you did, think about it logically, you can't keep getting away with these things, nobody can. People will work it out, they'll guess. You told me yourself that Violet-May knows what you did that day on the bridge. And Robbie obviously doesn't trust you around Oliver."

All the time I was talking Rosemary was looming over me, her eyes fixed on my face, but I still had no sense that she was really hearing me. I tried desperately to think of something that might get through to her.

"The diary," I said, "they'll find the diary. They'll find it and then everyone will know that Alexander's death wasn't an accident."

"They won't find it if I find it first," said Rosemary. "And I will find it first because you told me yourself where you put it. Did you forget that, Kay?"

I remember wanting to slap my own face for being the idiot I was. "I lied," I said. "It isn't where I said it was."

A gleam came into Rosemary's eyes. "And were you lying when you told me what was in it too, Kay? Were you lying when you told me you'd written that it was Violet-May who dropped Alexander into the river?"

I hesitated, unsure how best to answer, and Rosemary watched me and I saw that she was smiling once more, obviously amused at my confusion.

"You're not very bright, are you, Kay?" she said. "Well, never mind, either way I'll find it and if I need to I'll burn it. But if you were telling me the truth – well, think about it – there it is in black and white – Violet-May did that terrible thing to her poor little brother. After all, everyone thinks she did it anyway, dropped him by mistake, but now they'll believe she did it on purpose. And who knows what she might do in the future, who else she may try to harm?"

I knew she was thinking about harming Oliver once more. At the same time I became aware that her grip on me had slackened. The time for playing possum was over and I made a lunge for freedom. I took her by surprise and, although she clawed after me, all she got was a fistful of my hair. She yanked it brutally and I cried out with the pain as I pulled myself free of her and ran. But she was right behind me and then she was on me, felling me with the force of her body. Then she had me by the hair again, with both hands this time, and I screamed with pain as she used it to drag me toward the edge of the riverbank. She bent over me and attempted to roll me forward but I clawed at her face and that was when she kicked me in the side not once but twice and then she was bending over me again and the next thing I knew I was falling.

I hit the water hard on my back and it was so cold. My heart began to thump violently in my chest and I remember thinking – *I can't swim! I can't swim!* Water flooded into my mouth and I realised that I was actually shouting the words out loud. I was panicking which was what I most needed not to do. I tried to calm myself, seeking with my feet for the riverbed only to find I was out of my depth which made me panic all over again.

I looked up and saw Rosemary on the riverbank, watching as I struggled and I called out to her.

"Help me, Rosemary! Please help me!"

But she did not move and I floundered again, flailing my arms and legs wildly in a desperate effort to keep afloat. An image of my father came to me, trying to demonstrate the dog's paddle, and I stopped thrashing about and tried to splashily swim. I kept going under but did succeed in moving closer to the riverbank, and then a little closer still, enough that I was able to reach out and claw at the mud of the bank. I found a handhold in a rock that jutted through the earth but there was nothing else to help me pull myself out of the water and so I clung on with all my strength and peered up into the falling rain, calling to Rosemary, whom I could no longer see, to help me. She suddenly loomed above me and stood looking down at me, frowning. When she began taking off her jacket I had a moment of pure hope. Her shoes were next and I remember thinking that she had come to her senses. She disappeared again for a moment then reappeared a little further along the riverbank where it formed a natural curve and I saw her lower herself to the grass, then swing her feet over the riverbank and lower herself into the water.

I concentrated on keeping my grip on my single handhold then and waited for her to come for me. I heard the splash and fall of the water as she swam toward me and I turned and watched her drawing closer, her rain-wet face, her blonde hair spreading on the water behind her, her blue-eyed stare fixed on me.

"Hold onto me," she said, then her arm came out and I let go of the rock with my right hand first and grabbed hold of her before letting go with my other hand.

Rosemary drew me toward her, turning me in the water so that my back was against her chest. Her right arm tightened across my upper body and then she pushed away from the riverbank, taking me with her. Into even deeper water. I opened my mouth to protest and at the same time Rosemary's arm loosened its reassuringly tight hold on me and I felt a weight on the top of my head as I was pushed under. Water rushed into my mouth and throat. I struggled and thrashed and managed to surface though she still was pushing on the top of my head. I clawed at her face and, feeling something soft, knowing it was one of her eyes, I dug my nails in hard. She loosened her grip on me and I pushed myself free of her. As I floundered she came after me and grabbed my head again. She pushed me down but I grabbed hold of her and pulled her with me. Down, down, down we went and the last thing I remember before the reeds took hold was how different the water was there, so darkly, darkly green.

I did not feel frightened of them at first. Their touch was soft on my face and neck, a sort of gentle licking which as I wriggled to free myself became a gentle sucking. Then they wrapped themselves about me silently like great wet serpents and I became aware of Rosemary once more, still close to me but not near enough anymore to reach out and harm me. Even if she had been she posed no danger to me any longer. She had begun to thrash and kick and I knew that the reeds had her too.

That was when I heard my father's voice. I heard it so clearly it was as if he were there with me in that cold green water, and he was telling me what he had told me all those years ago when I first heard from him the story of the boy who had drowned in the Pool.

"*The trick is to stay calm,*" he said. "*Try to float through the reeds using your arms as paddles.*"

But it is not easy to be calm when reeds like giant green spaghetti are encircling your arms, your legs and your throat, when almost all your energy is focused on the overpowering need to breathe and the fight not to. But I tried, I tried for as long as I could until in the end I gave in as I had to and inhaled. In one great spasmodic breath I drew water into my mouth and it was like accepting death.

In the moments before death supposedly a person's life flashes before their eyes, the past spooling before them. That did not quite happen to me. After the struggle was over and I was surrendering to the inevitable, one thought came to me: *the heroine cannot die, she must live to tell the story.* It was followed by another: *you have never been the heroine, you are only Little Kay Kelly, the watcher-on.* Then I could see myself at Violet-May's play, standing behind the second garage, invisible, delivering my lines through the open window. And at that memory something rose up inside me, a shot of spirit, of rage – no, more than rage, of outrage – Kay Kelly should not die like this. But it was too late. The last thought that came to me was: *I'm sorry, Daddy, I did try, I really did, but I couldn't do it, I couldn't do it.*

Chapter 30

I was aware of a great weight on my chest, like something was pushing down on it. It hurt and a thought flashed through my mind that I could not be dead because dead people cannot feel pain. I opened my eyes to see Robbie Duff leaning over me, his eyes fixed intently on my face. The weight on my chest lifted suddenly and I knew then that what I had been feeling were his hands on me. Then something rose up in my throat and I felt myself being rolled over none too gently. My nostrils scented damp earth and I was violently sick into the grass. This time the hands that rolled me onto my back were gentle and Robbie was leaning over me once more, raising my head and holding me there against his arm. I saw Violet-May standing a little way back, her phone in her hand. She saw me watching and she smiled at me bleakly. The next thing I was aware of was my lungs which felt as if they were burning while the rest of me was cold, colder than I had ever been in my life before. I was aware that I was shivering violently and my teeth were chattering. I understood now why they called it chattering, it was like a cacophony of sound in my ears and it was coming from my mouth.

"She's freezing," said Robbie.

A moment later something came around me. My fingers

brushed against it and I realised it was his tweed jacket.

Then a young voice said, "Is she dead?"

I let my head drop to one side so I could see who was speaking. Two boys of about twelve or thirteen, each with a fishing rod in his hand, were standing a little way back, staring at me with avid eyes.

"I'm not dead," I tried to say but my voice did not work – instead I began to cough so violently it was more like choking.

Robbie leaned me forward some more and held me there until the spasm passed.

Then I tried again and a voice that sounded very unlike my own managed this time to say croakily, "I'm not dead."

"She pushed her," said the other boy. "The other woman pushed her."

And everything came back to me then in a flood of memory, Rosemary dragging me by my hair to the edge of the riverbank, the savage kicks, the shock of the cold as I hit the water and the moment of hope as I saw Rosemary taking off her jacket. The force of her hands on my head pushing me under and last of all the slippery softness of the treacherous reeds on my skin and the sight of her thrashing and flailing next to me.

I leaned back and gazed up at Robbie. "Rosemary?"

He shook his head gently.

"How did I ..." I began but I could feel another coughing episode coming on and I cut my question short.

"He went in after you, missus," said the first boy, pointing to Robbie. "He got you out first and then he went back for the other woman, the one that pushed you in the river and tried to drown you."

Too many pronouns I remember thinking, so confusing when there are too many pronouns. But I caught the sense of what he was saying and looking at Robbie I realised for the first time that he too was shivering and that his clothes were saturated and sticking to his body. I remember thinking, he

310

saved me, he got me out first and he saved me.

"She didn't push me," I croaked. "It was an accident. Nobody was to blame."

After all, it was what I had been saying, what we had all been saying for what seemed forever now. What was one more lie?

I was still shivering even with the jacket around me so Robbie sent Violet-May to fetch the blanket from her car. She came back with it just as two ambulances arrived within seconds of each other.

Robbie asked Violet-May to go with me and I was a little surprised when she nodded in silent acquiescence.

"But you'll stay here until they ... until they find her, won't you, Robbie?" she said.

"Yes, I'll stay," said Robbie.

I knew then that Rosemary was still in the Pool.

Then I was lifted off the ground and carried into the ambulance.

At the hospital I was examined and tests were run and then I was informed that I was being kept in overnight for observation. I was glad. I had no desire to go back to the Duff house and, even if it had been habitable, there was nothing and no one waiting for me at my parents' home. And so I let myself be put to bed in a hospital ward.

At some point I must have fallen into an unhappy doze, the pathway to unhappy dreams out of which I woke with an unpleasant little jerk and found myself once again staring into the face of Robbie Duff.

He was not watching me this time, he had fallen asleep in the chair next to my bed, the bag that had fallen to the ground in my struggle with Rosemary lying on his lap. I could see the little twitching movements of his eyeballs under the thin skin of his lids and, as memory flooded back, I remember wondering if he too was dreaming about the sullen dark waters of the Pool and I imagined what it had cost him to

311

leave his sister down there wrapped about in those cold slippery reeds. At the thought I almost felt their hold on me once more and I stirred in the bed and Robbie must have heard it because he started awake.

For a moment he just stared me as though puzzled to find me there.

"You're awake," he said.

"So are you," I said and my voice though still not my own sounded a little more robust.

We looked at each other then for a while without saying anything at all.

"Rosemary," I said then. "Did they ... have they ...?"

"Yes, they found her," said Robbie and he bowed his head.

"I'm sorry, Robbie," I said.

Then we were both silent for a long time.

"How did you find me?" I said. "How did you know where we'd gone?"

"You have Violet-May to thank for that," said Robbie. "She found Rosemary's phone – she'd left it on the kitchen table. She checked her messages. She'd been feeling uneasy after overhearing some of a conversation between you and her. And she saw the messages from Rosemary-June asking you to meet her outside of the house today. And there was the message you left me too, you mentioned Rosemary in that. As soon as I got it I booked the first flight back."

Of course. That would have been like an alarm bell to him.

"She'd seen Rosemary watching you and it worried her, so she decided to go and find you. I arrived back at the house just as she was leaving, so I came with her. We saw the car outside the park but we couldn't find you. Then I remembered that part of the river beyond the park proper."

"The Pool," I whispered.

"You were both at the bottom by the time we got there. But there was no way of knowing that and if it hadn't been for those two kids being there ..."

He got up and walked to the single small window and stood with his back to me. I had come to recognise that this was characteristic of him: he turned away to hide emotion or even perplexity.

After a while I said, "Those boys, they said you brought me out first and then you went back for Rosemary. You knew it was already too late for her?"

"I didn't know," he said, still with his back to me.

"But …"

He turned and looked at me. "The boys told me when we got there. Rosemary pushed you under, she tried to drown you. You tried to make them believe it was an accident but you and I know it was no accident. And I knew a great many other things by then. Violet-May told me a great deal today that I just wish I had been told before."

He was looking me fixedly and I thought I saw reproach in his eyes.

"I see," I said.

"So, if you're asking me if I made a choice, Kay, the answer is yes. I brought you out first and I left Rosemary there and I didn't know if she was alive or dead. But I made a choice, Kay, and I chose you."

"So Violet-May told you about Alexander," I said.

Robbie was sitting next to my bed once more. He looked up from the polystyrene cup he was holding between both hands. "Yes, she did," he said.

After our earlier exchange, he had gone to get himself a coffee, or that was the reason he gave, except that when he came back about ten minutes later he had a stoic smile on his lips but tell-tale red-rimmed eyes. It pained me to think of him crying in a hospital toilet or some corner of the car park.

While he had been gone I had lain in my hospital bed and thought about what he had done. I thought about him diving into the dark waters of the pool and finding us there, both of us caught in our prison of weeds, both of us only barely alive. His decision had to be made in a nanosecond. Surely every instinct should have sent him first to the aid of his own flesh and blood. But he had chosen me: he had closed his heart against his sister, saved me and left her down there all alone in the long weeds.

"But you'd already guessed," I said.

"Guessed?" said Robbie. "More than that. I'd known for a very long time that there was something wrong with Rosemary. It was she who poisoned Prince, you know."

"I know, she told me so today," I said.

"She admitted it? Did she say why she'd done it?"

"She wanted a kitten. She thought she'd be allowed to have one if the dog was gone."

"Christ Almighty, a kitten." He put his coffee down on the floor next to the chair leg and ran both hands over his face and into his hair. "I should have said something at the time, I knew I should have, even then. But I had no way of proving it was she who poisoned Prince and nobody would have believed me. I did let her know in my own way that I knew it was her. I'd like to be able to say I enjoyed that part but frankly I couldn't bear to be near her after that. Every time I thought of what she'd done, it made me feel ill."

"So ill you wanted to go away to boarding school."

"As ill as that," he said with a bitter twist of his lips.

"She knew you'd guessed about Prince. She thought you knew about Alexander too and that you'd told me all about it. She thought we were all in on it together, spying on her, trying to catch her out – that was what she kept on saying." I looked at him uncertainly, thinking about what I wanted to say. "You do know that it was she who threw Oliver's ball into the pond that time when he almost drowned?"

"I know, Violet-May filled me in. That thing with the attic-room window ..." Robbie got up from the chair and went back to stare through the window once more. "But why in

God's name? Did she say?"

"She thought he was Alexander," I said.

Robbie swung round. "What do you mean, she thought he was Alexander?"

"Just that," I said. "She thought Oliver was Alexander come back again."

"Jesus Christ," said Robbie.

He hand swept across his face once more then it dropped to his side and he stood for a moment, head up, eyes on the ceiling, and I saw from the way his neck was working that he was struggling for composure.

"Then that was why," he said. "I knew something was wrong about the way she was with him, and I knew that Violet-May was uneasy about it too."

"So you did think she might try to hurt him?" I said.

"It was just a fear, a suspicion. Prince was one thing – but her own child?"

"I think it was a bit more than a suspicion," I said. "I think you were really worried and I think that Violet-May always knew it was Rosemary behind all those near-misses with Oliver. And to think I suspected her – and Grace too!"

"Grace? Grace wouldn't harm a hair on either one of those kids' heads. Grace was a safeguard – as you were. But I didn't realise the level of the danger Oliver was in. I thought Rosemary was disturbed, not crazy. Christ, what a bloody nightmare!"

"You know you could have told me, Robbie?" I said and I was beginning to croak again. "When you asked me to move in you could have told me the real reason. Rosemary accused me today of being a spy – and, when you think about it, she was right. That was why you wanted me there, not for any of the reasons you gave me but simply to spy on her ..."

My voice gave out and Robbie hurried to pour me some water. While I drank it, he prowled about the room, his hands in fists by his side, throwing me occasional unhappy glances.

And when I'd put the glass down and was lying back against my pillows he came and stood next to my bed.

"I'm sorry, Kay," he said. "You're right of course, I should have been honest with you. But there was no proof, none and she's ... she was my sister after all. For crying out loud, I could hardly admit what I suspected to myself let alone to you!"

I said nothing and Robbie flung himself back into the chair and for a while he just sat there staring down at his hands. When he looked at me again there was an altogether different expression in his eyes.

"You know, Kay, I'm not the only one who hasn't been honest. I did ask you if there was anything you were keeping to yourself. Why didn't you tell me then what you knew about the day Alexander died?"

Afterwards I told myself it was because of what I had been through, because I was still in shock and completely exhausted, that I lost my temper with him then. And that was part of it – but I think now it was also down to a niggling sense of disappointment, the cause of which I had not yet examined.

"How dare you, Robbie Duff," I croaked. "You don't know what I knew or what I didn't know. You don't know what I felt, you don't know the first thing about it. So how dare you judge me, how dare you!"

I was aware of a stricken look on Robbie's face but just then a nurse burst in and, having taken one look in my direction, she promptly sent Robbie out.

After she too had gone, I was left alone and free to pull the sheets up around my shoulders and give in to misery and the comfort of tears.

Chapter 31

By the time my next visitor sailed into my room, I was already eating myself up with guilt. Robbie Duff had saved my life and his sister was dead and I had yelled at him – or come as close to yelling as a person can who has recently been half-drowned. Under the circumstances, I thought Violet-May looked almost indecently glamorous – she was even wearing her usual perfume – I smelled it when she leaned in to kiss me. That was when I saw the evidence that she too had been crying. No amount of make-up could quite cover up the ravages grief had wrought to the skin around her eyes.

"I brought magazines, lots of magazines," she said, her voice determinedly bright. "And flowers too, but unfortunately an impossibly stern nurse took them from me – apparently they're not allowed. They were meant as a peace offering, not from me but from Robbie. I was to give them to you with the message that he knew he'd been crass and insensitive and had upset you badly without meaning to. I was also to tell you that he's an idiot and he knows you're not to blame for any of this and would you please forgive him? There, I think that was the spirit of it."

"I upset him too," I said. "I shouldn't have done that, not with everything he's going through, everything you're both

317

going through. I'm so sorry about Rosemary, Violet-May, I'm so very sorry."

Violet-May, who had settled herself into the chair next to my bed and was busy spreading her long pale coat so as not to crease the silken fabric, glanced up suddenly.

"How can you be?" she snapped.

I watched as all pretence at levity drained from her face, leaving her looking bereft and suddenly every minute of her age.

"I'm sorry, Kay," she said. "I know you're a nice person, much too nice for the likes of me and Rosemary-June, that's for sure, but how can you be sorry? There wasn't any accident, and we both know it. Rosemary really did try to drown you, didn't she?"

"Fine," I said baldly. "Yes, Rosemary tried to drown me. She dragged me by the hair to the edge of the Pool and then she kicked me and pushed me in. Then she stood there and watched me flailing about trying to save myself without a lifting a finger to help me. Then she got in to finish the job." I saw Violet-May flinch and I said quickly, "I'm sorry. Robbie told me I have you to thank for the fact that you both turned up on time. He said you suspected Rosemary had it in for me. What made you think that?"

"It was just a feeling at first," said Violet-May. "I caught her looking at you with that expression in her eyes, the same expression I'd often seen when she looked at Oliver. What I couldn't really figure out was why she wanted to hurt you. I still can't."

"She thought Robbie had brought me to the house to spy on her. She believed, or at least she suspected I knew what she'd done that day on Bone Bridge." I looked away from Violet-May and said miserably, "Actually she couldn't have been more wrong. The truth is I never had the slightest suspicion it was Rosemary. I'm so sorry, Violet-May. I thought it was you."

"Everyone thought it was me," said Violet-May. "They were supposed to."

"No, you don't understand," I said.

"What don't I understand?"

"I heard you, Violet-May. I heard you and Rosemary-June talking on Bone Bridge that day. You were telling her that she had to say it was an accident, not just telling her, you were ordering her to say it. And there was something in your voice, you sounded so terrified, and then when I came through the gap and found the pram empty I just knew it hadn't been an accident.

"Well, you weren't wrong, were you?" said Violet-May bitterly.

"But I thought it was you. I thought you'd done it on purpose. It was the way Rosemary-June kept staring from me to you. I didn't know then that she'd seen me through the gap in the hedge. She thought I'd seen her too, that I knew what she'd done. And then when she began to scream, but you kept on looking terrified, that made me think all the more that you were guilty."

"Oh well, don't feel too bad, Kay," said Violet-May. "Easier to believe it was me than angelic little Rosemary, right? But, if you believed I'd not only done it, but done it on purpose why did you never say anything?"

"I don't know," I said. "It's complicated. I knew what you'd done or I thought I did, but I hadn't actually seen anything. It was just a feeling I had based on what I'd heard and I didn't want to believe it. Just thinking about it made me feel sick and so somehow or other I managed to forget about it. But then coming here brought it all back. Right from the very first day, seeing Oliver looking so much like Alexander – and then there was Rosemary telling me about the day your mother died, and how Oliver was almost drowned. And there was something about the way she told me too, almost as though she was making a point of it."

319

"How do you mean?"

"Well, she managed to make me feel that there was more to it all than she was actually saying. She went on about how your mother had taken a turn and been really agitated, how she'd kept repeating your and Oliver's name over and over again."

"She was putting you off the scent," said Violet-May dully. "Laying a trail that would lead you straight to me. She must really have hated me."

I looked at her in silence. How, I wondered, must it feel to mourn a sister, as I knew Violet-May was mourning Rosemary, and at the same time know the things she knew about her?

After a while I said, "Do you remember that day when I first came to stay at Robbie's house and you made some comment about feeling that you were being watched?"

"I did feel like I was being watched," said Violet-May. "Even before you came I'd had that feeling, and then you arrived out of the blue and that made me even more suspicious. I think I knew in my heart that Oliver was in danger but I began to wonder if Robbie thought the same thing and believed it was me who wanted to harm him."

"It wasn't Robbie who was watching you, it was Rosemary," I said. "She knew where the danger lay. She suspected Robbie knew what she'd done to Alexander but she knew for certain that you knew. I believe that's why she tried to point me toward you. And she did a good job of it, I'll give her that, she led me by the nose."

"And still she couldn't resist trying to harm Oliver," said Violet-May. "But she was clever – she only did it when I was around."

"Well, there was Grace too. For a while I suspected her." I looked Violet-May in the eyes. "I know about Grace, Violet-May. Robbie has told me that she's your half-sister."

Violet-May opened her bag and rummaged, head bent so I

could not see her eyes. "So he told me," she said. "So that's all the dirty linen out there for all to see now." She shut her bag with a snap and looked at me once more. "Robbie says Rosemary believed that Oliver was Alexander come back to trick her? I suppose that makes sense of it all in some twisted way."

"I suppose it did in her mind," I conceded. "And then of course I put the wind up her even further when I told her about the diary."

"What diary?"

So I told her about the diary, how I had remembered its existence and retrieved it. I told her what I had written there.

"I'm sorry, Violet-May, I got it so very wrong," I said.

"We all got it wrong," she said.

"But then I had to go and tell Rosemary that I believed you were trying to harm Oliver. She pretended to believe me, even told me she'd suspected the same thing. But all the time she was convinced I knew it was her who'd killed Alexander, and that I was trying to trick her. And so she decided to shut me up."

"Then knowing that," said Violet-May, "how can you say you're sorry she's dead?"

I considered the question, but only for a moment. "Because I am. I'm sorry for Rosemary herself and for you and Robbie too, but most of all I'm sorry for those two innocent little children. But do you know what else makes me sorry, Violet-May? You said just now that I'm too nice for the likes of you and Rosemary? You're wrong, you know. Don't put yourself in the same box as her, because whatever your sister was, whether she was sick or mad or just plain bad, you are not the same. Do you hear me, Violet-May? You are not the same."

"Please don't, Kay. Please don't be kind to me, I don't think I can bear it."

And I watched as the tears fell, tracking the make-up and cracking the carefully applied mask she had made for herself.

"Just tell me one thing, Violet-May. Why did you cover for

her? That day on Bone Bridge. Why did you cover for Rosemary and take the blame for Alexander's death yourself?"

The crying had eventually stopped and with the aid of a small gold compact Violet-May had repaired the damage to her face and reapplied her lipstick.

"Why did I cover for her?" Violet-May snapped the compact shut and dropped it into her bag. "Partly, I think, because I didn't know what else to do. Partly because I was terrified for her. I thought she'd be sent to prison or something. But Rosemary didn't seem to understand the implications of what she'd done at all. If anything she was put out that I wasn't more pleased that Alexander was ... that Alexander ... and all the time he was in the water, getting further and further away from us and I didn't know what to do to help him."

"Did you actually see her drop him, Violet-May? Couldn't it still have been some sort of terrible accident?"

It was a stupid question and I knew the answer before I heard it.

"I saw her, and she did it on purpose. I'd been leaning over the wall of the bridge waiting for a stick I'd dropped in to come out the other side. When I turned Rosemary was holding Alexander out over the wall, dangling him, you know, and then she just ... she just let him go. He didn't slip, she let him go, and she didn't scream or cry out. I screamed and when I did Rosemary gave a sort of start and she turned and I saw the smile on her face. As long as I live I will never forget that smile."

I felt myself shiver, then I said inanely, "So it was you I heard. I always thought it was Rosemary-June who screamed first."

"She saved that until she had an audience," said Violet-May. "She knew I'd seen her and she didn't even pretend she'd done it accidentally. And when I asked her why she'd done it, she said it was because I'd wished Alexander would go away. She reminded me that I'd said I hated him and wished he'd never been born. And the worse thing was, it was all true – I had said those things and wished those things.

"But you didn't mean those things," I said.

"But I did say them, Kay, you know I did."

"So what? Children say things like that all the time – it doesn't mean anything. You would never have wanted any harm to come to Alexander and you know that as well as I do, Violet-May."

"But Rosemary-June couldn't seem to understand that. "She was very angry with me. She told me she'd done it for me, that I'd wanted Alexander to go away and she'd made it happen, just like she'd made the stupid dog go away. It was she who killed Robbie's dog, Kay. Rosemary killed Prince."

"I know," I said, "she told me that too."

"She reminded me that I'd said I'd wanted him dead, that time he chewed my shoe. And it was true, I had said that, and so you see, I really did feel that I was to blame somehow."

"But why did it have to be you?" I asked. "Why not say it was Rosemary-June who'd dropped Alexander but that it had been an accident?"

"Because I knew instinctively that she'd give herself away," said Violet-May. "I knew she'd be incapable of behaving as she should if she'd been the one responsible, even if it was an accident. It was just easier if I took the blame. I could act the part. And you know, it really wasn't so bad. Moving away really helped and people felt sorry for us and were kind to us, the few who knew what had happened, because after all it was just a terrible accident that had befallen two children."

"Three children," I said. "There were three children on Bone Bridge that day, Violet-May."

"Of course, I know that, I'm sorry, Kay."

"It wasn't your fault," I said. "Whatever you chose to tell people, whatever Rosemary tried to make you believe, none of it was your fault."

"I don't feel that. I'll never feel that."

We were quiet for a while, then I said, "What was she like, afterwards? Didn't anyone ever realise there was something wrong with her?"

"Not as far as I know," said Violet-May. "There were things, I suppose, a coldness you might call it. She seemed incapable of seeing things other than as they affected her, and I don't just mean that she was selfish." She laughed suddenly. "I'm selfish, I'm very selfish and always have been, but this was different. No, there was no one big sign that she was warped inside, but then again I didn't spend my life looking for signs either. Just like you, Kay, I found a way to forget what had happened, or at least to push it to the very back of my mind and never look at it again."

"What about your mother," I said. "Did what happened affect your relationship?"

"You mean, did she blame me for what happened to Alexander? If she did, she never once let me see it and, honestly, I believe my mother blamed nobody but herself. She thought it was a punishment for something she'd done wrong in the past. An old sin, she called it." She gave a short mirthless laugh. "It was a while before I found out just what that old sin was exactly."

I quickly steered her away from the subject of Grace.

"So when did you begin to worry about Rosemary again – when the children came along, I presume?"

Violet-May nodded. "Even before Caroline was born I began to worry. I flew back so I could keep an eye on Rosemary. I asked Mummy to find a nanny." Her face hardened. "Well, you know all about that fiasco. But then Caroline was born and everything seemed fine. Rosemary didn't exactly dote on her, but she seemed to quite enjoy her. I stuck around until I was satisfied that I'd been worrying unnecessarily and then I went home again. I told myself that what had happened to Alexander was firmly in the past – a terrible tragedy to be put down to a moment of unthinking childish pique or jealousy or something. You have no idea how much I wanted to believe that and I almost did until Oliver came along."

"What happened?"

"I just knew from the start that we were in trouble. I could see it in her eyes when she looked at him. And when she'd mix up the names, call him Alexander instead of Oliver, it made me shiver."

"Me too," I said.

"Do you think your mother ever suspected the truth?" I asked. I tried to keep my voice casual.

"You mean about Alexander, that it wasn't an accident?"

"Or about Rosemary trying to harm Oliver," I said.

Violet-May's eyes widened in surprise, "No, why would she?"

"Well, I just wondered if maybe some maternal instinct might have meant your mother guessed more than you knew."

"Well, she didn't, and for that at least I'm grateful," said Violet-May. "And I'm glad she isn't here right now, that she's been spared all of this."

I knew then that I would never tell her or Robbie either what I had learned about their mother's death. It was, I realised, yet another lie in a family almost destroyed by lies and perhaps I was wrong to add yet another layer of deceit, but Violet-May and Robbie had suffered and would continue to suffer and I knew I would never be able to add to the sum of their pain.

And so when the two Guards came and stood by my bedside and asked me for my version of the story the two boys had already given them, I made light of their tale, insisting that I had fallen into the river and that Rosemary, far from trying to drown me, had tried valiantly to save me.

Rosemary was trying to save me – every time I said those words I forced myself to think of Caroline and Oliver and, like a little sugar, it helped me to swallow the bitter medicine.

The following morning they discharged me from the hospital. I had already decided that I would not return to the Duff house. It was a house in mourning and I felt I had no place there. I had the driver stop and wait outside my father's house while I went in. I was half thinking of camping out in the living room but, much as I wanted to convince myself otherwise, I could see that that was impossible. Most of the upstairs furniture had been piled up there for a start and it was also clear that I would only be in the way of the builders. Another week or so, they assured me, and I could move back in. Somehow I doubted it. I picked up the things I needed and left and had the taxi drop me at a local B&B where I took a room.

Chapter 32

It was four days before I saw Robbie again. We had spoken only once since the day that Rosemary died, and that was by phone when he realised I was not returning to the Duff house. He had not tried to talk me out of my decision and had promised to get my laptop and other belongings to me as soon as he could. For my part, I had assured him that writing was the last thing on my mind, and that me and my things should be the last on his. When he hung up I felt cold and curiously hollow.

Now he had come as promised, my bag in one hand, my laptop case hanging from his shoulder. I brought him through to the guests' lounge and I sat on the sofa and he sat in an armchair opposite.

He asked me how I was and I said I was fine. He asked me if I was comfortable there and I said I was. He looked about him and said it looked quite comfortable, then we sat for a while and said nothing at all.

I was beginning to wonder if he was ever going to speak again when he suddenly said, "We're taking Rosemary back to England. The funeral will take place there and she'll be buried there."

"Not with your mother?" It was an instinctive reaction and

my voice was sharper than I had intended.

Robbie looked at me. "You mean because of Alexander? But Mummy never knew what Rosemary had done to Alexander – thankfully she was at least spared that."

"Thankfully," I said, and wished with all my heart that it were true.

"Still, I take your point," said Robbie. "In any case Rosemary will be buried with Justin. It seems the right thing to do – after all, he worshipped the ground she walked on."

"Then I'm glad." I did not say what I was glad about, in truth I don't think I knew myself.

"How are the children?" I asked. "And Grace, how is Grace? Rosemary was Grace's sister too."

"She's sad and shocked and concerned for you but also fiercely loyal, even about Rosemary. And I might be imagining it, but I think I see a beginning of a thaw in Violet-May's attitude toward her."

"I'm glad." After all, I was thinking, Grace is the only sister Violet-May has now.

"As for the children," said Robbie, "Oliver is too young to really know what he's lost. Caroline is a bigger problem – she misses Rosemary of course. I've tried to explain, you know, all that she's gone to sleep stuff – sometimes I think she's accepted it then she asks when Mummy is coming back. I mean, how do you explain death to a three-year-old?"

"You don't. I mean you can't, not really – all you can do is your best and keep on loving her."

Robbie smiled briefly. "Well, at least that part is not hard to do."

"No, not hard to do at all," I agreed. "So what will happen to them? Will they stay with you or what?"

"They'll stay with me," said Robbie. "They have no-one else, except an elderly grandfather who couldn't possibly look after them, and a middle-aged bachelor uncle with no interest in raising children. So of course they'll stay here with me."

"I thought you might say that," I said. "Try not to worry. The children are going to be alright, just as long as they have you in their lives. Just give it time. I know it's the most infuriating platitude in the world, but time really does fix most things."

"Do you really believe that, Kay?"

I looked at him then, really looked at him and I saw that even in the space of time since I had last seen him, a change had come over his face. There were lines there around the eyes and mouth that I was almost certain had not been there before and his eyes, those swimming blue eyes which were still as beautiful as ever, had so much sadness in them I wondered if any amount of time would be enough to dilute it.

Before I could answer him, Robbie got up and began to move about the long narrow room, his hands in his pockets. "Perhaps you're right," he said. "Actually Caroline is taking a big interest in a cat that's turned up out of nowhere and seems intent on hanging around the house. I suppose that's a good sign, except that she wants to keep it."

"I hope you said yes?"

"Of course I said yes," said Robbie. "I just worry it will run away again – it's obviously a stray."

"They say if you put butter on a cat's paw, they won't run away."

"I've heard that," said Robbie. "I suppose it's worth a try. Perhaps I should have put butter on your paws, Kay, to stop you running away."

He turned and looked at me.

"Caroline misses you too, Kay. She asked me only this morning when you were coming back. She grew very fond of you very quickly."

"I miss her, and Oliver too, but they hardly know me – it won't take them long to forget about me."

My voice sounded brusque, hard almost, and when Robbie spoke again I heard the note of surprise.

"Do you think so?" he said. "Some people you don't forget as quickly as others."

"What about Violet-May?" I said. "Wouldn't she think of staying and helping out? She's quite good with the children when she wants to be."

"Violet-May is going back to America," said Robbie. "Her English actor has dropped her – seems the thrill of the chase was more attractive than the flesh-and-blood woman. She's hurting but she's putting a brave face on it. And I think she's decided it's better to be the adored, if bored, wife of a rich man than a discarded plaything."

"Perhaps she's right," I said. "It's always best to know where you stand with people, wouldn't you agree?"

Robbie bowed his head. "You mean me, don't you? You believe I used you when I asked you to move into the house. I'm sorry if it seems that way to you, Kay, but ask yourself if you wouldn't have done the same thing, in my shoes. Wouldn't you do anything in your power if you had the slightest suspicion that the life of a child was at stake?" He raised his head and looked at me.

It sounded like another accusation – after all, I hadn't done all I could.

"You're thinking again about what you said to me in the hospital, aren't you? You're thinking that I should have told you what I knew about what happened on Bone Bridge?"

"I had no right to say that, Kay," said Robbie. "I had no right in the world to judge you. I'm sorry for what I said. I hope you can believe me."

"I do believe you," I said.

Robbie studied me in silence for a moment. He said, "You believe me but you can't forgive me, is that it, Kay?"

"That's not true," I said. "I do forgive you. I really do."

"But you're still angry with me, I can see that you are. Please don't deny it, Kay."

He was right, I was angry with him, I was very angry with

him. But I had told the truth when I'd said that I forgave him. I did forgive him, I accepted his apology, his reasons for having acted as he did. I could even, as he had asked me to, put myself in his shoes and understand why he had done what he had. So why was I still angry with him?

"What is it, Kay? Please tell me." He came toward me, sat next to me and reached out and took both my hands in his.

I looked down at them, my fingers pale against his sun-browned skin. I said, "If I am angry, it isn't because ... I mean, it has nothing to do with ..."

"Oh, just spit it out, Kay!" said Robbie in exasperation.

I pulled my hands free of his. "All right then," I snapped. "You want to know why I'm angry so I'll tell you why. You come here and tell me you're sorry, that it was never your intention to lie to me or to use me, but you're still doing it."

"I don't understand," said Robbie. "What am I still doing?"

"Using me, you're still using me, Robbie. You've come here today and you're saying all the right things, making me feel sorry for you, making me feel guilty, saying that stuff about Caroline missing me – and all because you need me again. The next thing I know, you'll be asking me to move back into the house because you have to go away again and you need someone like me, someone safe and *ordinary* to come and look after the children. And it isn't fair, it isn't, because I adore Caroline and Oliver, I do, I really do, but the answer is no, Robbie because the truth is ..."

Robbie got to his feet abruptly and stood looking down at me. "You really think that's what this is about?"

He had spoken very quietly but there was something in his tone and something in his eyes too that cut through my rant and made me fall silent.

"What else is it about then?" I said.

"Not to make you take pity on me," said Robbie. "And not to use the children to make you feel sad and guilty, and not because I needed someone – what was it you said, safe and ordinary?"

"I didn't say that," I snapped. "You said that. You told me to my face that I was ordinary."

Robbie shook his head as though I were some sort of human puzzle. "You've lost me, Kay," he said. "When did I ever say any such thing?"

"That day in Malahide. You told me I was, and I quote, 'someone down-to-earth and ordinary and uncomplicated'."

Robbie's eyes widened. "I said that, to you?"

"Yes, you said that to me."

He put a hand to his head and closed his eyes and opened them again. "Then by the thrice-beshitten shroud of Lazarus, I have no memory of saying it."

I almost smiled. I too had read the book and at any other time I would probably have asked him if he had enjoyed it as much as I had.

"It doesn't matter," I said. "I shouldn't have said anything. Forget it, it really doesn't matter."

"It matters to me," said Robbie. "If I said that, it was unforgivable of me. I've hurt you, Kay, and that is unforgivable."

He sat down next to me once more and I saw the stricken look on his face.

"No, it isn't," I said. "It doesn't even matter really. With all that's happened it's just not important. I'm not important and I don't want you thinking about me or worrying that you might have hurt my feelings."

"Listen to me, Kay Kelly," said Robbie fiercely. "There is nothing unimportant about you, do you hear me? Whatever I said that day, clearly I made the most god-awful dog's dinner of it, but what I was actually trying to say was that I wanted you around precisely because you are so extraordinary, because you are everything my sisters are not. Because you are, and always have been, a breath of fresh air, and because

332

you are kind and lovely and sane, so beautifully fucking sane. But ordinary? You could never be ordinary, Kay."

I remember thinking: Robbie Duff just sworn. I had never heard him swear before. Robbie Duff had sworn and he had said that I was lovely. He had said other things too – fresh and kind – a fresh breath of kind air, or something like that anyway. But mostly I was lovely, not ordinary, lovely.

"And that day in Malahide you've just been talking about," said Robbie, "that was the day I came close to telling you how I felt, only I never did, because I was scared of frightening you off. I'm always scared of frightening you off, Kay."

"What did you almost tell me?" I demanded.

"You asked me if I'd ever come close to marrying," said Robbie. "Well, the truth is I did come close once or twice – but I never did. And do you want to know why? It was because of a snapshot I had somewhere in my head, a snapshot of a frowning girl with brown hair and very grey eyes, who was only short of stamping her foot at me every time I called her 'Little Kay Kelly'."

"You remembered me?" I said.

"I never forgot you, Kay. And I know how I feel about you, but if you don't feel the same way then just say so and put me out of my misery."

I put him out of his misery.

We went together to see Violet-May off when she flew back to LA.

"You probably think I'm a selfish bitch, don't you?" she said. "You think I should stay and do my bit for my sister's children."

"No, I don't think that at all," I said.

"Well, I do," said Violet-May. "I know I should stay, and I know I should want to stay, but the truth is I don't. And it isn't because I don't love them, and when they're older I'll be more than happy to have them come stay. I'll be the exciting

American auntie who flies them out and shows them the Hollywood Hills and takes them to San Francisco and New York and all that sexy stuff. But that's not what they need right now, is it, Kay?"

"No," I said. "I don't suppose it is."

"What they need right now is someone to run around after them, see that they eat the right foods and take their naps and have their baths but I wouldn't be any good at all that stuff, I simply wasn't cut out for it. Besides which I'm much too selfish. But you, Kay, you'll be good at it, and what's more you'll enjoy doing it."

"I think I will too," I said.

"I know you will," said Violet-May. "And you have no idea how relieved I am that it's so. I'd have gone back to the States either way – I won't pretend I wouldn't have. But it's so much nicer to be able to do what you want to do without having to feel too guilty about it."

What could I do but smile?

After we had kissed her goodbye and she was walking away, Violet-May turned back suddenly and called my name.

I left Robbie and walked to meet her.

"There's one thing I want you to know," she said. "I didn't hate him, Kay, I didn't hate Alexander."

"I know, Violet-May," I said.

"You do?" Violet-May's eyes were scanning my face as if seeking corroboration there of what I was telling her.

"He cried so much," she said. "But when he wasn't crying he was ... he could be really very sweet. He smelled good and I used to tickle him and make him laugh. Sometimes I even cuddled him and kissed him but not when anyone was round. I didn't want to be thought soppy and sweet on babies."

"I think I saw you kiss him once," I said.

"Did you?" Violet-May's eyes, blurry now, shone through her tears.

"Yes – it was at the garden party for Robbie's fifteenth

birthday." I decided not to mention that I had later wondered whether she had in fact kissed him or pinched him.

"I don't remember that," said Violet-May. "But I do know that I was very sad when he died, and I just wanted you to know that, Kay."

And then she was gone and I went back to Robbie and we watched her until we could not see her any longer.

And now, because every story must end somewhere, all that is left to tell is that exactly when she was ready to and not a moment sooner, Kay Kelly moved into the Duff house and lived happily ever after.

Except that there is no happily ever after, unless of course in fairy tales, but I do not believe in fairy tales and, unlike Violet-May, I have never wanted to be a princess, not in a play and not in real life either. I know only too well that the world in which we must make our way is a place where, unfortunately, monsters sometimes really do exist. And I also know that it is a world in which people very often take wrong steps and become hopelessly, sometimes irretrievably, lost. And, because it still seems to me that only the very lucky among us truly find what we were hoping for, I daily count my blessings, take nothing for granted and am grateful for the family I never dreamed could be mine. Robbie, Caroline, Oliver and the twins – what more could I ask for – unless it was to arrange it so that Lizzie and Florrie could have met their grandmothers. Those two strong and, each in their own way, wonderful women. I can only hope our girls have inherited the very best of each of their qualities.

But there – life is never Facebook-perfect and is, perhaps, the better for the imperfections.

THE END

Now that you're hooked why not try
The Last Lost Girl
also published by Poolbeg

Here's a sneak preview of chapter one.

The LAST
LOST GIRL

Chapter 1

1976

Lilly's radio is playing "Young Hearts Run Free".

Lilly is lying face down on the brown blanket. Her green bikini has a tiny frilled white skirt that flutters when the wind blows, but there isn't any wind today. Lilly's toes almost touch the glass bottle that glitters in the grass. Jacqueline can just make out the words on the bottle's greasy label – Red Lemonade – but there isn't any lemonade now, only oil mixed with vinegar to make Lilly's skin turn brown in the sun. Jacqueline closes her eyes, but the light seems to seep under her eyelids and there is no escaping the heat. Even the tar on the road is sweating – it clings to the soles of Jacqueline's white summer sandals like black chewing gum. Daddy says this is the hottest month of the hottest summer in living memory. Jacqueline supposes he means that only dead people can remember a hotter summer, but that doesn't make any sense. So many things don't make sense, like why Goretti Quinn gets to lie next to Lilly on the brown blanket when Jacqueline does not. But Lilly is my sister, Jacqueline thinks, not Goretti Quinn's. She opens her eyes. Goretti Quinn has rolled over onto her stomach. The waistband of her skirt is folded so far down that Jacqueline can almost see Goretti's bottom. Mrs Quinn won't let Goretti wear a bikini. "Big girls should wear big skirts," she says – and, looking at Goretti Quinn's thick pink thighs, Jacqueline thinks that she agrees with Mrs Quinn.

"Get us some water, Jacks, please? I'm parched."

Jacqueline is so surprised that for a moment she does not move. Lilly is smiling at her, calling her 'Jacks' and saying please. Then she jumps to her feet and runs all the way to the house.

Daddy and Gayle are at the kitchen table – Daddy is teaching Gayle how to gut fish. He looks up and smiles when Jacqueline comes in.

"What are you up to, pet?"

"Lilly needs some water – she's parched."

"Why can't she get her own water?" says Daddy. "You'd think she'd be glad to get out of the sun for five minutes. The pair of them must be roasted alive out there by now."

"Lilly is just trying to get a bit of colour – what's wrong with that?" says Jacqueline's mother, coming into the kitchen with Granny's vase full of red and white roses. She carries it the way she always does, as though, Jacqueline thinks, it were made of gold instead of glass. "Out of the way, Jacqueline. You've no idea how heavy this thing is when it's full of water."

She puts the vase on the dresser and steps back to look at the flowers, her head dipping from side to side.

"What's wrong with the colour she was born with?" Daddy gives Jacqueline a wink. "And do they have to stretch themselves out like that for the whole world to see? That Quinn girl looks like a Mullingar heifer."

Jacqueline laughs as loudly as if she has never heard the joke before. Through the open window, she can hear Lilly's radio playing "Let Your Love Flow" and remembers why she has come in. She takes the big jug from the press, and carries it to the sink.

"That's not fair," says Jacqueline's mother. "Goretti is a perfectly nice girl."

"All the same, she's no Liz Taylor," says Daddy.

"Everyone can't be Liz Taylor, Frank. And will you stop running that tap, Jacqueline Brennan. In case you haven't noticed, there's a water shortage. When are you going to be finished with that mess, Frank? You're stinking the house out."

"We're nearly there," says Daddy. "Now, are you watching this, Gayle?"

"Yes, Daddy," says Gayle.

Jacqueline turns off the tap and carries the jug carefully across the room. She stands next to her sister. Gayle's pale-blue eyes are staring at the fish lined up on the table. Her body is stiff – exactly, Jacqueline thinks, as though she has died standing up. Her long fair plait reaches almost to her bottom. Lilly says Gayle is too old at fourteen-going-on-fifteen to be wearing her hair in a plait all the time, but Gayle says who cares, it keeps it out of her way for running.

Jacqueline looks down at the blue-bellied mackerel – they stare back from dead eyes. The Irish Times *is spread across the yellow oilcloth – fish scales have fallen between the headlines like silver confetti.*

BANK STRIKE TALKS TO GO AHEAD BUT SHUTDOWN LOOKS LIKELY
THREE SHOT DEAD IN PUB OUTSIDE BELFAST

"Are you watching, Gayle?" Daddy's knife slides along the length of the fish's belly. "You want to make your cut here, at the gills. Then you stick your finger in and pull gently, just a little tug, like this, to detach the gut. Now, you see that little dark vein running along the backbone? Do you see it, Gayle?"

"Yes, Daddy."

"Well, you need to scrape that right out. There you are."

Daddy holds up the knife and Jacqueline sees what looks like a thin dark worm on the glinting silver blade. Gayle's hands go to her mouth and Jacqueline wonders if she will throw up all over the table. She kind of hopes she will.

"Why do you want to learn how to gut fish, Gayle?" she asks.

Gayle does not answer and Jacqueline remembers something Lilly once said: "You're such a lick, Gayle – always trying to make Daddy notice you."

Jacqueline had not understood what Lilly meant, because Daddy notices Gayle – he notices her all the time. The china cabinet in the sitting room is full of trophies and medals that Gayle brings home from running: "Look, Daddy, look at what I won today!"

Gayle is the one he wakes first in the mornings, to go collecting mushrooms. Gayle is the one he asked to hold the ladder when he mended the roof and it is Gayle he takes with him to gather sticks for the fire. Daddy taught Gayle how to repair a bicycle puncture and how to oil the lawnmower and how to pluck a turkey. Looking at Gayle's face now, Jacqueline wonders if Gayle really likes mending punctures or plucking turkeys either.

Daddy slides the fish onto a plate. "There we are, all done. Give those a rinse under the tap, Gayle love. Gently does it now, don't damage the flesh."

Gayle carries the plate to the sink with outstretched arms, as though she wants to keep the fish as far away from her as possible. Daddy gathers up the newspaper, folding it over the fish heads and guts.

Jacqueline carries the jug to the back door.

"Tell Lilly her dinner won't be long," says Daddy, "and maybe she'd like to put some clothes on."

Jacqueline turns in the doorway. "What's Lilly having for her dinner?"

"She's having fish like everyone else – what do you think she's having?"

"But Lilly doesn't eat fish, Daddy."

"Of course she does. Lilly loves a bit of mackerel."

"Not any more, she doesn't," says Jacqueline. "She's a vegetarian now. She says she's never going to eat anything with a face ever again."

Daddy laughs. "Lilly a vegetarian? I'll believe it when I see it. Lilly likes her meat too much." He walks to the sink and moves Gayle aside. "Here, let me do that – you'll be there all day."

Outside in the garden it feels hotter than ever. Lilly has turned over onto her back and Jacqueline puts the jug down carefully next to her head.

"I got your water, Lilly."

"Thanks." Lilly doesn't open her eyes and Jacqueline sits down at the edge of the blanket. Lilly prods her in the back with her toes. "You can't sit there – get your own blanket."

When Jacqueline doesn't move, Goretti Quinn raises her head and says, "You heard Lilly – now, go on, scoot!"

Jacqueline feels her face going red. She gets up as slowly as she can and takes a few steps away from the blanket. Then she sits down on the grass, folds her arms, and watches them. She wishes now that she had told Lilly to get her own water. She tries to think of something clever to say that will make Lilly and Goretti Quinn sorry.

"Daddy says you have to eat a big fat mackerel for your dinner, Lilly Brennan!"

Goretti and Lilly turn their heads and look at one another, then they burst out laughing.

"Top up my back, will you, Goretti?" says Lilly.

340

Goretti Quinn groans, but she gets to her knees and reaches for the bottle. She pulls out the paper stopper and pours the oil and vinegar mixture into the palm of her hand. Jacqueline watches as she rubs her hands together then begins rubbing the oil into Lilly's back.

Goretti looks up and sees Jacqueline watching her. "What do you think you're looking at?" she says.

"'I'm looking at you, your eyes are blue, your face is like a kangaroo!'" says Jacqueline.

Lilly and Goretti start laughing again.

"You smell like a chip shop, Lilly Brennan," says Jacqueline.

"Do I look like I care?" says Lilly.

Jacqueline sticks out her tongue at them but nobody sees.

Lilly has stretched out her hand and is turning up the radio. "Oh, I love this song!"

"Oh, me too!" Goretti Quinn pushes the stopper into the bottle and stands it in the grass. "I hope they play it at the festival dances. I can't wait, can you, Lilly? Did you ask your da yet?"

"Not yet," says Lilly and begins singing along to the radio.

Goretti Quinn rubs her oily hands against her thighs, then she lies down next to Lilly again, closes her eyes and begins to sing too. Jacqueline is the only one who sees Daddy coming. His shadow falls across Lilly's back.

"For God's sake, turn that racket down, Lilly!"

Jacqueline smiles. Daddy thinks all music is a racket, unless it's Frank Sinatra or Jim Reeves.

Lilly stops singing but she does not move.

Goretti Quinn jumps up. "Hiya, Mr Brennan!" She tries to pull her skirt down but it won't go.

"Hello, Goretti," says Daddy but he does not smile.

Jacqueline knows why. Daddy wishes Lilly wouldn't hang around with Goretti Quinn so much. Daddy thinks Goretti is as thick as two short planks. She heard him say so.

"What if she is?" Jacqueline's mother said. "Not everyone can be intelligent. And Lilly likes Goretti so that's all that matters."

But Daddy said, "That's all very well, but I like to think that Lilly is just that little bit above." Daddy is always saying that the

Brennans are "just that little bit above". When he says it, he puts one hand above the other like shelves. Jacqueline supposes he means that they, the Brennans, are the top shelf.

"Lilly, I asked you to turn that music down," says Daddy.

Lilly slowly reaches out and turns the silver dial. "There, are you happy now? And can you get out of the way, please, Daddy? You're blocking the sun."

"Do you not think you've had enough sun for one day?"

"I could never have too much sun," says Lilly.

Daddy, looking down at her stretched out on the blanket, scratches his head. "Well, anyway, your dinner will be ready in half an hour. I got us a nice bit of mackerel."

Jacqueline looks at Goretti Quinn as though to say: I told you so. Goretti Quinn starts to giggle.

"I don't eat fish anymore," says Lilly. "I'm a vegetarian. Daddy – please – the sun – do you mind?"

"Told you," says Jacqueline to Daddy.

Daddy opens his mouth as if he is going to say something else, but then he just turns and walks away.

Goretti watches him go. "Bye, Mr Quinn!" she calls.

Daddy does not answer.

"I think your da is lovely," says Goretti. "You should have asked him about the dances, Lilly."

"I'll ask him when the time is right," says Lilly.

"Do you think he'll let you go?" says Goretti.

"He has to let me go," says Lilly and she reaches out and turns up the radio again, just in time to hear the man say, "That was Dr Hook, and 'I'm Gonna Love You a Little Bit More'."